CW01590061

Derek Hansen is a former advertising man who walked away at the peak of his career to fulfil a lifelong ambition to write novels.

His first novel, *Lunch with the Generals*, became an immediate bestseller, followed by *Lunch with Mussolini* and *Sole Survivor*. *Lunch with a Soldier* is his seventh novel and the fourth in the Lunch series.

Derek Hansen's work has also been published in America, Europe and the United Kingdom. He is married, has two adult children, and lives on Sydney's northern beaches.

'[*Lunch with the Generals*] is a rare book and a rare story that blazes life and death and love from every page . . . the style sparse yet detailed, the sign of a brilliant storyteller'
— *Courier-Mail*

'Derek Hansen, take a bow. You have written one of the most entertaining, gripping and powerful novels of the year'
— *Sunday Telegraph* on *Lunch with Mussolini*

'Another fine effort from Hansen, with complex characters from wartime Germans to Italian fascists to Australian widows'
— *Courier-Mail* on *Lunch with Mussolini*

'Derek Hansen has a knack for making the immediate past come alive with contemporary pain'
— *Canberra Times* on *Sole Survivor*

OTHER BOOKS BY
DEREK HANSEN

Lunch with the Generals

Lunch with Mussolini

Lunch with the Stationmaster

Sole Survivor

Blockade

Perfect Couple

SHORT STORIES

Something Fishy

Dead Fishy

Psycho Cat

Lunch with a Soldier

DEREK HANSEN

HarperCollins*Publishers*

HarperCollins*Publishers*

First published in Australia in 2004
This edition published 2005
by HarperCollins*Publishers* Pty Limited
ABN 36 009 913 517
A member of the HarperCollins*Publishers* (Australia) Pty Limited Group
www.harpercollins.com.au

Copyright © Derek Hansen 2004

The right of Derek Hansen to be identified as the moral rights author of this work has been asserted by him in accordance with the *Copyright Amendment (Moral Rights) Act 2000* (Cth).

This book is copyright.
Apart from any fair dealing for the purposes of private study, research, criticism or review, as permitted under the Copyright Act, no part may be reproduced by any process without written permission.
Inquiries should be addressed to the publishers.

HarperCollins*Publishers*
25 Ryde Road, Pymble, Sydney NSW 2073, Australia
31 View Road, Glenfield, Auckland 10, New Zealand
77–85 Fulham Palace Road, London W6 8JB, United Kingdom
2 Bloor Street East, 20th floor, Toronto, Ontario M4W 1A8, Canada
10 East 53rd Street, New York NY 10022, USA

National Library of Australia Cataloguing-in-Publication data:

Hansen, Derek, 1944– .
Lunch with a soldier.
ISBN 0 7322 7547 4.
1. Secrecy – Fiction. 2. Friendship – Fiction.
I. Title.
A823.3

Cover design by Sharyn Raggett
Cover image: photolibrary.com (boy and horse);
Getty Images (background face).
Typeset by HarperCollins in 10.5/12.5pt Sabon
Printed and bound in Australia by Griffin Press on 50gsm Bulky News

5 4 3 2 1 05 06 07 08

For my wife, Carole,
who has been pushing me to write Neil's story
ever since Neil first opened his mouth.

FIRST THURSDAY

Chapter One

Gancio glanced across the bar towards the table where the four friends would soon gather for another afternoon of storytelling. His restaurant had already begun to fill, mostly with regulars and their guests, and he'd shown them to their tables with his customary charm. He had a good head for names and faces and a way of making his customers feel not just welcome but important, as though they were personally responsible for the success of his restaurant and its ambience, described by one reviewer as 'calculated to encourage the sharing of confidences and promote the clever retort'. But, in truth, Gancio was preoccupied with one of the empty tables. For the first time in nine weeks it had been set for four. In a moment of foolishness he'd considered making a Hungarian dish, but common sense soon prevailed. If the four friends wanted a traditional Hungarian meal, why would they come to an Italian restaurant?

Gancio glanced through the list of reservations, confirming what he'd already established many times over. He had one table free, which he was inclined to leave free in case any of his regulars decided to try their luck without a reservation. It was a courtesy that had paid off many times over, and rare was the lunch or dinner that passed with the 'free' table unoccupied. Gratitude, he'd learned, was bankable. The list also told him who would be late and who liked to linger over pre-lunch drinks — customer habits which were welcomed because they spread the load on both kitchen and staff.

'So I'm first here? Damn! It's my turn to tell a story and I'd planned on making a grand entrance.'

Gancio spun around. He'd developed a sixth sense that had him opening the door just as guests reached for it, but for once his instincts had failed him.

'Neil, my apologies. I didn't see you coming.'

'No worries, mate. I just fired my PA. She didn't see it coming, either.'

'You what?'

'Fired my PA. Discovered she's been sleeping with the enemy, a rival developer who'd just love to know what new projects we're considering. It's a bugger. She's been my PA for ten years.'

'Would you like me to show you to your table?'

'Why? I know where it is.'

'Perhaps you'd prefer to wait at the bar?'

'What do the others do when they're first here?'

'They go straight to the table.'

'In that case, I'll wait at the bar.'

'I'll get you a Peroni.'

Neil pulled out a bar stool and sat down. He glanced at his watch. He was early. Ten minutes early, courtesy of a nearby parking spot and a desire to get away from an office filled with tears and recriminations. Gancio placed a cold frosted glass in front of him and slowly poured a perfect beer.

'You do that better than anyone I know,' said Neil wistfully. 'You sure you're Italian, not Australian or German?'

'Italians drink lots of beer,' said the restaurateur. 'Now, please excuse me, I have more guests to seat.'

Neil studied his beer before slowly raising it and savouring the first mouthful. He had a story to tell which would demand his full concentration but he still couldn't clear his mind of the morning's drama. He'd thought it would be something easily resolved. He'd given his assistant a fair choice: her lover or her job. He'd pointed out that the job was hers for as long as she wanted it, but her relationship with his competitor would only be for as long as he wanted it, and his competitor's past record with women suggested that would be for about as long as it took ice-cream to melt. Neil thought her decision was a no-brainer. He was stunned and even a little hurt to discover she thought otherwise.

'A Peroni. Only an Australian would fill up on beer before a meal.' Lucio sat down heavily on the stool next to Neil.

'One beer doesn't begin to fill an Australian, Lucio.'

'In that case, I'll join you.' Lucio caught the eye of a waiter. 'The ability to drink large quantities of beer comes with Australian citizenship. We swore allegiance then sat down to a typically Australian meal at the local Chinese restaurant. No wine, just beer.'

'How come you're so early?' said Neil.

'Nine weeks is a long time on a diet of short stories, however entertaining. I want meat, Neil, substance and a healthy serve of deceit. I have enjoyed our lunches without Milos, but I enjoy them more when we're all together.'

'I know what you mean. Bloody hell, here comes Blind Pugh.' Neil checked his watch as Gancio guided Ramon to the bar. He took the blind man's hand and shook it. 'Lucio and I were just saying how much we've missed Milos and our regular stories. Seems you have as well. It's not like you to be early. Punctual, yes; early, no.'

'The absence of any one of us diminishes us all,' said Ramon. He shook Neil's hand and took Lucio's. 'Neil, I take it you are well? You too, Lucio? Gancio tells me you are drinking Peronis.'

'Would you prefer wine?'

'No, thank you, Gancio. If my friends are drinking Peroni, I will drink Peroni. Perhaps we can raise our glasses to the return of our absent friend?'

'And to the return of our storytelling,' added Lucio. 'Tell me, Neil, where are you taking us with your story?'

'That's privileged information, best kept till we're all seated. Besides, I don't want to have to repeat everything for Milos.'

'Just a hint?'

'No.'

'It's not fair. It's like being blindfolded and in bed with a beautiful woman. I know I'm going to have a good time but I don't know whether I like her.'

'Just lie back and enjoy it,' said Neil amiably. 'Here comes your beer, Ramon.'

'So what is the toast?' asked Lucio.

'To a successful story,' said Neil. 'One that lauds me, humbles Ramon, confounds Milos and embarrasses you.'

'To the story,' said Ramon.

'To the story,' echoed Lucio. 'I only hope it doesn't also embarrass the teller.'

'I hope it doesn't, either,' said Neil, suddenly serious. 'I guess that's a risk we all take when we choose to tell a story. Ah, here's the man himself.' He stood to greet Milos, effectively preventing Ramon or Lucio following up on his comment. 'Welcome back, old mate.'

Milos embraced each of his friends in turn.

'Beer before lunch? At last I feel like I've come home.'

'You're looking well, Milos,' said Lucio. 'You've put on weight. Are you sure you didn't go to Italy instead?'

'I thought I made it clear in my last story: Hungary is not a country for the diet conscious.'

'Perhaps we should sit at our table,' said Ramon. 'Then you can tell us all about your trip.' He slipped his arm through Milos's.

'First you have to tell me what I have missed out on. I have nine weeks of storytelling to catch up on. What stories did you tell? Gabriella would also like to know.'

'Tell Gabi she missed nothing,' said Neil. 'We just discussed ways in which terrorists could blow up Sydney. It's depressingly easy. Imagine a bomb in a container in the harbour tunnel or on the harbour bridge. Are you sure your wife wants to know about this?'

'Ignore him,' said Ramon. 'We took turns to tell each other short stories, a fresh story every Thursday. Some were better than others, but all of them left us hungry for something more substantial. They failed to satisfy. However, we are eager to hear about your trip before Neil commences his story.'

'What can I tell you? Hungary was a poor country when I left it and it is a poor country still. Oh, there are more cars on the roads and people have televisions and stereos and refrigerators, but these are little things. The country is still weary from its struggle for freedom. The buildings are tired and the roads are cracked. Some people will always make money in whatever circumstances, but, for the most part, people are poorly paid by our standards. For Hungary, becoming rich and decadent will be a very slow process.'

'Did you go back to Sarospatak?' asked Lucio.

'Of course, that was the whole point of the visit. The life of Sarospatak still revolves around the university, but it now has wine bars and smart cafés. We also went to Satoraljaujhely and I walked up through the hills where Tibor and I lay and watched the Jews being rounded up. Nothing has changed. Of course the town is bigger and the railway station is smarter, but nothing really has changed.'

'And Tibor's grave?'

'Moved. When Aunt Klari and Andras died there was no one to take over their farm. Their children — yes, they had children, two daughters and a son — had made lives for themselves in Budapest and Debrecen. I did not mention them in my story because they played no part in it.'

'What did they do during the war?'

'Neil, there are some questions you learn not to ask.' Milos sighed. 'I come to hear a story yet it is me who is doing all the talking. A glass of wine, or even water, would be nice.'

'Our apologies,' said Lucio and waved vigorously towards the bar.

'The new owners did not want the grave of a stranger in their back garden. My brother's coffin was dug up and his remains moved to the Catholic cemetery. It wasn't hard to find him. There was a small headstone with his name, date of birth and death, and an inscription which read, “In memory and honour of a loyal friend”. Who knows what loyal friends were responsible for this kindness. Whoever they were, railwaymen or gangsters, Gabi and I are grateful to them. Tibor’s grave was well tended, unlike those in the Jewish cemetery, which are overgrown. Perhaps such trifles shouldn’t matter, but they do.’ Milos paused while Gancio poured a pinot grigio into his glass.

‘Tibor was a gangster, that is a fact, and doubtless how Hungarian history will remember him, if he is remembered at all. For a while he became me and was the husband of my wife, but above all I remember the brother who loved me, who was my protector and who is the sole reason I am sitting here with you today and reminiscing. He was and will always be my hero.’

‘So how much of your story was true?’

‘The story was true, Neil. We have had this conversation before. There were embellishments, but the story was my story — mine, Tibor’s and Gabi’s.’

‘You never learn, do you, Neil?’ said Ramon. ‘Life is not a Hollywood movie. It doesn’t have tidy endings with everything resolved. We will never know how much of Milos’s story was fantasy and how much was fact. Your insistence on the truth only serves to shore up Milos’s fictions. You play into his hands.’

‘And I think you see games where there are none,’ snapped Neil. ‘Ever since your story, our lunches have taken on the tone of the confessional.’

‘This is more like it,’ said Lucio enthusiastically. ‘What is storytelling without friction? Enough of Hungary, enough of Milos’s story. It’s time to move on. I think we should call Gancio over and find out what we're having for lunch. Then Neil can enlighten us by telling us where he will be taking us with his story. Personally, I can't wait.'

'You insulted me,' said Neil. 'And, by implication, you insulted all Australians.'

He pushed away his cheese plate and replaced it with his wine glass so he could reach it more easily. He'd sat quietly through lunch while the others had probed Milos for more detail of his travels. Neil's mood had grown more sombre as the meal had progressed and even Gancio's signature saltimbocca with white asparagus, one of Neil's favourite dishes, had failed to lighten his mood. He'd decided to tell a story that would replicate what he'd condemned his friends for doing. He'd thought long and hard before he'd made his decision but, once made, it was irrevocable. How would they react? Now that the time had come to commit to his story, he was beginning to have doubts. But his decision had been based on anger and a sense of injustice and he used this to strengthen his resolve.

'Milos, you have said repeatedly how glad you are to be home, to be back in Australia, yet, consciously or unconsciously, you denigrate Australia at every opportunity.'

'That is not true.'

'Oh yes, it is, Milos, and Ramon and Lucio are no less guilty. You live in Australia and enjoy all its privileges yet you cling to and flaunt your Europeanness as though it somehow makes you superior. On that first day, when you began your story, you asked me what I was doing when I was twelve years old, while twelve year olds in Europe were being beaten up and pissed on at school. You asked if my father was plucked out of my happy home and taken away to almost certain death. You said my father was probably teaching me to play cricket while yours was teaching you to survive the Nazis. Your tone was accusatory, as though it was something I should feel guilty about. You accused me of resenting you because you had lived more as a teenager than I would in my entire life.'

'You take my comments out of context. It was you who accused me of "wallowing in my past", no? I was simply responding to your charge.'

'You made these statements, Milos, and they are not out of context. Furthermore, when you made these statements your two fellow Europeans supported you to the hilt.'

'I am South American,' said Ramon.

'Only by birth. In manner and habit you are European. Your Europeanness is something you have worked on so hard that your affectation has become part of who you are. You are a South American who came to Australia and adopted Europe.'

'Such a broad brush,' said Ramon.

'The broad brush is a weapon of your choosing. Milos virtually claimed ownership of post-traumatic stress syndrome, as though it was a condition peculiar to Europeans who have suffered. For God's sake! Australia is a country built on post-traumatic stress syndrome. Which country suffered the greatest number of casualties per head of population in World War I? Was it Germany? No. France? No. Great Britain, Russia? No. It was our big brown land. You asked if our fathers were dragged away from our happy homes to near certain death — well, the answer is yes. Yes, they bloody well were.

'And it happened again in World War II. Our fathers were sent away to fight another European war, only to be recalled and delivered into the hands of the Japanese in Singapore by an inept British high command. Can you imagine the state of the soldiers who survived Changi and the Burma Railway? Can you imagine what went through their minds when they closed their eyes at night? Can you imagine the effect on their lives and their families? Dear God, the suffering of those survivors virtually defines post-traumatic stress syndrome.

'Then, just when it seemed we might actually get a generation of Australians who hadn't been stuffed up, Vietnam happened. As you pointed out in your story, Milos, the impact of Vietnam actually brought about the identification and naming of post-traumatic stress syndrome. Perhaps you don't regard Vietnam as a real war because it lacked the scale of your European wars, but it was pretty bloody real to those of us who fought in it. So spare me. Please don't any of you ever suggest that Australians have no idea of what you Europeans endured.

'Then there is your conviction that post-traumatic stress syndrome is something you just have to learn to live with. You asked me what I thought sufferers were supposed to do about it. Forget about it, just because the sun was shining and the surf was up? Well, yes. That is what I expect you to do, or at least to try to do, because that is what we as a nation have done. We, as a nation, have faced our demons and got on with it. Yet you mock us. To use Ramon's words, you diminish us and our history.' Neil turned away from them, not so much in disgust as to rein in his anger.

'I assure you, Neil, I did no such thing. If that is how you interpreted my words, then I apologise for my clumsiness.' Milos was stunned by the vehemence with which Neil had made his points. They all were. And chastened, because there was at least a grain of truth to his accusations. This was not the Neil they knew and this was not how they had expected the day to develop.

'I concede we may have gone a little too far,' said Ramon heavily. 'I sensed what Milos was doing, how he was setting you up in the story he told, and simply added my weight to his cause. As I recall, there was a touch of facetiousness to our comments. None of us would deliberately set out to do the things you accuse us of. The comments were made to bait you, not to cause offence.'

'Ramon is right,' said Lucio. 'I can see that you've obviously thought a great deal about what happened, but no offence was intended. Milos may have exaggerated to make a point and we backed him because it was clear that, for some reason, he was targeting you. But, Neil, it was just a game. Our comments were made in the spirit of the game.'

'Oh, I accept it was a game, one of your precious, elitist, European games. What pisses me off most is that you're not even aware that you're doing it. I don't know why you just don't come out and admit it, admit that Australia is not good enough for you. I know it has its appeal and comforts but, in your hearts, Australia is just not sophisticated enough. You flaunt your culture in the face of our football, your café society in the face of our backyard barbecues, your urbanity in the face of our mateship.'

'Neil, your audience has extended far beyond this table,' said Milos quietly. 'Did you intend humiliation to be part of your retribution?'

Neil paused to compose himself and lower his voice. There was too much anger, too much aggression. It was time to pull back and Milos had provided him with the opportunity. He adopted the tactic of the man on the soapbox in the park who deliberately speaks softly so that people have to gather in close to hear what he has to say.

'I've thought long and hard about what story to tell. I have had many ideas but, in the final analysis, they all seemed too trite. This is not a time for fiction.'

'Neil, what are you saying?' Concern was etched into Lucio's face. He glanced at his companions but their expressions were no different to his and brought him no comfort. Neil's about-face was the last thing they'd expected.

'We no longer have any conventions,' said Neil. 'Our lunches are no longer a venue to exchange clever fictions. Ramon changed all that when he decided to air his sordid past. You, Lucio, compounded the error with the story of your aunt. All Milos did was continue down a path already established, but it was he who drove the nails into the coffin. These last nine weeks have not been unsatisfying just because the currency was short stories but because we were dealing once more with fiction. Fiction can never carry the weight of truth nor the substance. Milos, you brought Gabi to our lunches, not so that we could imagine her pain as we would if she were an invention, but so that we could feel her pain. So we could look her in the eye and see how she suffered. Ramon summed it up perfectly, as he always does, when he said that the presence of Gabi, and having Gabi share the storytelling, added an extra dimension to your tale. It did. My God, did it ever. Now, tell me, how can fiction compete with that?'

Neil looked around the table at each man in turn. He'd never seen them so uncomfortable. He'd fired his arrows and not one had missed its target.

'You disadvantage me and my preference for fiction. You leave me no choice but to do what I pleaded with you not to do or to face relegation to the second division. Lucio, you asked where my story was taking you, so I'll tell you. It's taking you to Australia, this country you treat so lightly. It's taking you into my past, a place you have no damn right to go. It is a story which, at times, will be as dramatic as any of your European epics and, yes, even as painful. It is a true story and one I never dreamed I'd tell.'

Neil paused. He had his friends' attention like never before. There was curiosity tinged with guilt, but, more importantly, he saw fear. They were scared of what he would say next. He smiled grimly to himself.

'My story is the story of my brother. He was a fabulous kid, younger than me but as gutsy as they come. He was my best mate. He was irrepressible. You couldn't knock the smile off his face with a hammer in each hand.' Neil's voice faltered at the memory and he stared down at the table so he wouldn't have to meet his friends' eyes. He was momentarily lost for words. When they finally came, his companions had to strain to hear them. 'His story has never been told. It is my family's darkest secret. If the secret is to be revealed, unfortunately, I am the one obliged to do it.'

'Why? Why you?' asked Lucio.

'Because I took my brother's life.' Neil's voice trembled with the admission. 'I took his life.'

His friends sat, shocked speechless, as they absorbed the implications. In all the years they had been meeting, Neil had told them nothing about himself, other than his occupation and the fact that he was single. Now he was preparing to lift the curtain on who he was and, worse, what he had done. They were intrigued, of course, but also wary. Ramon had once told a story that had threatened to break up the group and put an end to any future lunches. Neil's story had the potential to do the same. It was a risk Lucio was not prepared to take.

'Neil, you can stop now. You don't have to tell us this. We don't ask it of you. Please, my friend, stop now before it's too late.'

'But it's already too late,' said Ramon. 'Your story has already started, hasn't it, Neil?' A slow smile spread across the blind man's face.

Chapter Two

The tunnel was supposed to be cold. The engagement the previous day, plus the relentless air and artillery barrage, had forced the enemy to withdraw. The smell of cordite and scorched trees still lingered among the other smells: the earthy, rotting, fecund smell of jungle; the sticky, sweet smell of shattered palms; and the unmistakeable smell of death. The bloodied bodies of the two Vietcong lying in the dugout firing post was clear evidence of the speed of the enemy's forced withdrawal. The VC were zealous in their efforts to recover and conceal their dead. The fact that two precious AK-47 assault rifles lay with the corpses and had not been reclaimed was taken as another good sign, a clear indicator that the tunnel was cold.

The artillery shell that had killed the two Vietcong had landed just centimetres to the side of the trench, giving them no chance at all. Ironically, if the shell had made a direct hit on top of the metre-and-a-half-thick roof protecting the trench, both men would have probably survived. A soldier ignored the flies to inspect the two AK-47s for booby-traps. He did it more as good practice than precaution. All the evidence suggested the withdrawal had been too hasty and he was well aware that the Vietcong could ill-afford to lose the weapons. Nevertheless, he attached wires to both rifles and took cover outside the trench before hauling them clear. He repeated the procedure with the bodies using ropes. There were no nasty surprises. The tunnel was cold.

Billy 'Barb' Dwyer had already taken off his shirt and was practising tying his torch to the end of a half-metre-long stick. He tied it at an angle of around seventy degrees so that it shone away to the side of the direction he pointed the stick. The tunnels zigzagged and Barb liked his torch to look around the corners before he did in the event that the tunnel was hot. He untied the torch and jammed the stick through his belt. The torch, his knife and a 9mm Browning pistol were all he'd take with him into the tunnel. His backup, Costa 'Motsa' Peponis, would carry the radio to maintain contact with the rest of the section up top. Barb couldn't help glancing at the bodies, at the faces of the enemy, an enemy he hoped he'd never meet underground. They looked harmless enough and there was nothing to them except skin and bone. Yet they were the stuff of nightmares: resourceful little men who killed, maimed and crippled without warning, often in ways that didn't bear thinking about. And they'd made an art of killing underground.

Barb entered the tunnel opening midway up the side of the trench and began the gentle descent towards what he expected would be the main communications tunnel. The stink and staleness of the air intensified the further he descended. He paused to draw a deep breath and tried to calm his nerves. His pulse was racing and the pounding in his ears could obscure the sound of the enemy, the clink of a weapon in nervous hands or the more subtle, dreaded sound of breathing, of suddenly realising someone else was down there, waiting, waiting for him. This was Barb's fifth tunnel and they didn't get any easier. He took two big sucks of the putrid air as he tried to convince himself that the tunnel was cold; how all the signs pointed to the fact that the tunnel was cold. He felt Motsa's hand touch his right boot. A gentle reassuring tap, a she'll-be-right-mate. As if he'd know.

Four metres in, the shaft met with the communications tunnel. Barb paused, flicked his torch on and searched for trip wires or cord that could be rigged to a grenade. It was a tense moment. If Charlie was waiting for them and pulled out the pin, Barb could count the rest of his life in seconds. There were no wires or cords and no decision to make over which direction to turn. The firing post was at the furthermost reach of the communications tunnel. Barb took his time examining the tunnel ahead. It was barely point-eight of a metre wide and no more than one-point-three metres high. He guessed the roof was not more than a metre and a half below ground. There was nothing to suggest this tunnel was anything special.

Despite the tension he couldn't help checking out the walls and roof: laterite clay, dull red by the light of his torch, betraying the presence of iron. It was good tunnelling soil and dried as hard as brick, not unlike the off-white shin-cracker he'd grown up playing amongst. Even the cold feel of it reminded him of the sandstone roof of the worked-out lenses he'd explored with his brother, always hoping to find opals that might somehow have been overlooked. He pushed on into the communications tunnel. The brief distraction had helped ease his jitters and sharpened his concentration. The tunnel ran straight for a good seven metres before angling away, but Barb took his time, running his fingers through the dust of the floor, feeling for wires that would indicate the presence of trapdoors leading to storage areas or a more comprehensive network of tunnels. There were none. The smell grew fouler but he'd learned to ignore it. Smell didn't kill.

He paused at the bend, turned off his torch and, in the darkness, tied it to the stick. He crept as close to the bend as he dared, flicked his torch back on and extended the stick out in front of him. He braced himself for a burst from an AK-47. There wasn't one. He withdrew his torch, untied it and jammed the stick back in his belt. Sweat ran down his face and dripped off his nose and the point of his chin. He stank but it was just one more foul smell among the many. He turned the corner, checking first for irregularities in the floor that could indicate someone was watching him from beneath a slightly raised trapdoor, waiting for him to come closer and present a target that could not be missed. There was nothing suspicious that he could see and no shafts in the ceiling leading to tunnel exits. He crawled slowly forward, fingers still probing the dust for telltale wires.

His conviction grew that the tunnel would probably not amount to much, that it did little more than link four or five firing posts. There was a chance that another communications tunnel at a deeper level connected up with other firing posts or a more complex system, but Barb suspected that he'd just find a number of tunnel exits from which the Vietcong could make their escape into the jungle and to a more comprehensive tunnel system. With any luck he'd find a rice cache or a weapons cache, doubtless booby-trapped, but they'd become accustomed to dealing with them and the discovery would be compensation for the risks he was taking.

But a discovery added to the danger. Any storage area would be built below the tunnel he was in and accessing it usually meant dropping feet first down a vertical shaft. He'd heard enough stories to know a Vietcong could be waiting with a bayonet to thrust up into his groin, or with an AK-47 that would blow Big Jim and the twins to buggery and virtually cut him in half, but what was the alternative? Besides destroying anything of value, hand grenades dropped down the shaft also burned up the available oxygen, limiting further exploration. His job was to explore the tunnel and report, not blow it up. That would come later.

He paused again where the tunnel bent back, turned off his torch and reached for his stick. All his observations and instincts confirmed the belief that the tunnel was cold. His breathing was easier now, measured and shallow, and the throbbing in his ears long gone. He expected the next section to reveal a shaft leading up to another firing position or at least a trapdoor covering an exit. Experience had taught the Australians that firing posts tended to be grouped in threes in the shape of a triangle, so each position could lend support to the others. Barb didn't doubt that the second point of the triangle lay ahead of him, just around the bend. Behind him, Motsa crouched as still as a statue, having stopped when he'd stopped. He finished tying his torch to the stick and paused to listen before switching it back on. In that moment, in that fleeting moment when neither of them moved nor drew breath, Barb heard something. Fear shot through his body, as sudden and as paralysing as an electric shock.

What had he heard?

What had caused it?

Dear God! He stared wide-eyed into the blackness, his ears suddenly as large as an elephant's, every muscle in his body poised to spring but not knowing which way. His mind raced over possibilities, hoping to identify the sound as something harmless. He'd been frightened before and nearly emptied his pistol on a rat the size of a small cat. Maybe it was another rat. Tunnels were full of them. But he knew instinctively that no rat had made the sound and hoping otherwise changed nothing. The sound had been soft. And muffled. Almost inaudible. But almost certainly human.

Almost certainly human!

Barb had dreaded this moment, feared it with the fear of death itself. His elephant ears heard the sound again and identified it beyond any shadow of doubt. Someone breathing. In that instant, all his fears were realised. Ahead of him, in the darkness around the bend, someone was waiting.

But who? VC, obviously. Waiting in ambush. A wounded, desperate enemy with nothing to lose or why hadn't he fled? Dear God! Sweet Jesus! Barb slowly backed up as quietly as he could until his boots touched Motsa. He reached behind and patted Motsa's arm twice in a pre-arranged signal, letting him know he'd made live contact and to back up. Barb wanted Motsa far enough away to be out of range of a hand grenade, but close enough to help him or get help if he got wounded. Motsa didn't hesitate. He backed away like an engine in a shunting yard.

Barb tried to remember the times he'd been scared before, the scrapes he and his brother had got into and how he'd coped. Nothing compared, not even the time the wild pigs had nailed him. There was no brother he could rely on now, no sense of thrill or excitement that it was all just a dangerous game that would inevitably end happily. There'd be no rolling around on the ground afterwards between the heaps of mullock, laughing off a cave-in and celebrating their immortality. Barb had never felt such overwhelming fear before, would never in a million years have believed he was even capable of it. He lay flat on his belly, pistol and torch poised in front of him, cursing the pounding in his ears, waiting for his shock and fear to ease so that he could act. He knew what he had to do, but first he had to be capable of doing it.

His plan was simple. He'd use his torch to draw a response. If it came in the form of a hand grenade he'd have to hope that the bend in the tunnel shielded him from shrapnel and the worst of the blast. If the response was gunfire, he'd wait until his torch was shot to shit, then reach around the corner and fire three shots blind. If there was return fire, wait five seconds and fire another three rounds. If there was more return fire, he was out of there and Motsa had better not get in his way! He took three deep breaths as quietly as he could but the breaths seemed not to contain the oxygen he needed. He took another breath and held it as he rose back up onto his hands and knees and edged forward. Christ, if only his brother could see him now! His brother loved his recklessness and fearlessness, even boasted about it in front of their father. Oh Christ, let him have the chance to boast about this.

Where was the corner? Why hadn't he counted his steps? He didn't want to turn his torch on until the last minute, didn't want to risk revealing it was only attached to a stick, but, even more, didn't want to expose himself to the first burst of gunfire. He felt along the wall but it told him nothing. There was no hard edge on the bend, just a gentle curve. He pressed his stick against the wall and felt along it to see if there was a gap at the furthest tip. No. He edged forward and repeated the exercise. Yes! He edged forward a little further to make certain. The stick rolled against the wall when he tried to hold it flat. He swallowed. The moment of truth had come.

Barb lay still, his finger poised over the torch switch, all his senses attuned to what his ears would tell him. He heard the breathing again. This time it seemed more rapid, like someone panting but trying to do so silently and all but succeeding. Whoever was there had to be no more than four metres away and, more likely, no more than three. Oh Christ! Would his enemy be crouched down like him, lying down or peeping through the narrow slot of a raised trapdoor? The Browning felt welded to his hand.

He sucked in a deep breath, not caring if his enemy heard him. The time for silence had passed and he knew it was better if his enemy realised he was about to make his move. He flicked on his torch and pushed it along the floor of the tunnel and out around the bend. Barb braced for the shots, hoping like all hell that his hand was outside the line of fire. He closed his eyes, couldn't help himself.

Nothing happened. No shots, no hand grenade.

Oh God! What now? Maybe the Vietcong pulled the same trick. Maybe his enemy had glimpsed the stick. Barb withdrew his torch, switched it off and detached it from the stick. Out of habit he jammed the stick back in his belt. What now? He knew damn well what now. If his adversary was beneath a trapdoor, firing blindly around the bend would accomplish nothing. With his torch in his left hand and his Browning in his right, he inched his way forward flat on his belly so that he, his torch and his pistol had a clear sight along the tunnel. It was like the war games he'd played with his brother, using rubber bands stretched between finger and thumb to propel rolled paper pellets bound tight with sticky tape. Whoever had the fastest reactions and steadiest hand always won.

Barb switched on his torch, saw his enemy and fired almost instantly. Two shots because he wasn't fast enough to prevent the second. He turned away and vomited. Oh Christ, sweet Jesus ...

'Barb!'

He heard Motsa calling his name as he slumped against the side wall, exhausted, drained, beaten and sick in his guts.

'Barb! What's happening, for fuck's sake?'

'I'm okay, mate, it's okay.'

He heard Motsa crawling towards him, felt his hands on his legs as he pushed past to gawk.

'Holy shit.'

Holy shit. What did that mean? Under the circumstances, what did any words mean?

'You okay, mate?'

Motsa's torch was pointed right at his face. Barb flinched at the glare.

'Sorry, mate.' Motsa directed his torch lower. 'You hurt?'

'No. Get on the radio and tell Brennan what happened.' Lieutenant Brennan was the platoon commander and leading the section. 'Tell them it's secure.'

'Right-oh.'

Barb forced himself to turn and look back at his victim. The old Russian K44 rifle lay where it had probably lain since the artillery bombardment, centimetres out of reach and useless. The hands, which had been turned upwards in submission, now lay palms down, flat and lifeless. The fear-filled face, which for the briefest of instants had pleaded for clemency, was now destroyed and oozing blood. If only he'd known. If only he'd taken a microsecond longer to look. All the while he'd been crawling through the tunnel, his enemy had lain trapped from the shoulders back beneath tonnes of earth, helpless and terrified, listening to his approach and watching the glow from his torch that offered both the hope of rescue and the threat of death.

Barb started to shake uncontrollably. He'd faced his worst fears and come through. But he hadn't expected it to end this way, hadn't expected his enemy to be so helpless, or to be a young woman hardly more than a girl.

The tunnel felt unutterably cold.

Chapter Three

Billy gazed northwards at a view that changed little no matter which way he looked. The homestead was surrounded by baked red soil, sparse grass and strips of metre-high saltbush, which protected the garden and provided a wind and dust break. Beyond, the coolibahs, whitewoods, myalls, boonarees and belahs gradually combined to form a screen which limited his range of vision to not much more than a kilometre. The view hadn't changed since he was a kid, except that now it was impossible to look anywhere without seeing the green plastic water tanks and pipes that delivered bore water to his sheep and cattle. The tanks and pipes were a necessity, an expensive necessity, without which his six thousand, five hundred hectares of grazing land would be worthless, but it didn't stop him resenting their presence. They were an intrusion upon a timeless landscape and, like the spiky thorns from the Hudson pear, impossible to ignore.

He put his head back and swallowed the dregs of the tea in his mug. He liked his tea strong with just a couple of cat's licks of milk which did nothing much more than turn it dark red-brown, almost the colour of the soil. He reached forward and placed his mug on the veranda rail, alongside his crossed boots. A family of lousy jacks descended on the kelpie's food bowl and began to help themselves to the leftover dry dog food. Out of habit Billy picked up his packet of Drum and rolled himself a cigarette. He didn't take his eyes off the bush. When he was working around the house he always had a rollie after his mid-morning cuppa and his fingers knew what to do. They made their way unguided to his mouth, where his tongue made a practised pass along the edge of the paper. He cupped his hands out of habit, even though he was sheltered from the cool westerly wind, and struck a match. He pulled his head back as he took the first long drag, forced the smoke deep into his lungs where it'd do the most harm, and slowly exhaled.

The action momentarily disturbed the numbness inside his head that enabled him to drift off into daydreams about nothing. His daydreams were unusual in that they lacked dreams. Chair back, feet up, a cuppa and a rollie, and Billy could drift off into a state of meditation devotees took years to achieve. When Billy thought about these occasions, which was rare, he simply regarded them as 'white-outs' as opposed to 'blackouts' and just a bloody waste of time. But so much was wasted.

The day didn't look like it was going to amount to much. High grey clouds spread from horizon to horizon but brought no promise of rain. They hung motionless, aloof from the winds that swept the plains, a dull, depressing undercoat to a painting no one was inspired to finish. The grey day was just a part of the home Billy had come back to at a time when he needed to get his act together and when his being home served a purpose. But times changed, needs changed, and his purpose in being there had uprooted and cleared out. Billy stayed on for no good reason other than that he couldn't think of where else he fitted. People had told him he just needed time, but time was a trap laced with the comfortable and familiar, lacking in urgency. He'd stayed, and his white-outs made a convenient barrier that restricted the range of his memories and regrets as effectively as the scrub restricted his view.

Billy was good with his hands, especially where carpentry was concerned, and he'd fixed the family's old weatherboard home to suit his needs. He'd enclosed the veranda, which encircled the entire house, with mesh to keep out the sandflies, mosquitoes and bushflies, building screen doors at the head of each set of three steps leading down to the yard. There was a set of steps on each side of the house. Billy always had his breakfast on the veranda on the eastern side, which had a table and chair dedicated to that purpose. He had lunch at a table and chair on the northern side and dinner at a similar arrangement on the western side. Each side also had a day bed, though Billy spent most nights in his bed out on the veranda on the southern side, which was generally the coolest, until the sub-zero winter nights drove him reluctantly indoors. He kept his television on an old chrome tea trolley that had once borne his mother's prized cut-glass sherry decanter and glasses, so he could wheel it out to wherever he happened to be. The television and his transistor radio kept him up with the news. Bob Hawke had just been re-elected prime minister, which meant less to him than a one-cent shift in the price of wool.

Billy's thoughts began to take on shape and substance. They often did as he emerged from his white-outs. Normally they took the form of a repair he had to figure out or a problem he had to solve. He'd lost count of the problems he'd solved with his feet up on the rail and the glowing tip of a burnt-down rollie creeping up on his fingers. Today he worried about his lambs and the potential losses. His ewes were three weeks from lambing and the cold August winds still swept in from the west, taking the temperature down to freezing at night. Out of the wind, the mid-morning sun held a false promise, which Billy could feel through his shirt and the legs of his trousers. But the weather pattern was troubling and promised no let-up. On the positive side, his sheep were in reasonable condition for the end of winter and he could expect a healthy crop of lambs. But he worried whether they'd be strong enough to withstand the cold if the winds kept up. There was little margin for stock losses. He was wondering what his brother would have done, what other factors he would have added to the equation, when his working dogs began barking a warning and straining at their chains. He rose to his feet, puzzled. He wasn't expecting anyone. The lousy jacks abandoned their free feed and took off to the safety of a nearby tree. He didn't recognise the Range Rover emerging from the scrub lining the road to his property.

A Range Rover? Billy didn't know anyone who owned a Range Rover, or even anyone who knew anyone who might conceivably own a Range Rover. Around Glengarry, Grawin and Walgett you were either a Ford or a Holden man, unless you had the cash to spend on a four-wheel drive, in which case you chose between Toyota and Nissan, with Nissan a distant second. The Range Rover had no bull bar, no

CB radio antenna and, as far as he could see, no dents. Maybe it was someone from the bank paying a courtesy visit, a salesman or a representative from the National Party. But the election had come and gone, he was square with the bank and hadn't seen or heard from a salesman for years. Dust and reflections on the windscreen concealed his visitor's identity.

The kelpie had come out from under the veranda steps and stood motionless, head to the side and ears cocked, as the four-wheel drive pulled to a stop. Whoever was driving it knew enough to let the dust settle before opening the car door. Billy was prepared for just about anyone to emerge, except for the person who did. His visitor was from another world.

He could see that she'd learned to wait and let the dust settle the hard way because a film of red dust coated her denim jacket and jeans. The denim was so faded it all but matched the white paint on the Range Rover. She wore pale blue-rimmed sunglasses that had mirrored lenses and was quick to put on a broad-brimmed straw hat before the sun had a chance to get at her. Even from the veranda she looked amazing. His kelpie obviously thought the same, judging by the way it wagged its tail and danced around her.

'Billy Dwyer?'

Billy opened the screen door and held it for her.

'Yeah, I'm Billy.'

She stepped up onto the veranda and removed her hat and sunnies. Without them she looked even more amazing. Her hair was an intriguing combination of honey-gold and a rich gum brown. She was city beyond doubt and, without remotely intending it, made him feel like a hick. She overwhelmed him with her poise and confidence, the clarity and freshness of her skin and her scent. Her eyes had the quickness and brightness of a good working dog and were totally disarming. He wasn't good with women's ages but guessed she was probably older than she looked, maybe late thirties. That put her only a few years younger than him but somehow she managed to make him feel ancient.

'Come in,' he said pointlessly. She was already in. 'I'll put the kettle on. How do you have your tea?'

'With lemon.'

'Lemon?'

She laughed. Even her laugh was amazing; so pretty, so uncomplicated, so natural.

'Black will be fine. Not too strong.'

'That, I can do.'

She wasn't as tall as he'd first thought but she was still taller than most women he knew.

'I'm Linda Sinclair.' She held her hand out and he shook it automatically, swamped by unfamiliar sensations. Her touch was pretty amazing, too.

'I've been talking to Jimmy at the stock and station in Walgett,' she said.

'Oh yeah?'

'He sends his regards.'

'I bet. Sit down. I'll go make the tea.'

Billy escaped to the kitchen, leaving her to face the trees to the north. The dogs had begun to settle, saving him from the indignity of bellowing at them. He warmed the teapot, emptied it and shovelled in his usual two heaped teaspoons of Bushell's. He had two minutes at least before the water boiled, time to adjust to the fact that he had a visitor and try to come to terms with the kind of visitor she was. Christ Almighty! Where had she come from? What did she want? What in God's name was she doing out in the mulga and where the hell did he fit in? The kettle whistled its readiness and he tipped the boiling water into the teapot. How strong was not too strong? For some reason he was anxious to get it right.

'How strong is not too strong?' he yelled. 'How long before I pour?'

'Thirty seconds and a stir.'

He heard her laugh again. Such an amazing sound.

He poured her tea and sweated on his own. He liked to give it at least three minutes for the tannins to infuse. Bugger it! He couldn't keep her waiting that long. He filled his mug, splashed in the token drops of milk and one heaped spoonful of sugar. It wouldn't be quite right but it'd do.

'Here you go,' he said and put both mugs down on the table. Something was different and he picked it immediately. The woman had brought a second chair around from the east side.

'I hope you don't mind,' she said.

'Of course not.' He felt obliged to explain his system to her.

'That's brilliant,' she said, and sounded like she meant it. She took a sip of her tea. 'Perfect.'

Without thinking, Billy leaned back in his chair and swung his feet up onto the rail. Almost immediately he realised his error and how rude and hick he must appear. But then she surprised him. Everything about her surprised him.

'May I?' she said. He watched, fascinated, as she swung her legs up onto the rail as casually as you like. That wasn't something women generally did. Her legs were long and slim and ended unexpectedly in a pair of sneakers. She crossed her ankles.

'Don't you ever get tired of the view?'

'There's more to it than you think,' said Billy defensively. 'You'd be surprised at the variety of trees out there. There's a lot of coolibah and myall, but that's a belah tree over there where the crows are. It's as good a specimen as you'll see. Some people call it a scrub oak. You get other kinds that are stunted and don't have much of a spread on them. Over there you've got some boxes and a silver-leaf ironbark. That big dead gum is a favourite perch for cockatoos and galahs. They fight over it sometimes and the cockies usually win. Mostly it's the white cockies; the blacks seem to have their own favourite trees but they don't come round much. Everything changes with the light and the weather. Sometimes you can feel the struggle going on out there, but other times, you're right, it's just wallpaper.'

'Is that why you eat at different tables? For variety?'

He snorted.

'I follow the sun. Makes sense to watch the sun rise and set. Biggest events of the day. But west, I look out towards the Grawin and the sand ridge country where the property ends. That's hard country up there. Lots of black pine and gidgee. Some mulga. I've got the yards and races to look at, and power poles taking electricity out to the shearing sheds and the shearers' quarters. South, I look towards Cumborah. I've got the work shed and barns where I store feed and the road you came in on. The trees on the southeast corner are wilgas my dad planted. East, I've got the old windmill pumping water up for the house. With the new pumps it's a bit redundant, but I keep it going for old times' sake. The trees thin out a bit the closer you get to Walgett and, if you look hard enough, you can see through to the grey soil plains. In the end it doesn't matter much which way I look. I always find work to do.' Billy stopped talking to take a swallow of his tea. He had no idea why he felt the need to explain himself or why he was rabbiting on. Usually he wasn't much of a talker. But the sheer presence of the woman and her scent ... Jesus Christ! He had to drag his thoughts back to matters at hand.

'So what brings you here to the Downs, Miss ... uh ...?'

'Call me Linda.'

'Okay. What brought you here, Linda?'

'I want to rent a house.'

'Out here?'

'Yep. Out here.'

Billy focused on an old ironbark, which was the last individual thing he could see before the trees all merged into one. It stood head and shoulders above the others and was a gathering place for black cockatoos whenever rain threatened. Looking at it reminded him of the dead branch beneath it he'd been meaning to saw up for firewood. He was glad he wasn't standing under it when it fell. That would have hurt, but it was doubtful whether it would've stunned him any more than the woman had. What the hell did she want to rent a house out here for? There was nothing for her at Jindalee Downs and her soft, smooth hands were as ill suited to country life as a poodle was to mustering. Why here? He wanted to ask but didn't want to appear rude. She might tell him to mind his own business and he didn't want things to come to that. He sneaked a look at her and discovered she was watching him with a wry smile on her face. For some unaccountable reason he felt guilty.

'Jimmy said your parents' house might be available.'

Bloody Jimmy would. Jimmy knew all there was to know about people in the shire, not that it always amounted to much, and liked to keep the rest of the world informed. Billy had built a house up among the ridges at the opposite end of the property for his parents to live in once they'd retired and he'd taken over running the place. Somebody had to. Trouble was, both his sisters had families and had settled down, one in Dubbo and the other in Newcastle, and neither had the slightest desire to return. That had been one of the reasons Billy had come home and one of the reasons he'd stayed. But then his brother had delivered, as his parents had always hoped he would, and they'd had no further need of the house. They'd abandoned it with indecent glee. He thought of all the work and materials that had gone into building it and the months he'd spent on it. More waste.

Yeah, he thought, the house might be available. His parents had picked the site well. It was an anomaly and, but for the covering of trees, would have been a landmark in an otherwise featureless landscape. The house nestled on a geological fault where tectonic forces had pushed the rocky substrata up through the top of a sand ridge. The sand ridge was like a long, broad, gently rising ocean swell. It lifted the house more than twenty metres above the surrounding plains and the rocky outcrop lifted it another twelve. Together they provided enough elevation for the house to catch the breeze in summer and overlook the trees and scrub all the way to Lightning Ridge and further north towards Queensland. But for all its prominence, the site was no more than a wart on an elephant's hide; you'd never find it unless you went looking for it.

Water wasn't a problem. Tanks gathered rainwater from the roof and they'd also tapped into bore water at twelve metres at the foot of the sand ridge, which could be pumped up to the house. The Namoi County Council had run electricity out to the house at the same time they'd done the main homestead. Billy shook his head at the cost. It had set them back almost five hundred dollars for each pole, plus wires and transformer. All for what? He blamed his brother for the waste.

'Spent a couple of nights in it some months back, while I was repairing fences out that end.'

'Yes?'

By turning her response into a question, Linda had clearly hoped for some elaboration, but Billy's eyes remained fixed on some distant point and his tongue only moved to lick a rollie. He was trying to imagine her living in that remote house and struggled with the idea. But why? It wasn't the deprivation, because the house had power and water and, now that he came to think about it, even a phone line. It needed a good cleanup, curtains, furniture and a lick of paint on the outside. It needed a garden, which would take some digging, and a vegie patch. But even he had to accept these were the sorts of challenges women thrived on, if there was a will and if they put their mind to it. The problem wasn't the house, but why she could want to live in such a remote place. What would she do there? What could it possibly offer her?

Out of the corner of his eye he could see her long legs paralleling his on the rail. Her jeans seemed tailor-made and accentuated rather than hid the elegance of her legs. They were truly amazing, a sight he'd never expected to see resting on his rail over his midmorning cuppa. The longer he looked the more certain he became. They were too elegant, too shapely and, despite the sneakers, surely made to slip under restaurant tables and office desks. Whatever his parents' house had claims to be, it was no place for a city woman. He thought it would be a kindness, the right thing to do, if he knocked the whole idea on the head straightaway and made up his mind to do so. He decided to suggest she look elsewhere.

'How far away is it?' she asked.

Her question caught him unprepared and he answered automatically.

'About eight k's by road. Bit less through the bush.'

'How long will it take us to get there?'

Billy stubbed the butt of his rollie on the heel of his boot and dropped it into an apricot jam tin half-filled with soil which he kept by the right rear leg of his chair for that purpose. How long will it take us to get there, not how long does it take? He wondered if this surprising woman could also read his mind.

'Depends how much of a hurry you're in,' he answered dryly.

Billy drove her up in his ute, knowing that Rodney would recognise it. Rodney Webb owned the adjoining land on the western side and was as mad as a cut snake where strangers were concerned. The day was complicated enough without having to explain Rodney to Linda and vice versa. He drove through the bush, where left and right were no different to in front and behind, just to give her an idea of the kind of country she'd be dealing with. A city woman could get lost just going for a five-minute stroll. He also let her do the gates, well aware of what the bulldust would do to her hair, skin and clothes. Dust was a fact of life and something you had to deal with, except when it rained and became mud; then mud was a fact of life. After about ten minutes, Billy turned onto a track and followed it up a sand ridge to a narrow gravelly gully. A car shelter, which consisted of four poles and a vee-shaped corrugated iron roof without guttering, sat in a clearing at the foot of the gully.

'I'll take it,' murmured Linda.

Billy finally allowed a smile.

'The house is about seventy metres further up behind these mulga trees. I bulldozed a track up to it to get building materials in. Then the rains came and the water decided the track offered the quickest way down the hill. Should've thought of that, should've cambered it and run a drain down the side.' He parked the ute in the shade and got out.

'I didn't expect a house on a hill.'

Billy just grunted and let Linda fall in alongside. The track was pretty much the way he'd left it, cut with channels where the rains had run off and littered with sharp stones and gravel. For all that he resented the very existence of the house, he had to admit he liked visiting it on the rare occasions he made the effort. The stand of silvery mulga made a fine sight and trees that were rare elsewhere on his property had found a home to their liking in the narrow cleft between the ridges of the outcrop. Some shaded the track and kept it cool. There was a leopardwood and a couple of wilgas. He glanced towards Linda and she smiled back. Well, if she was looking for her Garden of Eden, this was as close as she was ever likely to get in the northwest.

'There it is.' Billy paused where the house came into view. It sat proud in an area that had been cleared and grassed but which was now infested with weed and scrub. Already he regretted bringing Linda to see it because its condition embarrassed him. It looked exactly as it was: unlived in, unloved, unwanted. The empty windows stared back like dead men's eyes. Only the leopardwood, which dominated the backyard and framed the house with the spread of its crown, made the scene in any way welcoming.

'I built it pretty much on my own.'

'When?' Linda was taking shots with a small camera.

'Ten, twelve years ago, thereabouts.'

'Looks like it could've been here since the first settlers arrived.'

'Thanks.'

Linda laughed.

'All I'm trying to say is that it looks like it belongs here.' Wide, shady verandas surrounded the house on the front and both sides, making it appear bigger than it actually was. Despite the presence of a chimney stack on the eastern side, Linda got the clear impression that most of the living was intended to take place out on the verandas, just as it did back at Billy's, although these weren't boxed in by screens. 'Shall we go up?'

The house had been built for the view and once they'd stepped up onto the veranda it was obvious why. The house overlooked a sea of treetops. To the sides, the gravel ridges and bush afforded shelter from the wind and sun, but ahead nothing impinged on the view.

'My God,' said Linda.

'I'll show you inside,' said Billy. The front door led straight into the living and dining room. Two doors led off the westward side into the main bedroom and a smaller guest bedroom where visiting grandchildren would have slept. A third door, opposite the front door, led to a large kitchen, laundry, bathroom and toilet.

'Waste goes into a septic tank,' said Billy. 'I always figured a vegie garden would go below the absorption trenches where that green patch is.'

'It's exactly what I'm looking for,' said Linda.

'And what exactly are you looking for?' Billy regretted his bluntness the moment the words left his lips. It was none of his business.

Linda studied him for what seemed like an age, as though assessing him and deciding how much to reveal.

'Solitude,' she said simply, and turned away to look at the stove.

Solitude. Billy shook his head.

'Well, you've sure hit the jackpot here.'

She offered him seventy-five dollars a week, cash in hand, and all his reservations about a city woman taking up residence vanished. He hadn't expected her to take the house, not for a moment, and under the circumstances even fifty seemed over the top. Seventy-five dollars. He did his sums and quickly calculated that it added up to three thousand, nine hundred dollars a year, which would buy a fair bit of feed if the rain held off and pay a few wages to shearers and the casual help he employed from time to time. He also figured it was about time his parents' house paid back some of the money that had gone into it. The prospect of having this amazing, apparently single woman living nearby didn't enter his calculations at all.

He showed her how to pump bore water up to the tanks and header tanks when the rainwater ran low and how to switch gas cylinders for the cooker. He promised to get a grader to have a go at the track so she could get a truck up with her furniture and gave her numbers to ring to get the electricity and phone turned back on. Thirty-nine hundred dollars a year! For doing nothing. He couldn't get the figure out of his mind. Maybe it was piss in a bucket to his brother, but it was thirty-nine hundred very welcome dollars to him.

She counted out a month's rent, three hundred and twenty-five dollars in crisp notes, handed them to him and then said something strange.

'The deal's off if you tell anyone. Okay?'

Billy nodded.

'Tell no one. I don't want anyone to know I've rented this place, or even moved into the area.'

'Fine with me.'

'I'll do all the arrangements from Sydney. I'll put the electricity and phone in a company name and give you a call when I've moved in. As far as anyone else out here is concerned, I don't exist, right?'

'Right.' Billy couldn't imagine how her arrival could possibly remain a secret for long. What about mail, supplies, her white Range Rover? She stood out like a prize rose in a cabbage patch.

'So, Billy Dwyer, we have a deal.' She offered her hand and Billy shook it. 'Oh, one more thing. Whatever you do, don't tell Jimmy.'

Billy's face cracked into a smile. He tucked the three hundred and twenty-five dollars into his back pocket. She had Jimmy pegged all right. She'd used him to make light of her need for secrecy, but a change had come over her, however fleeting, like a passing shadow.

Linda went home to the city and Billy went back to the job of crotching and spraying his ewes against flystrike. The procedure was simple enough, just a matter of shearing a horseshoe shape around the beasts' hindquarters and spraying the shorn area with Vetrasin, but with the lambing season hard upon him he borrowed a young Aboriginal man who worked for his neighbour to help out, paid him wages, fed him and provided him with a bed. The lad's name was Shane and Billy liked him because he was well mannered, quiet by nature and a genuinely hard worker. They got on well together, sharing meals, watching television and occasionally exchanging views on matters of common interest. The constant work and the presence of Shane crowded Billy's days and nights to the exclusion of everything else. He forgot all about Linda and was caught by surprise when a bank cheque arrived for the following month's rent. It helped pay Shane's wages and he was grateful for it.

The cold winds eased a week before the first lambs arrived and the seasons changed as abruptly as though someone had thrown a switch. With the prospect of rent money supplementing his income, Billy hung onto Shane for another few weeks to help him mend fences and gates. He also had some corrugated iron sheets to replace on the roof of his shed before the summer rains and it was a job more easily accomplished by two. When Shane departed, life returned to normal with spring lambing in full swing. But it also brought a brief period of lesser activity and time for Billy to put his feet back up on the rail over a midmorning cuppa and rollie.

By his reckoning, seven weeks had passed since Linda had appeared out of the blue in her Range Rover and he'd begun to wonder whether he'd ever see her again. Yeah, she'd sent him a cheque, but that could simply have been a means to buy time while she came to her senses. Then again, there was her need for a hideaway, otherwise what was the point of her conditions of secrecy? It occurred to him that maybe she didn't need a hideaway any more. If she did, he reasoned, she'd already have moved in. Billy shook his head to get his mind back on to the present and swung his legs down off the rail. Two rollies had hit the apricot jam tin, which was a sure sign that he'd wasted too much time thinking about her. He was pretty well resigned to never seeing her again.

He could hear his kelpie shuffling about under the front steps, getting impatient, reminding him he had a bit of mustering to begin, a bunch of steers he needed to bring in and get ready for market. He'd kept a paddock full of Mitchell grass for that purpose and bought in some corn to help fatten them up. He rose and rinsed his mug in the kitchen sink. His cattle dogs, chained to their kennels, started up a chorus of barking and by the time he'd put his hat back on and closed the screen door behind him they were straining at their leashes. He hadn't a clue how they knew there was work to do, but they always did. Maybe they'd heard him getting the trail bike ready, replacing the pin and float in the carburettor, cleaning the plugs and re-setting the gap. Maybe they saw him wiring up the front guard so that it stopped catching on the tyre. Maybe he gave out a hundred little signs that they noticed and he never gave a thought to. Maybe they were just more attuned to the cycle of things.

He set off with his kelpie up on the fuel tank, leaning back against his shirt front, and his working dogs chasing along behind, and decided to forget about the city woman. It was a decision easily made but not easily adhered to. He'd spent so much time thinking about how he'd use the rent money, what should've been a bonus now felt like a loss. And there was something else too, no less disquieting. He hadn't undergone an epiphany or been blinded by sudden revelation, but something had happened, something which he couldn't ignore no matter how hard he tried, something that felt strangely like an awakening.

Chapter Four

Although things hadn't always been so, Linda prided herself on her management and organisational skills and her ability to handle people. She was a fast learner, which had taken a lot of people by surprise, none more so than her ex-husband. The Range Rover had gone, replaced by a second-hand drab green Toyota Land Cruiser, little different to the others she'd seen around Walgett, Coonamble and Collarenebri on her earlier reconnaissance. People wanting to keep a low profile did not drive Range Rovers. She'd left the Castlereagh Lodge at Coonamble at 2 am and motored steadily up the Castlereagh Highway so she would arrive at her new home well before dawn and still have time to attach bright yellow ribbons to poles at each turn-off to guide the furniture truck. She'd rung around to find a removal company that had an unpainted truck, and settled on one that was using a Budget rental to cover for a truck that was in for repairs. She'd given the company detailed maps but still didn't trust them not to get lost. Although the ribbons might attract attention and some curiosity, they were a far better option than having the driver ask locals for directions. The driver and his mate were also under instructions to stop and remove the ribbons as they passed by. Linda was satisfied she'd done all she could to conceal the fact of her arrival.

Wherever possible she attached the ribbons to poles immediately before turn-offs, to give the driver time to wake up and react. Country driving had a way of dulling the senses, particularly of those driving a slow, heavy vehicle. She left the ribbon ends loose so that they'd flap if there was any breeze. Experience had taught her that the eye was drawn to even a small amount of movement. She turned up the track that led to the car shelter beneath her new home just as her watch ticked past 5 am and the sky had only just begun to hint that another day was in the making. Her timing was about right, she figured. First, a stretch and maybe a light doze in the car until it was time to make breakfast. She'd brought a kettle, toaster and a pot to boil two eggs. A cup of tea, buttered toast cut into soldiers and two runny eggs out on the steps of her veranda sounded like the perfect way to take up residence, until she realised she'd forgotten to include an eggcup. The eggcup hadn't even made it onto her checklist. The oversight made her smile. So she wasn't Miss Efficiency after all.

She parked the Toyota and got out. With the headlights off, night still held a firm grip on the land despite the soft glow in the east. She decided to cancel her loosening stroll and simply do a few stretches. It wasn't that she was scared of any specific thing, she just didn't know what to expect at that time of the day. She knew some snakes were nocturnal and that there were feral pigs about and maybe even dingoes or wild dogs. Just because nobody had mentioned dingoes didn't mean they weren't there. Maybe whatever was around would take off once she started shining her torch about. Maybe. But maybe wasn't good enough for Linda, who liked to do her homework and deal with certainties. She climbed back into her Toyota, wound down the front windows a little to let in some of the cool dry air, reclined her seat and closed her eyes.

Billy had been good enough to give her the plans to the house, so she'd bought furniture that would not only suit in terms of character but also dimension. By the time the truck arrived around eleven, she'd have strips of tape or chalk marks on the floor indicating where each piece had to go so she wouldn't have the problem of moving furniture around single-handedly later. She began practising the breathing rhythms she'd learned at meditation classes to ease herself into a light sleep. Ten minutes later, the first stone thudded into the side of her Toyota.

Linda shot bolt upright and looked anxiously around. She could make out the shape of bushes and trees against the lightening sky but not much more. Maybe something had fallen from a tree but it sure hadn't sounded like it. When a second stone thudded into the Toyota she realised she had a problem and she made a desperate grab for her torch.

'Bar-tid! Bar-tid! Pid off! I know whad you're af-da!'

Linda pointed her torch in the direction the voice had come from and jammed it hard against her side window. It took a few moments for the torch to find its target and then Linda almost wished it hadn't. All the horror stories and myths about outback psychopaths and murderers flooded back in one nerve-jarring instant. She didn't know what scared her most: the rifle pointing at her or the face of madness behind it.

'Garn! Pid off be-fore I toot you! Garn, ya thie-vin' bar-tid, git lod!'

The sentences were delivered in a strange staccato fashion, with every second syllable stressed, which made them hard to understand. But there was no misunderstanding the sentiments or the consequences if she ignored them. Dust blurred her vision as she dropped her torch, jammed the gear selector into reverse and spun the Toyota around so it faced back down the track. She hit the lights and accelerated away, expecting to hear a crack from the rifle at any second, sobbing with relief when it didn't happen, only slowing once she'd negotiated a bend. She had to slow down, not just because of the condition of the track but because her hands were shaking so badly she barely had control. She'd never stared down the barrel of a rifle before or into the eyes of a madman. The combination had been nothing short of terrifying. Her life could have ended in a blink of an eye, through no fault of her own and for no good reason. Linda was shaken to her core.

Once she'd put a kilometre between herself and the madman, she pulled to the side of the road to give herself a chance to calm down and take stock of her situation. The obvious thing to do was to drive into Walgett, contact the police and make the madman their problem. But then she'd become a talking point for the entire district, and everyone would know about her and where she was living, all of which negated the whole point of the exercise. There was only one other option besides turning around and driving back to Sydney. If he was up, she figured she'd find him with a mug of tea in his hand, sitting feet up on the eastern side of his house. But what if he wasn't there?

* * *

In fact Billy had only just put the kettle on when Linda's Toyota came tearing up the driveway towards his house, lights on high beam even though the sun's imminent arrival made it debatable whether she needed lights on at all. It had taken him a couple of days to round up and walk his steers to the good pastures near the homestead. It had been careful, patient work rather than tiring, with most of his efforts going into restraining the enthusiasm of his dogs. He could've finished sooner, but mustering could knock the beasts around so that they lost condition and that was the last thing he wanted. His dogs might have preferred a bit more excitement but, as much as they loved to belt around, Billy knew they'd rather work a couple of days than just one. Besides, he always gave them a good run racing them home at the end of the day.

Billy didn't recognise the Toyota and hadn't a clue what idiot was driving it, only that someone was in a God Almighty hurry and kicking up enough dust to damn near bury the house. Keeping things clean was hard enough without such stupidity. He knew it couldn't be a local. Locals knew better than to do that. The Toyota had woken the dogs and they'd reacted as they always did to excitement by getting excited themselves. They strained at their chains, barking and snarling. The kelpie, which had come out from under the steps, was standing poised for action, ears pricked and tan eyebrows raised. The Toyota stopped and was momentarily lost from sight as dust billowed over it and headed for the house. The dogs copped it too and voiced their disapproval.

The kelpie took off, tail not so much wagging as thrashing, giving Billy his first inkling as to who his uninvited guest might be. Despite the discourtesy of the dust he began to smile, but his smile vanished the moment he saw her running towards him. He'd seen that look on people's faces before and it was something he'd hoped never to see again. An instant after he opened the screen door she was in his arms, sobbing on his shoulder, trying to speak between sobs.

'It's okay,' he said, without having a clue what was okay. He kept an eye on his driveway in case whatever or whoever had scared her was still chasing her. But the only thing moving was the dust and that was settling. 'It's okay,' he repeated, holding her tight until her sobs subsided and she began to calm down. He led her around to the eastern veranda and made her sit down. Only then did he become aware of the whistle from his kettle and wondered how long that had been going on.

'Black with lemon, thirty seconds and a stir,' he said, and finally drew a ghost of a smile from her. 'Yeah, I got some lemons in. Tried it. Not my thing. I'll get another chair and you can tell me what happened to you over a cuppa.'

Billy went the long way to the kitchen so he could check his driveway. Nothing moved. The dust had settled, the dogs had crawled back into their kennels and the kelpie was back under the steps. When he rejoined Linda she was more like the cool, confident, amazing city woman he remembered. But, Jesus Christ, something had shaken the living daylights out of her.

Linda began to tell her story and she'd hardly begun before he was assailed by guilt. He let her go on, thinking she needed to get it out of her system.

'That was Rodney,' he said eventually. The sun was up but hadn't yet cleared the trees. Soon it would flood the veranda and take the night chill off the air. Not far away, kookaburras were having a discussion of their own and magpies were tuning up. 'You should have let me know you were coming so I could've had a word with him.'

'You know him?' Linda was incredulous.

'He's your neighbour.'

'My neighbour!' She was angry now. 'Why didn't you tell me I had a gun freak madman for a neighbour? Don't you think that's pertinent information?'

'Rodney's all right.'

'The hell he is!'

Billy leaned back in his chair, focused on a distant box gum that was among the first to have its upper branches highlighted by the sun, and began rolling a cigarette. She was upset but had no call to contradict him or question his knowledge. He decided to give her time to calm down. He noticed she hadn't swung her feet up onto the rail and thought perhaps things would go a bit better if she did. A couple of grass parrots flew by at breakneck speed, a blaze of red and green. Forty or fifty zebra finches clustered around the dripping tap at the edge of his vegie garden, busily filling up ahead of the heat. His tea tasted dusty but that didn't surprise him.

'Secrecy is one thing,' he said finally. 'But what did you stand to lose by telling me you were coming?'

'You were supposed to be my litmus test. If I could move in without you knowing, then I could be pretty sure nobody else would know.' She swung her feet up onto the rail, which Billy took as a good sign. The fact that she was wearing heavier, more utilitarian jeans this time and ankle-high boots made her legs less distracting, but only marginally. He gave her time to settle and find something to focus on. Some grey kangaroos were foraging no more than a hundred metres away. He wondered if she'd noticed them.

'No harm done,' he said. 'Rodney has to know anyway, and he's not going to tell anyone.'

'Want to tell me about him?'

Billy took a final drag on his rollie before stubbing it out on his boot heel and dropping it into the apricot jam tin. There were apricot jam tins strategically placed on each veranda.

'I've known Rodney all my life. Went to school with him. He's a bit odd but he's okay. He's got some diggings up on his land, which occasionally produce some pretty decent opals. They're black seam opals, like you get down on the Grawin. Funny thing, his dad was just like him, same affliction, same addiction to opals, same fierce determination to guard his patch.'

'What affliction? Are you saying he's insane?'

'Rodney, insane? No, he's sane enough, just sane in a different way. What time's your truck due?'

'About eleven.'

'Let me make breakfast and I'll take you up to meet him.'

Linda tagged along behind in her Toyota as Billy set off across country in the ute with the kelpie up on the tray, driving slowly so that he didn't choke her with his dust. She realised he was only being considerate but that did nothing to ease her growing impatience. It had passed eight and the truck was due in less than three hours. There were things she had to get done up at the house and had hinted over breakfast that she was anxious to get on with them. But nothing she said appeared to have any effect on him. He did things as she supposed he always did them, with the unhurried efficiency that typified country folk. But she sensed his mannerisms weren't exclusively the product of geography or his solitary life and that there was something else governing him. There was a remoteness to him that showed in the faraway look in his eyes, as though he wasn't quite rooted in the present. Although she hardly knew him, and realised any speculation was, to say the least, premature, it seemed to her that he'd made a conscious effort to remove all the peaks and troughs from his existence. She'd arrived unannounced on his doorstep, more than just a little hysterical, and thrown herself weeping into his arms — hardly the sort of thing that happened every day. Yes, he'd done all the right things, calmed her down and made a cup of tea, but there'd been no emotion in his response, not even surprise, and that puzzled her. Her own life had known too many ups and downs in its thirty-eight years and she readily conceded she'd have been happier if there'd been fewer, but peaks and troughs, the highs and lows, were ultimately what made life interesting.

Ah, what the heck, she thought, maybe he's just the strong, silent type. Everyone was a bit strange in their own way and she didn't have time to worry about Billy and his peculiarities, not with her furniture due almost any moment. Besides, she had another hurdle to negotiate. Somewhere up ahead there was someone even stranger: a madman who was both armed and her neighbour.

She watched the kelpie run from one side of the ute to the other with the regularity of a metronome and wondered if she should have a dog. Maybe a dog was just what she needed to keep feral animals and freaky neighbours at bay. But dogs spoke of a commitment she was in no position to make. She dismissed the idea as the ute swung onto the track and turned up towards her house. She stiffened in her seat when she recognised the spot at the side of the track where she'd pulled over to dry her eyes and failed utterly in her attempt to stop shaking.

Billy parked short of the carport so she could have the shade and his ute would be out of the way when the truck arrived. She backed into the carport so she could make a fast getaway if need be. The panicky two-point turn she'd been forced to execute earlier felt like it had taken for ever, despite the fact that she'd chipped the odd cog with her desperate gear changes. The last thing she wanted was a repeat of the experience. By the time she'd turned off the motor, Billy had got out of the ute and was leaning up against his bullbar. She jumped when he put two fingers in his mouth and let fly a piercing whistle, but realised almost immediately it wasn't her attention he was trying to attract. He motioned to her to stay in the Toyota and slowly began to roll a cigarette. She was happy to oblige, even to the extent of locking her doors. Billy had smoked his rollie down to the butt before Rodney appeared out of the grey bush on the passenger side of the track, shotgun in hand.

Linda almost screamed. He looked even more frightening in broad daylight than he had by the beam of her torch. He glared at her through the window, head slightly angled away, eyes filled with suspicion. Lank black hair, matted and choked with dust, hung in long greasy strands beneath a battered Akubra and met up with an equally unkempt, greying beard. But what held her riveted was the constant flow of expressions across the madman's face: anger, malice, frustration? His jaw worked furiously as if he was trying to summon up insults to hurl at her, but no words came. His shotgun was jammed hard against his shoulder but, mercifully, not pointed at her but down. His whole body seemed alive with barely restrained energy. Her mind wrestled with what she was seeing and tried desperately to make sense of it. His head kept bobbing angrily up and down behind the rifle and Linda suddenly realised what she was witnessing. The last emotion she'd expected to feel was compassion but it washed through her. The other thing she noticed in that instant was his size. Her neighbour, her terrifying neighbour, was barely a metre seventy even with his hat on.

He turned from her and strode down the track towards Billy. Linda watched him go, confused by the sudden change in her feelings. She saw the kelpie dash out from under the ute and run to greet him. While the two made a fuss of each other, Linda took a more measured look at her strange neighbour. He wore a jacket over what appeared to be a collarless shirt or undershirt. God only knew what colour his jacket and trousers had been originally but both had aged and worn down to roughly the same filthy charcoal grey. Linda thought she saw tinges of dark green still in the jacket, but had to concede the green could've been anything from stains to mould. His boots had probably once been black but were now a cracked, crazed, indeterminate grey. A whitish dust and soil coated everything.

Billy lit up another cigarette and handed it to Rodney, before lighting one for himself. If a word had passed between them, Linda had missed it. She watched as both men drew smoke deep into their lungs and exhaled. Then Billy started talking and Linda would have given anything to hear what he had to say. She began to feel foolish, but then remembered how different things had been earlier that morning, when she'd had every reason to react the way she had.

Her nerves were more or less under control when Billy waved to her to come down. The 'thunk' as her doors unlocked sounded embarrassingly loud. Both men were watching as she climbed out of the Land Cruiser and probably laughing to themselves. She hadn't exactly distinguished herself. Damn them, she thought, it was time to assert some kind of control. She stopped and bent over, hands on knees.

'Here, boy,' she called.

The kelpie didn't need to be told twice. It bounded over to meet her as if it hadn't already gone through that ritual with her earlier. She rubbed its ears and the spot in front of its tail, keeping the two men waiting, determined not to behave like a frightened city woman. She stood up, straightened her back, made a beeline for Rodney and held out her hand.

'Hi, I'm Linda.'

'Bitch.'

Bitch? Linda tried to withdraw her hand but Rodney already had hold of it and hung on. His bottom teeth hammered uncontrollably against his top teeth.

'The dog. Id a bitch.' He let go of her hand.

'Oh.' He was talking about the kelpie. She half expected to read amusement in his eyes but saw only suspicion.

'Rodney's sorry for frightening you but he didn't know who you were.'

'That's okay.' She listened to Billy but kept her eyes on Rodney and even offered a smile. It wasn't returned.

'He thought you were one of the prospectors up from the Grawin, after his opals.'

'I'm not.'

'He knows that now. Also, he didn't realise you were a woman.'

'A lot of people make that mistake.' She glanced at Billy who snorted and crushed his rollie beneath his heel.

'I told Rodney you needed someone to dig a garden for you.'

'You told him what?' Linda glared at Billy, clearly questioning his sanity. She glanced back at Rodney whose expressions ranged from suspicion and distrust to outright rage.

'You need someone to break up the soil and dig out the stones. It's hard work for anyone but Rodney's kind of used to it. He charges ten dollars an hour.'

Rodney's restless jaw jutted forward in defiance, making the point that his fee wasn't negotiable.

'Sounds fair,' said Linda, though the look she gave Billy was nothing short of withering.

'He says he can start next week.'

'Lucky me.'

'Good, then it's agreed.' Billy spun around and opened the passenger door of his ute. He pulled out a slab of Tooheys Old and handed it to Rodney.

Rodney took the slab without a word of thanks, glared at Linda one last time and retreated back into the scrub.

'Thank you, Billy Dwyer. That's all I need,' said Linda once she thought Rodney was out of earshot.

'A drunken madman with a gun doing my gardening.'

'Yeah, sorry to drop the garden thing on you, but I figured it was the best way to solve two problems.'

'Specifically?'

'Well, you need someone to dig your garden and Rodney needs to become accustomed to you.'

'What do you mean?'

'Give him a week or two and he'll have forgotten he met you. How many times do you want him to greet you with his shotgun?'

'Shotgun?' It sounded so much more threatening than a rifle.

'The shotgun's his weapon of choice but he has a rifle as well. One day you'll recognise the difference. I figure if he digs your garden and you give him a few dollars to come over and help you with it, he'll get used to you being around.'

'And what about the beer?'

'Rodney's not much of a drinker. The carton will last him a month. He doesn't go into town much so I usually get him what he needs. The basics, beer and a block of chocolate.'

'Chocolate? Very generous.'

'He pays for everything I get him out of his disability pension. They don't know he sells the occasional opal and he's smart enough not to tell them.'

'Doesn't tell them about the gardening, either?'

'What do you think?' Billy paused as if deciding whether or not to continue. He sighed heavily. 'Look, there's something else you should know about Rodney. Sometimes he loses things a bit.'

'What do you mean?'

'He'll start shouting and swearing at you for no good reason. He doesn't mean to and doesn't want to, but something just takes hold of him. Sometimes he gets this helpless look in his eyes, like he knows what's going on but can't stop himself. He won't harm you, but it can be a bit off-putting until you get used to it.'

'For heaven's sake, Billy, have you got any more surprises? I've got to tell you I'm damn near surprised out.'

Billy shifted uncomfortably.

'Look, I'm only doing what I think is best.'

'I hope in a week or two I'll share your point of view. Now, shall we go on up?'

The truck arrived on time and managed to negotiate the newly graded track without too many dramas. While the removalists unloaded the van, Billy drove home and returned with fresh eggs, bread and a dozen cans of VB. Linda didn't realised he'd gone anywhere until the smell of curried eggs began to waft through the house.

'What on earth are you doing?' she asked.

'Protecting your interests.'

'By currying eggs?'

'Look, Linda, these guys are hot, hungry and thirsty and they're going to want to eat before they head back to Sydney. Do you really want them shooting their mouths off in the first pub they come to?'

'They know to be discreet,' she said defensively.

Billy just stared at her before turning his attention back to his eggs.

'So how come I took down the ribbons?'

Linda closed her eyes and silently cursed the removalists before realising she should be giving thanks.

'It's nice to have someone watching over me,' she said. 'I don't know how I would have managed without you. I do my best but sometimes it's hard to think of everything.'

The faraway look crept into Billy's eyes.

'Sometimes it's hard to think of anything.'

Lousy jacks woke Linda on the first morning in her new home, but she stayed in bed until the light flooding into her bedroom made dozing impossible. She couldn't recall the last time she'd slept right through a night or enjoyed a sleep as deep and restful. The day before had been long and eventful and she'd gone to bed worn out, but, for her, that was a normal state of affairs. What wasn't normal was the silence of the night and she credited that and the cool night air with the soundness of her sleep. There'd been no noise at all. No traffic, no sirens, no aeroplanes, no boats, no voices, no barking dogs, no possums on the roof, no wind ruffling trees, no arguing neighbours. When she looked out through the window she could see an unbroken blue sky above the ridge line and decided to make hanging her prefabricated cedar blinds a priority. But then she looked at the pale lemon and lilac floral wallpaper and realised there was no point in hanging blinds until the walls had been stripped and all the painting had been done. When she'd planned her escape from Sydney it had been with the clear intention of getting back into her painting, but painting walls wasn't quite what she'd had in mind.

Hey, she thought, slow down. She had to get used to the idea that there were no longer any deadlines and no time pressures. The day was hers to use however she wished and, furthermore, so were all the tomorrows. She decided to make a cup of tea and go for a walk before breakfast so she could get a feel for the land surrounding her.

The gully peaked on a ridge about thirty metres behind the house and the grey gidgee scrub thinned out the higher she went. Their twisted trunks suggested that life was not easy in her gully, but Linda was in no mood for anything negative. Billy had told her there was nothing on the other side except another ocean of treetops stretching to the horizon, interrupted only by a few sand ridges that obscured the one feature of any interest, Narran Lake. All the same, she wanted to see for herself. To avoid ripping her sneakers on the hard stony ground, she wore her boots and took the advice Billy had given her about walking in the scrub.

'Keep your eye on the track in front of you at all times while you're moving,' he'd said. 'If you want to look around, stop first. That way you won't go stepping on something you shouldn't. Oh,' he'd added as an afterthought, 'make a lot of noise so if there is something up ahead of you, it's got time to get out of the way.'

Linda made a point of stepping on twigs and crunching up leaves. A pair of hares startled her when they broke cover and took flight. She smiled. Hares, she could deal with. Although she knew what to expect, when she reached the top of the ridge she was still stunned and in awe of the view. As far as she could see to the south there were no signs of human habitation: no roads, no houses and no electricity poles or pylons. Somewhere in the distance were the Macquarie Marshes and, when she looked hard, she could see the darker green lines that marked the courses of the Barwon River and the Big Warrambool. The disappointed ahh-ahh-ahhhhh of a solitary raven only served to underscore the loneliness of the vast expanse. The view to the west was blocked by the sand ridge a kilometre away where Rodney lived. It was little different to her own, except that it had no upthrust of rock on top of it and, wherever gaps in the cypress pine and coolibahs allowed, she could see mounds of off-white soil among the red gravel that were quite clearly man-made. She guessed they were Rodney's diggings, but distance made detail elusive. Movement caught her eye and she stood motionless while a pair of pale-headed parrots, like small sun-bleached lorikeets, flitted among the branches of a nearby tree.

She slowly picked her way back along the western ridge line, looking down on her bedroom window as she passed her house, before pausing on a ledge that gave her a commanding view north and northeast where the rolling hill of Lightning Ridge eased above the plains. Although she knew where the road should be, she couldn't find a trace of it, nor could she see any sign of Billy's house. Only the track leading to her home and the power poles gave any indication that her world was inhabited. An argument broke out among galahs far away on the undulating plains and the sun put a shine on her perspiring forehead. A grim smile crept over her face. People always claimed that the best place to hide was in a crowd, but they'd obviously never stood where she was.

* * *

Neil pushed himself back in his chair to let his friends know it was time for a break. When he glanced over to the bar he saw that Gancio had already begun to make their coffees: long black for Ramon, macchiato for Milos and Lucio, cappuccino for Neil. But what Neil was really looking forward to was the mid-afternoon shot of grappa. He still had a long way to go before he was finished for the day.

'I didn't realise you were a country boy,' said Ramon.

'Well, now you know.'

Lucio and Milos exchanged glances. Neil's earlier hostility seemed to have carried through his storytelling.

'I can see it is also going to be a romance,' said Lucio, trying to lighten the mood. 'I see the first signs of the *grand amore*.'

'Any love will be more than matched by hate,' said Neil. 'Count on it.'

'It's clear you weren't your brother's favourite person,' said Ramon. 'Yet in your introduction you made it sound as though the two of you were close.'

'That was also my impression,' said Lucio.

'So what?' said Neil. 'My story has hardly begun. You don't know anything yet. You don't know my brother, you don't know Linda and, God knows, you don't know me.'

Chapter Five

Two things were anathema to Billy and both were hard to avoid. Debt was something the northwest lived with, as much a fact of life as the red dirt and as common. A few years of good rains and good beef, lamb and wool prices could easily deceive as graziers began to feel indestructible. They paid back loans to the banks, built up their breeding stock and looked forward to a life easier than the one they'd known. But it didn't take much to bring them crashing down to earth and for the debt to start piling up again. Too little rain brought drought, and too much rain brought floods, and each brought its own set of hardships.

Billy could remember the magic days as a lad when the wool cheque had arrived. For those brief moments they'd felt like millionaires and, in a relative way, even acted like millionaires. His dad would eye up a good second-hand car or tractor, while his mother shopped for new clothes and shoes for everyone. He and his brother liked new clothes, but his sisters were like butterflies emerging from their chrysalises. They adored their new clothes and could hardly wait to show them off. But for Billy, the temporary affluence expressed itself in much more overt and immediate ways. The family drove down to Dubbo for a couple of days so they could go to the pictures. They bought ice-creams and chocolate bars and, for a brief time, enjoyed the kind of luxuries city kids took for granted. Those were the days when dynamite couldn't wipe the smiles off their faces, but they never lasted. The cheques might have borne his father's name but there were others with stronger claims to the amounts written on them. There were banks to placate, the stock and station, the service station and everyone else who'd given them goods on tick. Throughout all his childhood there'd never been a time when his parents didn't owe more than they had.

Billy had turned things around and it was a source of pride to him that the station now operated debt-free. Of course, his brother had helped initially, by paying off the debt he'd inherited, and was always there as a backstop when things got desperate, but Billy did his best to keep him out of the equation. As far as he was concerned, it was the least his brother could do, but, all the same, the less he had to do with him the better.

Billy had always listened when Neil and their dad discussed farm business. It had sounded so easy back then, but it had taken him years to understand the signs and variables that made the difference between operating at a profit or a loss. His brother had explained how maximising profitability lay in anticipating the market, in doing what everyone else planned to do but doing it first. Billy did his best but he still made misjudgements. He hadn't adjusted the balance of his stock to favour cattle at the expense of his labour- and cost-intensive sheep to the extent that he'd like, and he hadn't hedged his bets by sowing crops. But he'd managed through the droughts of the early eighties that had destroyed four crops out of five and brought his neighbours to their knees, somehow getting his starving stock through with minimal losses.

He'd watched the southern oscillation index for indications of rain in the early days of the droughts and talked to the local Aborigines, who had their own ways of forecasting which were as accurate as anyone's. The sight of rainbirds, the grey-coloured cuckoos, never failed to encourage him although they frequently let him down. The black cockies tended to be more reliable. People were often surprised when he began to stock up on cattle nuts and hay while there was still feed on the ground, but that was also when feed was at its cheapest. Once the droughts bit, he hand-fed his beasts and lopped the middle out of fodder trees to make his supplies and cash last longer. He'd managed to hold onto his cattle and sheep while his neighbours had sold, and cleaned up selling breeding heifers once the rains had come. True, on a couple of occasions he'd had to turn to his brother for a handout, but he dismissed them as irrelevant because the amounts were small and he would probably have got through anyway. Billy wasn't prepared to give his brother any credit for the fact that the station traded in the black. He wasn't prepared to give his brother credit for much at all.

The other thing Billy hated was handling and spraying herbicides, but that was a legacy of Vietnam and another fact of life he had to deal with. He often sprayed after the summer rains, particularly when the rivers had come up and there'd been a bit of a flood to spread seeds. The burrs and thorns were the worst of his problems. Along with the Hudson pear there were African boxthorn, Bathurst burr, Noogoora burr and roly-poly. The burrs played havoc with the wool, hooking onto sheep as they passed by. The matting they caused knocked dollars off the value of the fleece. The business of wool-growing was marginal enough without working for half-price. Thorns, like the six-centimetre-long thorns from the Hudson pear, could cripple sheep and cattle, and Billy had lost count of the times he'd had to get a pair of pliers to pull them out of his beasts and even out of his own hide. The pain was something you never forgot.

Billy was happy to contract out the spraying where extensive areas were involved, although he resented the cost and the threat to his liquidity. He did his best to maintain a reasonable grass cover so the roly-poly couldn't take over, and kept a sharp eye out for any infestation by introduced weeds which poisoned stock: the pigweed, cat head, blue heliotrope, mother-of-millions, mintweed and liverseed which occasionally snuck into the fertile eastern end of his spread. He attacked the weeds almost on sight.

To keep his costs down he'd cobbled together his own spray rig, a 600-litre tank, pump and spraying arm which he could mount on the back of his ute. He'd used it at the beginning of winter to kill a couple of outbreaks of mother-of-millions before it had the chance to seed and spread. Still, it was a job he hated even though he knew he was doing the right thing. The whole idea of spraying herbicides made him so uncomfortable he wore gloves, full-length overalls, a hood made from an old sheet that covered his head and neck, and an industrial mask to filter out the chemicals. None of his skin was exposed. Neighbours who'd seen him in his full attire laughed, but also felt some sympathy for him. While he tried to do his spraying when it was cold and still, some days grew a lot hotter than expected and then Billy really suffered.

His desire to always keep ahead of the game got him into his ute and on the road to Walgett to replenish his stocks of Roundup. On trips off his station he let the kelpie ride in the cabin alongside him with its head out the passenger window, licking the breeze. On really hot days that called for air-conditioning, the kelpie just curled up on the seat and slept off its boredom. Either way, Billy enjoyed the silent companionship. Given that Walgett was sixty k's from Jindalee Downs and a hundred and twenty k round trip, Billy never went there for just one reason. There was Rodney's pension cheque to cash, a bit of shopping for both of them and beer and chocolate to buy. His only concern was whether or not he should be buying for three.

He had no idea how Linda planned on getting her supplies. He hadn't asked and the subject had never come up. Obviously she couldn't go into Cumborah, Walgett or even Coonamble without setting tongues wagging. Maybe she could get away with a few trips to Lightning Ridge posing as a tourist. The Ridge was never short of tourists blowing through and she could pass herself off as one, for a while at least. But the Ridge offered no long-term solution to her problem and, when Billy thought about it, neither did he. There were just some things he couldn't buy without raising suspicion and revealing Linda's presence. But surely he could've bought her staples like potatoes, tea, coffee, sugar, flour, bread and tomato sauce. If he could split a sack of spuds with Rodney, he could easily do the same for her.

The issue stayed with him all the way into Walgett, but the fact remained that she had his phone number and hadn't rung once in the two weeks since she'd moved in. If she'd needed him to get her something she would've rung. Then the thought occurred that maybe she was waiting for him to ring and offer. But why would he ring her when she'd made it as plain as day that what she wanted was solitude? Did a phone call breach her idea of solitude? Probably. Would his good intentions be interpreted as interfering? Possibly. Was his silence indicative that he didn't care about her? Did he care about her? This was the toughest question to answer. Did he care? Why was she always creeping into his thoughts? Why was she always waiting for him unbidden when he emerged from his white-outs? By the time he pulled up outside the stock and station the issue had begun to bother him.

When he walked into the stock and station he hoped he'd find Peter serving but saw Jimmy holding court with a couple of graziers from down Carinda way. Jimmy ran the business but everyone Billy knew preferred dealing with Peter, or Elders down the road. The difference between the men was chalk and cheese. Peter knew his stuff, was straight as a die and always tried to do the best by you. He was the kind of bloke who looked you in the eye, was good company over a beer and didn't go sticking his nose in where it didn't belong. The same could not be said for Jimmy.

'G'day, Billy,' called Jimmy, as though they were inseparable mates. Jimmy liked to give the impression that he was best mates with everyone, when nothing could be further from the truth. He waited until Billy came close. 'How'd you go with that good-looking city sheila I sent you?' He winked at the graziers from Carinda. 'The one that wanted to rent your parents' house. Did you get to throw a leg over?'

Billy suppressed the sudden fury that threatened to engulf him. His first instinct was to defend his integrity and Linda's honour, but just as quickly he realised the pitfalls. Jimmy's customers were smiling expectantly so he took his cue from them.

'Hell are you going on about, Jimmy?' he asked affably. 'You didn't send me anyone, good-looking or otherwise.'

'Bloody did.'

'Well, I never saw her. Maybe she couldn't find my place, or called in when I was out in the paddocks. Be just my luck.' Billy nodded greetings to the graziers. They looked embarrassed but he also knew they were more than a little interested in the exchange.

'Way I hear things, she's already moved in,' said Jimmy smugly.

'Moved in where?'

'Your parents' place.'

'When?'

'About two weeks ago.'

'If only. Someone's winding you up, mate. I dossed down in the old place a couple of nights ago when I was moving some sheep around. There was no city sheila living there.' He turned to the two graziers. 'I think I would've noticed.'

The graziers laughed. They liked that bit. It was a line they could use later in the pub.

'Now, Jimmy, how about you finish serving these gentlemen while I find what I need?'

'We're about done,' said one of the graziers.

'Don't hurry on my account,' said Billy. He sauntered slowly and deliberately back to the front of the store and the open doorway, but all the while he was quietly seething. He knew Jimmy was just fishing but how many people had the bastard been talking to? How many people had he told about Linda? It was another reality of country life that people were so hungry for interesting local news that gossip became fact once it had been repeated often enough. But what could he do? If he tried to kill the gossip he would only succeed in arousing suspicions. The graziers said their goodbyes as they headed out the door.

'Last time I do you any favours,' said Jimmy as he caught up with him.

'Does that mean you won't help me load up my ute?'

'What do you want?'

'Roundup.'

'I'll get the trolley.'

Jimmy helped load the three drums of herbicide onto the ute but Billy could see he still wasn't finished with him.

'What about the yellow ribbons then? How do you explain them?'

'What ribbons?'

'I heard there were yellow ribbons tied to poles leading from Walgett through Cumborah up to your parents' place.'

Billy just shrugged. Cumborah was the last town before the turn-off. If you sneezed driving through it you missed it. Even so, people lived there and someone might have seen ribbons, but he couldn't imagine anyone following them to see where they led. No one would have any reason to. Jimmy was just speculating.

'When was this?'

'Told you. Two weeks ago.'

'Two weeks ago? No, I didn't see any ribbons.'

'Would you tell me if you did?'

'Of course.' Billy pulled on the ropes to make sure the drums were secure. 'We're mates, aren't we?'

He left Jimmy glaring down the road after him as he headed for the post office. Billy collected Rodney's cheque, cashed it and went straight to the supermarket. He completed his shopping without incident and wandered over to the RSL club for a glass or two to settle the dust before making the trip home. There were a couple of deadbeats watching the horse-racing on television and a few blokes standing around the bar having a beer before lunch. As he ordered a schooner he spotted the graziers from Carinda by an open window, talking to Peter from the stock and station, and decided to join them. Peter was on his lunch break.

'G'day, Billy,' said Peter. 'These blokes have just been telling me how Jimmy gave you the third degree.'

Billy shook Peter's hand.

'Third degree's about right.'

'I dunno what drives that bloke,' said Peter. 'He's got half the town convinced you've got that woman set up in a love nest.'

'I wouldn't know a love nest if I fell in one.'

'Want me to tell him to back off?'

'Do you think it would do any good?'

'Probably not.'

Billy sipped his beer thoughtfully.

'I don't know whether to feel pissed off or flattered,' he said. 'What was the woman like?'

'I'd feel flattered if I was you,' said Peter. 'That woman had real class. If you ever had a love nest, she's the one you'd want sitting on the eggs.'

Laughter ended the conversation and they got down to the serious business of discussing the likelihood of rain, how Collarenebri had got a brief downpour that missed everywhere else, and how long the wool prices would hold up. Billy always took note of other people's opinions because it was more information to help him make his decisions. He quit the pub after buying Peter a middy. The blokes from Carinda declined because they didn't want to get involved in a shout where everyone started buying rounds. He stopped at the Imperial bottle shop for a slab of VB and one of Tooheys Old and set off back home.

Linda had been on his mind when he'd pulled into Walgett and he was thinking about her as he left. Jimmy's speculation and gossip had gone beyond the point of containment and he just had to hope that the rumours would die in time through lack of nourishment. But it wouldn't take much to keep them alive or revive them, and he had to make that patently clear to Linda. Walgett was out of bounds if she wanted her presence kept secret. Collarenebri and Brewarrina were probably off limits too. Maybe she'd still get by up at the Ridge because of all the tourists passing through, but not before people started forgetting about her. So where did that leave her besides a prisoner in her own home? And how was she going to get her mail and supplies? He worried about her need for secrecy and the possible reasons behind it. But there was another matter that also troubled him, stemming from the comment Peter had made in the pub about a love nest. It wasn't something he wanted to think about, but it just wouldn't leave him alone.

Rodney banged on Linda's door on the dot of seven o'clock and scared the daylights out of her. She hadn't seen another living soul for two weeks and had grown accustomed to the fact that the only sounds she'd hear apart from the birds and the wind were those she made herself. She'd risen early and was preparing to undercoat walls newly stripped of wallpaper. Rodney's knock had come with the suddenness of a shot from a cannon.

She found him standing on the kitchen doorstep with a shovel over his shoulder, keeping his shotgun company, and a heavy hexagonal crowbar and mattock in his other hand. He didn't appear to have changed his clothes since she last saw him, or his attitude towards her.

'I've come to do your gar-den,' he said. His jaw worked furiously and the muscles in his face refused to be still. Linda found it less disconcerting to look him straight in the eye.

'Gun-na do the pot-ted dog fird.'

'What?'

'The pot-ted dog.' He raised his voice as though volume and anger would somehow aid comprehension. 'Got-ta get rid of the mid-dle toe.'

'Middle toe?'

'Yed. Ped-ly the yel-low mid-dle toe. Roo-win the pot-ted dog if you led it.'

'Show me,' said Linda. She hadn't a clue what he was talking about.

Rodney threw down his shotgun and tools and led her straight to the leopardwood. He pointed to the mistletoe that had taken hold of it, clearly frustrated by her lack of comprehension.

'Mistletoe!' said Linda.

'Thad what I daid. Mid-dle toe.'

'And the tree's a spotted dog.'

'Yed.'

'Billy said it was a leopardwood.'

'All-wade been a pot-ted dog to me.'

'Okay, get rid of the mistletoe,' said Linda. 'Want a hand?'

'All-wade work alone.'

'Okay. Let me know if you want a cup of tea or anything.'

Rodney ignored her. He was already trying to work out the best way of tackling the mistletoe. Linda went back inside and watched him briefly through the kitchen window. On the one hand she resented his intrusion into her little world, but, in a funny way, it wasn't unpleasant having someone there. His frustration had been obvious and she realised she'd have to work harder to get used to his staccato up-and-down speech and strange pronunciations. She wondered if it was frustration that triggered the mood swings Billy had warned her about. The line of thought terminated abruptly when she walked back into the living room and saw the magnitude of the task ahead of her. She wanted the painting finished and the blinds hung before she invited Billy over. As had happened so often in her life, proving her competency had become an issue with her. She poured undercoat into the tray and dipped the roller in, smiling to herself when she remembered the encouragement she used to give her students.

'A masterpiece begins with a single brush stroke,' she said out loud, and pushed the roller up the wall.

Shortly after ten she stopped to make a cup of tea and take a break. She'd managed to paint the living room and one of the bedrooms, although the corners and edges still needed cutting in by brush. Nevertheless, she was pleased with the start she'd made. After removing the fleece from the roller and soaking it in a bucket of water, she wandered around to the front of the house to see how Rodney was getting on digging the garden. The longer she watched her neighbour swinging the mattock, the more she appreciated how difficult the ground was to dig and how much strength there was in the little man's arms and upper body. She realised digging the garden would've worn her out in minutes and she could only stand and admire Rodney's application, willing to concede that Billy's idea wasn't so stupid after all.

'Want to break now for a cup of tea?' she called.

Rodney spun around with his mattock poised mid-swing and glared at her from beneath his battered Akubra. His face was streaked with sweat and dirt.

'Bar-tid!' he screamed. 'Bitch! Hoo-wah, bar-tid, bitch!'

Linda's jaw dropped and she stood momentarily stunned. What had she said to provoke him? But for Billy's warning about his turns, she'd have been convinced Rodney was about to turn the mattock on her. She retreated to the kitchen, not sure what to do next. Hiding until he'd calmed down seemed a good option. Instead, she decided to take her courage in both hands and face up to her neighbour. If Rodney had to get used to her, she had to get used to him. She made two cups of tea and put both on a tray along with milk, sugar and a plate of chocolate-coated biscuits. The biscuits were her indulgence, kept in the fridge and eaten one at a time as a reward for hard work. Filled with trepidation, she carried the tray out onto the front veranda. But she needn't have worried. Rodney had calmed down and was sitting in the shade on the top step. He also seemed in need of a break.

'Bar-tid, hoo-wah, bitch,' he said as she passed him his cup but the sting had gone out of his invective.

'Milk and sugar?' said Linda.

He ignored the milk but took two heaped teaspoons of sugar.

'Biscuit?' She offered him the plate and instantly realised her mistake. Rodney took one look at the chocolate coating the biscuits, took the entire plate and began hoeing into them. Oh well, she thought, he'd earned them. Rodney's never-still face reflected the conflicts raging inside his head but slowly the fire and anger in his eyes subsided.

'Put-tin the vege-ta-ble gar-den he-yah,' said Rodney between mouthfuls. He pointed towards the absorption trenches. 'Roded and ger-ran-i-um a-round the ver-an-da.'

'Sounds great. I love roses.'

His demeanour had changed so much she wondered whether the bastard, whore, bitch bit was directed at her or the unyielding soil. Maybe it was the effort that brought it on. Maybe it was stress. She smiled at her strange, tormented neighbour and the mistrust with which he regarded her wavered momentarily.

'You won't tell anyone I'm here, will you, Rodney?'

'Bil-ly told me not to tell an-y-one.' His eyes blazed. 'I'm not an id-i-ot, Lin-da. Dum people think I am, but I'm not.'

'I'm sure you're not.'

'I'll tell you who id an id-i-ot.'

'Who?'

'Bil-ly id,' he said angrily. 'And you, you're not much mar-ter.'

Chapter Six

Billy was as close to anger as he'd ever been since he'd left Sydney. He dealt with it by sitting down on the eastern veranda with his feet up on the rail, a mug of tea by his side and his tobacco pouch in his lap. He had to choose between the rifle and the phone, and his preference for the rifle was what really made him sit down and think things through.

While he was out spraying the day before, he'd found a campsite where pig shooters had trespassed onto his property with their dogs. He didn't mind that. They'd lit a fire to cook by and sit around, and he didn't mind that either, because they clearly knew what they were doing and had doused and covered the ashes. They'd drawn water from a tap to a watering trough to cook with and wash themselves, and he had no problem with that either. Billy didn't mind pig hunters coming onto his property and killing a few pigs, as long as they knew what they were doing, respected his property and livestock and asked first. But these guys hadn't asked permission and that irritated him, though he didn't really mind so long as they observed his other conditions. But they hadn't. They'd killed a pig but apparently wild boar wasn't to their taste. They could have shot a grey kangaroo and cut a feed out of it, but hadn't bothered. Instead, they'd slaughtered one of his sheep and that was unforgivable.

The bastards knew exactly what they were doing and had shown absolute contempt for him. He'd found the branch where they'd strung the sheep up and cut its throat so it would bleed to death. He'd found the bloody fleece and its shape told him whoever had skinned the beast was expert with a knife, probably a butcher by trade or at least someone who'd worked in a slaughterhouse. The hunter had probably butchered the carcass into hind and forequarters, cut the ribs into racks and taken the back straps so it could fit into their eskies. This was no thoughtless opportunism; it indicated a clear intention to live off the land at other people's expense. Billy knew the type. They stole diesel from unattended homesteads, robbed vegetable gardens and killed stock for meat. His inclination was to track them down, which wouldn't be hard given the unusual tyre pattern on their four-wheel drive, demand compensation and order them off his property. He'd done it before with other shooters, even gone as far as waving his Ruger semi-automatic around to convince them of his seriousness. It occurred to him that the businesslike approach of these hunters probably meant he'd have to go the extra step and squeeze off a couple of rounds. But, in his anger, he didn't mind that, didn't mind that at all.

Billy made himself another mug of tea and rolled another cigarette, deliberately stalling. He needed time to calm down, to regain control and get the incident into its true perspective. He wanted to frighten, not kill or injure, and he was aware how easily the situation could blow up. If one of the hunters caught a bullet there'd be an investigation and, even though he knew the local cops would be sympathetic to a point, they'd want to know why he hadn't called them so they could deal with it. And he'd wind up in precisely the situation he was trying to avoid.

He examined other options. The four-wheel drive was heading west. He could just forget about it and let the hunters become someone else's problem. But that wasn't his way and they had killed one of his sheep. He figured he'd track the four-wheel drive through the scrub on his trail bike, then thought better of it. The hunters would hear the bike coming a mile off and that would alert them, either send them packing or put them on guard. On the other hand, they wouldn't hear him coming if he took the mare. The idea began to appeal to him. The mare was due some exercise and he could tether it a kilometre or so back from their campsite once he'd located it. He rolled another smoke, liking the way his thoughts were heading.

The lousy jacks were back at the kelpie's food bowl. Billy liked them because of their strong sense of community. If there were twelve birds in the family and twelve pellets of dog food, you could pretty well guarantee every bird would get its share. A wedge-tailed eagle hovered about half a kilometre away. They always came around lambing time, when they could peck the eyes out of the newborn and the weaklings, and rip into the dying before the pigs came to clean up. Bleeding hearts reckoned that eagles, ravens and crows were carrion eaters and only attacked or killed live lambs that were sick, but Billy wasn't so sure. Few things made him as angry as the sight of the big birds ripping into a lamb carcass.

Every year he dropped a few with his shotgun, but that didn't stop them coming back.

He'd made his decision by the time he drained the dregs of his tea. His anger had subsided and he'd come to accept that settling a dispute with rifles was something best avoided. Sneaking into their camp while they were sleeping and stealing their four-wheel drive was a much better option. The keys would be in the ignition because the hunters would have no reason to remove them. He always left his keys in the ute except when he went into town, and even there he left them in the ignition as often as not. Who was there to steal their four-wheel drive out in the bush? Their dogs would probably make a bit of a racket but they'd be tied up for the night. As for getting the mare home, he'd tether her to the bumper and she could just trot along behind.

The beauty of his plan was that the hunters would have no choice but to follow the tracks of their four-wheel drive to the homestead, where they could buy the ignition key back off him. It would be a fair old walk carrying their gear and he didn't expect much fuss from them when they finally arrived. They'd know exactly why he'd taken their four-wheel drive and, as well as being hot, tired and thirsty, they'd be burdened by their guilt. Billy figured fifty dollars for the ewe, and fifty for the trouble they'd put him through and for not calling the police. He'd also remind them of the rules and let them know he'd be contacting every station between Walgett and White Cliffs and putting them on the lookout. One way or another, he was determined to send the hunters packing back to Sydney, or wherever they came from, with their tails between their legs.

He wandered into the kitchen to wash his mug and stack it on the draining board, making a mental list of things he needed to take. The Ruger was at the top of his list, followed by oats for the mare, torch, knife, sandwiches, tea, sugar, a billy and matches. He decided to tie up the kelpie so she didn't follow, then thought better of it. It wouldn't harm to have the kelpie keep an eye on the mare when he went off on foot.

Billy was well into his preparations when the phone rang. He stared at it, trying to guess who the call could be from and the reason for it. Maybe the hunters had moved on to another property and killed another sheep. Maybe one of his neighbours was ringing to alert him to their presence. The phone didn't ring often, but when it did there was always a good reason. He picked up the handset.

'Billy Dwyer.'

'Billy, hi, it's Linda.'

'Linda.' She was the last person he expected. His mouth felt suddenly dry.

'You remember me. Your tenant?'

'I'm sorry, Linda, I was expecting a call from someone else.'

'Is this a bad time?'

'Not at all.' It had been a week since Billy had made the trip to Walgett and he still hadn't rung to warn her about the gossip. He'd meant to, but was deterred by the comment about the love nest. What if she laughed at the absurdity of it? After all, she was a sophisticated city woman and he was just a hick. What if she didn't laugh and interpreted his warning as a cheap try-on? Even now he lacked the confidence to raise it. He decided to duck the issue and stick to the immediate problem. 'I was just thinking of you,' he said.

'Thinking of me?'

'Yeah. I've got this problem with some pig shooters trespassing on my property. They slaughtered one of my sheep.'

'And that made you think of me?'

'Of course.'

Linda started laughing.

'What's funny?' said Billy. 'If I called the police and they decided to come out, how long do you think your presence here would stay a secret?'

'I'm sorry, Billy, it's just that I couldn't quite see the connection.'

'It's because of you that I've decided to go after them myself.'

'When?'

'Now.'

Billy thought the line had dropped out when the phone went silent.

'Hello? Are you still there?'

'Yes, I'm still here. What time do you think you'll be back?'

'Dunno. Why?'

'I've finished painting and hanging blinds. I rang to invite you over for dinner so you could see the results.'

Over for dinner? Billy froze, torn between an obligation to deal with the pig shooters and the unexpected opportunity to spend an evening with Linda.

'Hello, Billy? You still there?'

'Yeah, I'm still here.' In the overall scheme of things, what was the loss of one more sheep? Between pulpy kidney, worms, flystrike, cold winds and poisonous weeds, there was no shortage of ways sheep could — and did — die on him. He decided the pig shooters could wait. All the same, he hated to think of them getting away with their thieving. 'What time would you like me to come?'

'You can make it? Fantastic. Come early while it's still light. Say, about five. Rodney's started on the garden. It's really coming on.'

'Five it is. Can I bring anything?'

'No. Just yourself.'

'See you at five then.' Billy hung up and stared at the phone, still recovering from the effect of her call. Her voice was so bright, so bubbly and so full of promises and expectations, none of which he dared put a name to. It picked him up and blew him away, like roly-poly before a westerly. He had the wit to realise that he'd had no decision to make, that once he'd heard her voice and what she had to say, all choice was taken from him. The funny thing was, he didn't mind.

The sandwiches he'd cut and left sitting on the kitchen bench reminded him that he had new plans to make to get some use out of the day. First he had to clear up a few loose ends. He rang his neighbours and told them about the pig shooters, the sheep they'd slaughtered and the tyre tread marks so they could keep a lookout for them. Finally he called the police to alert them in the event that the shooters stopped somewhere to refill their eskies with ice, or had a thirst and called into one of the pubs in the Grawin or Walgett to slake it. Depending on how much meat they still had in their eskies, they'd be charged or warned off. Either way the police would get fifty dollars off them as compensation for the sheep. But first the police had to find them and there were no guarantees they'd do that.

There was a spring to Billy's step as he gathered up his sandwiches, put away his Ruger and pulled his shotgun off the rack. He was looking forward to seeing Linda again but ambivalent about what she might have done to the house. The bit about painting worried him, although she had asked permission. He'd taken his mother all the way down to Dubbo so she had a decent choice of wallpapers and spent another couple of days hanging them. More wasted effort. He slipped a couple of shotgun cartridges into his pocket. He could've kept on spraying the Hudson pear and the barley grass that was creeping in where the sheep had been grazing, but being covered from head to toe for three days on the trot was about all he could stand. The mare still needed a bit of a gallop and he knew it wouldn't do any harm to check up on his lambs and shoot a few eagles or ravens while he was at it. It was a funny thing, people thought birds were stupid and even used expressions like 'bird-brained'. But the ravens knew the difference between his shotgun and his Ruger and spotted it the instant he stepped off the veranda. They knew when to make themselves scarce.

When she saw Billy making his way up the track towards her, Linda's face broke into the broadest smile. Even from the front veranda she couldn't help noticing the almost military crease in his moleskins and the freshly ironed shirt. He looked scrubbed and shaved to within an inch of his life and even the kelpie was fluffed up from a bath. He clutched a bunch of roses in his hand the same way he'd hold a hammer, some a dark crimson and others a creamy yellow, colours which didn't quite complement each other.

'Right on time,' she called.

He just nodded in his matter-of-fact way, having no reason to contradict her or anything to add. His hat was as battered and dusty as always, but, as he drew closer, she could see that he'd also polished his boots. The effort he'd made and the naivety of his innocent country formality touched her, and she would have likened him to a nervous schoolboy on a date but for the fact that he didn't show the slightest bit of apprehension. He paused at the foot of the veranda steps and looked up at her.

'I brought you these roses because it didn't seem right to come empty-handed.' He turned and took a measured look around the front garden at the work Rodney had put in. 'Pretty soon you'll be growing your own.'

'Don't let that stop you bringing more. The woman hasn't been born who doesn't like being given roses.'

Linda stepped down from the veranda to greet him and was intercepted by the kelpie. The kelpie's feelings were obvious but the same couldn't be said of her owner. There was no indication of whatever it was that had made him press his clothes and even shine his boots. She glimpsed again the remoteness of a man held in check that she'd noticed when she'd run to him after her first encounter with Rodney. She kissed him on the cheek and took the roses from him, already mentally separating the red ones from the yellows and deciding they didn't even belong together in the same room. 'What kind are they?'

'I'm not much into roses. My mother planted them. The red ones might be Crimson Glory and I think the yellow ones are Golden Delight. Could be wrong.'

'They're beautiful whatever they are. Now, come and see what I've done to the house before we sit down and have a drink.' She took his hand and led him up onto the veranda, wondering whether her handiwork would elicit some kind of reaction from him.

'You don't like wallpaper,' he said.

'No, do you mind?'

'Each to his own.' He took his time looking, mentally comparing what he saw with what had been. 'You've done a good job, Linda. I never thought the place would scrub up so well.'

'You like it?' She couldn't hide her delight.

'Of course.'

She sensed him hesitate, that he had something more to add.

'What's the problem?'

'I don't know whether this is some modern thing, but I don't see much point in the paintings.' Bare canvases hung on every wall where there was space.

Linda laughed. 'That's because I haven't painted them yet. That would be carrying minimalism too far. I hung them because that's the best place to store them, and they're also there to remind me to pick up my brushes.'

'You're a painter?'

'Not exactly.'

'What does that mean?'

'Make yourself comfortable on the veranda and I'll tell you over a drink. I haven't any beer so I've made a jug of Bloody Mary. Okay?'

'Sounds good to me.'

She watched Billy wander out onto the veranda, pull up a chair, swing his feet up onto the rail and begin to roll a smoke, pleased that he already felt comfortable and at ease with her. She poured the drinks and joined him.

'There you go.'

Linda handed him a Bloody Mary in a tall glass rattling with ice and pulled up a chair alongside him. She'd decided to wear her olive-coloured Country Road blouse and shorts, both of which boasted an array of button-down pockets, and matching sandals. She thought she'd hit the perfect balance between informality and elegance and felt mildly disappointed that her appearance hadn't provoked an appropriate comment, or indeed any comment.

'Cheers,' she said. 'Welcome to my home.'

'Cheers,' Billy responded. 'Thanks for inviting me.'

Linda squinted over the bush landscape, trying to see in it what Billy saw and allow a little breathing space. Pauses and companionable silences went against her grain because she was accustomed to deadlines, delegating and putting out fires when things went pear-shaped. She made a determined effort to adjust. The bush stretched out below them, grey-green, flat and lifeless, as though exhausted by the heat of the day. There were a few high clouds, which looked like they might catch the sunset and throw a bit of colour. Far off a raven cawed as though mourning the recent depletion in its numbers. Finches had begun to arrive at the tap around the side for an evening drink. They made a nice sound even though they were probably arguing over whose turn it was to drink.

'Why is it that crows always sound as though they've trodden on something unmentionable?' Linda was unable to let the silence continue.

A smile slowly spread across Billy's face.

'Those crows are ravens.'

'I sit out here every night at sunset,' she said. 'This is my evening treat. I love the timelessness of it. I sometimes get the feeling nothing has changed here for hundreds of thousands of years. It's like stepping back into the distant past. One of these days I'm going to try to capture it on canvas.'

'How long have you been a painter?'

'Ha! I'm not a painter, not yet anyway. Oh, I've done a few paintings but that was some time ago. I used to teach art at high school.'

'You're a teacher?'

'Was.' This time Linda was happy to let the silence hang while she decided how much of her story to tell him. It was too early to begin sharing confidences, and maybe it always would be. She heard Billy strike a match and for the first time noticed how thin he rolled his cigarettes. It was about half the diameter of a tailor-made. He caught her watching him.

'Old army habit,' said Billy. He drew smoke deep into his lungs, exhaled and turned back to face the expanse. 'So, you're running away from school?'

His question caught Linda completely off guard. There was a slight smile on his lips as though he was teasing her, but she could see that he was looking for an answer that went beyond her professed need for solitude. She laughed, but her laugh sounded insincere even to her own ears.

'What makes you think I'm running away from anything?'

'Aren't you?'

He unnerved her by turning to face her, his eyes locking onto hers, looking not so much at them as through them, as though searching her soul. She stared back, but realised she was no match for eyes accustomed to spotting distant sheep through thick scrub. She blinked and turned away defensively.

'I'll have you know I came here of my own free will.' There was a touch of indignation in her voice, which she regretted and tried to laugh off. 'I'm not trying to escape anything, other than the pressure of work and living in a big city. What about you?' She threw the question back at him with the practised touch of someone who knew how to manage people.

Billy rocked back on his chair and looked for somewhere to ash his rollie, found nothing and simply flicked the ash onto the deck. The ash was cold and would blow away without trace. If he was disappointed in her answer he gave no indication.

'I was born here,' he said with finality. He rattled the ice in the bottom of his glass. 'Getting to be a dry argument.'

'I'm sorry,' said Linda, though she was anything but. She poured him another drink from her jug. It was time to move on and they both knew it. 'Excuse me for a moment and I'll go and get our first course. We can eat it out here.'

'I prefer to sit out,' said Billy. He finished his rollie, stubbed it out on his heel and tossed the butt over the balcony.

The bruschetta had crisped up a little more than Linda liked, but not so much that it would shatter. His question had caught her by surprise, but she should've realised he'd guess she was in hiding and be curious to know why. His slowness belied a thoughtfulness and intelligence. The question was, how much to tell him and when, and whether to tell him anything at all. Did she really need to air the dirty linen? She decided to wait and see how things developed between them. Maybe some time in the future she could let him into her secret. Maybe. Maybe she'd have no choice if someone turned up in town asking questions about her. But how would anyone find out where she was? She carried the tray back out to the veranda.

'Cheese on toast?' said Billy. 'Great.'

'Italian cheese on toast, if you don't mind.' She couldn't help smiling. 'It's a kind of bruschetta. Normally I make them with tomato, onion and basil, but fresh ingredients are a little hard to come by. I made these ones with anchovy and baked capsicum and these with Italian salami and dried tomato. The cheese on both is mozzarella. I'm learning to use what's frozen, canned, cured or keeps.'

Billy bit into one with anchovy and was taken aback both by the strength of flavours and the crunchiness of the bread.

'You don't like anchovies?'

'Only ever had them on pizza before. Had something similar. Fish sauce. Long time ago, though.' His eyes seemed to lose focus and drift off into the distance. Linda waited to hear what he had to say when they came back, what thought had made a connection. Instead he carried on as if nothing had happened.

'Mind if I try one of the others?'

'You'd better,' she said. 'I'm not expecting anyone else.'

They were halfway through the bruschetta when the kelpie shot to its feet and stood, ears cocked, gazing out over the scrub below. Billy stopped chewing immediately and stared where the dog was looking.

'What's up?' said Linda.

Billy motioned her to be quiet. She held her breath, staring hard at the kelpie, eyes widening in apprehension as she realised the possible implications.

The dog had clearly heard something, something not too far off and where it had no right to be. She glanced at Billy. He sat statue still, waiting for the breeze to pick up and carry the sound to them again. Christ! The finches were hard at it around the tap and she wished they'd shut up. Overhead, the clouds had at last begun to colour up. Dry bush rustled and somewhere a small dead piece of tree branch crashed through foliage to the ground. Linda held her breath once more as the breeze came in and lightly ruffled the kelpie's coat. It cocked its head one way and then the other, ears up and straining, but didn't lock onto anything.

'What is it?' whispered Linda.

'Probably nothing,' said Billy. The kelpie lost interest, settled back on its haunches and lay down. 'Dog heard something. Thought I heard something too. Could've been a motor.'

'A motor?'

'Or Rodney letting go of his windlass and dropping a bucket of claystone. It was too faint and indistinct to tell, although the sound didn't appear to come from Rodney's. There again, the bush can play tricks on you.'

Linda sighed and allowed herself to relax back into her chair. Her heart rate slowed as she silently berated herself. It was a false alarm. Of course it was a false alarm! How could it have been anything else? She wondered if any of her anxiety had shown and decided it hadn't. She decided to continue on as though nothing had happened.

'What's claystone?'

'The dirt dug out of opal mines. It dries out and sets like concrete. Then it's called shin-cracker, for obvious reasons.'

'I guess it would make a bit of a noise falling. That's one of the things I love about this place,' she said. 'I never hear anything except the birds and the bees and the sounds I make myself. Occasionally I hear your sheep or cattle.'

But Billy wasn't listening. He'd reverted to gazing with unblinking eyes onto the plains below. Ordinarily she would have been offended by the rudeness but she quickly realised that rudeness played no part in his actions. He had no artifice and no hidden agenda. Something had disturbed him and it was in his nature to try to understand what it was. She smiled to herself. Billy was complicated but in a nice way, and it felt nice to have a man around, to have him there with his feet planted solidly on her rail. She was beginning to appreciate how warmly satisfying companionable silence could be.

She'd planned to eat indoors by the subdued light of cleverly placed lamps, but Billy persuaded her to eat out on the veranda. His arguments were reasonable. The late spring nights had lost the chill of winter and not yet realised the full heat of summer. The temperature was at that pleasant in-between stage where it was a little cool for just a shirt but not cool enough for a cardigan or jumper. Even the sandflies were absent, in transition to adulthood. Billy claimed this was the best time of the year and helped her carry the table out onto the veranda. She placed three candles on the table and lit them, aware but not alarmed by the romantic implications. She was certain Billy would see them as utilitarian, the only option in the absence of any alternative. Besides, she recalled his opening remarks when he gave her the roses, saying it didn't feel right to arrive empty-handed. Those weren't the sentiments of a Romeo intent on having it off with his Juliet.

'I hope you like prawns,' she said, taking a seat opposite him.

'I love them. Every so often I get a craving for seafood and drive up to the Bowling Club at Lightning Ridge. Usually on my birthday.' He smiled slightly, as though surprised or embarrassed. 'Sort of caught up on me this year. Ought to be up there now.'

'What? What are you saying? Don't tell me today's your birthday.'

'It is if it's still November twelve.'

'Why didn't you say?'

'Didn't think it was relevant.'

'Not relevant? My God! Happy birthday, Billy Dwyer.' She leaned across the table and kissed him. 'So you're having your birthday dinner anyway. I hope it's up to Bowling Club standard.'

'They do it well, Linda. The seafood's flown in and it's as fresh as anything you'll get in Sydney. One day I'll take you there.'

'You're on. When?'

Billy shifted uncomfortably. His mood changed.

'Yeah, well, we've got to think about that.'

Linda sensed there was more and kept her silence.

'There's a story doing the rounds that I've got you set up here in a love nest.'

Linda nearly choked on her drink. She started laughing and instantly regretted it when she saw the look on Billy's face. Briefly, for not much more than the flicker of an eye, she thought she glimpsed a breach in his self-control, a flash of hurt or vulnerability. It suddenly dawned on her how her reaction could have been interpreted.

'This is serious, Linda.'

'I'm sorry. It's just that "love nest" is such a quaint, old-fashioned expression.' She smiled and touched his hand reassuringly. 'I thought only naughty politicians had love nests, and even then only in tabloid newspapers. Please go on.'

She listened intently as Billy told her about his conversation with Jimmy in the stock and station and the sequel in the bar of the RSL.

'You're going to have to sit tight for a while,' he concluded. 'Dinner at the club is on hold.'

'In that case, you're just going to have to come here, even though my prawns are frozen.' She rose. 'Now excuse me, the water's boiling for the pasta.'

The brief chink in Billy's façade, coupled with the pressed clothes and polished shoes, were signs too obvious to ignore. It was her first inkling that he entertained hopes that their friendship might extend beyond the merely neighbourly, and the prospect was not at all disagreeable. She liked Billy, and there was certainly more depth to him than she'd expected. A relationship hadn't figured in any of her plans but, if the cards fell that way, would it be such a terrible thing?

She quickly fried the prawns in chilli, garlic and olive oil and added the pulp of a few tinned Italian tomatoes for colour and texture. It was a simple dish and done well but she didn't expect quite the response she got. Billy raved about it.

'Better than the club,' he said.

'High praise indeed.'

'It is, Linda. The restaurant at the club does good food.' He paused to swallow another mouthful and looked her squarely in the eye. 'People don't learn to cook this well just making dinner for themselves.'

Linda smiled wryly. No one she knew back in Sydney would be so blunt, but, in a strange way, she appreciated and even liked his frank honesty. He was curious and had every right to be. She decided to be equally frank in her reply but nonetheless miserly in the amount of information she gave him.

'I'm divorced,' she said. 'I have a daughter who has just turned fourteen.' She expected a reaction, a raising of eyebrows, something, but Billy simply accepted the information and waited for her to continue. It was an interviewing technique she'd learned on a management course, but Billy just did it naturally. Her mind raced as it examined options: how much to tell him and how much to tell him now?

'My daughter is in boarding school.'

Billy nodded and waited. Linda sighed and made a quick judgement.

'My daughter is in boarding school and … and my ex-husband is in gaol. I helped put him there.'

'I figured it would be something like that.' Billy showed no surprise or shock. His only concession was to look away from her, pick up his glass of wine and take a sip. 'There had to be a reason why you came here. You're worried what he'll do to you when he gets out. If he finds you.' It wasn't a question but a statement.

Linda bit her lip. It had never been her intention to go so far so soon.

'I also needed a break,' she said defensively. 'Coming here suits both purposes. If I've been circumspect it's because I don't want to get you involved in my problems. My ex-husband can be quite violent.' It was time to revert to her training and deflect the discussion to him. 'What about you? Have you never been married?'

Billy smiled apologetically, even guiltily, as though acknowledging he had no right to pry, and accepted the switch of focus as a rebuke. Courtesy demanded similar admissions.

'Yes, I've been married, briefly and foolishly. Cut a lot of scrub since then. Cheryl-Lynne was her name. Not just Cheryl and not just Lynne. Local girl. Divorce was a blessing for both of us.'

'What happened?'

'She ran off with a travelling salesman she met in Walgett. She finally got what she wanted. A ticket out of here.'

'What was she like?'

Billy's eyes lit up as though he was enjoying a private joke, surprising Linda with their unexpected warmth.

'She was nothing like you. She wasn't quick, she wasn't clever and she certainly wasn't beautiful.'

Linda's jaw dropped. She sat stunned, open-mouthed, amazed. At the start of the evening she'd bemoaned the fact that he hadn't complimented her on her appearance. Now she had no idea how to deal with the compliments he had paid her. She was the one who was supposed to be quick and clever but his compliments — and their implications — left her gasping. She laughed while she stumbled for the appropriate response, knowing full well where that could take them and not wanting to make any mistakes. She reached for his hand, which seemed the logical next step, but her hand froze in midair. The sound of the gunshot reverberated up the gully, bouncing from ridge to ridge. Billy was on his feet before Linda had a chance to draw breath.

'Rodney,' he said. 'That was a shotgun. I've got to go.' He raced for the steps, ran down them and disappeared into the night, hot on the tail of his kelpie. A second shot set the birds screeching and wheeling into the air.

'Be careful!' she shouted. She was on her feet now, pulse racing. Surely it couldn't be her ex-husband. Surely he couldn't have found her. But what if he had? She felt suddenly alone and vulnerable. No, she realised, it couldn't be, not midweek, not yet. She slumped down in her seat, trying to come to terms with how quickly things had changed, how with the mood of the evening and the exchange of confidences, a new depth or at least a better understanding had entered their relationship and, incredibly, how inevitably and naturally they seemed headed towards her bed. The image of him suddenly leaving the table was imprinted on her brain: his grim face, the table napkin still tucked between the second and third buttons of his shirt, and in his eyes the apprehension of a man hurrying to somewhere he didn't want to go.

Billy gunned the ute down the track towards the road before spearing off left into the scrub, headlights and spotlights blazing. The second shot had come from a rifle and that had him worried. He could imagine the scene waiting for him up ahead if Rodney had accosted the pig shooters. It would be a confrontation Rodney was unlikely to win. Roos broke cover ahead of him and bounded along parallel to the ute. He cursed and slowed, well aware of their habit of suddenly cutting across in front of vehicles. He leaned on his horn, not just to frighten off the roos but to warn the people ahead that he was coming. The imminent intercession of a third party, a witness, might just be enough to cool passions and ease the pressure on triggers. That was what he hoped.

Billy had fashioned a gun rack behind the ute's seats but only ever carried his rifle or shotgun when he had a specific use for it in mind. As he raced through the scrub he began to wonder what he'd do if shooting did break out. What could he do? He hadn't heard any more shots and wasn't sure if that was encouraging or a sign that Rodney had stopped a bullet. He swung wide around the banks of a dried-up warrambool filled with dead and blackened trees, slowed to a stop and turned off the motor. There was a track in front of him winding between the myalls and coolibahs. It was one of the few tracks that ran through to Stony Creek Road and he figured the shooters would've known that and chosen this part of the bush for their campsite. He heard shouting directly ahead of him; one of the voices was unmistakeably Rodney's. At least he was still alive.

Billy restarted the ute and drove slowly forward in second gear. This was no time to go barging in like the cavalry. A cool head was called for and he wanted the shooters to know that he was unarmed and represented no threat to them. His spotlights bounced off glass and sheet metal about a hundred metres ahead. He leaned on the horn again for three long blasts. The trees thickened around the edges of the warrambool and their branches spread closer to the ground. Billy slowed even more as he picked his way through them and the clumps of thorns. The kelpie stood on the seat alongside him, alert and on edge.

As Billy crossed the dry stony creek linking the water holes he got his first good look at the vehicle in front of him and groaned involuntarily. It wasn't a four-wheel drive and there'd be no match-up for the tyre tracks he'd seen. Worse, the vehicle was a Volkswagen Kombi converted into a campervan, the kind in which adventurous young tourists bummed around the outback. It even had flowers painted on the side. A young woman leaped out of the door and sprinted towards him, waving her arms in the air.

'Oh, Christ,' said Billy under his breath. The kelpie turned towards him sympathetically. He slowed to a stop and let the young woman run up to his open window. He knew exactly what she'd say.

'Help,' she said. 'There's a madman shooting at us.'

'Take it easy,' said Billy. 'I know him and he's harmless. I'll sort it out.'

He slipped the ute into first gear and crawled towards the campsite. The young woman was careful to keep the ute between her and Rodney's shotgun. He could hear Rodney shouting abuse and someone yelling back at him. He turned the wheel slightly so he could pick them up in his spotlights and stopped. If the situation hadn't been so fraught he would have laughed. Rodney and a young bloke wearing shorts and nothing else stood facing each other with their weapons at the ready, as though rehearsing a scene for *Gunfight at the OK Corral*.

'Would you two jokers put your weapons down,' he said calmly. 'Neither of you want to shoot anybody.'

'This bloody madman took a shot at us!'

'Yeah,' said Billy, 'he does that. This is his land you're on.'

'Bar-tid, thie-vin bar-tid!' said Rodney. 'I know what thede thie-vin bar-tid want!'

'They're not the Grawin mob, Rodney. All these people want is somewhere to spend the night, that's all. Now put the shotgun down.' He turned to the young man protecting his VW. 'You too, mate. The shot was just to frighten you off. Rodney can shoot the legs off a mozzie at a hundred metres. If he'd wanted you dead, you would be.'

'That prick's insane,' shouted the girl.

'No, just territorial,' said Billy. 'The best thing you can do is pack up your gear and follow me back onto my property. You can spend the night there.'

'We're not staying anywhere around here,' said the young man. 'We're outta here. That bloke's a screamin' nutter.'

'Please yourself. Just pack up while I talk to Rodney and calm him down.'

The guy and girl began throwing things into their Kombi: their little fold-up table and chairs, their Hibachi barbecue, esky and dirty plates. At least they'd had time to finish their dinner. Rodney stood by quietly as though exhausted. Even his juddering jaw had slowed. The couple threw the last of their belongings — two sleeping bags and two lilos they didn't bother to deflate — into the van and slammed the door shut.

'Do you want me to guide you back out onto the road?' asked Billy.

'You just keep an eye on that freak,' said the young man. He started the motor. 'Make sure he doesn't follow us. We're heading back to Walgett. That bastard ought to be locked up.'

'There's no need to involve the police,' said Billy hastily. 'There's no harm done.'

'No harm done? The bloody freak could've killed us!' The young man dropped the clutch and the Volkswagen lurched back towards the creek bed and the track to the road.

'Bloody hell, Rodney,' said Billy as they watched the tail-lights disappear off into the scrub. 'You've really done it this time.'

'They-yad no right to come on to my land.'

'You'd no right to take a shot at them.'

'I did-din doot at them. I dot o-ver their head.' But Rodney's defence lacked conviction and Billy could tell by the way he stood that he knew he'd done wrong. He looked exactly like he had years earlier when he'd been caught trying to sneak out of the general store with a chocolate bar he hadn't paid for. Billy had tried to teach him and so had his brother, but Rodney had no talent at all for shoplifting.

'Let's hope the police agree with you. I'll ring them in the morning and try to head them off. If they turn up on your doorstep, don't greet them with your shotgun. You understand me? In fact, if you threw the bloody thing down a mineshaft you'd be doing yourself a big favour. Now go home.'

'Tor-ry,' said Rodney. If the little man had a talent for anything it was for looking guilty.

'Yeah, mate, I know.'

The kelpie nuzzled sympathetically into Rodney's hand.

'Bar-tid, bitch, hoo-wah,' he said.

'Let's go,' said Billy. The kelpie sloped back to the ute and jumped up onto the passenger seat, ears flat as though sensing her master's dismay. Billy turned the ute around and slowly started picking his way through the scrub towards home. He thought briefly about returning to Linda's, but knew in his heart that the evening had effectively ended the moment he'd heard the blast from the shotgun. He felt the loss keenly.

Now that he had time to think, he mentally scrolled back through the evening and he couldn't help wondering what possessed him at times. Sometimes his mouth had a mind of its own, operating independently from his brain. His questioning had been nothing short of rudeness and had embarrassed Linda into evasions. Yet he'd still persisted with his probing until she'd been forced to turn the question back on him. A flood of guilt washed over him. He'd had no right to stick his nose into her business in the first place. She paid him rent and, in doing so, bought privacy.

Yet he couldn't help smiling. Nice things had taken place, things that couldn't be ignored, and it had been a long time since that had happened.

He reached the point where he could turn back onto the track that led up to her place and stopped. He thought of her laugh, and her quickness to protect his feelings when he'd mentioned the love nest. He remembered how her hand was reaching for his. Was it too late to go back? He looked at his watch and saw that it was pushing ten o'clock. The night had ended. He decided he'd call her in the morning, after he'd rung the police and hosed down the situation with Rodney. There was nothing else he could do, except hope the evening had meant enough to Linda that she'd invite him over again. If not, nothing was lost except a deal of wishful thinking. He reluctantly engaged gear and turned for home.

* * *

'That's it for today?' said Ramon.

'It's enough,' said Neil. 'We normally finish about this time. Milos might think it's cute to keep us sitting around until our bums ache, but I'm more considerate.'

'Neil,' cut in Milos, 'can't we please finish the day on a more civil note? After all, this is my first day back. I came here delighted to see you all again and I would like to leave feeling the same way.'

'Me too,' said Lucio. 'I think we should all have another drink. There's wine left in the bottle.'

'This anger isn't like you,' said Ramon. 'But I sense it in the character of your brother, Billy, and that's to your advantage. Your anger becomes his anger and it adds tension to the telling.'

'I'll take that as a compliment.'

'I meant it as a compliment.' Ramon picked up his glass and raised it as though preparing to make a toast. 'I'd like to congratulate you on a successful start to what promises to be an interesting and intriguing story.'

'Thank you, Ramon, but your congratulations are misplaced. They'd only be appropriate if my story was an invention, which unfortunately it isn't. I don't deserve congratulations for relaying events over which I had no control and ultimately emerge from without credit. Your comments are nothing more than flattery.'

'They are an olive branch,' said Milos. 'An apology for putting you in a position where you feel obliged to tell this story.'

Neil snorted and pushed his glass of wine away. 'Frankly, I'd rather have a beer.'

SECOND THURSDAY

Chapter Seven

Lucio and Milos arrived together and found Neil once more sipping a beer at the bar. Ramon joined them just as Gancio was pouring two more.

'What is this? Do you want to make this a regular occurrence?' asked Ramon. 'If so, I think we should vote on it. I for one will stick to wine.'

'Relax, Ramon, I'm not forcing anyone to have a beer. It doesn't matter a damn to me whether you guys join me or not.' Neil smiled and swallowed another mouthful. 'I got here first and decided to have a beer by way of celebration.'

'Oh yes? And what are we celebrating?'

'I'm celebrating the return of my PA who chose to resign rather than give up sleeping with my main competitor.'

'Congratulations,' said Lucio. 'What brought about the change of heart?'

'The enemy found her decidedly less attractive when she no longer had access to my confidential files. The *grand amore*, as you like to put it, didn't even last a week.'

'So you took her back?' said Milos. 'That was a very gracious thing to do.'

'Gracious be buggered,' said Neil. 'Have you any idea how much recruitment agencies charge these days? Or how much time and money it takes to hire and train a replacement? Christ, I was so glad to see the tart back I was tempted to give her a raise. Gave her a kiss and threw my leg over instead.'

'You what?' said Lucio. He started to laugh. Ramon joined in while Milos just shook his head in wonder.

'Hey, we always had a close relationship. Sometimes, when we were away on business together, we kind of gravitated to my bed. When she returned, cap in hand, asking for her job back I just wanted to let her know I had no hard feelings. I think she appreciated the personal touch.'

'You have a very individual way of doing business,' said Ramon.

'Not so,' cut in Lucio. 'I once had a secretary who thought an invitation to lunch was a request to remove her knickers. I tell you, I put on so much weight. I took her out to lunch every day.'

Ramon smiled. He couldn't see the faces of his friends but he could feel them enjoying themselves. This was how the first day should have gone.

'What about you, Ramon?' asked Neil. 'Don't tell me you never played hide the sausage with your staff.'

'I'm South American. We have siestas every afternoon. What do you think?'

'What about you, Milos?'

'I have only slept with one woman in my life.'

'What?'

'You heard me, Neil.'

His admission stunned his friends into silence. Their smiles faded into looks of awe and disbelief.

'Only one woman?' said Lucio incredulously.

'Only Gabi.'

'I don't know whether to give you a medal or damn you as a fool,' said Neil. 'That's unnatural. Worse, it's un-Australian.'

'Stop it there, Neil,' said Milos sharply. 'I don't believe in sex without love, and I don't believe in love without trust and respect. This is nothing to be ashamed of and not something to be treated lightly. It is a question of values, no?'

'I agree. We should all have values,' said Lucio. 'For me, I don't believe in sex without passion. Fortunately, when a beautiful woman offers me sex I can't help but feel very passionate.'

Even Milos had to laugh.

'So,' said Ramon, judging it was time to move on, 'where are you taking us today, Neil? Back to the red soil plains? Back to your childhood, perhaps?'

'Where am I taking you?'

'Yes.'

Neil looked steadily at the blind man.

'I'm taking you back a few years in time to a place you should've gone long ago.'

'Really? And where would that be?'

'To gaol, Ramon. To gaol.'

* * *

'Guilty.'

Grant Sinclair had not taken his barrister seriously when he'd warned him to prepare himself for an 'unfavourable' verdict because he didn't expect one. The word hit him with the force of a bullet. Guilty? He was stunned by the jury's stupidity. For Christ's sake, couldn't they see he was innocent? He was not guilty!

Definitely not guilty! Why hadn't the morons listened to him? Nobody in their right mind could take his ex-wife seriously. She was nothing, a nobody, a liar. She didn't matter! He wanted to scream his protestations to every corner of the court, correct the jury and alert the judge to the miscarriage of justice, but his breath seemed to jam up in his throat so no words could pass. His brain wouldn't hold still, wouldn't lock onto a single thought long enough for it to be grasped and considered, wouldn't stop spinning, wouldn't halt in its dizzying ride from outrage to blind panic. What would happen? This didn't happen to people like him. It couldn't be happening. *What would happen to him?* All the stories he'd heard of beatings, gang rapes, suicides and deaths in custody roadblocked in his brain, piled up on top of each other, forming walls, insurmountable walls, from which there was no escape.

The judge addressed the court but Grant's whirling brain struggled to grasp what he was saying. The words formed into recognisable phrases but their meaning — their significance and relevance — eluded him. Surely the judge was talking about someone else. How could he be talking about him?

'Given the seriousness of the offence ... bearing in mind the history of violence ... the likelihood of a custodial sentence ... no continuation of bail ...'

When the judge stood and left the court Grant wanted to race after him and make him understand the horrendous mistake that had occurred. The jury had got it wrong! They were morons. Anyone could see they'd got it wrong! He felt a tugging at his sleeve and spun around, wide-eyed, to confront his barrister.

'You've got to do something!' he gasped. 'They've got it wrong!'

'Grant, listen to me,' said the barrister. 'Listen to me. The judge has asked for reports and adjourned for six weeks while he determines the sentence.'

'Sentence? I haven't done anything wrong. Get me out of here!'

'I'd like to, Grant, but I can't. The judge has denied a continuation of bail.'

'What?' Denied bail? Grant remembered hearing the words but hadn't connected them with himself. 'For Christ's sake, do something! Appeal, do whatever you have to.'

'We can appeal to the Supreme Court for bail and we can appeal the verdict.'

'Then do it, do it now.'

'I think we should talk about this.'

'Talk about it? What's to talk about? Just bloody do it!'

'We'll talk when we have a little more time. We'll be in touch in a day or two.'

'A day or two! Bullshit! Get me out of here now!'

'I'm sorry, Grant, but right now there's nothing we can do.'

Grant watched disbelievingly as his barrister turned his back on him and walked away. He wanted to grab the inept bastard and force him to earn the exorbitant fees he'd paid him, but instead became suddenly aware of an issue of far greater immediacy. There were two officers waiting for him.

'Hands.'

It was an order. Grant was not accustomed to taking orders. He watched numbly, incredulously, as they took his hands and handcuffed them, and walked him on legs shocked into compliance down the stairs to the cells below the courthouse.

'Remove your belt and shoelaces.'

'Why?'

'In case you decide to hurt yourself.'

'Oh for Christ's sake! I shouldn't be here.'

'But you are.' The older of the officers moved so that he stood squarely in front of Grant, invading his space. It was an act of intimidation that under normal circumstances would have been met with a solid right hand. 'Look, son, I don't think you really want to cause trouble. That's the one thing you don't want to do. You with me? Just do as you're told, when you're told, and keep your nose clean. Understand?'

'I can't believe this is happening.' Grant undid his belt.

'That's the idea,' said the officer. 'Now, are you on any medication?'

'No.'

'Have you taken any drugs recently, either legal or illegal?'

'No.'

'Do you have any pills, tablets, powders, medication of any kind about your person?'

'No. Can I ask a question, please?'

'Make it quick.'

'What's going to happen to me?'

'An escort will be along shortly to take you to the remand centre.'

'But I shouldn't be here. It's a mistake!'

'Sure it is.'

The cell door clanged shut and one of the officers turned the key that took away his freedom. They were treating him like he was a piece of shit. Grant slumped down on the edge of the bunk, trying to comprehend what had happened. He had meetings to attend, a restaurant reservation for dinner, people to call. He had plans, had commercials to shoot, had a whole life happening on the other side of the bars. Why was that so hard for people to understand? People like him didn't belong in gaol. He wanted out. Now! He'd stood before he realised there was nowhere he could go and no one to listen to his pleas or even give a damn. He grabbed hold of the bars of the cell, felt their coldness, their thickness, their strength and their purpose. The cold steel registered on him more than words ever could and cut through the whirring disorder of his mind. Had the bars been electrified they could not have shocked him more.

He sat back down on the bunk and tried to take stock. Apprehension vied with outrage. Of course he'd appeal. Demand bail, demand the verdict be overturned, quashed or whatever. He was not guilty. Cell doors clanged as prisoners came and went; someone was shouting, someone wept. Toilets flushed. There was a smell of vomit, urine, faeces and body odour. Through all the noise and the assault on his senses, words Grant had never expected to hear came back to him: seriousness of the offence, history of violence, custodial sentence, remand centre. What was a remand centre? What was it like? He sat on the edge of the bunk for over two hours, trying to rein in his fears and curb his anger in preparation for whatever happened next. But his composure slipped the moment his cell door opened and his escort came to take him away.

'Where are you taking me?' he demanded.

'Remand centre. Long Bay.'

Long Bay. Whatever vestiges of hope and courage remained vanished instantly. Long Bay. That was where they sent murderers, bank robbers, thugs and drug dealers. It was home to hardened criminals and the most violent offenders in the state. Why the hell were they sending him there? When would someone wake up to what was happening? When would someone realise he was just the victim of a terrible mistake?

They put him in the back of a van which was little more than a canvas-covered steel cage on wheels. He'd seen them around but had never dreamed he'd ever ride in one. Bench seats ran along both sides and he sat as close as he could to the back door where there was a small window in the canvas. The inside of the van didn't smell much better than the cell he'd just left, but at least he was the only passenger. He took some consolation from that.

To his surprise, the van headed north instead of south. Maybe the guards had been wrongly informed. Maybe he wasn't going to Long Bay after all. When the van began crossing the harbour bridge he breathed a sigh of relief. He didn't know where they were taking him but he knew it had to be better than Long Bay. Surely anything would be better than Long Bay. The van continued north across the Spit Bridge and turned right towards Manly. Grant searched his memories but couldn't recall anything even remotely like a prison in Manly. The van turned into a courtyard alongside Manly Court and stopped. Grant waited for someone to come and let him out. Maybe he was going to be held in a cell beneath the courts. Maybe his barrister had got on the ball with a bail application. Yes! Hope surged. At last people had come to their senses. When he heard the bolt on the door being pulled back he began to rise to his feet.

'Where the hell do you think you're going?' The officer pointed towards the far end of the cage. 'Make room. Get right in back.'

Crushed and confused, Grant did as he was told but not before he'd caught a glimpse of two surly handcuffed prisoners. Suddenly the inside of the cage shrank. He took a fleeting glance at the prisoners as they were loaded into the wagon and the fear he'd felt back in the cells returned in force. He'd always fancied that he could handle himself, but knew instantly he was way out of his league. These guys were hard. They could swat him like a fly and think nothing of it. He stared straight ahead, avoided all eye contact and tried his best not to show his fear.

As the van lurched away Grant suddenly became aware of the suspect springs and worn shock absorbers, now apparent under the extra load. The two prisoners sat across from each other, not directly opposite, but giving each other and him space. They didn't seem any happier to be where they were than he was. The one closest to him sat with his head in his hands, muttering and swearing to himself. The one by the door stared out through the barred window. Grant's back was beginning to ache from the jolting and from having to continually brace himself against the top-heavy swaying of the van.

It took a while for him to realise the direction they now travelled. West, it was heading west. Why west? Why not south? He didn't want to go to Long Bay but he didn't want to spend too much time locked up in the van with the two criminals.

'Ah, fuck you!'

Grant spun around, automatically raising his arms in self-defence. The prisoner by the door had lifted his feet up onto the bench opposite.

'Ya filthy pig!'

Grant was suddenly aware of a sound, an all-too-familiar sound, but couldn't believe what he was hearing. Incredibly, the other prisoner had pulled out his penis and was pissing onto the floor of the van. Instinctively he lifted his feet up as the unmistakeable steamy smell filled the van.

'Ya stinkin' pig!' The prisoner by the door lashed out with his boot and caught the other prisoner on the thigh. It didn't stop him pissing. The noise of it drummed on the metal floor.

Grant tried to shut out the sound of his unwanted companions as they continually niggled at each other. He expected their niggles to blossom into a full-blown fight at any second, in which it would be impossible for him not to get caught up. It was almost a relief to arrive at the Parramatta Courts. The van took on two more prisoners, jamming them up on the benches so he had no option but to put his feet back down on the wet floor. Fortunately most of the urine had run off but the stench remained. Grant tried to ignore the man pressed up alongside him but couldn't. The newcomer was shivering constantly with his arms crossed in front of his chest, groaning and swaying every time the van hit a bump or went over a speed hump. Without warning the man vomited. Grant shrank further back into his corner amid a torrent of abuse. Boots lashed out at the culprit. There was no escaping the stench, no escaping the horror, no escaping the brutal reality of his situation. What kind of men were these? He had absolutely nothing in common with them. They were like some kind of troglodyte suborder, a species closer to animals than humans. Where did they live? What did they do? Why were they allowed? It suddenly dawned on him that he'd probably end up sharing a cell with one of them or with someone just like them. The prospect liquefied his bowels.

Cramps took hold of his belly and he couldn't help doubling over. What if he fouled himself? What would they do to him? He glanced at his watch, tilted it until enough light came in through the barred window for him to read it. Five-thirty. When had he left the cell? Three-thirty. Two hours, he'd been in the van for two hours and they were still nowhere near Long Bay, crawling along roads jammed with peak-hour traffic. He needed a toilet urgently, needed to ease the pressure and pain in his bowels, winced each time the van's shot suspension bottomed out on a bump. The prisoner alongside vomited again and kept retching even though his stomach had emptied. The curses and abuse only subsided as they drew close to Long Bay.

Grant's fears heightened the moment the van passed through the main gates yet he was comforted by the knowledge that he was close to a toilet. It was dark inside the van and not much brighter outside, except when they passed directly beneath a light. As hard as he tried, he couldn't make out anything through the tiny barred windows.

'Everyone out!'

Grant filed out of the van behind the other prisoners into a floodlit area. Armed guards stood by in case anyone got it into their head to resist. Armed guards, for Christ's sake, with semi-automatics! He glanced up to get some idea of the building he was being taken into and looked straight into the barrel of a rifle held by a guard up on the parapet. Not even the hours in the van had prepared him for this. It couldn't be happening to him, but it was happening to him. It was happening to him! He followed the other prisoners into the prison reception and was about to be locked in a holding cage to await processing when he pleaded his desperate need for a toilet.

'Come with me,' said the custodial officer. He guided Grant to a cubicle along the wall of the reception room. A filthy toilet was jammed into the narrow space.

'Is this it?' asked Grant incredulously.

'Get on with it!'

'There's no door,' said Grant.

'Just do what you have to do and be quick about it.'

Grant's dignity dissolved in a noisy eruption of diarrhoea. The CO watching him screwed up his face in disgust. The smell was overwhelming but there was nothing Grant could do about it. Prisoners yelled abuse at him as he was led back to the holding cage thoroughly humiliated and defeated.

He could find no comfort anywhere, nobody he could relate to, nothing to ease his sense of alienation or shame. Prisoners were being interviewed one at a time at a long counter and then moved on for further processing. Grant waited and watched, not knowing how to feel when eventually his turn came.

'Name?' The officer hardly bothered to look at him. He wrote with his pen jammed between his second and third finger so that his hand bunched up like a claw. Grant had always been dismissive of people who held pens that way, considering them uneducated and ignorant. He was used to people like that deferring to him.

'Look, there's been a mistake. I shouldn't be here. Is there someone I can see?'

The officer looked up from the pad he was writing on and gave Grant a long, hard, contemptuous stare.

'Name?' he repeated.

'Sinclair. Grant Sinclair.'

'Right. Did you give your name, address, date of birth and next of kin to an officer at court?'

'Yes, but —'

'Are you on any medication?'

'I've already told people that.'

'Now tell me, smart-arse.'

'No, I'm not on any medication.'

'So you've got no pills on you or tablets, stuff like that?'

'No.' Grant found it hard to hide his impatience.

'Right. Now I'd like you to hand over all your money and valuables.'

'Look, can I see your superior?'

'Money and valuables.'

'What about my watch?'

'Let's see it.'

'It's a Rolex.'

'Hey, Ryan, bloke here's got a Rolex. Wants to know if he can keep it.'

Grant was aware of other officers laughing but what struck him most was the way the other prisoners waiting to be processed and those helping out in reception all turned as one to look at him, all with the same sudden interest.

'You can keep a watch if it's worth less than fifty bucks, which yours clearly isn't. And if I were you, sunshine, I wouldn't let on that you owned a Rolex, or had ever owned one, or even considered owning one. I wouldn't let on that I even knew what a Rolex was. Understand?'

Grant handed over his watch, his gold chain from around his neck, the silver-and-turquoise ring he'd bought on location in Arizona, the keys to his Porsche, his apartment and office keys, his wallet and the coins in his pocket. The officer gave him a typed sheet with carbon copies to sign listing the items and amount of money.

'The money will go into your account and you can use it for buy-ups,' said the officer. 'The rest will be handed back to you on release, or you can give permission for a visitor to collect it, which is what we recommend. Okay? Now I'm going to give you a list of questions and you just have to tick yes or no. Don't spend all day doing it.'

Grant took the eight-page tick-and-flick and scanned through the questions. Had he taken any illegal substances in the previous forty-eight hours? Was he coming down? Was he suicidal? Did he need to see a doctor? No, no, no, no, no!

'Now, is there any reason you should ask for protection?'

'Protection?' A ray of hope flickered.

'The Department of Corrective Services is responsible under legislation for the care of people placed in our custody. Is there any reason why you should think that your life or welfare is threatened?'

Any reason? Grant didn't know where to begin. Once again he was aware of the other prisoners watching him. He didn't understand the wry half-smile on the officer's face.

'I should warn you that if you ask for protection you will spend the rest of your time in prison in protective custody with rockies and be regarded by other inmates as one of them.'

'What are rockies?'

'What are rockies? Rock spiders. Paedophiles. Do you want to be put in with them?'

'No way.'

'Okay, so protective custody refused.' The officer ticked a square on his pad.

Grant wished he hadn't been so quick with his response. What was worse? Taking his chances in the open prison, where God only knew what could happen to him, or taking protection and spending every waking and sleeping moment with child molesters? Given that he would only be there for as long as it took his legal team to get him out, protection suddenly seemed a better option than sharing a cell with one of the animals from the van.

'Okay, now I'm going to give you an ID card which you have to keep about your person at all times, understand?'

'Yes. Look, about protection —'

'We've done that. Don't lose your card. Lost cards cause us a lot of aggravation, which means we'll cause you a lot of aggravation. Got that? I'm also going to give you a six-digit MIN, which is your master index number. Remember it like it's your name because, as far as we're concerned, your MIN is your name. You can be asked for it any time of the day or night right up until the day you're released. Your number is 1012_ _. Got that?'

Grant nodded, even though the last two digits eluded him. His mind was still wrestling with whether or not he'd done the right thing by refusing protection. He again thought of the prisoners in the van, their tattoos, and their shoulders bulked up by doing weights.

'Right. This your first time in gaol?'

'Yes.'

'Okay. You're probably feeling a bit scared and a bit angry, right? Since you're a cleanskin I'll give you a bit of advice. It's okay to feel scared but put the anger away. You've got attitude and that's only going to get you into trouble. Got it? Nobody comes here unless they've done something wrong, so button it. Just do what you're told when you're told and no ifs or buts. You might be a big man outside but here you're just another piece of shit. Now, a CO is going to come and take you to be fingerprinted and photographed and then searched. After that you'll be given a shower and your greens and then you'll be handed over to staff whose job it is to deal with all your questions. Until then, I'd keep a lid on it if I were you. Okay?'

Grant was photographed, fingerprinted and taken into another doorless cubicle.

'Strip.'

'What?'

'You heard! Take your bloody clothes off!'

'In here?'

Grant obeyed although his sense of vulnerability escalated with each item he removed.

'Put your clothes in the tray. You'll get them back for your court appearance.'

Grant had changed often enough in football changing rooms but never before under such an unflinching gaze. He felt inadequate and humiliated.

'Open your mouth.'

The officer peered into his mouth.

'Lift your tongue.'

Grant pulled his tongue back as far as it would go.

'Turn your head to the left.'

The officer checked behind his left ear before repeating the process with his right.

'Lift your scrotum.'

'What?'

'Lift your nuts so I can see behind 'em.'

The officer crouched down in front of him and squinted between his legs.

'Jesus Christ,' said Grant. 'Is this really necessary?'

'You say something?'

Grant decided he hadn't and shook his head.

'I thought you did. Okay, now bend over and spread your cheeks.'

Grant turned around and did as instructed, his humiliation now absolute.

'I am authorised to call a doctor to conduct a full-body cavity search if I feel it is warranted. Is that what you want?'

'No.'

'No, *sir*.'

'No, sir.'

'Then learn to keep your mouth shut. Okay, stand.' The officer led Grant naked into a tiled cubicle alongside the one he'd just vacated. 'Shower and be quick about it.'

Grant stumbled beneath the shower and turned on the taps. The tiles were broken and chipped and covered in a film of soap and hair. The grout between the tiles was black and a breeding ground for tinea. Soap was shared. All his anger had gone and his fear put on temporary hold. He could scarcely comprehend what had happened to him, the indignities he'd endured, the deliberate dehumanisation. Unbelievably, he felt close to tears.

He dried himself and got dressed in his greens. Underpants, T-shirt, tracksuit pants, sloppy joe, socks and Dunlop Volleys. Dunlop Volleys, for Christ's sake. He was accustomed to two-hundred-dollar Nikes. He clutched his spare T-shirt, underpants and socks, two pairs of shorts and a toilet kit containing a toothbrush, toothpaste, shampoo and disposable razor hard against his chest. The officer led him away to a room where more COs and a welfare officer waited to interview him.

'Is there anyone we need to inform of your whereabouts? Landlord?'

Christ! His mortgage, what about his mortgage? There were so many things to think about. If his legal team didn't get him out he'd lose his townhouse. That was something else he'd have to get his solicitor onto.

'Is that a yes or a no?'

'No.'

'Employer?'

Oh God, what would happen to his business?

'No.'

'Any relatives who need to be informed? Wife, parents, children?'

If only. His parents had moved to Forster on the New South Wales mid-north coast and divided their time between their crappy little brick-veneer house and the RSL club. Even if they sobered up, he doubted they'd care. His daughter was another matter, but not something he or anyone else could address in one phone call.

'No.'

'Any pressing personal or family problems?'

He could think of one, oh yes, he could think of one, but it was a problem he'd have to deal with himself.

'I shouldn't be here. I'm not guilty. Someone's stuffed up.'

'So you'll be in good company. This place is full of people who haven't done anything. You've been classified B(u): B unsentenced, bail refused. That's pretty clear. The B classification means that, in the opinion of the Commissioner, you should be confined behind a secure physical barrier at all times. If there's any reason you shouldn't be here tell your solicitor not me. Now, please answer the question.'

'I have no personal or family problems.'

'Do you have any medical problems that require you to see a doctor?'

'No.'

'Right-oh. Some time over the next few days you will go through screening and induction by trained officers to help keep you safe and assess you for services and programs such as alcohol and drug dependence. They'll want to know why you're here and address your problems so that you don't re-offend. A psychologist and a probation officer will prepare pre-sentencing reports to be forwarded on to the judge. It is in your best interests to cooperate at all times. Any questions?'

'Will I have my own cell?'

'Slot. We call them slots. You will be allocated a slot two out in the remand centre, which means you share a slot with another prisoner.'

'Can I phone my solicitor?'

'You're entitled to make one phone call now and three local calls a week up until sentencing.' The welfare officer pointed to a phone attached to the wall. 'You're limited to six minutes.'

Grant's hands were shaking so much he had to concentrate hard so he didn't hit the wrong buttons, get a wrong number and blow his one chance at a call. He heard his solicitor's receptionist answer by reciting the name of the law firm. He nearly wept at the sound of her voice, a voice from another world, a voice that could lead to his release. But then she continued. 'The office is presently unattended. Please state your name and phone number and the name of the person you wish to contact after the beep. Thank you for calling.'

A recorded message? Grant was stunned that his solicitor hadn't waited back for his call. What the hell was he paying him for? He wanted to rip the phone off the wall with frustration. That was what he did under normal circumstances. He'd lost count of the number of times he'd smashed handsets by hurling them to the floor or against walls.

'It's Grant Sinclair for Richard Challoner. Tell him I've wasted my one and only phone call on him,' he said bitterly. 'And tell him to get in touch urgently. He knows where to find me.'

He thought of the thousands of dollars he'd paid his solicitor to get him off, money he was no doubt drinking away in some watering hole, money that was supposed to buy the right verdict. His solicitor owed him big-time. It was his fault that he was in gaol. Challoner should've been there to take his call. He slammed the phone down, attracting immediate attention from the welfare officer and the nearby CO.

'If you've broken that phone you're going to be very unpopular,' said the CO. He strode purposefully towards Grant who threw his hands up in apology.

'Sorry, sorry ...'

'Do you want to lose phone privileges?'

'I'm sorry.'

The officer checked the phone to make sure it was still working.

'You don't know how lucky you are. One more outburst like that and you're going on report.'

Lucky? Grant had never felt less lucky in his life. He was in gaol and about to be locked up in a cell with someone no better than an animal. And he was scared, more scared than he'd ever been or thought he could be.

'You're now going to be taken to your slot in Twelve Wing. Here is a copy of the inmate handbook,' said the CO. 'Read it carefully and give it back tomorrow or when you finish it. You've missed dinner but we've kept you some sandwiches. Okay?' He handed Grant two halves of a sandwich in cling-wrap.

Grant was escorted outside and across a narrow access road into a forbidding old Victorian building. He expected the interior to be dingy and threatening but it was way beyond his worst imaginings. Metal doors clanged shut behind him until he found himself standing on the ground floor of a three-storey building, surrounded on all sides by walls of cells and steel walkways reaching all the way up to the roof. There were nets strung between each of the levels and Grant guessed immediately what their purpose was. Hard men stared out at him from behind bars. Some made wisecracks but his numbed brain couldn't take them in. His escort stopped abruptly before a cell door and unlocked it. Grant was almost too scared to look inside, frightened of who he might find in there. He was dimly aware of a man stretched out on the lower bunk watching TV. Suddenly he was inside the cell. His escort said something that didn't register above the sound of canned laughter coming from the TV, but he heard the man on the lower bunk grunt, he thought, with irritation.

He put his bundle of clothes, toilet kit and sandwiches on his bunk but had no idea where to put himself. There was a small table and two metal chairs opposite the bunks, but occupying either of the chairs meant eyeballing his cellmate and he wasn't yet ready for that. He hauled himself up to the top bunk and lay down, too scared to move.

'You're the wrong fucking way round, man.'

'What?' Grant froze. Yet the voice beneath didn't seem to carry any menace.

'The toilet, man. Bad news. You wanna keep your head as far away from that as you can.'

Grant peered over the end of the bunk. There beneath him, jammed in the corner against the wall, was a filthy stained toilet with no seat. The only concession to privacy was a brick wall less than a metre high. A toilet roll sat on the wall. Grant instantly recalled his noisy humiliating defecation on admittance. He'd thought it would be a one-off experience that he'd get over, never imagining for a second it would become the norm for the duration of his stay. In the corner opposite was a handbasin no more appealing than the toilet. This was where he had to wash his face and clean his teeth? How were people expected to live like this?

'You got a name?'

'Grant.'

'I'm Dave. Some people call me Dopey but that's got nuthin' to do with my IQ. You're a cleanskin, right?'

'Cleanskin?'

'First-timer.'

Grant swung his legs hesitantly over the bunk and dropped down to the floor. He'd expected his cellmate to be a tattooed, hairy Neanderthal with a penchant for sodomy, but his preconceptions went straight out the narrow barred window. His cellmate was thin and pale-skinned, with a weedy moustache and goatee he was wasting his time trying to cultivate. He looked exactly like the sort of loser Grant had always done his best to ignore and categorised as a waste of both oxygen and food. Yet he almost smiled with relief. The man was a dope fiend and no threat. No threat! He shook hands and slumped down into one of the metal chairs.

'I shouldn't be here.'

'Oh, man, there's one hundred and eighty other guys in Twelve Wing who think that. Including me.'

'What are you in for?'

Dave shook his head.

'Man, there's some things you gotta learn. You don't ask questions. Nobody tells no one nothin' in here. And don't tell no one nothin' about yourself. Got any smokes?'

'Don't smoke.'

'Shit, man.' Dave seemed to take the absence of cigarettes as a personal affront. 'What kinda sandwiches they give ya?'

'I've no idea.'

'Take a look.'

Grant reached up onto his bunk for his sandwiches and unwrapped them. There was something sodden, brown and disgusting between two thin pieces of white bread. Whatever the filling was he couldn't face it and handed the sandwiches to his cellmate.

'Baked beans,' said Dave. His face brightened. 'Hey, good one, man.'

Over the next few days Grant's anger and depression grew as the hopelessness of his situation became increasingly apparent. While he had all the attachments of the young and successful, he had no money. The townhouse, the Porsche and the lavish lifestyle were all dependent on cash flow, on paying leases and mortgages. Even his production company operated on an overdraft. For fifteen months his lawyers had applied successfully for a series of postponements contrived to delay his trial and the cost had been a serious drain on his funds. The trial had exhausted what remained and strained the viability of his company. Even though his solicitor urged him to appeal his conviction and denial of bail, Grant decided to wait until after sentencing in the hope that an appeal would not be necessary. Besides, appeals to the Supreme Court did not come cheaply and he no longer had the means to pay. His parole officer suggested legal aid, but Grant couldn't see how legal aid could get him off where his expensive silks had failed. He needed cash and needed to be on the outside, running his company, to generate it. His frustration fuelled his anger.

Despite the horrors of his daily existence and the suffocating fear he experienced every time the prisoners in Twelve Block were released into the yard or out onto the 'killing fields' for sport, he decided to concentrate his few remaining resources on presenting the best possible case when he appeared in court for sentencing. He'd learned that there were three options the judge could consider as an alternative to a custodial sentence: supervision in the community, a community service order and periodic detention. These options gave him hope.

His solicitor suggested preparing a psychologist's report of their own to counter any negative comments from the prison psychologist and Grant agreed. He provided a list of people who could testify to his good character. Once again he put his faith in his high-powered silks to make the judge see reason. He treated the tests and reviews he was obliged to undergo in prison with barely concealed contempt.

Both his parole officer and the prison psychologist tried to make him show remorse for the victim and sympathy for the victim's family but Grant refused. He interpreted their intentions as a way of tricking him into accepting his guilt. How could he accept guilt when he was not guilty, despite the jury's findings? He was not guilty and, as far as Grant was concerned, that was the end of it. He believed that the fact that he stuck to his protestations of innocence would stand him in good stead with the judge. By the time he went to court for sentencing, he'd convinced himself that the judge would realise that the jury had stuffed up and that he'd be released with no more than the judicial equivalent of a slap on the wrist. He thought a community service order or, at worst, periodic detention was a mere formality.

The moment the judge opened his mouth, Grant began to suspect that things might not go quite the way he'd hoped. The judge reviewed his case and, from time to time, looked up from his reading to peer down at him like a stern father to a wayward child. He noted that Grant had not been in trouble before and had no prior offences, but also noted his lack of remorse and unwillingness to accept responsibility for the crime of which he had been convicted. He cited precedents as a basis for his decision. Grant listened in dismay. The precedents seemed to have little in common with his situation. They involved serious offences by violent men, while he was just guilty of being party to an unfortunate accident.

It slowly dawned on Grant that there was a very real possibility that he'd be sent back to gaol and that there was absolutely nothing he or his legal team could do to prevent it. He began to speculate on worst-case scenarios. What would he get? Twelve months with nine months non-parole? At worst, eighteen months? The thought almost made him sick. Eighteen months! He'd lose his townhouse, lose his business, in fact lose everything that defined who he was. Eighteen months! No! It couldn't happen. It couldn't.

When the judge passed sentence all the air exploded from Grant's lungs. He felt his legs begin to collapse beneath him, felt his hands cling to the rail in front of him for support. He glanced around wildly but neither his barrister nor solicitor was prepared to meet his eye. Instead, his eyes locked onto his ex-wife's. She seemed as stunned as he was. In the midst of his panic, two words bounced around inside his skull, unable to find a place that would accept them. Eight years! Eight years! Eight years!

Chapter Eight

Grant Sinclair walked out of Long Bay Gaol and onto Anzac Parade to wait for the bus that would take him on the first step of his cross-town journey to his mate's duplex in Manly. For the first time in five years and six months he was free to spend the night in a real bed instead of a bunk, in a bedroom instead of a slot, and with a woman instead of a masturbating cellmate. Weekend release was a milestone which one thousand, nine hundred and ten interminable days earlier had seemed impossibly remote, beyond both reach and hope. Like most prisoners on weekend release, Grant walked out through the gates anticipating pleasures too long denied. But his anticipation was leavened by the knowledge that weekend release, like the day releases which had preceded it, was just a brief illusion of freedom, just another element in a custodial sentence he still had to serve, and a stinging reminder of a life rightfully his that had been taken from him.

There were only three other people on the bus when Grant boarded it and he found a seat as far from them as he could. Grant still refused to accept that he was guilty or had done anything to deserve his term in gaol. Fear, resentment, bitterness and a burning desire for revenge had been constant companions every second of every minute of every hour of every day. There was no shortage of people he blamed for his incarceration, but his ex-wife stood out head and shoulders above the others. She had to pay. Pay for her lies and pay restitution. She had to pay for the fear that had enveloped him the moment his world had come to a shuddering halt, and for the outrages, humiliations and the bottomless despair that had stripped him of everything he was. Memories were the whetstone for his anger. They kept his spirit alive when everything else conspired to crush it. They got him out of his bunk every morning, got him through the tedium of the day and the bitter loneliness of night. They honed his need to get even, reinforced his determination to exact revenge.

The bus seemed to stop at every lamppost and corner but tedium was something else Grant had grown accustomed to. In the scheme of things, a forty-five-minute ride was nothing compared with a twenty-four-hour lockup in a slot. A poster advertising baked beans caught his eye and interrupted his thoughts. Baked beans. He'd made a commercial for baked beans once and had become an expert on them for as long as it had taken him to do pre-production, shoot and edit. He hadn't given baked beans another thought until he'd wound up in gaol and discovered that they carried a premium over whatever else was put in sandwiches. The weight-lifters were prepared to fight for them because they believed the protein in the beans helped build muscles. Most of the other prisoners just wanted them for the taste. Tins of baked beans were a big-selling favourite in the buy-ups and Grant had never known a cell block that didn't smell of them being warmed. The commercial he'd made had squarely targeted children below the age of eleven and, as far as he was concerned, that just about summed up the mental age of most of the inmates. He'd gone for the cheese and salad or cheese and pickle sandwiches, even though the cheese was bland-tasting, a plastic-looking cheddar any self-respecting mouse would turn its nose up at. But it was better and more reliable than whatever passed for cold meat. God only knew what animal it had come from and when. There'd been times when he'd had to choose between baked beans and cold meat sandwiches and gone for the cold meat so as not to deprive the weight-lifters in the line behind him of their protein. His thoughtfulness didn't earn him thanks, just spared him a cuff around the ears.

He stepped off the bus at Circular Quay and into a cool spring breeze blowing in off the harbour. People zipped up jackets and hunched down into sweaters but the breeze made no impression on Grant. He was used to it. Heat and cold were things you learned to handle. There'd been times when he'd thought the architects of Long Bay Gaol had deliberately chosen the site as further punishment for the inmates. When the cold southerly winds blew straight in off the sea there was no escaping them. But, in truth, Long Bay wasn't as cold as Bathurst Gaol and nowhere near as bleak as Goulburn. The winds that roared down off the snowfields and into Goulburn Gaol were as cold as a psychopath's heart.

Grant copped an eyeful of grit as he crossed the road to the ferry building. Being Saturday morning, the street wasn't exactly deserted but had nowhere near the midweek numbers of people. Sheets of newspaper caught the wind and tumbled along the road. Grant couldn't help wondering what the town planners were thinking of when they allowed the giant glass and concrete towers to be built. What they needed was a spell in Long Bay to give them a dose of reality and bring them back down to earth. That would do it. The wind freshened as the ferry pulled away from the Quay. The sun was on the water and along the harbourside, seagulls circled for handouts from tourists. The gulls probably ate better than he did. Grant found a seat outside and looked forward to the thirty-minute crossing to blow away the cobwebs of five and a half years of incarceration and blunt the edge of his anger and bitterness. Despite what his probation and parole officer thought, Grant believed he had his anger under control. He wouldn't let it spoil his weekend.

* * *

'Hello, Dad.'

Gaol had hardened Grant to the point where murders, bashings and rapes could take place right in front of his eyes without making him blink, but no armour is without flaw.

'Hello, Jammy.' Grant smiled, kissed his daughter's cheek and gently hugged her. 'It means everything to me, you know,' he said softly. 'You coming to see me.'

'I know.'

'You look fabulous. What did I do to deserve you?'

Grant hugged her again then held her at arm's length so that he could look at her. She was so young, fresh and innocent, absolutely gorgeous, but with a little too much of her mother in her. That was something else her mother would have to pay for:

she'd robbed him of the opportunity to watch Jasmine grow up, to see her change from a gawky eight-year-old to a half-child, half-woman of fourteen. He'd refused to let her visit him, refused to let her see him in gaol, and had seen her for the first time in five years just three months earlier, on his first day release. He had her letters and her photographs to know that she still loved him and hadn't turned her back on him, despite what had happened and despite the poison her mother must have breathed into her ears every single day he'd been inside. He'd had to wait two years — two years! — for her first tentative letter, but after that she'd written once or twice a month and he'd phoned her in between. How hard had it been for her to have her father sent to gaol, to have someone whose love, affection and presence she took for granted suddenly taken away from her? Even now as he looked at her he could sense the hurt. He took in everything about her, the streaking in her hair and the spot on the side of her chin that she'd tried to cover. What did she see when she looked back at him? He stared at her until her face flushed from embarrassment.

'I'm sorry, Jammy. It isn't like I've seen a lot of you these past few years. I was just trying to imagine what I'd missed.' He looked around. 'Where's Cameron?'

'He's waiting for us in a café on the seafront. He thought it would be nice if I met you off the ferry by myself, you know, give us a chance to talk.' She slipped her hand in his and they headed off down The Corso.

'Boarding still okay?'

'Yes, it's fine. I have fun.'

'But you'd rather be at home.'

Jasmine didn't answer because to respond took them into forbidden areas.

'I can't help feeling you're being punished because of me.'

'It's okay, Dad, really. I don't feel like I'm being punished. I'm with friends and I'm enjoying myself.'

'Does your mother keep in touch?'

'She phones every second day and on weekends when I stay over with Aunt Fran and Dave.'

Fran was her mother's sister. Grant had never liked her and the feeling was openly mutual. He could imagine how much sympathy and understanding he'd get from her. But at least they were kind enough to take Jammy out of school for weekend leave. Weekend leave, he thought bitterly. Anyone would think she was in gaol too. Christ Almighty, his ex had a lot to answer for.

'Do you call her?'

'No.'

'So how do you get in touch if something happens to you? What if you fall sick or break an arm or something?'

'They ring Aunt Fran. She rings Mum.'

Grant sighed. Statues would weep blood before Fran gave up the number.

'But what if it's an emergency? Is she still in Sydney, is she nearby if you need her?'

'Dad, you know I can't answer those questions. I'm not allowed to tell you anything.'

Grant cursed silently. He was aware of the sudden flatness in his daughter's voice and decided to change the subject. Her loyalties were divided, and where there was division he'd find opportunity soon enough. It was all a matter of building trust and waiting for the unguarded comment, the unthinking little slip of the tongue.

'Tell me about yourself. How are you getting on with your studies?'

Grant listened attentively as she ran through her latest marks and boasted of her prowess at netball. The smile was back in her voice and that was enough for now.

They found Cameron sitting at one of the café's prized pavement tables, which was sheltered from the wind and had a view right up the shore to the headland at Queenscliff. It was exactly the sort of table Grant would have demanded and been given years earlier.

'Pity about the table,' he said as he shook Cameron's hand.

'Yeah, and pity about the view,' said Cameron.

When his production company was still small and growing, Grant had given Cameron a job and taken him under his wing, teaching him all he knew about producing. At the time, Cameron had been just a pimply street kid with not much formal education, no training at film school and few prospects. His only assets had been his persistence and a burning desire to work in films. He'd offered to work for nothing, to sweep floors, clean Grant's car and be everyone's lackey, just for a chance. He'd hung around reception and turned up on shoots, sometimes in the middle of the night, until Grant had weakened and given him what he wanted. They'd got on well but Cameron had never really numbered among Grant's friends, at least, not among those who mattered. Yet it was Cameron who'd stuck by him when the shit had hit the fan, who'd visited him in gaol and kept him sane by taking care of and taping his collection of jazz records, who'd handled the sale of his townhouse and his Porsche, topped up his gaol account so he could afford the necessities and bribes to get by, who'd sponsored him for day release and now weekend release, and had even provided him with the clothes he was wearing. It was Cameron who picked Jasmine up from boarding school on his days out and who delivered her to her aunt's safekeeping afterwards. Grant had once tried to tell Cameron how much he appreciated what he'd done for him and how much he owed him. 'Forget it,' Cameron had replied. 'Ever stopped to think how much I owe you?'

Grant gave the waitress his order and stretched his legs beneath the table. Billie Holiday was softly wishing on the moon from tiny speakers strung over the doorway. Out of the wind the sun was pleasantly warm and there was a brightness to the day. He'd woken up that morning locked down in a slot and had suffered the usual breakfast of rice bubbles with milk and artificial sweetener, because sugar wasn't allowed in gaol in case inmates used it to brew up alcoholic concoctions. Now he was sitting at a prized seafront table with his daughter and closest mate, while a parade of beautiful people passed by. He knew if he looked over the seawall there'd be young women sunbathing topless and young men whose only concern was to ride waves better than their mates. When his coffee arrived, he could put as much sugar in it as he liked and no one would object. All in good time, Cameron would take him and Jammy to a restaurant where his entrée alone would cost more than he earned in a week inside learning to operate a forklift. His daughter interrupted his thoughts.

'Because this is your first weekend out, Aunt Fran said she'd pick me up off the ferry at Circular Quay so you and Cameron don't have to drive me home.'

'We don't mind.'

'I know that, Dad. But it's your first weekend out and she thinks you're entitled to have a bit of fun without me holding you back.'

'Tell Fran I appreciate her thoughtfulness.' So there was some good in the woman, not much, but some. His coffee arrived and he put two heaped teaspoons in it and stirred until every grain had dissolved. The smell was sensational, the taste even better. He closed his eyes as he sipped. More than anything else, good coffee with real sugar seemed the definitive expression of freedom.

'Take your time,' said Cameron. 'There's no hurry.'

No, there was no hurry. He had the weekend off but he still had six months to serve before being released on parole. He had another one hundred and eighty-two days to endure before he could set about rebuilding his life. Another Christmas would come and go, although they'd probably let him out for it. They hadn't been so considerate on his fortieth birthday. He'd always figured he'd be rich by then and celebrate that particular milestone with a lavish party and more booze than a single truck could deliver. Instead, he'd celebrated with an overcooked lamb chop, mashed potatoes and some mushy grey-green peas with less than one hundred dollars in his gaol account.

Grant took his daughter's hand and squeezed it. She was his until four o'clock and he was determined to make every moment special for her. After that, he and Cameron would get down to business. Cameron had arranged a barbecue for him so he could renew contact with old colleagues still in the business, people who might prove helpful further down the track. He knew his protégé would do things in style, with film caterers preparing the food, grog by the truckload and enough snort to make sure everyone had a good time. That was the one thing that worried Grant. Just being on the same premises as illegal drugs could see his weekend leave revoked and his parole put at risk. But what choice did he have? The use of coke was so rife in the industry it was considered a cost of doing business. And there'd be girls, among them enough one-time lovers to guarantee his first night out of gaol would not be lonely. That still left him an entire day to sit down with Cameron and start making plans for the film company they intended to start.

There was other important business to attend to as well. He had to begin the process of finding an ex-wife who'd gone into hiding. He noticed Jasmine looking at him curiously, as though trying to read his thoughts, and smiled. Good luck to anyone who tried. He'd grown accustomed to ignoring people around him and showing nothing of what he was thinking or how he was feeling. He decided his ex-wife could wait. What were another few hours when he'd waited five and a half years?

* * *

Neil leaned back in his chair and signalled to Gancio that he'd reached the break in his storytelling. His timing caught both the restaurateur and his friends by surprise.

'No comments?' he asked dryly.

'What are you doing to us?' said Ramon. 'I enjoyed last week in the outback with its wide open spaces. I didn't expect to spend the first half of the afternoon in a cell.'

'In a slot, Ramon, get it right.'

'You haven't told us what Grant did to get sent to gaol,' said Lucio.

'You'll find out soon enough.'

'It must have been something serious to get treated the way he was.'

'The nature of the crime has nothing to do with the way he was treated,' said Neil. 'Everyone who goes on remand at Long Bay gets treated the same way.'

'What about corporate criminals? What about people like Alan Bond? They get special treatment, no?'

'No, Milos. Not when they first enter the gaol system. They might get classified low risk and ultimately be sent to a low-security prison or section of a prison, but processing takes days and in the meantime they take their chances along with everyone else.'

'But they wouldn't be strip-searched and humiliated like your character was. They get looked after. Money talks, no? Even in prison.'

'Everyone gets strip-searched. That's policy. Even corporate criminals and traffic offenders.'

'Traffic offenders?'

'Have an accident and seriously injure someone when you've had too many grappas and you'll find out.'

'That's barbaric,' said Lucio.

'Maybe, but it's nothing compared to what happens to you when you get thrown in gaol in Argentina, is it, Ramon? And as for Hungary — well, it's just a stroll in the park, right, Milos? We Australians, we think we're hard bastards, but we're just amateurs compared to you blokes.'

'Don't start that again,' said Milos. 'The times and circumstances were entirely different.'

'Ignore him,' said Ramon evenly. He made room for Gancio to serve his coffee and grappa. 'The real issue is whether we should feel sympathetic towards this Grant Sinclair and whether or not he deserved to be sent to gaol for eight years. The whole point of Neil's story today is to give us a sense of a man wronged. Every detail is designed to heighten the sense of injustice and outrage and justify his desire for revenge, while, at the same time, putting a question mark over Linda's character. Am I right?'

'Are you ever wrong?' said Neil glibly. He took a sip of grappa and washed it down with coffee. 'Now, do I have your permission to proceed?'

'If you're taking us back to gaol I'd like to enjoy my grappa — and my freedom — a little longer,' said Lucio.

'Relax, we're not going back to gaol. We've spent enough time with the guilty. I think we should now spend some time with the innocent.' Neil acknowledged the quickening of interest with a slight smile. 'There was a time when we were all innocent, even Ramon. I'm not going to bore you by taking you right back to my earliest childhood, but I want you to understand what my brother was like when he was a kid. I was only eighteen months older but I couldn't wait for him to grow so I had someone to play with. It can get bloody lonely growing up on an isolated station. My sisters weren't good at many things but they were bloody geniuses when it came to ignoring my existence. There were times I got so lonely my dad used to tie a bone to my leg to see if the dogs would play with me.'

Chapter Nine

Billy lay in bed too excited to sleep. He looked forward to his elder brother's tenth birthday as keenly as if it were his own. And he had every reason to. Money was tight and his parents tended not to waste a birthday on a present that would only benefit one of the boys. He couldn't wait for morning to discover what the present was. His eldest sister had got a hairdryer on her birthday, a gift clearly intended to be shared with her younger sister, and some clothes, which really didn't count. Just the thought of clothes made Billy shut his eyes tighter, cross his fingers and make a wish so he didn't put the mockers on his brother's present. Clothes were the worst thing that could happen. The worst! Clothes were a total waste of a birthday. Things were tough when Neil turned nine and his parents had given him a new pair of jeans and a sweater. They thought it was a neat way to solve two problems: Neil got a birthday present and his younger brother got hand-me-downs to replace the jeans and sweater he'd worn holes through. The boys could hardly credit the scale of the disaster. They'd pinned their hopes on a second-hand air rifle a kid two properties away was selling. Billy tried to banish the thought of clothes from his mind because Neil had warned him that just thinking about things could sometimes make them happen.

The build-up to his brother's birthday had been nerve-racking. They couldn't give their father a list of presents to choose from because they knew from experience that it would only make him angry. To the boys it was a wish list, but to their father it was a catalogue of his failure to provide them with things other kids took for granted. The best the boys could do was contrive conversations in the kitchen in which various desirable items like a new cricket bat, Monopoly set and a new football featured. Their mother pretended not to hear them but they reckoned the smile she tried to hide was a dead giveaway.

A new football was top of their list because the one they used at school had finally split its seams and burst. When they played rugby league at playtime they had to make do with a prune of a basketball the netball team had discarded. They managed, but only a proper football could make the game real and make it feel right when they dummied, sidestepped and pretended they were playing for South Sydney. A football was definitely top of the list, but it had to be a proper one not a kid's one, leather not rubber. There again, an air rifle would be fantastic.

Both boys knew how to handle guns. So long as he had guns in the house, their father insisted they know how to handle them so they'd hold no mystery and they'd not be tempted to play with them when he wasn't around. All the same, he let the brothers know that if he ever found out that they'd so much as touched his guns without permission, he'd belt the living daylights out of them. But that hadn't stopped the boys sneaking looks at them in the cupboard and imagining an air rifle on a rack beneath them. Billy finally fell asleep diving over in the corner for the winning try.

Neil woke him up by shaking him.

'There's no present.'

Billy sat up, stunned. He looked over at his brother's bed, leaned forward so he could see around the foot of it. There was no sign of a present. No wrapping paper, nothing.

'Have you looked under your bed?'

'Of course.'

Billy stared at his brother in horror. His parents always snuck into the bedroom in the middle of the night and left their birthday present on the bed or alongside it. Except ... except when it was clothes. Billy fell back on his pillow in disappointment, unable to look his brother in the face. He sensed Neil was close to tears.

'They might have forgotten or got the day wrong.' It was the only thing Billy could think of to say that would give his brother some cause for hope.

'Your shoes are okay, aren't they?' said Neil.

'Yeah. And my boots.'

'What about your shorts?'

'I've got lots of good shorts and shirts.'

'What about your jacket?'

'Mum sewed it up.'

'Can you think of anything you need?'

'No, honestly, Neil.'

'Maybe they did get the day wrong,' said Neil unconvincingly. 'Let's go get breakfast.'

They wandered through to the kitchen, half expecting to see new jeans or a jacket draped on Neil's chair at the kitchen table, or maybe, if they were really lucky, a big present like a bike resting up against the wall. There were no clothes and nothing that looked remotely like a present. Their mother, Millie, was making toast. There wasn't even anything special for breakfast, just Weet-Bix as usual.

'Happy birthday, Neil,' said Millie. She gave Neil a big kiss and a hug.

'I didn't get a present,' said Neil. 'I looked everywhere.'

'Your father thinks you're too big now to get presents in bed. That's for little kids. You're ten now.'

'Where is Dad?'

'He's out in the yard somewhere. You can go look for him after you've had your breakfast.'

Neil stared down at his bowl and splashed milk over his Weet-Bix. Neither boy was a cry-baby but Neil didn't want anybody to see his face just in case. Why hadn't they warned him, he wondered, why hadn't they told him he was too old for presents? His sisters, Gloria and Kathleen, still got presents and Glory was thirteen. It wasn't fair. Maybe his dad was teaching him a lesson. He was always saying things were tough and that if people wanted to get on they had to learn to handle disappointment. Well, if it was a lesson, Neil decided he'd show his father he was up to it. They could all get stuffed.

'He's not too old, Mum,' said Billy. 'Honestly, he's not too old to get presents in bed. You're not too old, are you, Neil?'

'Hush, Billy,' said his mother. 'Are the girls awake?'

'I don't know.'

'When you finish, go wake them. And remind them to wish Neil a happy birthday.'

Happy birthday? Billy couldn't believe the way things had turned out. How could a birthday possibly be happy if there wasn't a present? He finished first and ran to wake the girls. When he came back, Neil was pulling on his sandals at the kitchen door.

'Wait for me,' he said. 'Where are we going?'

'I'm going to look for Dad.'

'I'm coming too.'

'Please yourself.'

The late summer rains had been and gone and the ground outside had returned to its normal hard dusty condition. Grass had given up trying to grow anywhere near the house and the only green came from the orange and lemon trees, the rose bushes and their mother's gardens. Keeping them going was hard enough without trying to grow a lawn.

Neil looked around defiantly, squinting in the glare of the morning sun. He had a point to prove and he was determined to prove it. He wanted to find his dad, look him in the eye and show him he was as tough as he was. Then he heard the sound that changed everything, clear and unmistakeable in the morning air. His spirits soared as his eyes turned skyward, searching for then picking up the flight. Billy had heard it too and was already screaming in rapture.

'Get out of my way!' Neil yelled.

Billy backed away as was only right. It was Neil's birthday and he was entitled to first go. The football reached the apex of its flight and began to arc downward. Neil raced into position, his eyes firmly on the ball. He backed up so he wouldn't be caught inside the line of flight and rose on his toes, ready to dash forward if the ball swirled and changed its angle of descent. Even with the ball falling, the boys could see the shine on it and realised it was a new one and a real good one. It hit Neil high on his chest and his arms wrapped around it in a grip that threatened to burst it.

'Mark!' screamed Neil.

'Yes!' screamed Billy. He ran to his brother, desperate to examine the football and find out exactly how good it was. He stopped short, his eyes filling with awe. He guessed he had the same dazed look on his face his brother had. Seconds earlier he thought Neil wasn't even going to get a present. Now they had this. And it was nearly almost partly his.

'Can I hold it?'

Neil handed the ball to his brother. Billy ran his disbelieving fingers over the stencil, over the brand name and the magic words 'Official NSWRL'.

'Will that do you?'

Billy looked up as his father stepped out from behind the chookhouse. Neil was already racing over to hug him. Would it do? Billy had never seen a better rugby ball in his life, never thought the day would come when he'd even hold one as good. It wasn't just good, it was the best you could get. He glanced over towards the kitchen. His mother and sisters were standing out on the veranda with big smirks on their faces. Billy thought Neil's birthday was the best day of his life.

'Make sure you look after it,' he heard his father say.

The school bus picked the boys up a kilometre away on Stony Creek Road, directly opposite their letterbox. The boys ran ahead of their sisters, passing the football all the way. They practised long raking passes from the scrum base, little flicks behind their backs and palm-offs, honing their skills for the big test that would come when they reached school. By happy coincidence, Neil's birthday also happened to be sports day, when the bus taking the kids home arrived an hour later than usual. The boys thought they could talk their teacher into having a City versus Country match instead of normal skills practice. The City kids were the Walgett kids and anyone else who lived within eight kilometres of the town. The Country kids were those who lived further out.

On the strength of his football, Neil became an instant hero to all the boys already on the bus and even more so when it stopped to pick up Rodney. The nature of Neil's birthday present had been the main topic of conversation for more than a week and Rodney had become almost as excited as Billy as the day had drawn closer.

'Id a bew-dy,' said Rodney in awe. 'And thad a-fid-dle.' Damn right it was official.

Neil let Rodney hold the ball for a couple of stops. The fascination with the football continued throughout the two-hour journey into Walgett and right through the day. In the entire history of rugby league, no football was more admired or handled with greater reverence. Even their teacher was impressed enough to grant their wish to play City versus Country. Country won a fiercely contested game, but it was only a last-ditch tackle by Billy on a kid twice his size that clinched the victory. Billy was a hero momentarily, but it was Neil's day.

They left the school to wait for the bus, which pulled up outside a house alongside the school. The house had a special place in school lore because its yard housed what everyone agreed was the fiercest mongrel in the far northwest. It was a big brute of a thing called Blackie. Its owner kept it on a long chain, not just because it was vicious but because it could chew through a rope in minutes. The kids knew exactly how long the chain was and which parts of the yard the dog could reach. Sometimes, when they got bored waiting for the bus, they did what they called 'Blackie runs', which involved dashing across the yard as close to the limits of the chain as they dared. This, of course, drove the mongrel insane. Every kid had to do the Blackie run at some time, and those who were brave or smart gained extra kudos by timing their run so that they made a fleeting incursion into Blackie territory. That really drove the mongrel nuts and the boys all knew that if they ever got caught there'd be nothing left to bury.

The boys weren't interested in teasing Blackie as they waited for the bus because they had the football to play with. They concentrated hard on their behind-the-back passes because they didn't want to drop the ball on the sealed footpath and scuff up the shine. They were concentrating so hard that they didn't notice the older black kids until they were almost upon them. Rodney shouted a warning but it was too late. Both Neil and Billy recognised the threat instantly.

There were plenty of Aboriginal kids from the Dewhurst Reserve in the school and the boys got on as well with them as they did with everyone else. They saw them as mates, not much different to themselves, except that some of the black kids could run like the wind and had the fastest, slickest hands of any of them. They were great league players and the boys envied their skills. In fact the only thing they didn't like about them were the head clashes. When you bumped heads with a black kid you knew it. Their heads could crack concrete. But for all that the boys got on with their mates in school, the older black kids were from the Namoi Reserve and they were something else altogether.

'Hey, good footie,' said one of the blacks. He was about fifteen and towered over Billy. His mates were all about the same age and size. Neil and Billy knew they were on a hiding to nothing.

'Gis a look at it,' said another of the boys.

'It's just a footie,' said Neil defensively. 'You can see it from where you are.' Neil knew that if he handed the ball over the black kids would take off with it and he'd be lucky if he ever saw it again. He also knew that if he was lucky enough to get it back, it would be battered, scraped and unrecognisable from the shiny football his father had kicked to him earlier in the day.

'We jus wanna look at it,' insisted the first boy. He put his hands around the ball and tried to wrench it out of Neil's hands. He pulled so hard Neil's feet lifted off the ground, but he managed to hold onto it.

'What you worried about, mate? Tole ya, we jus wanna look at it.' He pulled again, this time more fiercely. Neil hung on grimly, but everyone could see it wasn't a contest he could possibly win.

'Leave him alone!' said Billy. He pushed the kid trying to steal the football. The black kid let go of the ball to shove Billy aside. Billy staggered backwards but kept to his feet.

'Pass!' he shrieked.

Neil didn't hesitate. He unleashed a pass any first-grade halfback would be proud of. Billy took it on the fly and kept running but the black kids were on him in a flash.

'Pard!' shouted Rodney.

Billy passed, even though he knew Rodney was hopeless at league and just about every other sport.

He threw a bit of a floater, what commentators called a 'Hail Mary' pass, but Rodney took it cleanly and continued running down the road, the black kids hard on his heels. Neil sprinted after him, out wide onto the road.

'Pass!' he screamed just as Rodney was about to be tackled.

Rodney threw a wobbler, a real shocker back over his head, but Neil managed to pick it up off his shoelaces. As he regathered his balance he could see instantly that all their heroics had got them nowhere. He was surrounded.

'Kick!'

Neil heard the desperation in Billy's voice, had no time to look for him and had to guess his position from the direction of his shout. He kicked, a spiralling torpedo punt back over his shoulder towards the first house by the school. Blackie's house.

As soon as he saw the trajectory of Neil's kick, Billy knew he was in trouble. He began to back-pedal. He thought he could take it if he jumped. He had images of Aussie Rules players in his mind as he leaped, but barely managed to get his fingertips to the ball. The football, their precious official football, glanced off his fingers and cleared the fence into Blackie territory.

'No!' screamed Neil. He stood in the road, too stunned and horrified to move. They'd lost a footie over the fence into Blackie's yard once before and the mongrel had ripped it to shreds in seconds. If the black kids had taken his ball there was always a chance that he could get it back. But there was no chance of getting his ball back off Blackie. His despair had no sooner taken hold when he saw Billy leap the fence. Even the black kids froze. They knew that was the wrong place to jump. That was right in the middle of Blackie territory and Billy had too far to run before the dog reached the limit of his chain.

'No, Billy!' Neil rushed towards the yard in a crush of black kids all heading in the same direction, all thoughts of nicking the football forgotten. Rodney, who'd already started running back towards Billy in support when Neil had kicked the ball, reached the fence first and climbed on top of it.

'Run!' he yelled. 'Run, you tu-pid bar-tid!'

But Billy wasn't running anywhere. He stood defiantly in the middle of the yard, feigning attacks on Blackie who stood drooling over the football, uncertain which to maul first. In the end it was an easy decision. The ball was just a toy. The boy was one of his tormentors and flaunting himself in his territory. Blackie spun around and charged.

'Get the ball!' screamed Billy as he began to sprint for his life.

Rodney didn't hesitate. He jumped down from the fence and grabbed the ball.

'Run!' screamed Neil.

The advice was good for both boys but Neil only had eyes for Billy. It didn't seem possible that his little brother could reach safety before Blackie got him, but fear and the dog's bloodcurdling snarl put wings on his feet. Billy had never run faster. He got past the roses and was level with the geraniums when disaster struck. Billy tripped on a discarded plant pot and went flying. Neil knew exactly where Blackie's territory ended and it was a good metre and a half past the geraniums. He knew with absolute certainty that his brother hadn't made it. All the boys knew.

'Billy!' Neil's shriek said everything, expressed all their fears. He was about to shut his eyes so he didn't have to witness his little brother being torn apart when Blackie pulled up like he'd hit an invisible wall. Neil knew instantly what that meant. They'd seen it happen a million times before. Blackie had reached the end of his chain. But how? He spun around to see that Rodney had had the presence of mind to toss the slack in Blackie's chain around an old tree stump his owner used to chop kindling on, and was sprinting away with the footie tucked under his arm as fast as his spindly little legs could carry him. Rodney's quick thinking had saved Billy. The dog was beside itself with fury, its slavering jaws centimetres from Billy's feet. Yet, above the cheers and the mongrel's snarling frustration, he could hear Billy's laugh. Their mother often said that when Billy laughed it was a sound so sweet even the angels stopped to listen. For the first time Neil understood what his mother meant.

'I'm going to tell Dad.'

Neil started at the sound of Glory's voice. Judging by the ashen look on her face, he guessed his sisters had arrived just in time to witness Billy's narrow escape. Neil sighed.

'Don't bother. I'll tell him myself.' He couldn't understand what it was about girls that made them want to ruin everything.

Neil's official NSWRL footie had as much to do with Japan's economic recovery as it did with his father's generosity. Japan couldn't get enough fine merino wool and pushed the price up to the point where wool-growers all over Australia rubbed their hands together in glee. But every time it looked like the Dwyer family could break the cycle of borrowing, something always stuck its leg out to trip them up. Nobody suspected as they moved into winter that the late summer rains were destined to be the last good fall they'd get for two years. Even with the Japanese buyers pushing wool prices to record levels, the family couldn't afford the hay or grain they needed to supplement the scrub they cut for their stock.

Braden Dwyer, the boys' father, worked himself to a standstill cutting scrub but had no hope of cutting enough. At first he did the right thing by cutting the middle out of the fodder trees so that regrowth would stand him in good stead during the next drought. But even with the boys pitching in on weekends and his wife, Millie, lending a hand, he couldn't keep up with the need. He resorted to the short-term solution of cutting down entire trees, but still his sheep lost condition to the point where they were little more than bags of bones. Left with no choice but to reduce the number of sheep to a more manageable level, Braden began selling off half of his stock. It was a heartbreaking decision whichever way he looked at it.

While the remaining beasts would probably get by on the scrub he cut, he'd effectively halved their wool cheque, something that wouldn't impress the bank. All he could look forward to was another round of belt-tightening, of patched trousers, cracked boots and making do, of squeezing more service out of equipment and vehicles already held together by baling wire. Of course he got a few dollars for the stock he sold, but the beasts were in such a sorry condition that it wasn't much, not after the costs of transportation. That was the thing that galled him most. The drought was selective and hadn't touched properties further east or over the Great Dividing Range. The wool-growers there had snapped up his sheep for a pittance and put them on lush pastures that would have them back in prime condition in less than eight weeks. He explained all this to his kids around the dinner table as he faced another sell-off. Like most fathers on the land, he expected at least one of his boys to follow in his footsteps and he never missed an opportunity to teach them the realities.

The boys listened attentively, taking in everything their father told them, trying to find solutions to the problem that their father hadn't thought of.

'Why can't we just take the sheep to where there's grass?' said Billy. 'Fatten them up and bring them back again.'

'That's called agistment.' His father smiled. 'Some wool-growers do that but they have to pay to put their stock in other people's pastures. You have to add that to the trucking costs and then sit down and work out how much you reckon you're going to get for the wool. I've thought about it and I reckon it'd end up costing us more money than we'd get back.'

'Couldn't we walk them?' asked Neil.

'Maybe if we'd started two years ago, but the sheep couldn't handle it now. They're too weak. Besides, there's only weeds left along the side of the road. A lot of the beasts are hungry and stupid enough to eat them and poison themselves to death.'

'Can't we just buy more feed?' asked Billy.

'We're buying all we can afford now. If we buy more, we won't have enough to feed ourselves.'

'We can eat snakes, goannas and frill-necks like the abos do.'

'Billy!' said his mother sharply.

'Well, like the blacks do,' said Billy.

'Are you going to catch them for us?' asked his dad.

'Yeah,' said Billy eagerly. 'If you get us an air rifle.'

His parents burst out laughing and even Neil, who always stuck up for him, had a broad smile on his face. They discussed other options, not letting the situation get them down but using it to generate discussion and more laughs. The boys loved these occasions because they gave them a chance to impress their dad. Even so, when Neil and Billy finally took off for bed, they went with hearts burdened by the family's plight, both of them desperate to find a way to help out.

'I've got an idea,' said Billy as the boys lay awake in the dark.

'What?'

'We could ask Rodney's dad if we can noodle through his mullock heaps. Maybe we can find some opals.'

Neil thought about the idea. It wasn't bad. They could put in a few hours after school before it got dark. Stories abounded at school about kids up on the Ridge who found good opals noodling through the mullock. One black kid had found a beauty of a black harlequin worth more than eight thousand dollars. The trouble was, a lot of the opal found on Rodney's place was pretty poor quality, light-coloured and brittle, though his dad had found a couple of lenses which had yielded some really good-quality precious opal. Neil supposed Rodney's dad must have found enough to keep him interested.

'We could give it a go, I suppose,' said Neil. 'But Rodney's dad sifts through everything pretty thoroughly. Rodney reckons he can spot a good black opal on a dark night through half a metre of claystone.'

'Yeah, but every digger misses something some time,' said Billy. 'That's a proven fact.'

Neil nodded. Whether or not it was a proven fact, it was certainly local lore. Everyone had a hard-luck story of digging out mountains of opal dirt, only to have their quarry slip through their fingers and into someone else's.

'We'll talk to Rodney tomorrow. If we do it, we've got to keep it secret, okay? Dad'll only get cranky if he finds out. Now go to sleep.'

Billy closed his eyes and imagined searching tirelessly through giant mullock heaps and the glory that would come with reversing the family's fortunes. He fell asleep just as a flash of colour caught his eye.

Rodney's father was wary about letting anyone near his diggings but gave the boys permission on three conditions. His first condition was one that had been drummed into them from the time they could crawl. Under no circumstances were they allowed to go underground. The boys nodded obediently, although, in truth, they'd secretly searched more mine shafts and tunnels than they could count. There was no way of stopping them so long as there were lengths of rope and ladders left lying around. Exploring tunnels on their hands and knees with just one torch between them was just about the most exciting thing anyone could do. And there was always the possibility that there were precious opals lurking just millimetres away in the claystone walls. Different eyes saw different things down in mines.

With Rodney's help, the boys had become pretty adept at picking bad ground that could collapse in on them and tunnels where props had been removed. Once Rodney took them down a shaft to show them a booby-trap his father had made which would cause the tunnel to cave in. His father was paranoid about other miners sneaking in and making off with his opals. He'd rather bury the bludgers alive than let them get away with it.

The second condition was that they only picked through dumps Rodney's father had marked with a stick and a piece of cloth. That way he could save the boys the effort of working through mullock that would only yield a smattering of potch, or common opal, at best and put some brakes on their ambitions. He'd sunk shafts all over the place, wherever he'd found wild orange or large box trees growing. The trees liked to sink their roots down into disturbed ground caused by joints or minor faults in the strata, which was where opals tended to be found. The last thing he wanted was overexcited kids racing around open shafts.

His third condition was that they showed whatever they found to him first. To keep them honest, he offered to polish their finds for them before they took them home. Rodney's father didn't expect them to come across much, but he gave them every chance by marking heaps of Finch claystone from shafts that had given him a bit back.

Rodney was allowed to work with the boys provided he gave any opals he found to his dad. Both Neil and Billy thought that was a fair deal because just working alongside Rodney improved their chances. Rodney knew all there was to know. He could tell Finch claystone from Coocoran claystone and knew at a glance which soil was good opal dirt and which wasn't worth bothering with. When he saw the mullock heaps they were allowed to fossick through he knew they came from good diggings.

The three boys were pretty excited when they got off the school bus at Rodney's place, especially Rodney because they were going to do something he was good at for a change. He'd told them how he'd salvaged one of his dad's old rumblers. It was a revolving mesh drum through which loosened dirt could escape, leaving only hard material like sandstone and, with a dint of luck, opals. Rodney had helped his dad sift through mullock since he was four years old and had only found opal of any value on a handful of occasions. Even with the rumbler, Rodney knew their chances of finding anything worthwhile were remote, but in the way of boys everywhere, they'd managed to talk themselves into believing otherwise. They walked up the red gravel plateau in a landscape so dotted with shafts and their surrounding off-white doughnuts of mullock that it looked more lunar than terrestrial, as though a thousand meteorites had impacted there. Both Neil and Billy were used to the sight but now they looked at it through the eyes of fossickers. Finding a needle in a haystack was a pushover compared with the task ahead of them. They walked to the nearest dump that Rodney's dad had marked and got ready to attack it.

'Rodney, you take the pick, I'll take the shovel and Billy can turn the rumbler,' said Neil. 'We'll change jobs after every six loads.'

The boys set to work but it was hard going. The top strata of soil, the Coocoran claystone, had dried out and turned into shin-cracker, and there were lumps of Wallangulla sandstone taken from the second strata which were equally solid.

'Dad worked a good deam where thid duff come from,' said Rodney. 'Went in a-bout three metre. He won't day but I rec-kon that wad where he found hid but-ter-fly wing black.'

The butterfly wing black? It was one of the few opals Rodney's dad had ever shown to them. It was smaller than the nail on Billy's little finger but the greens and reds in it were electric. What more incentive did they need? If this stuff came from the same seam they had every chance of finding something precious. Neil and Billy worked with a will and no thought of pacing themselves. They were puffing long before the sixth load went into the rumbler. But Rodney, who was used to the work, looked like he could go all night. The boys had rarely seen him looking so happy.

'Why don't we sort through what we've got?' said Billy. 'Give us a chance to get our breath back.'

'Okay,' said Neil. He divided the heap of stones and rubble tailed out from the rumbler into three roughly equal piles. 'Billy, you have first pick, Rodney second, me third. Next time Rodney chooses first and then it's my turn.'

Neil and Billy copied Rodney and nipped any promising lumps with pincers. The first round yielded nothing but that failed to dampen their enthusiasm. They did another six loads for the same result. Billy was halfway through the smallest pile in the third round when he caught an unmistakeable glint of something emerald.

'Opal!' he screamed. He couldn't believe it could be so easy. They'd only been at it for less than two hours and he'd already solved his family's problems. He could feel his father's hand patting him on his back, the hug from his mum and something approaching genuine respect from his sisters. He held up a piece of rock-hard claystone about the size of a boiled egg yolk.

'Led me dee,' said Rodney. He took the piece of claystone from Billy, looked at it critically and nipped it with his pincer. He gave his verdict. 'Jud pekd,' he said and nonchalantly tossed the claystone back to Billy.

'Bulldust!' said Billy. 'They're not just specks.'

'Give me a look,' said Neil. He gave Billy's stone a quick once-over and, without warning, smashed it with the shovel.

'What are you doing?' shrieked Billy.

'Take a look,' said Neil.

Billy looked and all he could see was a flattened pancake of dust. He ran his fingers through it but couldn't find any colour at all. The disappointment was no less crushing.

'If Rodney says there's just specks, there's just specks,' said Neil quietly. 'He knows what he's talking about and you don't. You put him down when you don't listen.'

Billy accepted the rebuke and apologised.

'Id oh-kay,' said Rodney.

'At least it was better than nothing,' said Billy.

'That's right,' said Neil. 'And if there's an ant around here looking for a stone to put in a ring, I'm sure it'll be grateful.'

The boys managed a few more laughs but found nothing that day or in the next two days. By the fourth day their enthusiasm had really begun to flag.

'We're never going to find anything in the dumps,' said Billy. 'Rodney's dad has already picked through them and he's too good.'

Rodney's chin drooped, as though he'd let his mates down. He loved it when the boys came around to his place, loved to be in a position where he was important and they listened to what he had to say.

'We knew that right at the start,' said Neil.

'I reckon we're going to have to look underground to have any hope of finding anything,' said Billy.

'He'd ride,' said Rodney.

'We've been down plenty of shafts and never found nothing before,' said Neil.

'Yeah, but we weren't really looking before,' said Billy.

'I dunno,' said Neil. 'Rodney's dad'll go off his brain if he finds out.'

'How's he gunna find out?'

'What if we find something?'

'We'll tell him we found it in the mullock.'

'What do you think, Rodney?'

Rodney hesitated before answering. He knew far better than the boys what it was like when his father went off his brain. He was the one who had to cop the abuse and the beltings that covered his arms, legs and back in bruises. But if they didn't go looking underground, he knew they'd give up looking altogether and the boys would find something else to do which, more than likely, wouldn't include him. Even if they did include him, it wouldn't be like searching for opals. It wouldn't be something he was good at. Rodney agonised but in the end he had only one choice.

'Don tell dad nuf-fin un-led id me that find the o-pal.'

'I dunno,' said Neil. He wasn't worried about cave-ins because Rodney's dad was cautious. When he drove in along a seam he always left plenty of stone pillars in place to shore up the back of the stope and arched the roof so it was supported by pressure from the sides. Sometimes he moved props from diggings he thought were no good to use in other tunnels, but their soles always left an imprint which was easy to spot. They never went into tunnels where props had been moved. It wasn't the risk that got Neil thinking but the breach in trust and in protocol. It was one thing to play in the tunnels and explore them, but another matter entirely to pick through someone else's diggings. Everyone knew that. It was okay to bend the back in mines that had been abandoned, but, as far as Rodney's dad was concerned, these were all still active.

'Oh, come on,' urged Billy. 'It's our only hope.'

'Thad ride,' said Rodney.

They were so keen and eager to do it, Neil had to give in.

'All right, but we're gunna need torches,' said Neil. 'We'll do it tomorrow.'

'Yes!' Billy threw his arms up in delight.

'You and Rodney can go down and I'll stay on top to haul up the bucket. Any dirt you loosen has to go in the bucket or Rodney's dad will know someone's been down there, okay?'

Of course it was okay. But Neil still felt a sense of disquiet. What they planned to do amounted to stealing and that was wrong. He also had the problem of disposing of the material they brought up after they'd checked it for opals. Anyone could tell new dirt from old so they'd have to bury it under a load of shin-cracker.

The following morning he and Billy each smuggled a torch into their schoolbags so they wouldn't give the show away. They spent all their free time during the day arguing over which mines were more likely to deliver the goods. In the end they let Rodney decide, which made him feel like a million dollars. His father was working a new patch he'd marked out half a kilometre away, giving them a clear run over the main workings. The newer mines offered the most hope, but Rodney was smart enough not to go near those. His dad lived and dreamed opals, and sometimes his dreams took him back down his recent diggings in search of recalled or imagined signs. Instead he took the brothers over to a shaft where they'd found plenty of potch but never found anything worthwhile. Rodney's dad had always maintained that, given the traces, there had to be good opals there, but as hard as he'd looked, his labours had come to nothing. Billy thought the choice of tunnel was inspired. Different eyes see different things. He convinced himself that his eyes would see what Rodney's father had missed.

The shaft descended about ten metres to the level where the Finch claystone bisected the sandstone. While the shaft was no deeper than the others around it, the horizontal tunnels were wider and higher. There were three of them, running off at different angles, where Rodney's dad had searched for the lens which he hoped would deliver precious opal. There were marks on the tunnel roofs and walls where Rodney's father had barred down the scale, and little dead-end pockets where he'd gouged out dirt on a whim or under the direction of a dream. The system was a monument to lost labour and the miners' most constant companions, optimism and disappointment. But to Billy it was Aladdin's Cave, at least potentially.

He followed Neil's instructions and let Rodney lead, dragging a bucket and spade along behind him while his mate carried the picks. They ignored the higher tunnels and entered the lowest, which was the last one Rodney's dad had worked. Even though the ceiling was so high they could almost stand up, they crawled through on their hands and knees until they came to a gallery. At some stage Rodney's dad had obviously thought he was on the right track, because he'd used roof bolts to support the roof and braced it with two props while he scoured out around.

Billy's eyes opened wide. He'd never been in a tunnel that opened into a gallery before, which made it special and the perfect place to begin gouging. He stared at the walls looking for inspiration, any small variation or difference in the claystone that indicated a divergence in the seam. Different eyes see different things, but Billy's eyes saw nothing that was any different to anywhere else. Undeterred, he began to chip away at the wall nearest to him with the extra pick Rodney had carried. In no time at all he'd filled the bucket with soil, and that didn't take into account any of the claystone Rodney had chipped away.

'We're gunna have to take turns,' said Billy. 'One of us digs while the other fills the bucket and takes it back to the shaft.'

Rodney just nodded and kept scratching away with his pick. His small build wasn't much good for rugby league but it was perfect for working in tight places. He loved working down mines. It was something he was good at and, besides, opals were in his blood.

Billy dragged the bucket to the shaft and tied the rope they'd shimmied down to the handle. He stood back from the shaft as Neil hauled the heavy bucket up to the surface, taking cover to avoid getting pelted by any debris the bucket might dislodge. When he crawled back to the gallery Rodney had another load ready for him. He filled the bucket again and dragged it back to the shaft. On his eighth trip he began to run out of steam and enthusiasm. Rodney showed no sign of letting up or taking over the bucket.

'It's my turn to dig,' said Billy. 'Your turn to pull the bucket.'

'Nod yed,' said Rodney. 'One more, jud one more.'

'That's what you said last time.'

'Jud one more.'

'Okay, just one.' Billy dragged the heavy bucket back to the shaft and called up to Neil. 'Rodney won't give me a turn digging. He always wants me to take one more bucketload.'

'Tell him he's gotta give you a go,' said Neil. 'Tell him I said so.'

He gathered the slack out of the rope and began lifting. Rodney's dad had built a good collar around the top of the shaft so he had something to brace his feet against, but even so the effort of hauling up the bucket had already made the muscles in his arms burn. They needed a windlass, but Rodney's dad only had a couple and they were always in use. To ease the burden he let the rope run against the side of the collar. He knew that would tip the bucket and gouge the shaft wall and also cause some of the claystone to tumble out, but he was just too hot and tired to do it any other way. He felt the bucket dig in against an irregularity in the wall and gave it a heave. Almost immediately he heard Billy cry out in pain.

'You all right?' he called.

'Yeah,' said Billy, but the tone of his voice made it clear that he was close to tears.

'What happened?'

'Something fell and hit me.'

'Where?'

'On my head.'

'It's your own fault for standing in the shaft. Get back in the tunnel while I pull the bucket the rest of the way up.'

'I've got a lump. It's really big.'

'Is it bleeding?'

'No.'

'Then you're all right. Try to find the rock that hit you and we'll smash it up to get even. But wait till I get the bucket all the way up.' Neil hauled the bucket up to the top and emptied it. Nine bucketloads didn't look much for all the effort they'd put in. 'Okay, Billy,' he called. 'Find the culprit before I drop the bucket back down.'

'Found it.' Billy put the stone in his pocket.

'Great, now stand back.'

Rodney did six trips with the full bucket but his small body wasn't up to doing any more. Billy, who'd just got into the rhythm of chipping away at the claystone, didn't feel at all disposed to swapping back to their original jobs. He was certain opal was just another chip of the pick away and he wanted to be the one who found it. But Rodney was worn out, so was Neil, and so were the batteries in their torches. They decided to call it a day and run their pile of opal dirt through the rumbler. They found no more than Rodney's dad had. They couldn't believe that all the effort had come to nothing.

'Give me a hand,' said Neil. 'We've got to bury all this stuff under shin-cracker.'

'Do we have to?' said Billy. His disappointment hung over him like a cloud. He knew they wouldn't come back looking for opals and he had to face the fact that he had no hope of solving his family's financial problems and even less of becoming their hero. It was a bitter pill.

They broke up enough shin-cracker to hide the evidence of their illicit endeavours and headed back to Rodney's shack to get a drink of water and lie down somewhere in the shade. Rodney was no less disappointed than Billy.

'Give me a look at the bump on your head,' said Neil. 'If Mum sees it, she'll want to know how it happened.'

'It's going down,' said Billy. He sat up. 'Can you feel it?'

'Jeepers,' said Neil, as he ran his fingers over the bump. 'Have a feel, Rodney. You could break your neck falling off something like that.'

The boys started laughing and suddenly the day didn't seem quite so disappointing.

'Did you ged the rock that hid you?' said Rodney.

'Yeah,' said Billy. He reached into his pocket. 'Look at the size of it.'

He handed it over to Rodney, who saw instantly what the rock really was. There was a glaze where the bucket had scraped it. They'd already put their picks and pincers back in the toolshed so Rodney spat on the opposite side and rubbed it vigorously with his hand. It glowed.

'Id an o-pal,' said Rodney. 'Id a big black like the one that they ged up on the Ridge.'

It wasn't just what he said but the awe and wonder in his voice as he said it. Rodney had clearly never seen an opal like it.

'Yes!' screamed Billy. 'Yes!' He threw his arms into the air triumphantly. 'I knew we'd do it.'

'Good on you,' said Neil, but it was doubtful Billy even heard him. He was dancing with joy and relief, the bush ringing with his magical laugh.

'Did id real-ly my dad,' said Rodney. He was almost in tears over the magnitude of the sin he'd committed. 'My dad nev-ver god one thid good.'

'That's not the deal,' said Neil.

'My dad will kill me if he find oud. Id far too big to come from mul-lock. He gunna kill me.'

'Then we won't tell him,' said Neil. 'My dad can sell it secretly to someone up on the Ridge.'

'Id not fair.' Tears fell from Rodney's eyes and splashed onto the opal.

Neil didn't know what to say. Rodney was right. It wasn't fair. But one of the boys had to come second: either his dancing ecstatic brother or the despondent Rodney. He thought of the effort they'd put in, all in good faith, and the deal they'd made. Okay, they shouldn't have gone underground and, by rights, they should show it to Rodney's dad. But if they did that, Rodney's dad would either beat the daylights out of Rodney or keep the opal. Neil realised that fairness was all a matter of where you stood. Rodney's dad had dug out the mine and Neil now had a good appreciation of the hard work involved. But Billy had found the opal fair and square. In his eyes, that meant Billy was entitled to keep it. He reached over to take the opal out of Rodney's hand. Rodney clung onto it, tears streaming down his face.

'It's Billy's.'

'No id nod! Id my dad!'

'I'm sorry, Rodney, I really am. I wish you'd found it, but you didn't. Billy did.'

Rodney let go of the opal and that made him cry worse. His small body was racked with sobs. Neil turned away, unable to witness his friend's grief.

'Billy, come here.'

Billy stopped dancing and looked at his brother suspiciously. There was something in the tone of his voice that put him on guard.

'What?'

'Come here.'

'What's wrong with Rodney?'

'What do you think?'

'Yeah, but I found it, Neil, I found it.' Billy stared at Rodney defiantly. 'I found it, Rodney.'

'Look at the size of it, Billy. We're not supposed to find opals that big. It's bigger than anything Rodney's dad has found.'

'It's my opal!'

'Is it?' said Neil.

'Yes!'

'Can you imagine what will happen to Rodney if his dad finds out? Can you imagine what he'll do to him?'

Rodney's sobbing doubled at the thought.

'The truth is, Billy, we weren't entitled to even look for opals underground. Up at the Ridge you can get lynched just for looking in someone else's mine and you know it.'

'Oh, please don't make me give it to him, please.' Billy was distraught. 'Please!'

'I'm not going to make you do anything, Billy. You just have to do what you think is right.'

Billy howled in anguish and buried his face in his hands.

'It's not fair!'

Neil had rarely seen his brother so upset but made no move to comfort him. In his mind the tide of the argument had changed and he knew with absolute certainty what was right.

'Do I have to?' pleaded Billy.

'Look at Rodney and you tell me.'

Rodney looked pitiful. His face was lined with streaks of dirt turned to mud by tears, and snot streamed from his nostrils. He looked pleadingly at Billy, too choked up to speak.

Billy grabbed the stone out of his brother's hand, stared at it as hard as he'd ever stared at anything, as though burning its image into his memory. Without saying a word he stuck it in Rodney's hand, turned and ran off into the scrub.

Rodney's hands clasped tight around the stone in case Billy changed his mind. Whatever else happened, he was determined not to let go until he'd delivered it safely to his father. He looked up at Neil, at first wary then filled with a flood of relief when Neil stood and offered him a hand up.

'Let's get Billy and go find your dad. What do you say?'

They found Rodney's dad sitting by a pile of mullock at his newest site, washing the disappointment of the day away with a mug of tea he'd brewed up in his billy. His weary body shook with the tremors that Rodney would one day inherit. Dust and grit covered his clothes and skin and his tired eyes regarded the boys suspiciously.

'Dad!' said Rodney. 'Ged whad? We found an o-pal. A big black.'

Whether it was the words Rodney said or the tone in his voice, his father shot to his feet as though struck by a cattle prod.

'Led me dee id!'

'Look!'

Rodney's dad snatched the opal from his son's hand and examined it closely. His hands began shaking violently but that had less to do with his tremors than with excitement.

'Where'd ya ged id?'

'Ad the trip-ple. The one you al-wade daid wad good.'

'Da trip-ple? Knew id! All wade knew id!' At that moment, Rodney's dad didn't give a hoot that the boys had disobeyed his instructions and gone underground. He was too wrapped up in the opal and the vindication of his beliefs. But something triggered an alarm bell inside his head. Maybe it was all the disappointments he'd had to live with and his conviction that nothing ever came easy or without a catch.

'Who found id?' he demanded.

Rodney seemed to shrink in size. His father looked angrily from Billy to Neil.

'Who found id!'

'Billy found it, Mr Webb,' said Neil. 'But we all agreed it really belongs to you.'

'You bed id be-long to me.' He glared at them. 'You bed id dud. Come wid me.'

The boys followed along behind Rodney's dad, feeling guilty and ashamed but still excited.

'Do you think it'll be another butterfly, Mr Webb?' asked Billy cautiously.

'I dun-no.'

'Mide ev-en be a har-de-quin,' said Rodney.

'I reckon it'll polish up with a heap of red in it,' said Neil. 'I reckon I could see red in it.'

'There'd red in id,' said Rodney's dad.

The sun was just dropping behind the sand ridges when they reached the shed where Rodney's dad polished his opals. Usually Neil and Billy had left for home by this time, so they could get back before it was completely dark. But neither boy gave a thought to leaving. They had to know what it was that they'd found. Typically, Billy was excited by everyone else's excitement and not brooding over his sacrifice. When Rodney's dad started the diamond-studded wheel, they crowded around to watch.

Rodney's dad had fashioned braces which he could rest his hands against to stop them shaking while he worked. Even more than the boys, he wanted to know exactly what it was they'd found, yet he worked with painstaking slowness, continually stopping his polishing to examine his progress.

'Whad do you think?' asked Rodney.

'Dun-no yed,' said his dad.

Rodney's dad slowly worked across the top of the opal and then gently around the top half of the sides. Even his audience could see colour refracting when he stopped to examine it. He turned the opal to the light and slowly revolved it.

'Thad'll do for to-night,' he said. 'I know whad id id.'

'What?' asked Billy. The tension was unbearable.

Rodney's dad smiled, a sight so rare the boys almost didn't realise what it was.

'Id will polid up in-to a nide har-de-quin. Pud mon-ey on id.'

'A harlequin!' said Billy. 'Oh boy, I found a harlequin!'

Rodney's dad stopped smiling and his face darkened ominously. The juddering of his jaw and the constant play of the muscles in his face made it hard for the boys to guess what he was thinking but they were suddenly wary. Rodney's dad pointed an accusing finger at Billy.

'You come wid me.' He turned to Rodney and Neil. 'You two day he-yah.'

Billy's eyes filled with fear and apprehension. He remembered what Neil had said about how trespassing in other people's mines was a lynching offence up at the Ridge. He recalled the bruises he'd seen on Rodney's arms and legs after his dad had dished out a hiding and turned pleadingly to Neil. His brother looked as scared as he felt but made no move towards him.

'Come!' commanded Rodney's dad. He took Billy's arm and dragged him out of the shed.

'What's he going to do to him?' whispered Neil.

'I dun-no,' said Rodney fearfully.

Rodney's dad took Billy into his shack and sat him down at the kitchen table.

'You day he-yah.'

Billy stayed. He waited wide-eyed as Rodney's dad disappeared into his bedroom, expecting him to return with a leather strop or wooden spoon, whatever it was he used to punish Rodney. Instead Rodney's dad emerged clutching a Smith Kendon sweets tin. Billy almost fainted with relief.

'I god dom-thin for you.'

Billy watched as Rodney's dad began unscrewing the lid, certain now that he was going to be rewarded rather than beaten. A boiled sweet didn't seem much for finding the opal, but it was a far better alternative to the hiding he'd expected. Billy's jaw dropped. There were no sweets in the tin. Instead, Rodney's dad pulled out pieces of cotton wool, opened them and lay them on the table. Billy's eyes nearly burst out of his skull.

'You chood.'

Billy stared at the opals. There were five in all, none of them as big or in remotely the same class as the one he'd found, but all of them were beautifully shaped and polished, and similar in size and colour. The dominant colours were green and red although some had a pale, slightly milky field.

'Go on, chood.'

'Choose?'

Billy hesitated, barely able to grasp the opportunity he was being given. He'd have been delighted to find any one of the opals out on the mullock. There was one in the shape of an elongated oval that took his fancy. His hands shook as he reached for it.

'Thad a good one,' said Rodney's dad. 'But thid one id word more.' He picked up a more regularly shaped opal and passed it to Billy. The field was emerald green, and it burned with reds, oranges and traces of blue. 'If you wan id, id yourd.'

Billy took the opal and rotated it in the light so that it refracted different colours at him.

'It's a real good one, Mr Webb. You done a real good job on it.'

'Id yourd.'

Billy's eyes were watering when he turned to Rodney's dad.

'Do you really mean it? I can keep it?'

'Yed. Take id.'

'Yes!' screamed Billy. His plans were back on track. He'd found an opal. He'd solved the family's problems and he'd be a hero. Life just didn't get any better. 'Thanks, Mr Webb! Thanks a million!' He got up off his chair and raced out of the door towards the work shed to show Neil and Rodney, shrieking with delight.

Braden Dwyer was waiting out on his veranda, ready to get the car to go looking for the boys when they came running up the driveway from the road where Rodney's dad had dropped them off. He was ready to bawl his kids out for being late for dinner but couldn't get a word in. He'd never known them to be so excited and, once they were inside with the whole family crowding around, they showed him why.

Braden instantly saw an opportunity to get the bank off his back and an easing of the pressure the family was under. Millie saw the prospect of actually being able to go shopping with money in her purse. Glory and Kath saw the prospect of new underwear and other essentials. Surely the bank wouldn't get all the money.

Neil told the whole story over dinner, making sure that Billy got the credit for the idea and for finding the opal. His father had a strange look on his face, which Neil finally realised was pride: pride in what they'd done.

'So you spent all your time after school for an entire week looking for opals?' Braden said. 'Just so you could help out?'

'You can sell it up at the Ridge,' said Billy enthusiastically. 'And pay off the bank.'

His father laughed. Kath had found a matchbox and stuffed it with cotton wool to make a protective nest for the opal while it was passed from hand to hand.

'It's going to take a few more opals than this to pay off all we owe, but it's not a bad start.'

'Then we'll find some more,' said Billy.

'No, you've done enough,' said his father quickly. 'I support this family. Besides, your mother and I have told you to keep away from mines. You know as well as I do how dangerous they are. You've disobeyed us once and I don't want you doing it twice.'

'But, Dad!'

'No buts, Billy. You got lucky. Lucky you didn't kill yourselves and lucky you found an opal. You've used up all the family's luck for the next ten years. I want you to promise me you won't go down any more mines. Okay?'

The boys promised.

'Did Mr Webb say how much he thought the opal was worth?' asked Millie.

'No,' said Billy. 'But he said it was worth more than any of the others he showed me.'

'It looks the goods,' said Braden. 'Got to be worth a few thousand. I'll take it up to the Ridge and ask around. See how much the bank's going to get for it. The way they're carrying on they'll be happy to get anything.'

'Do we have to give the bank all of it?' asked Millie.

'Not quite all of it. I'll have to give them some so we don't have to sell more sheep. Might be a few bucks left over.'

'I think you should give the bank the minimum and use the rest to buy more sheep,' said Neil.

'Buy more sheep? There are a heap of things we can do with the money, Neil, but I don't know that we should buy more sheep.'

'I reckon we should buy more ewes to replace some of the ones we sold. We can make do with what we've got a while longer.'

'No, we can't,' said his mother emphatically.

'I'd like more sheep, Neil, but we can't feed them. Not unless we get rain.'

'That's the whole point, Dad,' said Neil. 'The papers are saying there's a good chance of the drought breaking inside the next four weeks.'

'The papers are always saying that.'

'This time the blacks are saying so as well.'

'Are they?'

'That's what the Dewhurst kids at school reckon. Their dads told them it's going to rain soon. It's all to do with what blossoms are out and what birds are around, but they reckon the signs are good.'

'I'll believe it when I see it.'

'But if you wait till it rains, the price of stock will go up. Everyone will want to build up their numbers with the wool price the way it is.'

'It's a big "if", Neil.' He picked up the matchbox and stared at the opal. 'Don't you think we've used up all our good luck for the time being?'

'It's a question of judgement, not luck,' said Neil.

'You're still asking me to take a punt, however you put it.'

'If we get the timing right, we'll really make up for some of our losses. If we get it wrong, we're no worse off than we are now.'

'Except that if we get it wrong we'll have wasted Billy's opal,' said Braden.

'Don't do it,' implored Billy. 'Please, please! Don't do it!'

'Don't do it,' echoed his mother and sisters.

Chapter Ten

'You're not doing yourself any favours with your attitude.' Grant's parole officer stared at him across the metal table.

'And what favours are you doing me, Alan?'

Grant didn't dislike his parole officer. He was a Tony Bennett fan and from time to time they traded jazz tapes. Under any other circumstances he'd probably find him interesting and even entertaining. They were about the same age and Alan had been nothing if not straight with him. But there was a barrier between them and neither was prepared to give an inch.

'You're in the Training Centre, on work release, and you've got weekend leave. I think what I've done for you speaks for itself.'

'You wouldn't have to do anything for me if you'd done the right thing in the first place.'

'God give me strength ...'

'You and that dickhead of a shrink had the chance at sentencing to keep me out of gaol. You had the opportunity to recommend a community service order or, at very worst, periodic detention.'

'Grant, you're like a cracked record. You've been kidding yourself for six years. You've been kidding yourself for so long you're starting to believe it. I couldn't get you PD. No one could have got you PD. Periodic detention was never an option. Even Mother Teresa, if she'd done what you did, would've got a full custodial sentence.'

'But that's the point you and dickhead always miss. *I didn't do anything.*'

'Here we go again.' Alan turned away and gazed at the wall, folded his arms and put his feet up on a vacant chair. 'Fact: you killed a woman. That might not have been your intention — we know it wasn't — but you nevertheless put her in a position and acted in an irresponsible way that caused her death. The problem for me and for the psychologist is that you won't accept responsibility for your actions and you show no remorse for what you did. And you show no sympathy for the relatives of the victim. Those are the facts.'

'How can I feel sorry for something I didn't do? Jesus Christ, if there's a victim here, it's me. I shouldn't be here.'

'Yeah, yeah, yeah ...' The parole officer swung around so that he faced Grant again. 'You just don't get it, do you? It's precisely this attitude that prompted the judge to give you eight and six. Anyone else would have got away with six years and parole after four. For once you're right, Grant. You shouldn't be here. You should've been out of here two years ago. These last two years are down to you and your attitude.'

Grant stared at the wall above Alan's head. Staring at walls was something he'd become good at. Alan may be bored with the cyclical nature of their conversations and their lack of progress but so was he. And damned if he was going to admit to something he didn't do. How could he feel remorse for an accident? Accidents were accidents. They happened. Sure, he felt for the victim's family, but his sympathy was tempered by the fact that they had no sympathy for what had happened to him. They blamed him when they had no right to blame him for anything.

'Have you seen the drug and alcohol counsellor like I asked you to?'

'Why waste my bloody time? I don't have a problem.'

'That's where you're wrong.' Alan leaned across the table so he was close to Grant and held his eyes. 'I asked you to see the drug and alcohol worker and undergo counselling so that I've got a piece of paper that unequivocally states you have no drug or alcohol problem. May I remind you that you were legally drunk when arrested and there were traces of cocaine in the victim's blood.'

'She might have had a problem. I don't.'

'I want proof, Grant, I want the piece of paper that says so.' The parole officer sighed and leaned back in his chair. 'Okay, let's play a game called "Get out of Gaol". You're eligible for parole in four months and you seem to be under the impression that it will be granted automatically. Let me tell you something. The psychologist is worried about you and concerned that you'll commit further acts of violence after your release. He's particularly concerned about your attitude towards your ex-wife. He's against parole unless you agree to counselling. The truth is, Grant, if I went solely by his report I couldn't recommend parole either.'

'Don't play games with me, Alan. I've got a clean sheet. We both know I've been no trouble to anyone.'

'Unless you start cooperating you may be forced to take your case for parole before the Offenders' Review Board. I'm not saying they'll knock you back, but you're giving them no shortage of reasons to. A young woman is dead because of you. If you accept responsibility, demonstrate remorse, sympathy for the relatives of the victim and have a favourable report from drug and alcohol, no power in the land could keep you in here. That's how people get out of gaol on parole. That's the game you have to play if you want out. Why are you so determined to make it hard for yourself?'

'How many times do I have to tell you? I'm not going to admit to something I didn't do.'

Alan sighed again and closed his interview book.

'Your mate Cameron doesn't mind you staying with him every weekend?'

'He looks forward to it.'

'And Jasmine's well?'

'As well as any teenager dumped into a boarding school can be.'

Alan shook his head at the tone in Grant's voice. Domestic violence cases were always convinced of their innocence and carried more anger than even the most hardened crims.

'Are you seeing her this weekend?'

'No, her aunt's taking her up to the Blue Mountains.'

'Have you heard from your ex-wife?'

'Not likely.'

'Have you made any attempt to contact or approach her?'

'Why would I bother?'

'Yes or no?'

'No. I don't even have the faintest idea where she is.'

'How's the job going?'

'Good. If I ever give up the film business I'll make a good forklift driver. You've got reports from my esteemed employers. You blokes trained me well.'

'How are your plans for getting back into the film business working out?'

'Fine.' It was a lie but Grant wanted to keep his disappointment from his parole officer. He fought back the flood of bitterness welling up inside him. When Cameron had suggested they go into business together, Grant had assumed they'd be equal partners. His pride had suffered a crushing blow when he'd learned otherwise. All Cameron was doing was throwing him a bone, but what else could he expect? He was contributing no capital and bringing no hip-pocket accounts. Things had changed a lot in six years and in that time he'd gone from hero to zero. A lot of the bright new advertising agency people who handed out work had never even heard of him. A lot of his old mates had been eased out. His reel, the showpiece of his skill as a director, was now hopelessly out of date. Any business he brought in he'd have to go out and hustle for while Cameron paid him a retainer. A retainer! When Grant had plucked Cameron out of the gutter, he'd never imagined that one day he'd wind up working for him. The reversal of roles was the cruellest of blows. If only he had cash to bring to the party, things would be different. Oh, yes! If only he had cash. An image of his ex-wife swam into focus.

'What are you thinking?'

Grant started. He was too used to time alone in the slot when his thoughts were free to go where they liked and he didn't have to account to anyone.

‘What?’ he said.

‘I asked how your plans were going and you went off somewhere. Where did you go? What were you thinking?’

‘I was just thinking how good it’s going to feel getting back to normal, to the way things were. Cameron’s already out looking at premises. He’s already got some work lined up.’

‘Glad to hear it.’ The parole officer leaned forward across the table until he was eye to eye with Grant. ‘Now I know I’m only a stupid parole officer, Grant, but if I had a good job waiting for me, I’d make damn sure I was there on the start date. Want to think about what I’ve been telling you?’

Grant had other things to think about when he got back to his cell. Gaol was full of druggies who broke into homes and stole to support their habit, but he thought he could teach the lot of them a thing or two. A few weeks earlier, while he and Jasmine were out at a movie, Cameron had taken Jasmine’s key ring from her handbag and had a copy made of her Aunt Fran’s front door key. Jasmine’s keys were back in her bag long before the movie finished. After that, it had simply been a case of Cameron taking Jasmine home at a time when he knew her aunt and uncle were out, seeing her to the door and watching over her while she deactivated the burglar alarm. The four-digit code was the year of her aunt’s birth. Grant thought he could’ve guessed it. Now, with everyone away in the Blue Mountains for the weekend, the time had come to take the first step in locating his ex-wife. Somewhere inside the house there was a clue to her whereabouts: a number in a teledex, a notation on a note pad, an entry in an address book. There’d be something and he'd find it. Crime was so easy, it amazed Grant that people were ever caught.

Fran's Federation home in Putney was a reminder of what Sydney looked like before councils caved in to developers and planning departments took their pieces of silver. The house had been painstakingly restored to the original. It was a jewel in a street dominated by two-storey blocks of units. Of the three other surviving houses in the street, two were occupied by families from the Middle East who had inflated ideas of the value of their property and were hanging on for the right offer. The third house was rundown and owned by an elderly widow who'd lived there all her married life. The developers were hovering, waiting for her to die so they could move in.

While Cameron sat in the car two streets away, Grant simply strolled up to Fran's house, opened the gate and continued up the path to the front door. Any casual observer who didn't know better would have assumed he was the owner, or at least had every right to be there. Even so, Grant would have preferred a weekday when people were at work, but a lot of people also worked Saturday mornings.

The house sat towards the back of a block that sloped upwards from the street. If he'd turned around, Grant could have seen the road and the footpath over the top of Fran's shrubs and the low picket fence. Anyone passing by could see him from the street. But who was there to see him? There was nobody around: nobody in the street and nobody watching at any door or window. Nevertheless, he had his fingers crossed as he pushed the key into the lock, hoping that the duplicate was a faithful copy. The last thing he wanted was to be seen fiddling with a key at the door. Any hesitation would be a clear sign that he had no right to be there. The key turned easily and he slipped inside.

He punched the code into the alarm system, breathing a sigh of relief when the red light switched to green. He was in. Grant had visited the house many times with his ex-wife and knew the layout and where things were kept. He went straight to the phone table, opened the drawer and flicked open the teledex. His old phone number was listed under 'S' but there was nothing for Linda. He selected 'L' and found numbers for her home, which she'd let, and for her office. The familiarity of the office number stopped him dead in his tracks. He'd always imagined that she'd have changed it and it stung him to realise that she hadn't. Six years earlier it had been his number, the number for Film Gate, the company he'd founded and which his ex-wife had stolen from him. For a moment his bitterness distracted him but then it was back to business. If Grant had needed further motivation, the unchanged number provided it. He searched under all the letters, looking at the bottom of the lists for new numbers, but found nothing that might be a code for his ex-wife. They had a new plumber and someone to tidy their garden and take their rubbish away. There was a recent entry for a Colleen Farmer, somebody called J Downs, a W Mynott and a Brian Williams. None of the names rang a bell.

He checked the inside covers of the phone directories. Numbers had been scribbled there, but again he had no reason to think any of them belonged to his ex-wife. He checked note pads. The plumber was coming or had come on Thursday at three. There were numbers Fran had written for her husband to call back and vice versa. Linda's name did not appear anywhere.

Grant went straight to the main bedroom and into the walk-in wardrobe Fran was so proud of. His ex-sister-in-law was compulsively neat and kept all her handbags except the one she was using lined up on a shelf. Grant checked each of them, looking for her address book and failing to find it. That didn't surprise him. He'd never known Fran to go anywhere without it. Nevertheless, it was another setback. He sat down on the bed to think. Clearly Fran had deliberately excluded his ex-wife's number from the teledex to prevent Jasmine from finding it, thereby eliminating any possibility that she could inadvertently pass the number on to him. Fran had the number written down somewhere, but where?

Fran was the family bill payer. She'd turned one of the spare bedrooms into an office from which she paid bills and kept track of accounts, receipts, bank statements, guarantee forms, their investments, tax returns and the rest of the paperwork people had to deal with. While it was an obvious place to look, there was no obvious place to start looking. Fran had two two-drawer filing cabinets and files, it seemed, for everything. Grant looked under 'Family' and found only birth certificates and her wedding certificate, school certificates of merit and certificates for sporting achievements. Grant hadn't a clue where to look next. He had no interest in their bank accounts or tax returns, or in quotes from painters or people to sand the timber floors. Yet he knew the answer lay somewhere in the files.

He read through the file headings, looking for cryptic associations which might link the file to Linda. Nothing stood out. He stopped once more to gather his thoughts. What had Jammy said? Her mother rang the school and rang Fran, but Fran had a number to call in emergencies. Emergencies! He left the office at a run and again grabbed the teledex out of the phone table drawer. The teledex didn't begin with an 'A' but an 'Em' for listings of emergency services. Typically, Fran had listings for everything: the police, fire brigade, ambulance, hospital, CES, poisons advisory service, gas company, 24-hour electricians, 24-hour vets, but there was no emergency listing for his ex-wife. He closed the teledex, put it back in the drawer and slumped down on the phone stool. What was he missing? He stared at the phone and the answer hit him like a bolt from the blue. He raced back into the office, pulled open the file drawer, lifted out a folder he wanted, thumbed through it and removed three pages.

Grant smiled to himself and checked his watch. He'd already been in the house for twenty-five minutes. Cameron would be beginning to wonder what the hell he was doing. He tidied up the files, closed the drawers and made sure everything on Fran's desktop was back in its rightful place. Before leaving he took the precaution of peering out of the front bedroom window to see if anyone was about. After re-arming the alarm, he stepped out onto the veranda and closed the door behind him. The sun was blazing down from a clear blue sky. Grant paused on the top step, as though in appreciation of the morning, and discreetly checked the windows of the house opposite and the units next door. For all intents and purposes the buildings could have been deserted. He walked briskly down the path, out through the gateway and onto the footpath. It had taken him forty minutes to get what he wanted and he knew that

Cameron would probably give him a serve for keeping him waiting so long. But he didn't care. The main thing was that he had what he needed.

* * *

Neil pushed his chair back to signal that the day's storytelling had concluded. His throat was dry and he would have killed for a beer, but he was mindful of the fact that he had to drive home. He scanned the faces of his friends, wondering who would be first to comment. He didn't have to wait long to find out.

'I take it we are finished for the day?'

'Yes, Ramon.'

'Good, I need a coffee.'

'Sorry I kept you waiting.'

Smiles spread across the faces of Lucio and Milos. Ramon's intentions were patently clear to them. He was getting in first with a touch of levity so the day would end pleasantly.

'I like the way the story is going,' said Milos. 'You're not usually this patient in constructing your stories. I like the way you are allowing the suspense to gather its own momentum.'

'Truth doesn't have the flexibility of fiction. The construction is determined by the events.'

'Even so, you have choices,' said Ramon. 'There is any number of ways you could tell this story, though I have no dispute with the way you are telling it. Milos likes the construction because you have copied his techniques and devices. Milos likes to build his stories block by block, like you are doing. First the foundations, then the events that develop from them. There were times I thought I was listening to Milos.'

'I'm glad you managed to stay awake,' said Neil.

'You have also stolen his device from his last story by referring to yourself in the third person,' said Ramon.

'Some would say he stole the idea from you. Still, it worked for him so I figured it would work for me.'

'It does,' said Milos. 'I particularly like the way you describe your childhood, your brother and your relationship to him, though I find it difficult to relate the thoughtful, generous young Neil in your story with the Neil telling the story. Where did you go wrong?'

It was Ramon's turn to smile. His friends had picked up on his intent to keep the mood light and gone on with it. He heard Gancio approaching with their coffees and made room.

'This is more like it,' said Gancio. 'Everyone smiling. You know, it used to be that I hesitated to bring your coffee because I didn't want to interrupt the laughing. This last year I've been hesitating because I didn't want to interrupt the arguing. I take it, Neil, you're telling one of your funny stories?'

'No,' said Neil.

'No?'

'No,' confirmed Ramon. 'A killer is stalking his ex-wife. Somewhere along the way Neil will take his brother's life. And, if he convinces his father to buy more sheep, it looks very likely that his sisters will miss out on getting new underwear.'

'What?'

The four friends laughed at the restaurateur's perplexity.

'I think I had better get back to my work.' Gancio withdrew to the sanctuary of his kitchen.

'You're a cynical bastard, Ramon,' said Neil. 'But I wonder if you'll still be laughing when I finish my story.'

THIRD THURSDAY

Chapter Eleven

'Today, to begin, I have a new dish which is West Australian sardines, butterflied with the bone removed and stuffed with prawn, garlic and herb risotto. They are breadcrumbed and fried and served with parmesan, parsley and just a drizzle of light tomato sauce made with fresh cherry tomatoes. You'll like it.'

'I can't think of anyone who wouldn't,' said Lucio.

'Got me,' said Neil.

Gancio glowed, clearly in his element.

'For the main, roast spatchcock with Italian roast potatoes and roast tomato.'

'Sounds wonderful,' said Ramon.

Gancio fussily topped up the wine glasses before retreating to the kitchen.

'It sounds to me like Gancio has decided to involve himself in the cooking again,' said Lucio. 'The sardines have his name written all over them. Most people don't eat this well even in Italy.'

'I'm glad you said that, Lucio,' said Neil. 'You guys can rave about your wonderful European cuisines, but the fact is you eat better here in Australia. Italian food is usually better in Australia than it is in Italy because we have better, fresher ingredients. The same can be said of French cooking, unless you're heavily into offal.'

'Neil, that is outrageous,' said Ramon.

'Bear with me,' said Neil. 'We may never compete with the elite Michelin three-star restaurants because there isn't much of a market for that kind of cooking here. What we've done in Australia is create our own cuisine by adapting other styles. Our French and Italian are Australianised and, I think, better for it. We prefer light sauces to heavy sauces. The sauce Gancio described to go with the sardines is a good example. In Italy, the tomatoes would have been simmered for hours and the sauce heavier. It is the same with Asian food. The Chinese will tell you they eat better food here than they do in Hong Kong and Singapore. The ingredients are better, cheaper and more readily available. Even so, there will be dishes we won't do so well. I think you have to go to Singapore for the best chilli crab and Hong Kong for the best shark fin soup. Doubtless there are other dishes, but generally Chinese food is better here.'

'I agree Australia has its own style, but whether or not it is better is highly subjective.'

'If every food critic in the world judged Australian cuisine best, you would still disagree, Ramon.'

'Don't worry about it. It will never happen.'

'It's happening, Ramon. One day you might have to sit here and eat humble pie, a dish I'm sure you'd choke on. Both Tetsuya's and Rockpool have been voted in the top ten restaurants in the world. And what's Tetsuya's style? Try his carpaccio of scallop with foie gras and lime. Carpaccio? Does that mean the dish is Italian? Raw scallop? Does that make it Japanese? Foie gras? Does that make it French? No. The combination makes it peculiarly Australian. To

Gancio's credit, he is adapting his dishes and making them more Australian. The only thing that surprises me is that the stuffing for the sardines doesn't also contain zest of lime, chilli and, maybe, a Thai influence.'

'Heaven forbid,' said Ramon.

'The only reason Australian cuisine does not yet have the recognition it deserves is because diehards like you refuse to believe that the new world can ever be better than the old world at anything besides sport. They should never have let you take up Australian citizenship, Ramon, because you'll resist to your death ever becoming an Australian.'

'Here comes Gancio with the sardines,' said Lucio. 'How about we give the subject a rest?'

'No way,' said Neil. 'I mean, just look at this.'

Gancio placed a plate of sardines in front of him. There were three fish, tails resting on a small moulded mound of risotto sprinkled with parsley and radiating out like the spokes of a wheel. Tomato sauce was drizzled on top of them. The grated parmesan was concentrated in three star bursts about the thicker part of the fish.

'Tell me, Gancio, how do you describe your cooking? Northern Italian, Southern Italian, what?'

'Better. It is Australian Italian, Neil,' said Gancio emphatically. 'I take the best of my country and the best of my adopted country. You don't like it?'

'On the contrary, old mate. I love it.'

Chapter Twelve

Billy parked the ute and began the long walk up the ridge to Rodney's shack, wishing he'd set out earlier. Summer was on its way and letting everyone know. The sun beat down from a cloudless sky that offered no relief. A couple of rabbits broke cover and bolted, which was more temptation than the kelpie could bear. It took off after them but Billy's whistle quickly brought it shuffling, head down, to heel. Some kangaroos moved warily away into where the bush was denser and cooler. On the drive over Billy had noticed some grass parrots flitting about, looking for new seed to pick at, but few birds were hanging around the ridges. All the signs pointed to the day being a scorcher. Billy thought about just parking and whistling till the little man came down, but suspected he could whistle till the cows came home. Nothing was going to budge Rodney, not when he thought he was in trouble, and certainly not when he thought the police might be waiting for him.

Billy maintained a slow, steady pace up the hill, wishing Rodney had the phone on which would save him a whole lot of trouble. But Rodney had never bothered to put the phone or power on and probably couldn't afford the expense anyway. He ran his generator for a few hours every day for the sake of his fridge, and intermittently to run his machines and the old concrete mixer he'd converted into a rumbler. His lights ran on kero, his cooker on gas from cylinders, his radio on batteries, and he went without a television. Unfortunately for Billy, the only way to put Rodney out of his misery was to make a house call.

He found him standing in the shade of a silver-leaf ironbark with his shotgun cradled in his right arm, as angry and suspicious as ever but also apprehensive. The kelpie raced ahead to renew acquaintance and get a pat for its trouble.

'Jesus, Rodney, why didn't you come down?' Billy slumped down and leaned his back up against the ironbark and began to fan his face with his hat. 'You could've met me halfway at least.'

'I'm nod lea-vin he-yah,' said Rodney. 'If they wan-na take me a-way they gun-na have to come and ged me.' He raised his shotgun and pretended to sight along it. The kelpie knew about guns and took cover behind Billy.

'No one's coming to get you, so you can relax and put the shotgun down. What did I tell you anyway? What did I tell you last night about your shotgun? What do you think would happen if the police came and found you standing here with a shotgun in your hands?' The heat and effort of climbing had made Billy irritable and in no mood for Rodney's theatrics. 'Sometimes, mate, I give up on you.'

Rodney lowered the shotgun angrily and made an elaborate display of laying it on the ground out of reach.

'Thad dad-id-fy you?'

Billy wiped his brow with his handkerchief and put it back in his pocket.

'I came to tell you I fixed it with the police. No one's coming to get you.'

'Fair din-kum?'

'Fair dinkum.'

'Whad did you tell them?'

'I told them the campers fired first. They didn't believe me, but it's my word against theirs and I have the distinction of being the only witness.'

'Thank, Bil-ly. I owe you one.'

'I don't want you owing me one. I don't want you owing me anything. I'm sick of lying for you, Rodney. This isn't the first time people have complained to the police about you and, God knows, you scared the crap out of Linda. What if she'd gone into Walgett and complained too? They'd come and take you away, Rodney.'

'Them and whad ar-my?'

'See? You don't listen and you don't learn. I'm not cleaning up after you any more. You're going to have to stop shooting at people and pointing your shotgun at them or the police will come. They will come, Rodney. They'll take you away and all those thieves from the Grawin will be all over your diggings in a flash. Is that what you want, mate?'

'Don led them take me a-way, Bil-ly.' Rodney hung his head. Anger and frustration still played across his face but there was a scared look in his eyes.

'Mate, you make it hard.'

'I'm dor-ry.'

Rodney looked so abject Billy relented.

'Ah, what the hell. Forget it.'

'I god a cup-la be-yah in the fridge.'

It was a bit early in the day but Billy needed something cold to drink and improve his frame of mind. Beer was the only option anyway.

'You get the beer,' he said. 'And a bowl of water for the kelpie.' He pulled out his tobacco pouch. 'I'll make us a couple of rollies.'

He watched Rodney scrabble away across the moonscape between the scrub and piles of mullock, wondering how long it would be before his little mate finally went too far.

Billy didn't drive straight home but made a right turn up towards his parents' house. He could've rung Linda to bring her up to date with everything that had happened over the previous night and morning, but, since he was in the area, it seemed rude not to tell her in person. He breathed the sigh of a man resigned to disruption. He had his lambs to mark, and a handful of barren ewes to weed out and sell. There was enough work to keep two men flat out.

The kelpie guessed where they were headed and began whining in anticipation. Billy reached the point where he'd stopped the night before and turned up onto the track. The dog was keen but Billy was suddenly hesitant. He knew he was doing the right thing, but phoning had the advantage of distance and detachment. They didn't have to look into each other's eyes. What if she was embarrassed? What if it had all been an unfortunate mistake, brought on by wine and the novelty of companionship? Not for the first time he wondered if he'd imagined the intimacies that had occurred or misinterpreted them.

He parked beneath a gum which was doing its best in soil not entirely to its liking. Its growth was stunted but, perversely, that had only served to thicken its canopy, which was why Billy had chosen it. He knew that by the time he got back to the ute he'd be grateful for every little bit of shade it provided. He let the kelpie race on up the drive, thinking Linda would probably appreciate a little advance notice of his arrival. Under the circumstances, he figured he'd probably benefit as well.

Linda was down on one knee on her front veranda when he spotted her, making a fuss of the kelpie. It was hard to know which of them was more pleased to see the other. A slow smile of relief spread across Billy's face. Linda didn't look like a woman harbouring regrets.

'You'll wear each other out in this heat.'

'Hello, Billy.'

Linda stood just as Billy stepped up onto the veranda and he was instantly at a loss to know how to greet her appropriately. They were long past the hand-shaking stage, but had they reached the point where a kiss was expected? Linda solved the problem by kissing him lightly on both cheeks.

'To what do I owe the pleasure?'

'It's a long story.'

'I was about to put the kettle on. Make yourself comfortable and tell me over a cuppa. By the way, you've never told me your dog's name.'

'It's Bella.'

'Good name. How come you never use it?'

'Dog doesn't need reminding what its name is.'

Billy found a chair along the veranda, rocked back on it and put his feet up on the rail. His earlier optimism had begun to fade. She seemed more interested in the kelpie than in him. Her kiss had been perfunctory and there'd been no hug, quick or otherwise. Although she'd smiled and seemed genuinely pleased to see him, she seemed to be holding something back. He wasn't sure what to make of it, but suspected they'd both fallen victim to the harsh light of day. It occurred to him that Rodney and the campers might have saved them both from further embarrassment. Nevertheless, he thought of the shotgun blast with genuine regret. What if there'd been no shotgun? What if her hand had reached his?

'Your tea. And jam tin.'

Billy smiled. The tea was in a mug, not a cup, and a healthy billabong brown. But it was the tin for his cigarette butts that revived his spirits. Clearly she expected to see more of him. So why the hesitation? He waited until she'd pulled a chair up alongside him and sat down.

'Are you going to tell me what's wrong?'

'Wrong?' said Linda.

'You seem distracted.'

Linda stared out over the plains, a habit she'd unconsciously borrowed from Billy. He rolled another cigarette while she thought through her answer. A blowfly droned somewhere behind them, but apart from that and a gentle soughing of the wind there wasn't a sound to be heard. No birdcalls, no bleating sheep or lowing cattle, no crickets. It seemed as though every living creature apart from them and the blowfly had decided to lieup somewhere cool. Billy hoped that the day was an anomaly and not indicative of a long, fiercely hot dry summer. What Billy wanted was a few days of light rain to soften up the ground followed by a good downpour now that his neighbours to the east had completed harvesting their winter crops. The flawless blue sky gave little hope of either but you never could tell. He'd lit up his smoke and taken a couple of deep pulls before Linda responded.

'It's a long story,' she said.

'I've got all day.'

'Oh, no. Your story first.'

Billy told her all about the campers and how he'd squared things off with the police by lying.

'I had to do it or else we'd have them up here wanting a chat with Rodney. They'd want me to act as go-between so Rodney didn't start shooting.' He turned towards Linda. 'They'd want to know what I was doing up here at the house and probably welcome the excuse to come nosing around. They'd be aware of the rumours Jimmy's been spreading and want to check them out.'

'Poor Billy,' said Linda. 'You've got Rodney to look out for and now me.'

'I've warned Rodney not to cause any more incidents. For what good it'll do, I've told him to chuck his shotgun down one of his mineshafts.'

'Well, maybe that wasn't such a good idea,' said Linda.

'What wasn't?'

'While Rodney's riding shotgun on his diggings, he's also riding shotgun on me. I feel a lot more safe and secure knowing he's out there on patrol.'

'Safe from what? Where's the threat? No one knows you're here and most people wouldn't be able to find this place anyway.'

Linda turned her gaze back across the expanse of plains to a horizon that couldn't be flatter if it had been ironed.

'My turn,' she said eventually. 'I had a phone call this morning. I have the phone for outgoing calls and so I can be contacted in an emergency. Besides you, only four people have my number: my sister, my solicitor, my accountant and my general manager from work. When the phone rings, chances are there's a problem.'

'Go on.'

'It's probably nothing.'

'People don't become distracted for nothing.'

'My sister, Fran, rang. They'd taken my daughter away for the weekend to the Blue Mountains. The little old lady across the road claims she saw someone — a man — go into their house on Saturday morning while they were away.'

'You mean, break in?'

'No, she said he had a key and stayed in the house for more than half an hour.'

'Anything missing?'

'Fran's not sure. The whole thing is weird. The house has an alarm and nobody outside of her immediate family and my daughter know the code. The alarm didn't go off and it was still armed when they got back from the mountains.'

'So someone had a key and knew how to disarm the alarm. Or the little old lady is imagining things.'

'She's old and her eyesight's not the best, even with glasses. But she's not senile. Fran also thinks someone has been in her office rifling through her files.'

'Thinks?'

'You have to know my sister. Everything has to be neat and tidy and in its rightful place. Every cushion has to be just so and magazines on the coffee table have to be neatly stacked and aligned with the edges of the table. If she suspects someone has been in her office I'm inclined to believe her.'

'But nothing's missing?'

'That's not the point. A normal burglar would have made a mess, tipped files out onto the floor and not just picked through them. Whoever went through those files was looking for something.'

'What?'

Linda took a deep breath.

'Fran thinks it was my ex-husband looking for my address and phone number.'

'I thought he was in gaol.'

'He gets weekend leave.'

'Does he also get your sister's front door key and alarm code?'

'Billy, the little old lady is not an idiot or a drama queen. If she says she saw someone then I'm inclined to believe her as well. Fran says someone was in her office. Her writing pads weren't properly aligned. There were gaps in the drawers of her filing cabinets, as if someone had pushed files back to make it easier to remove one of them. She's not making this up just to frighten me.'

'Does your sister have your address?'

'No.'

'But she has your phone number.'

'In her teledex.'

'No one would think of looking there.'

'It's under a false name. My sister's family have their own lives. There's probably a hundred names in the teledex that my ex-husband wouldn't recognise.'

'Is that the only place she's written your number down?'

'Yes. Absolutely.'

'Then what are you worried about? If someone entered your sister's home, and if it was your ex-husband, he wouldn't have found anything.'

'I think I've got a lot to worry about. If Fran is right then we know my ex is determined to come after me. So determined, he's prepared to break the law and risk getting caught. If he'd been caught, he would've lost all chance of parole and served out his full sentence. He was risking another two years in gaol.'

'But he didn't get your number.'

Linda bit her bottom lip. Billy was surprised by how tense she was and how worried.

'He might have. We can't be one hundred per cent sure that he didn't.'

'Okay, let's assume your ex-husband somehow got a key and the code and your telephone number. What does it tell him? It tells him you live somewhere in the northwest of the state covered by the Walgett exchange.' Billy waved his arm expansively over the plains below them. 'If you were him, where would you begin?'

Linda gazed at the bush that stretched as far as her eyes could see whichever direction she looked. Her number was unlisted and in the name of a company which existed only on paper in her accountant's office.

'If I were looking for you, Linda, I'd go around all the towns asking questions and showing your photograph. You came up here the first time over three months ago and people are still talking about you. In the unlikely event that some bloke comes up here asking questions and flashing your picture, don't you think I'd get to hear about it?' Billy slowly rolled another cigarette. The blowfly made the mistake of settling on Billy's knee and got swatted for its trouble. The silence didn't augur well for a wet summer.

Billy stayed for lunch and managed to convince Linda that someone had called in at her sister's house, found nobody home and called back half an hour later. It seemed quite plausible that the old lady had seen the man arrive the first time and leave the second time and drawn the wrong conclusion about the period in between. Linda also conceded that her sister's husband and teenage children used the office and didn't share Fran's obsession with tidiness. It wasn't just Billy's arguments that helped her relax but the quiet, unhurried way with which he presented them. His calmness seemed to rub off on her. Their conversation came as easily as it had the previous night and she promised him dinner on her return from a trip to Dubbo to buy fresh food and supplies.

Billy left Linda far happier than she'd been when he'd arrived. He also left in a happier mood. Despite the heat and the loss of a day's work, he felt like celebrating. He was convinced that his next dinner with Linda would deliver what Rodney's shotgun had postponed.

Billy's good humour didn't last long. Disregarding the heat he took a circuitous route back to his homestead so he could check on parts of his property he didn't often get to. Rabbit burrows had become full-blown warrens while his back was turned, harbouring God only knew how many of the pests. If the summer turned out as hot and dry as he feared, he'd need every blade of grass and edible shrub. He didn't want it wasted down the throats of rabbits. Bulldozing the warrens offered the best solution, but bulldozers cost money to hire and the infestation didn't justify the expense. The best he could do was hit the warrens with poisoned carrots. It wouldn't wipe the bunnies out, but that was about all his budget ran to. What was really needed was someone to come up with a successor to myxomatosis before the rabbit population built up to plague proportions again. As much as Billy had an aversion to poisons, he made a mental note to return with some strychnine.

His dark mood deepened as he continued on his way past more warrens and patches of roly-poly which had taken over where the sheep and rabbits had grazed out the buffle grass. His inventory of jobs that needed doing continued to grow. Apart from the lamb marking, he had calves to castrate and brand and the mob of steers to send off to market. He could feel things slipping away from him and that only added to the tension and made matters worse. Rodney was partly to blame and so was Linda. He just wasn't accustomed to outside influences deciding how he spent his days, but conceded he was as much to blame for letting them.

Thinking about Linda only brought another worry to the surface. When she'd mentioned she was intending to stay in Dubbo from Monday to Friday he hadn't said anything, but that hadn't stopped him wondering why she would need five days to shop for supplies. Why would she need five days? How did a person spend five days in Dubbo? Sure Linda had some shopping to do and would probably visit a hairdresser and maybe go see a couple of movies, but that didn't take five days. It puzzled him, adding another concern at a time when he needed his load lightened.

He almost groaned out loud when he saw the tyre tracks, recognising immediately what vehicle had left them. But when? Were they old marks or were the pig shooters still prowling around somewhere on his land? Billy could feel the pressure building inside his skull and heard the pounding in his ears that always came with it. He stopped the ute, closed his eyes and kept them shut till long after the dust had settled, only opening them when the kelpie began whining and licking his face. His hands were still on the wheel and reasonably steady, which was a good sign. But Billy knew he was pressing his luck. He cursed his brother, engaged gear and pointed the ute directly towards the homestead. Time healed, and he needed time to calm his mind and create some kind of order so he could deal with things one at a time. One at a time, one at a time, one at a time. That was the only piece of advice he'd been given that had ever made sense. He needed to put his feet up on the rail, smoke a few rollies and maybe suck a beer. Just the one, because that was all he had cold — all he ever had cold, just in case. But, more than anything, he needed to look aimlessly out over the scrub towards the sand ridges and let his mind drift off down any road it liked to oblivion. Before he could think of doing anything, he needed to think of nothing.

Chapter Thirteen

The corporal and a private from Wagga helped Billy up out of the tunnel. One of them patted him on the back and someone slipped him a rollie already lit. The guys were smiling and making wisecracks, but the truth was no one dared to look at him directly or catch his eye. They didn't want to see their hero damaged, didn't want to see the most capable and courageous man in the platoon broken down by the contact underground, didn't want to see their own fears and weaknesses exposed. They wanted Billy to laugh off the experience like he always did, or say something that made them laugh, or do something that added to their respect, anything, so long as they could cling to their belief that they could emerge from Vietnam with their minds as well as their bodies intact.

The regular grunts liked having Billy attached to their platoon. When they went out on patrol the sergeant put him fourth in line behind the forward scout, the second scout and the lieutenant. Most platoons liked to stack a bit of firepower up front and fourth place normally went to the man with the M60, while the first sapper went in midway through the section. But Billy's eyes picked up irregularities other soldiers didn't and the lieutenant liked having him nearby. Billy could see small things, insignificant things, things that were apart from the natural order: pieces of bamboo arranged in patterns, the deliberate cross-hatching of leaves, wilting plants and other subtle man-made indicators of mines, booby-traps, trip wires and tunnel entrances. Neil had always claimed Billy had 'abo eyes' because of his ability to track wild pigs and locate straying stock. When they went out looking for emu eggs amongst the lignum, Billy always led because of his knack for picking up emu tracks and following them over rock-hard ground until they'd found what they were after. But keen eyesight was just a part of Billy's ability. Equally impressive was the fact that he'd developed a sixth sense for booby-traps, whether above ground or below. Whenever the patrol stopped for a break, the lieutenant always let Billy check the site out first. Like the forward scouts, Billy took risks on behalf of the entire section.

Billy wanted to sit down somewhere shady, lean back against the trunk of a tree and shut his eyes, not for long, just long enough to get his thoughts back together and everything under control. But even with his mind screaming for time out, instinct stopped him in his tracks. Experience and training had drilled into him the fact that the Vietcong booby-trapped the area around their firing positions and Billy had no reason to think this firing position would be an exception. He also noted that the tree he was heading for was precisely the sort of nice shady tree hot and tired soldiers like to rest under, and precisely the sort of place the Vietcong were likely to booby-trap. He took a drag from his rollie, holding his hand hard against his lips to stop the shaking, and scanned the ground for telltale signs. It took all of his self-control to look thoroughly and, although he saw nothing suspicious, he nevertheless dropped to his hands and knees and began to prod the dirt between him and the tree with his knife. Certain that he'd be left alone, he didn't search for mines all around the tree, just along a strip where he could stretch out with his back against the trunk.

'Barb's back in business!'

Billy had no idea who had called out, or who laughed in response, only that the laughter sounded relieved. The trunk felt coarse against his bare back and he was momentarily aware of how much he stank. But both things were irrelevant. Now that he could finally relax he wanted to scream, cry and turn back time, but mostly he wanted to crawl away into a hole somewhere and stay there. He butted his rollie because he had no chance of holding it steady enough to bring to his lips. He crossed his arms tightly across his body to stop them shaking, crossed his legs for the same reason, and all the while his inner voice shrieked at him desperately.

'Think it through, don't lose it, don't lose it, think it through ...'

Don't lose it. Think it through. Billy tried to think it through, to come to terms with both the events and his fear, but he didn't want to go back down the tunnel, didn't want to bear witness a second time, didn't want to face up to what he'd done, didn't want to remember. The tunnel had changed everything. He'd survived, but the experience had pulped his confidence, trashed his convictions and torpedoed his strategy for getting out of Vietnam alive and intact. If he couldn't rely on himself, on his wits and on his skills, who could he rely on? The tunnel had taught him how vulnerable he really was. It didn't matter that he was good. He could be good and still get killed because circumstances took his skill out of the equation. His thoughts raced out of control, ricocheting around inside his head like a pea in a whistle. He fought for control and finally let his thoughts free to run away wherever they liked, so long as they got him away, away from his fears, away from the tunnel, away from his enemy and her desperate silent plea for help, and away from the lottery of his existence.

Though Billy was a crack shot with a rifle, he decided that if he had to join the army he'd try for the Engineers. Probably through watching old war movies or reading war stories, he'd got the idea in his head that Engineers were people who built or repaired bridges for an advancing army and blew them up when it was retreating. The thought of building bridges or building anything appealed to Billy, as did the notion of repairing vehicles and operating heavy machinery. Nothing about Holdens, Fords, trail bikes or tractors was a mystery to him and he could rip a gearbox out, replace clutch plates or do an engine rebuild with his eyes shut. He figured that by becoming an Engineer he'd spend most of his time in Vietnam well away from the shooting and serve something like an apprenticeship at the same time, which might come in handy when he got back home. When they told him about mines, booby-traps and tunnels he paid attention, even though he thought the information would have no bearing on what he did. He was a Plant Operator and a Plant Operator when posted to Vietnam.

During his first month in Phuoc Tuy, Billy's duties lived up to his earlier expectations. He was put to work on a variety of constructions and roadworks, sometimes at the control of machines, but mostly with a pick or shovel in his hands. He spent a couple of days laying wire, which was how he earned his nickname. It was hot and dusty most of the time, and hot and muddy when it rained, but, apart from the oppressive humidity, these were conditions that he was used to and he'd no real cause to complain. His first mission out of Nui Dat was to clear trees for a firebase and that was something else up his street. During his school holidays he'd picked up a few dollars helping farmers down Coonamble way clear scrub for crops. He was actually looking forward to going out into the countryside because his work up to this point had all been around the base and because the job was comparatively low risk.

Knocking down the trees for the firebase and clearing them away went off without a hitch. Billy had grown up around tractors and agricultural machinery and loved being at the controls of the big bulldozers. In no time at all he had the Caterpillar D8 up and dancing. Judging by the encouragement and comments he received, Billy thought that in carving out the firebase he'd also carved out a career for the duration of his Vietnam service. But armies have their own way of doing things and, in recognition of his skills with the big Cat, he was sent out to lay mines.

He was paired off with a bloke called Tom who'd been in Vietnam for six months and was dedicated to survival. He was anything but impressed at being partnered with someone who had so little experience.

'What do you know about these M16 mines?' asked Tom.

'Not a lot.'

'Then you watch what I do,' said Tom. 'You watch everything I do and make sure I do everything right.'

'Fair enough,' said Billy.

'Then I watch what you do and make sure you do everything right, okay? You don't argue, you don't question, you just do what I tell you, okay?'

'Okay,' said Billy.

'Only work at the speed you're comfortable with, no matter how much shit the NCOs throw at you, okay?'

'Okay.'

'Don't try to impress me. Don't try to outdo me.'

'Okay.'

'You get us blown up, mate, I'll fuckin' kill ya.'

Billy looked for a trace of a smile but there wasn't one. Maybe because of his inexperience they were assigned to testing fuses and spent the day pulling pins in a deep cut a dozer had made, making sure they moved smoothly, and replacing them. The job was tedious and undemanding and made even more insufferable by the heat and the NCOs who accused them of slacking off. But Billy followed his partner's advice to the letter. He worked steadily rather than quickly and maintained his concentration as the day dragged on.

'Do everything as though every mine's got your bloody name on it,' said Tom. 'I know we're only testing but act like you're arming. Get used to being methodical, get used to checking everything. Tomorrow we could be arming the friggin' things.' That was the closest Tom ever got to small talk.

To Billy's surprise, Tom looked for him the following morning and made sure they were partnered up again.

'You got good hands,' said Tom. 'And you listen. Keep listening and I'll keep you alive.'

'Thanks.'

'Some of these pricks, mate. Fuckin' cowboys.'

'Hey! You two lovers. Over here!'

Billy looked up and realised the NCO was calling to them.

'Oh shit!' said Tom.

'On the truck.'

'Give us a break,' said Tom. 'This bloke's straight out of Kapooka. He needs help to find his prick to take a leak. Testing's his limit.'

'Has to learn some time,' said the sergeant. 'Get on the truck.'

'Shit!' said Tom.

Billy suddenly realised Tom's true motives. He'd been using him and his inexperience to try to get out of laying and arming the mines.

'I'll be careful,' said Billy. 'Don't worry.'

'Ain't just you, mate, it's the other friggin' cowboys. These bloody "jumping jack" mines, Jesus, mate, I'm telling you. I heard some poor bastard got killed when one went off and he was just standing around minding his own business seventy metres away. Seventy metres! Ripped his throat out. Just pray we get digging.'

If Tom did any praying, it didn't help. Their section was put straight onto arming. The deal was they had to arm twenty clusters before rotating to digging.

'Jesus,' said Tom. 'At least it won't be too hot. There's nothing worse than arming mines when it's stinking hot.'

They ditched their rifles, gear and webbing and assembled by the area where mines had been laid ready for arming.

'You have to wear a helmet and flak jacket,' said Tom. 'They stink like pigs shat in them but at least they won't stink as badly as they will when we've finished with them. There's nothing worse than a friggin' sweaty flak jacket.'

Billy pulled on a flak jacket, surprised by how much it did smell like a pig had shat in it.

'Do what I say when I say. Twenty clusters is fuckin' eighty mines. Concentrate on every one. Work with me. Don't do anything on your own, understand?'

Tom had a way of working that was slow and methodical and had more to do with staying alive than killing Vietcong. He seemed to move into another realm. Sweat poured off his brow from both the heat and the effort of concentrating. Billy knew what had to be done but Tom automatically talked through each step of every mine they armed. By the time they'd armed the last of the mines, the heat and Tom's droning, repetitive litany was beginning to fray Billy's nerves. Yet he could see the sense of Tom's caution and admired the way he could shut out everything except the job at hand. Nothing changed the pace at which he worked and nothing broke his concentration, not even the urging and threats of the NCOs.

They shed their helmets and flak jackets, lay them in the sun to dry out for the next section, and wandered over to where they'd left their gear for a well-earned break and a drink.

'Got a stiff neck,' said Tom. 'Always get a stiff neck arming mines. Friggin' tension gets me every time.'

'Wasn't so bad,' said Billy.

'It's not us I worry about,' said Tom. 'You saw those cowboys, arming single-handed while their mate nicks off for a smoke. You heard them, talking about their girlfriends and the bar girls. You think they've got their mind on the job? They fuck up and we cop it as well. Pricks.'

Tom's whining and negativity ran contrary to Billy's nature. Arming mines was dangerous but the procedure was straightforward enough and he was convinced they could have worked half as fast again without any increase in risk. Still, he decided, better safe than sorry. He'd swallowed two bottles of water without making much impact on his thirst when they got hustled away to start laying mines. The heat and humidity felt as though it had doubled since morning. Billy looked across at the section taking over the job of arming. He'd sweated enough in the flak jackets but the new blokes would cook.

Billy was busy digging when he heard the mine go off. Tom hit the dirt so quickly Billy thought he'd been hit.

'Fuckin' arseholes!' said Tom. 'What did I fuckin' tell ya?'

Billy spun away from his whinging mate. Someone had started screaming and others joined in. A puff of blue smoke looking like nothing, looking harmless, drifted slowly away. Uninjured sappers near the site of the explosion stood motionless, either in shock or counting their blessings that they'd escaped relatively unharmed. As quickly as he could, Billy retraced his steps and, once he was clear, ran back to the armed mine area. A sergeant who'd given him an earful for being too slow was standing white-faced by the edge of the minefield, yelling at everyone to stand still. Billy ignored him and walked straight in, stepping in the footsteps of others who'd gone before.

'What are you doing?' screamed the sergeant. 'Enemy mines! It wasn't one of ours. I saw it happen. Stand still! Use your bayonets. Follow procedure!'

Billy ignored him. Following in the footprints of soldiers in army boots and flak jackets through undergrowth was a piece of cake compared with tracking a wild pig across the concrete-hard country he was used to. By the time he reached the site of the explosion, the uninjured and lightly injured were already trying to help their mates. Other soldiers came racing in to help along the same path he'd taken. Billy stopped dead in his tracks, stunned by the carnage. Someone elbowed him aside. One soldier had taken the blast full in the face and upper body. He'd lost both arms and blood squirted intermittently from an artery among the pulp that had been his neck, the volume and pressure fading till it became no more than a trickle then stopped flowing altogether. Others had lost hands, arms, legs, had torn faces and throats. Somebody grabbed his arm.

'Go get some pins to put back in these mines. And tell the fuckin' sergeant to jam it. It was one of ours that went off.'

Billy turned and ran back towards the sergeant, grateful to be doing something to help.

'It was one of ours,' said Billy. 'It's confirmed. I need some pins.'

'Pins!' shouted the sergeant. 'Who's got pins?'

'Here!'

The reply came from a sapper who'd just reached the scene.

'Retter, you go with this man,' ordered the sergeant. 'Disarm the mines around the site and along the route in. Goddamn it! Where're the company medics?'

Billy and his new partner raced back to the site and began to disarm the mines. Retter was at least ten years older than Billy and worked at four times the speed of Tom. Billy had to ask him to slow down.

'What's your problem? You new or something?'

'Yes,' said Billy.

'Tough.'

Billy couldn't keep up and was reduced to handing pins to his partner as he needed them. Everything Tom had told him about cowboys came flooding back and Billy grew more apprehensive by the minute. There was no need to hurry. The infantry company medics had arrived and the word was, the dust-off choppers were already on the way.

'Slow down, for Christ's sake,' he said. 'The last thing we need is another fuck-up.'

'Relax. Ain't gunna be another fuck-up.' The sapper looked up from the mine he was disarming and locked eyes with Billy. He kept working while he stared at Billy, his smile widening as Billy's terror bloomed. 'You heard of Mad Mike? Mad Mike Retter? That's me. The best mine man in Vietnam. I can arm and disarm these suckers with my eyes closed.' To make his point, he closed his eyes.

'For fuck's sake, watch what you're doing!' Billy's voice was shrill and almost pleading. Mad Mike just laughed. In horror, Billy looked down to see what Mad Mike's hands were doing. They never missed a beat, which was more than could be said for Billy's ticker.

He returned to base that afternoon burdened by the knowledge that three of his fellow engineers, three men who'd left camp with him on the truck that morning, were now dead; four more would live the rest of their lives missing a leg or an arm, if they were lucky enough to pull through; and five or six others had injuries serious enough to get them sent home. All because of what? All because someone got careless, lost concentration, goofed off, got too hot, what?

What?

It was all so pointless, so needless.

Up until the mine went off, the war had been something that happened to other guys in other sections and his war experiences had all been second-hand. 2 Platoon C Company had been ambushed on patrol and suffered two dead and five wounded. A soldier in B Company trod on a mine which killed him and two others and made a mess of another four. Some positions had been mortared but he wasn't sure of the casualties there. And one of those freaky things that happen in wars occurred when a sapper out on patrol caught a stray bullet in the head while he was fast asleep under his hoochie.

Billy had heard the stories, but they meant no more to him than road accidents had back in Jindalee Downs. For as long as he could remember, accidents had taken the lives of young people in the northwest. Everybody felt bad about them at the time, but life went on as normal. He was largely untouched by the tragedies, even when two-twenty-year olds from Walgett, who'd been a couple of classes ahead of him at school, wrote themselves off against a tree on their way home from an all-night party. Accidents happened, people got killed but it didn't really touch him. That sort of thing didn't happen to him. But suddenly his whole universe had changed. What if the guy who fucked up had been in his section? What if he'd been alongside? What if Mad Mike had finally got it wrong? He could, so easily and without fault, have been one of the casualties, even one of the dead.

He realised then and there that he somehow had to take more control over his destiny.

The first time he was sent out on patrol he made sure everyone knew about his special skills, his bushcraft. He talked to forward scouts and sappers coming to the end of their tour and learned how the Vietcong operated and signposted their traps. Once he was reasonably confident, he put his hand up for a more active role. If someone had to check out a rest site he wanted it to be him, because he trusted his ability to find mines and booby-traps more than he trusted anyone else's. If there were claymore mines to be laid around the perimeter of their overnight positions, he made sure he got the job so there were no fuck-ups. When they found tunnels, he volunteered to go down first for the same reasons. He was more scared of being killed by someone else's mistake, oversight or lack of ability than he was by the Vietcong.

For two months his system had worked like a charm. He'd found mines out on patrol and on cordon and search operations, and had either disarmed them or blown them up. When the forward scouts had found something unusual, Billy had gone up to help them work out exactly what kind of surprise the Vietcong had prepared for them. By taking responsibility and not relying on others, Billy believed he was taking the best possible care of himself.

Underground, it had been the same story. He'd found one booby-trap in a communications tunnel, a trip wire connected to a grenade, and neutralised it. He'd found trapdoors leading to rice and weapons caches, all of them booby-trapped, and dealt with them. By going first into the tunnels and keeping his wits about him, he genuinely believed he was minimising risk. But then all of the earlier tunnels had been cold.

'Time to go, Barb.'

The sound of Lieutenant Brennan's voice brought Billy back to the present. The lieutenant had followed Billy's tracks and was crouching over him, concern evident in both his face and his voice.

'We're about ready to move out.'

Once again it was time for Billy to face the enemy, to pit his wits against their mines, booby-traps and ambushes. When he'd first arrived in Nui Dat, the battalion CO had told all the new arrivals that they would never be off-duty so long as they were in Vietnam. He'd told them their job was for twenty-four hours a day and seven days a week and they should accept that and never relax their guard. He warned them that Australian soldiers in the province saw action as much as six days out of seven. Billy had thought it was just the usual bullshit pep talk. Now he'd learned differently. The war made no concession to him or anyone else, regardless of what they'd done or been through. He rose heavily to his feet.

'You okay?' The lieutenant hadn't moved.

'Yeah,' said Billy. 'Laughing.'

Chapter Fourteen

'They're calling their company Camera.'

'Camera?'

'I guess that's as close as Cameron could get to putting his own name on the shingle. That's what he wants but that would be just too much of a blow to Grant's ego.' Albert Larkman, Linda's office manager, rose from his chair and wandered over to the bench above the mini-bar to pour himself another coffee. 'Get you one?'

'No,' said Linda. She'd booked a suite at the Country Club in Dubbo with a large living area that could double as her temporary office. 'As much as we can do without the competition, I hope they succeed. In fact, I'm counting on them succeeding. I can't come back to Sydney until Grant gets back on his feet and the money starts flowing. I won't be safe until he's got something to lose.'

Al Larkman put his coffee down on the table and slumped into the chair opposite Linda.

'Camera will succeed because Cameron will succeed. He's driven, the classic poor kid made good. But whether Grant can cut it again, or even be sucked along in Cameron's wake, is another matter. A lot of agency people will boycott Grant out of loyalty to you and right now you've really got the sympathy vote. We're picking up business for no other reason than people want to show their support. So long as our quote is in the ballpark, we're in.'

'Tell them if they want to help, give Grant the job.'

'I'm not going to do that,' said Al. 'Right now your exile is working for us, but what's going to happen down the track, six months to a year from now? It's your company. People want to deal with you.' Al took a sip from his coffee and screwed his face up in disgust. 'Must be the water. Look, Linda, I know you want Grant to succeed but don't count on him getting an easy ride. It's going to be hard for him. You know better than I do that there are a lot of new directors around with interesting ideas. Agency people want edgy stuff and these new whiz-kids are probably the ones who are going to provide it. We've brought two in as a matter of fact — at the request of the agencies involved — working on a couple of our current jobs. There's a lot they don't know but, by the same token, there's a lot they're teaching us. It's been fun.'

'And profitable?'

'Of course.'

'I wish I was there,' said Linda.

'We all wish that.' Al sighed and leaned back in his chair so he could look out over the golf course. He was an anomaly in the commercial film business in that he was an accountant by profession and preferred a suit and tie to the standard office garb of jeans and T-shirt. Prematurely bald, overweight and entirely unathletic, his concession to Dubbo was to wear casual slacks and remove his tie. His strength lay not only in his financial expertise but also the fact that he had a touch of the entrepreneur about him, which made him ideal for the film business. In an industry noted for brilliant creative but poor commercial judgement, Al provided a voice of sanity Linda could rely on. 'God knows Dubbo makes me appreciate Sydney, Linda, but I don't think either of us can expect an early end to your exile. I think you'd better face up to that and factor it into your plans. Okay?'

'Let's just wait and see.'

'Your call. Now, where do you want to start? Do you want to review our quote/win ratio, review individual quotes, check the numbers, review personnel, what?'

'I want to review everything. I want to be convinced that my absence hasn't made way for bad habits or slackness. But first I want you to assure me that you're the only one who knows my phone number and that you haven't written it down anywhere.'

'Linda, for God's sake —'

'Indulge me.'

'I even have the phone accounts passed through to me unopened so I can black out your phone number.'

'What?' said Linda. Colour drained from her face.

'The numbers for all STD and international calls we make are listed on the account. You know that. That's how we allocate calls to the cost sheets of each job. I black yours out so nobody sees it.'

'Oh my God …'

'What's the matter?'

'Excuse me, Al, I've just got to make an urgent call to my sister.'

Knowledge enlightens but also crushes. Linda spent the rest of that day and the following day reviewing the operations of her business while trying to come to terms with the revelation that pages from one of Fran's phone bills, which almost certainly contained her phone number, had been taken from the files. Her ex-husband was not yet released on probation but he'd already managed to narrow his search down to the Walgett telephone exchange. Worse, she'd discovered her sister had listed her number under J Downs in her teledex. Had Grant taken note? It was little consolation that Jindalee Downs was too insignificant to be recorded on most maps. It was recorded on local maps and maps of the opal fields. Anyone who asked around Walgett would have no trouble getting directions. But would Grant have realised what J Downs represented and picked it out from the hundreds of names listed in her sister's teledex?

Linda took her anxiety out on Al. She grilled him on all aspects of the business and even gave him a hard time over producers and directors not keeping records of how they spent the contingency cash on shoots. This was a notoriously difficult area to police. While the cash was meant for emergencies and to solve problems on location, it was common knowledge that a substantial part of the money often went into booze or into the producer's or director's pockets. The practice was so entrenched, some directors even regarded the contingency money as theirs, one of the perks of the job. Linda knew she was being unfair and that Al was as vigilant as anyone could be. Her irritation grew as she failed to find anything other than minor discrepancies and oversights. Al had risen to the occasion and done an excellent job of managing her business in her absence. He deserved to be praised for his efforts. Nevertheless, Linda kept him on the defensive until they had no further issues to discuss.

Al took the assault on the chin. On his last night in Dubbo, he took her out to dinner, plying her with more wine than was healthy in the hope that alcohol would succeed in calming her where his words of assurance had failed.

'At least you know your business is in good hands,' said Al. 'You can relax on that score.'

'For heaven's sake, Al,' said Linda. 'My success is only going to provoke Grant even more. I'll relax when he's successful.'

'Sorry, sorry,' said Al quickly. 'That didn't come out quite the way I meant.'

Linda bowed her head.

'Yeah, I know. I'm sorry.'

She thought about her plans for the following day. She'd intended to get her hair done and go shopping, not just for food and supplies but also for furnishings for her little homestead between the ridges. But what was the point? As much as she'd grown attached to her new home and to Billy, and even Rodney in a funny sort of way, she couldn't ignore the fact that her ex-husband was closing in on her. It was time to move on. But if she did, would there be another Billy or a home as secluded? And, even if there were, how long would it take Grant to track her down again?

'What am I going to do, Al?' she said. 'I don't want to move on.'

'How long before Grant gets out?'

'Two months.'

'And what do you think his priority will be?'

'I know what it is. Getting even. He left me in no doubt about that.'

'Wrong. He won't have time to get even. He'll have his work cut out just getting going. Grant won't have time to scratch himself when he gets out. He'll be flat out flogging his reel around town, trying to drum up work, and he'll probably fly down to Melbourne to do the same. Start-ups gobble cash, you know that. His number one priority will be to get work in and get some cash flowing. He also needs to get new, up-to-the-moment work on his reel. That's not going to take days or weeks, it's going to take months.'

'Grant's got a lot of hate and it has to go somewhere.'

'Even good haters have got to eat and to eat they've got to earn. My guess is it's going to take Grant at least six months to get some momentum going.'

'Six months?'

'Sure, to get the work and then do it.'

Linda thought over how long it had taken her to go through the quoting process, pre-production, the shoot and post-production. Six to eight weeks was the norm and there was no guarantee that Grant would get jobs back to back. Six months looked a conservative estimate.

'I guess you're right.'

'I am right. Like you said yesterday, the best thing that can happen for you is if things go well for him. If I were you, I'd stay where you are, at least for the time being. A lot can happen in six months.'

Linda took a long sip from her glass of wine. Everything Al had said made sense and she wanted desperately to believe him. But Grant was Grant and she knew what he was capable of. His one phone call to her from prison almost six years earlier had left her in no doubt where his priorities lay. She was his priority. He'd made that perfectly clear. Al ordered another bottle of wine and, as far as she was concerned, it couldn't come quickly enough.

After a restless night, Linda dropped Al off at Dubbo airport and returned to town to do her shopping. She was tempted to check out of the Country Club and drive straight home to Jindalee but decided to stay and go to the movies as she'd originally planned. *When Harry Met Sally* was playing in the afternoon session. It was exactly the kind of light, slick entertainment she needed to take her mind off her problems. That evening she had dinner in her room and lay in bed watching 'Hill Street Blues'.

Linda checked out of the Country Club at two-thirty the following morning so that she could get through Walgett and Cumborah while it was still dark and nobody would be about to see her or recognise her. The weather reports on her car radio talked up the possibility of good falls of rain on the northwest plains. Linda thought about Billy and how pleased he'd be if the skies decided to open over his property. Thinking about Billy brought the first smile to her face for days. It also occurred to her that her own place could do with a few drops. The first shower splattered onto her windscreen a few kilometres north of Coonamble. Just short of Walgett she drove through a much heavier fall but thought of it as nothing more than a minor inconvenience necessitating the use of windscreen wipers. After all, the Castlereagh Highway was sealed and there was no traffic on the road. Her only concern was whether or not the rain also fell on Billy's property. She knew how disappointed he'd be to miss out. It continued to drizzle as she drove through the dark, deserted streets of Walgett.

In one of those quirks that drive graziers to an early grave, the rain seemed to have bypassed the area west of Walgett. As soon as Linda turned onto the dirt road leading out to Cumborah she switched off her windscreen wipers. She could see in her high beam that there'd been some rain but not much, not enough to do any good or do any more than lay the dust. The steering wheel felt strangely light in her hands, almost skittish, and she put it down to the fact that she hadn't adjusted to the change from the tar seal to the dirt. Nevertheless, she slowed down. Her one remaining imperative was to clear Cumborah while it was still dark or at least gloomy and she figured she had plenty of time up her sleeve. Occasionally she saw the eyes of animals reflecting back from the sides of the road and pinned the odd kangaroo in the glare of her headlights. Billy had warned her about their erratic habits and she slowed whenever she spotted them. Strangely, the thing that was beginning to concern her most was the sheer blackness of the night. The darkness seemed to absorb the light from her headlights and she found she had to concentrate hard just to stay on the road. Then the rain came.

At first there were just a few drops but they were soon joined by others until Linda found herself driving through a heavy shower. Rain mixed with the dust on her windscreen and the area covered by her wipers became streaked with mud. The road became even harder to distinguish through the falling rain. Instinctively Linda lifted her foot from the accelerator. Nothing happened. The Toyota failed to slow down and, worse, started sliding slowly to the left into the heavy soil and shallow ditch that lined the side of the road. Linda began to panic. What would happen if she got bogged in the slurry along the side of the road? She'd be stuck there and have to be towed out. The implications almost paralysed her. What were the chances of keeping her presence secret then? She turned into the direction of the slide just as the Toyota at last began to slow, found traction and gingerly steered back into the centre of the road. Previously she'd wondered at the lack of camber on the road and assumed it was because they got so little rain. The real reason was now painfully apparent. Rain penetrated the soft dust but sat on the concrete-hard clay beneath, making the road as slippery as an ice rink. The slightest camber caused the four-wheel drive to drift off line. Even a moderate camber would cause vehicles to slip off the road altogether.

Linda gradually slowed to ten kilometres an hour but still found it hard to keep in the middle of the road. Her pulse raced and her heart hammered in her chest but everything else seemed to be happening in slow motion. The only similar experience she could draw on was when she'd driven through a blizzard on an icy road up to Mt Perisher, and then she'd had the benefit of chains on her wheels. She groaned out loud when she realised the road was curving away to the right. It was difficult enough just keeping the Toyota in a straight line. She turned gently, hoping that her tyres would find enough grip to get around and, after a few heart-stopping skids, they did. That was enough. Linda wanted to stop until it was lighter and she could see better. But the thought had no sooner formed when she realised that if she stopped she probably wouldn't find the traction to get going again. Just as she was starting to despair she drove through the other side of the shower. The rain eased and the road became a little drier and marginally less slippery.

Linda slipped and slithered her way into Cumborah, past the few buildings that justified its position on the map, and turned right at the windmill. Although she was hours behind schedule and the country around her had turned from an impenetrable black to a uniform dull grey, she was comforted by the fact that no one noticing the Toyota pass by would have any idea who was at the wheel. Her windscreen and side windows were streaked with mud. Believing the worst was behind her she began to relax.

She was halfway between Cumborah and the track up to Billy's when the storm broke overhead. Rain lashed her windshield. She flicked her wipers to high speed but they still struggled to cope. In desperation she lifted her foot from the accelerator but once again experienced the ice-on-ice sensation that had frightened her earlier. She tried desperately to hold the car in a straight line as it slid, but nothing she did had any effect. With agonising slowness the Toyota began to turn sideways. She applied opposite lock and held on. The car suddenly jiggled over corrugations, caught snatches of traction, began to straighten then resumed its slide. It had slowed to less than five kilometres an hour but Linda still had no control over which direction it went. She tried applying a little power to straighten the car, but the wheels spun uselessly; tried dabbing the brakes but they had no effect either. Inevitably, and with maddening slowness, the Toyota slid off the road into the slurry and stopped. Linda slumped over the steering wheel and turned off the motor and wipers. As if to confirm her defeat the rain intensified and hammered like a thousand mad drummers on her roof. Her windows turned opaque.

She closed her mind to the pounding rain and tried to get a grip on her predicament. How long before the rain eased up? Was it just another shower? How long before the road dried up enough to be driveable? What were her chances of getting mobile again before someone came and offered to help her? She groaned inwardly. If only the rain had held off for another twenty minutes, she could have got as far as Billy's or at least to the track leading up to his house. That would've solved all problems. She examined her options. From time to time her film crews had got their cars bogged while shooting commercials on beaches or in the bush and she recalled them saying how they jammed rocks and scrub under the wheels for traction. That was something she could try. There weren't many rocks around but there was plenty of scrub. The only other alternative was to get out and walk to Billy's some seven or eight kilometres away, without boots, raincoat or umbrella. One thing was certain, if she couldn't get the car going she had to abandon it. She couldn't risk staying put and having her presence discovered.

The rain eased briefly but just as quickly picked up again. When a gust of wind hit the Toyota side-on and actually moved it a few centimetres, Linda realised she really had no choice. It was going to take hours, if not days, for the road to dry out enough to be driveable. She waited for another two hours, hoping that the rain would stop, but instead it settled into a steady drizzle. With no sign of any break in the clouds, Linda opened her car door and stepped out. As the first drops landed on her she thought of her hair and the money she'd wasted in Dubbo having it cut, tinted and styled. She was thinking of the pathetic figure she'd cut on Billy's doorstep, all soaked and bedraggled, when her feet shot out from beneath her.

It hadn't occurred to her that if the road was too slippery to drive on it might also be too slippery to walk on. That oversight cost her dearly. She landed heavily on the flat of her back, banging her head and knocking every wisp of air from her lungs. She lay there, dazed and in agony, desperately trying to draw breath. Slowly, ever so slowly, the pain in her diaphragm subsided and she managed to get some rhythm back into her breathing. Now she only had to worry about the pounding in her head. Her hand found the Toyota's front mudguard and she dragged herself up into a sitting position. The effort and movement, as small as it was, drove a thousand long nails through her skull and into the part of her brain that registered pain. Cautiously she reached behind her head with her free hand to assess the damage and groaned when she felt the wetness. Blood. She forced herself to look at her hand to try to gauge how badly her head was bleeding and almost sobbed with relief. Her hand was red and wet all right, but the culprit was mud not blood.

Linda dragged herself to her feet and waited for the throbbing in her head to subside. Mud covered her from head to toe down her back and sides and had splashed over her front. Filled with trepidation she tentatively prodded the road surface with the toe of her shoe. The mud was only two or three centimetres deep. The ground below was still as hard and unyielding as ever and as slick as ice. Once again she was forced to examine her options. The Toyota was going nowhere and she'd already accepted she couldn't stay with it and await help. That left her no choice but to walk to Billy's.

Now that she knew how slippery the road was she stepped gingerly over to the softer ground alongside it.

Mud oozed over the top of her shoes before sucking them off her feet altogether. Barefoot, soaked, muddy, her head hurting like hell and with at least seven treacherous kilometres to walk, she set out grimly for Billy's. Twenty metres on she fell for the second time.

Chapter Fifteen

Billy lay flat on his belly against the embankment, his feet in the ditch and his eyes staring along the length of his SLR and across the sea of rice plants to a barely visible village erupting in flames three hundred metres away. The roar of the jet planes and their explosives was all but drowned out by the pounding of torrential rain on a million leaves. The rain hid the aircraft from sight but not the damage they did. Rain was no defence against napalm and HE, and nothing, least of all rain, stopped play in Vietnam.

He saw movement on the road leading from the village — someone or something coming towards him — and automatically took aim. He wiped rain from his eyes and concentrated, focusing all his attention on the shapes slowly resolving in his sights. People running. Old people, women and children. Someone in black pyjamas. Vietcong? No. A woman. A woman and her kids. All scared shitless. Screaming. Waving. Billy held fire.

Before Vietnam there'd never been a time in his life when he wouldn't have rushed to the help of any woman in distress, especially one with kids, especially when they were screaming, especially when they were running for their lives, especially when they were so helpless. He would've acted instinctively, without regard for his personal safety, his duties and obligations as automatic as the act of drawing breath. Instead, Billy held his fire. There were stories, dozens for every incident, cautionary tales repeated to the living to help them survive: of fleeing women dumping grenades minus their pins into the hands offering to help them; of children exploding in the arms carrying them to safety. Safety? In Vietnam, safety was a concept with little application. Nowhere was safe, nothing was safe and no one was safe.

Billy watched the woman running towards him, saw her throw up her arms and fall. He listened for the report from the gun that had felled her, heard none, saw her get back up on her feet and run after her kids. The remains of the village ripped apart under the weight of ordnance. The woman fell once more, toppled by the blast, rose and resumed running. Billy held fire, the only act of compassion left to him. Other shapes emerged from the rain behind her but he wasn't interested in them. His sights were trained on the woman, on the saturated clothes clinging to her body in case they concealed a weapon, on her hands in case they clutched a grenade. She was within seventy metres and he still held fire; within fifty when she called out to him, when she called out his name, when she collapsed in front of him and did not get back up.

She called his name. She knew his name? How could she know his name? The rain still hammered down but the sound changed, became sharper and more metallic. She waved to him, beckoned him, helplessly, wearily, desperately. The children had gone and so had everyone else. Where had they gone? Billy held fire. A dog raced to the fallen woman, stood over her. Where had the dog, his dog, come from?

Billy rose unsteadily like a man awoken suddenly from sleep, disorientated and disconnected, his mind straddling different places and times and struggling with the shift.

'Billy!'

Linda?

He stepped down from the veranda. The rain, the sudden feel and weight of it, dragged him into the here and now, washing away the fog clouding his brain and dispatching memories to their hiding place like fleeing dreams. The woman began to rise to her knees, one arm pushing down on a stick, the other held out imploring. Linda? He started running. Linda.

By the time he reached her, she'd collapsed back onto her heels, sobbing. She held her arms out to him and, even through the pouring rain, her tears were plain to see. She was light in his arms when he picked her up and carried her back to the house, where he laid her down on his bed on the veranda. It didn't matter that she was soaking wet and covered in mud. What mattered was her obvious distress, exhaustion and uncontrollable shaking. He noticed her shoes were missing and there was blood mixed in with the mud on her feet. She was crying like a child.

'Shhhh. It's okay. You're okay.' He stroked her forehead. 'I'll get you a blanket.'

Billy raced indoors, went straight to the bathroom and began running a bath, grabbed a blanket from the storage cupboard, paused to put the kettle on the stove and finally returned to Linda. He found her lying on her side with her knees pulled tightly into her chest, threw the blanket over her and tucked her in. The kelpie sat guiltily by the side of the bed level with Linda's head. It knew its place and it definitely wasn't on the veranda but under it. It flattened its ears in expectation of a reprimand but Billy ignored it.

'Why didn't you come ... why didn't you ... when you first saw me?'

'Shhhh.'

'Why?'

'Shhhh.' He sat on the bed, took her hand and began stroking it. 'The kettle's on and the bath's filling.'

'Why, Billy? Why did you ignore me?'

He leaned over and kissed her forehead. It worried him that she'd got so close to the house before he'd noticed her and he tried to work out why. He knew he'd had one of his white-outs, when his mind emptied, but there'd been something else, something when he was emerging from his white-out, something elusive and distracting. Something ... exhumed. When the kettle whistled he retreated to the kitchen and poured the water into the teapot. Something had happened but for the life of him he couldn't nail down what it was. While the tea was drawing, he carried Linda into the bathroom, gently lowered her feet to the floor and helped her stand.

'I'll go fetch your tea.'

'Billy ...'

'What?'

'You'll have to help me undress.'

He hesitated.

'For God's sake, Billy. I can't do it myself.'

Billy undressed her while she leaned against him for support, picked her up again and lowered her into the bath.

'Oh!'

'Too hot?'

'No. It's just my feet.'

'I've got some Radox.'

Linda sank back into the bath, rested her head on the enamel rim and closed her eyes. Billy pulled the packet of bath salts from the bathroom cupboard and realised immediately that he should have added the crystals while the tap was still running. He glanced up at Linda for guidance, saw that her eyes were closed and also saw that she'd left him no choice but to stir the crystals in by hand. He did it bit by bit, trying hard not to touch or disturb her. When he'd finished, he gathered up her clothes and tiptoed away to the laundry where he immediately began soaking them in NapiSan. That was the only way he knew to get the red soil out of clothes. As an afterthought, he went out to the veranda and gathered up the sheets from his bed and threw them in with her clothes. When he returned to the kitchen he found the kelpie had taken up station by the door out to the veranda and sat, head cocked, watching him anxiously.

'I dunno, Bella,' said Billy. He had no lemon and was beginning to think that Linda would prefer not to be disturbed and have a cuppa after her bath. The tea was stewed anyway but not so strong that he couldn't drink it. He poured himself a mug and took it out onto the veranda, slumped into his chair and put his feet up on the rail. He thought he'd got everything back under control, sorted out his priorities and begun to work through the jobs on his list one at a time. One at a time, just like the doctor ordered. His tea had a bitter aftertaste despite the spoonful of sugar. Something had been going on inside his head when Linda had appeared and it troubled him that he couldn't remember what. Maybe he needed more time out, or maybe the time out was the problem. He felt the kelpie nuzzle into his hand and rubbed its ears. 'I dunno, Bella,' he repeated. 'I just dunno.'

The kelpie looked up at him helplessly. It didn't know either.

Billy made up the spare bed for Linda but she declined it. Instead she borrowed a set of his winter pyjamas and a pair of football socks and sat with him on the veranda, wrapped in a blanket.

'You did bloody well to keep the Toyota on the road as long as you did,' said Billy.

'That was the easy part,' said Linda. 'God only knows how many times I slipped over.' She sipped her tea. 'You saw how many times I fell over just out here.'

Billy looked away.

'I guess it didn't help that I lost my shoes.' She reached across and put her hand on his arm. 'Once again you've had to rescue me. I feel so useless and pathetic.'

'You didn't know,' said Billy. 'It's my fault for not telling you. No one moves around here until the rain stops and the sun's had a chance to dry the roads. Everyone's been caught at some time and learned the hard way. You just have to pull over and wait it out.'

The previous evening a pair of rainbirds, channel-billed cuckoos, had swooped low across the trail in front of his ute. He'd thought nothing of it until he noticed the black cockatoos settle on the old-man ironbark, an event which only days earlier had seemed as unlikely as snow falling.Their appearance was just what he needed to give his spirits a lift. Now when he concentrated he could hear them negotiating between themselves way over by their favourite roost. He looked for them, but they'd obviously decided to take cover from another shower heading in from the southwest. He made a quick appraisal of the soil around the homestead. The rain had deepened the colour, made it less orange and more a rusty red, but it was too soon to count on any benefit. It all depended on how much more rain they got over what period and how deep it penetrated. He looked at the rain pooling in tyre tracks and figured they'd had enough to bring the weeds on but still needed a bit more to give the Mitchell grass a kick-along. Nevertheless, things were looking up. The cockatoos had not only brought rain, they'd brought Linda.

'I may not be a burden on you much longer.'

'What do you mean?' Billy sat upright, alarmed. Her comment had caught him completely off guard.

'I know for sure Grant has my phone number. It was listed on my sister's phone account. That was what he was after all along.'

'The shire's a big place. He still has to find you.'

'My number was listed under J Downs in the teledex. If he makes the connection — and he will — that kind of narrows down the field.'

'No one knows you're here, Linda. If you can hide from the locals, you can hide from anyone.'

'That's the reason I'm here and not sitting out the rain in the Toyota.'

'Have you made up your mind?'

'No, just thinking out loud.'

Billy settled back thoughtfully into his chair.

'What are we going to do about the Toyota?' asked Linda.

'Nothing. Not until the rain stops.'

'What if someone sees it?'

'Who? You won't get anyone out on that road for another two days at least.'

'How am I going to get home?'

Billy shrugged and rocked back on his chair.

'I suppose you could try taking the mare.'

'Uh-uh.' She tried to play as deadpan as Billy but was unable to contain a smile. Nothing was less likely and both of them knew it. Their conversation had swung to a much more agreeable subject and she had no doubt where it would lead.

'I guess you'll just have to stay here with me.'

'Is that why you made up the spare bed?'

'It's yours if you want it.'

'What if I don't?'

Billy ran a rollie across his tongue, sealed it, cupped his hands and lit it. He drew hard so that the tip glowed, then exhaled.

'You can always share mine.'

'Maybe.'

'Only maybe?'

'I might need persuading.'

'Go on.'

'I don't need a dozen roses, but you could cut me six. The red ones not the yellow ones.'

'No problem.'

'And I will definitely require dinner. Nothing less than a baked whole snapper and an entrée of calamari will do.'

Billy closed his eyes and let his head slump forward so that his chin rested on his chest. He knew what was coming next.

'They're in an esky in the back of the Toyota. Do you mind?'

Billy glanced up at the threatening sky, looking for an encouraging sign, but found none. The shower was almost upon them. Maybe it would blow over by the time he'd saddled up the mare and dug out his Drizabone, but if he ducked one shower another was sure to find him. The mare had handled similar conditions before and he figured she would do so again, though they'd both need to keep their wits about them. He stubbed out his rollie and rose slowly to his feet. Fourteen k's on horseback in the wet, seven of them with an esky plus whatever vegetables needed saving on his lap, but what choice did he have? He bent over Linda's upturned face and kissed her on the lips. It was meant to be a parting kiss but she made sure it was much more than that.

'You're lucky I like seafood,' he said eventually.

Billy insisted they have dinner out on the veranda, which Linda found strange given the strength of the wind gusts and the almost constant rain. Even in the lee on the southern side eddies still found them and there was an inescapable dampness to the air. Yet Billy would not be deterred. They ate by the flickering light of an old oil lamp, a relic from the pre-war, pre-mains electricity days when the generator was turned off at night, and to the music of rain on the tin roof and wind in the trees. Linda was still wearing Billy's pyjamas and socks, a turn-off for any man in any other circumstances, but it didn't seem to matter. In its own odd way, the evening was as romantic as any she'd experienced. But later, when she heard him wheeling his bed around to the eastern side, she decided it was time to put her foot down. She'd noticed that there was a perfectly good double bed in the master bedroom and had assumed that would be where they slept. The idea of squeezing together on Billy's four-footer out on the veranda, exposed to the elements and the magnitude of the outback, held no appeal. She found sheets in the bottom drawer of the tallboy and made up the bed. She'd just spread the cover over the top when Billy appeared in the doorway.

'What are you doing?' he said. 'I've already made the bed up outside.'

'Love nests have walls, Billy. They're supposed to be intimate and cosy.'

'I always sleep outside.'

Linda decided to put an end to any chance of the debate developing. She slipped off her socks, pyjama jacket and pants and climbed naked into bed.

'Your call.'

Billy hesitated.

'Is it okay if I open the window?'

'Of course.'

To Linda's surprise he lifted the sash window as high it would go, causing the lace curtains to billow inwards and dance like hyperactive ghosts. When he pushed the bedroom door back hard against the wall and jammed it there with a doorstop the significance of what he was doing slowly dawned on her. Here was a man who slept on the veranda, ate on the veranda and, when he'd visited her for dinner, insisted they sit outside even though the evening was barely warm enough.

'How long have you been claustrophobic?' she asked.

'I didn't know I was.' Billy seemed genuinely surprised by her question. He turned off the room light and undressed by Linda's bedside lamp. When he went to switch it off, she stopped him. He stood there awkwardly, acutely aware that his genitals were at the same level as her eyes and exposed in the full glow of the lamp.

'Now that we've both seen all there is to see,' she said, 'what have we got to hide? Leave the lamp on.'

It had been a long time since Linda had shared her bed with anyone, but for Billy it had clearly been longer. For both their sakes she decided to take control. She patiently kissed away his awkwardness and hesitancy and slowly brought him to the point where he reacted both instinctively and appropriately. During her days with Grant there'd been times when she'd fantasised about having a lover who adopted her agenda, allowed her to play the dominant role, willingly and patiently following her guidance, surrendering his needs to hers, giving rather than taking. Billy became that lover.

They made love twice more, still exploring, still discovering, before finally giving in to sleep. Linda closed her eyes knowing that the depth of her contentment went far beyond the pleasure of their lovemaking. She felt safe and secure with him, revelled in his steadfastness and solidity, and wanted to be part of him, to hold fast to him like an oyster to a rock, impervious to wave, storm and everything else thrown at them.

At some point she awakened and in her half-sleep reached for him to snuggle up to and enjoy the pleasure and comfort of having him alongside her. She reached for his waist, expecting a warm softness, but encountered his knees instead. She forced her eyes open but the darkness yielded nothing. Her hand traced along his thigh to his waist and she realised he was sitting up.

'What's wrong?'

'Nothing. Just thinking.'

'What are you thinking?' Linda propped herself up on her elbow. Even though he was only centimetres away she still couldn't see him.

'I was thinking about your ex-husband. I think it would be safer if you moved in with me.'

'Just safer?'

'No, not just safer.'

Linda reached up and kissed him.

'I can't think of anything I'd like more. I think I'm falling in love with you, Billy Dwyer.'

Billy liked the way she sometimes called him by his full name.

'So you'll move in?'

Linda's heart screamed yes but her brain urged caution. There were bridges to cross, hazards to negotiate. She couldn't help wishing that she'd stayed asleep so they could have this conversation at another time. More than anything she wanted the night to end as it had begun, with lovemaking, tenderness and time out from reality.

'Can we talk about this in the morning?'

'Why not now?'

'Because I'm scared, Billy. Scared of what Grant might do to me. Scared of what he might do to you if you get too close. Scared of what he might do to us.'

'I'll take care of you, Linda. I won't let him do anything to either of us.'

Linda shivered, even though the night was warm despite the rain.

'Just hold me, Billy. Please? Just hold me.'

* * *

Neil relaxed back into his chair. He didn't need to try and catch Gancio's eye because he was certain the restaurateur would have been awaiting his cue. A sudden hissing from the espresso machine provided confirmation.

'The situation with Linda is interesting,' said Milos.

'Thank God for that,' said Neil. 'Now I can sleep tonight.'

'Let me finish. The situation with her is interesting because it raises a question about menace, no?'

'If you say so.'

'There is a parallel with my story in how we tried to get on with our lives back in Hungary at the beginning of the war despite the shadow the Nazis cast over our futures. I understand well how Linda must feel. We did our best to put the menace out of our minds, but it was always there and it didn't take much to bring it to the fore. There was an inexorability about the threat, just as there is for Linda, no? It is interesting to speculate whether the menace to us of the Nazis and Eichmann was more terrifying than the menace of just this one man to Linda.'

'If you are in fear of your life, I personally don't think it matters whether the threat comes from an army or an individual. The intended victim's fear is the same.' Ramon turned to Lucio. 'What do you think?'

'I think you're getting ahead of the story. Neil has been careful not to tell us exactly what Linda did to Grant or what form his revenge might take. I suspect Linda is not quite who she appears to be.'

'Really?' said Milos. 'Care to enlighten us?'

'Sure, why not? But first let Gancio serve our coffee. Neil, you can correct me if I'm wrong.'

'Don't count on it,' said Neil. 'I'm not playing your games. You can speculate as much as you like. It changes nothing.'

The shadow Milos had spoken about seemed to find Neil and settle there, a reminder that soon the story would take a twist and Neil would not emerge from it with honour. Lucio and Milos exchanged glances, as though accepting a collective responsibility to keep him from reverting to the bitterness that had marred their first lunch. There was his awful admission to consider, though they couldn't begin to guess how it fitted in with the story he'd told so far. The moment Gancio finished serving the coffees and grappa, Lucio continued.

'What do we know about Linda? I tell you what I think. I think she is precisely the kind of woman I would like to go to bed with.'

'Great. That narrows her down to ninety-eight per cent of the adult female population,' said Neil sarcastically.

'Maybe the top ten per cent, even five per cent. Why not? She is beautiful, confident, intelligent and sexually accomplished. You have told us that. To my mind, that makes her extremely desirable but, maybe, also extremely ambitious. Is she also calculating and ruthless? If she is, consider the weapons at her disposal: her intelligence and her sexuality. She says she was a humble schoolteacher teaching art, but now we learn that she has a successful film production company making television commercials. Quite a jump for an art teacher, wouldn't you say? How did that happen? Neil has suggested that she stole the company from her husband but didn't elaborate. Think about that. It was her testimony that sent him to gaol, yet he has consistently protested his innocence.

What if he was innocent? If he was innocent, look to see who stood to benefit. Perhaps her ex-husband has good reason to want revenge, which raises the question of what form his revenge will take. We fear violence, but maybe he simply wants back what he considers is rightfully his.'

'You're forgetting he killed a woman,' said Ramon.

'He claims it was an accident.'

'He had a history of violence.'

'According to his wife.'

'No. According to the judge, Lucio, according to the judge. Everything Neil has said about this man tells me he is violent: selfish, egotistical and violent. And my knowledge of domestic violence cases, limited though it is, also tells me that the perpetrators rarely accept their guilt. It is a well-known characteristic that they consider themselves the victim. Of course this man Grant would protest his innocence. He is just conforming to type.'

'I disagree,' said Lucio. 'What do you think, Milos?'

'I'm sorry, Lucio, I agree with Ramon. I think Grant is a violent man and after more than financial compensation, although that may well be part of it. As for Linda's testimony being the reason he was sent to gaol and the accusation that she stole his company, that is only Grant's perspective on events, the perspective of someone who considers himself the victim.'

'Well, Neil, are you going to tell us who is right?'

'You'll have plenty of opportunity to work that out for yourselves. But tell me, Lucio, you prefaced your remarks by saying Linda is the type of woman you'd like to take to bed. Given your suspicions about her, do you still feel the same?'

'I admit I would think twice about it.'

'Yes, but would you let her into your bed?'

'Of course! What kind of a man do you think I am?'

The friends were relieved when a smile spread across Neil's face.

Chapter Sixteen

If Grant had ever thought he could pick up where he'd left off six years earlier, reality soon proved otherwise. He struggled to win work. Some producers and creative teams wouldn't even consider him because of his past, while others invited him to quote out of morbid curiosity. They were more interested in his time inside gaol than in his ideas and had no intention of using him. He did one job, an uninspiring thirty-second spot given to him by a writer who thought he owed Grant from the old days, but the truth was, he was getting nowhere. For six years he'd thought of nothing but exacting revenge; instead, he found himself constrained by his obligations to his parole officer and the necessity to rebuild his life. His bitterness grew with each passing day and each missed opportunity, particularly when he lost out to Film Gate, his old company, now owned and run by his ex-wife.

His latest loss had hurt most. He'd worked hard on the writer, who he'd quickly figured out was the decision-maker, and had been sure he'd done enough to win the job. He'd been devastated to learn otherwise. Grant was in The Escape, kicking on from a long boozy lunch with old mates in the industry and bemoaning the passing of the good old days, when he spotted the writer and his art director mate wandering up to the bar for a drink. He couldn't let things be and got up from his table to intercept them.

The Escape was one of the advertising and film production watering holes. More sorrows had been drowned there than successes celebrated. He was aware that he'd had too much to drink and that he was in danger of letting the booze do the talking, but the creative team represented everything that was wrong with the business. He resented their cockiness, their assumption of infallibility and their hyped-up opinion of their meagre talents. But mostly he resented the fact that they had the power to make or break him.

'So why didn't we get the job?' he demanded.

The writer and art director exchanged looks, which only irritated Grant more. They were just kids, barely half his age, and didn't know shit from shine. But they were also his clients, at least potential clients, and he needed them more than they needed him. An editor, one of Grant's drinking mates, saw the impending confrontation and called out to him.

'Give it a miss, mate. It's your shout.'

Grant ignored him. All his training and experience told him to move on, to laugh off the confrontation and shout the creative team a drink in exchange for a promise to keep him in mind next time they had a commercial to shoot. Instead he stepped between them and the bar so they couldn't avoid him.

'You haven't answered my question.' Grant's voice sounded thick and ugly even to his own ears.

'You win some, lose some,' said the writer. He was as tall and as solidly built as Grant and not intimidated.

'You win some, lose some,' mimicked Grant. 'Thanks for the scoop, but that still doesn't answer the question. You know how much effort I put into the quote. I made sure it was right on the money.'

'If it was just down to money you would've got the job,' said the writer. 'We gave it to Film Gate because they came up with better ideas for the execution.'

Grant drew a deep breath but the red film was descending. Film Gate. Once again his ex-wife was turning the screws. He wondered if the two upstarts in front of him even realised he'd founded Film Gate and made it the hottest shop in town before they were out of short pants.

'Better ideas, eh?' Grant knew he'd gone too far but was powerless to stop. He'd survived gaol, been locked up with hard men who'd smash his face in over a baked-bean sandwich, seen men stabbed to death with the sharpened handle of a toilet brush and watched men get kicked to a pulp just for using the phone out of turn. Now he was supposed to lie down and cop it sweet while two jumped-up, baby-faced twats with peach fuzz on their faces shat all over him. He was dimly aware of his friends calling to him but it was too late. Someone had to pay for his humiliation. Someone had to pay for the fact that he was getting nowhere. And someone had to pay for the fact that, somewhere, his ex-wife was laughing at him. He moved in closer to the writer till their eyes were just centimetres apart.

'And, of course, you'd be the judge of that.'

'In the end it comes down to the best response,' said the writer. 'Yours was thorough but predictable. We wanted something edgier. Now, if you don't mind, I want to order a drink.'

There it was, the suggestion that he was past it, a has-been. It was the final straw. Grant's fists clenched, but just as he was about to start swinging he felt someone grab his arms. It was Cameron. Grant had no idea where he'd come from and in that instant his anger was swallowed by guilt.

'Hi,' said Cameron to the creative team. 'I heard we came a close second. What are you drinking?' He subtly let go of Grant's arms.

'Vodka tonic,' said the writer.

'Same,' said the art director.

Cameron passed the order on to the barman and turned to Grant with a wry smile. 'Now what the fuck's all this about?' He took a pack of cigarettes out of his shirt pocket and offered it around. 'For the last four weeks Grant's been a scratched record about how much he liked working with you guys and how much he liked the spot. Christ Almighty.' He handed the creative team their drinks. 'Grant doesn't give compliments very often but he reckons you guys are among the few who still have the brains to come up with original ideas. You don't get higher praise than that.' He passed a beer to Grant. 'I thought you guys were best mates.'

The writer just shrugged.

'Grant?' said Cameron.

'I was out of line. It's a great script and I was really looking forward to doing it. Sorry, guys. No hard feelings?'

'No worries,' said the writer. He took Grant's hand.

'No worries,' said the art director.

No worries, thought Grant. He kept the smile on his face but he knew, come morning, he'd have to face another of Cameron's lectures, another galling dressing-down from his one-time employee and trainee. The worst part was, he knew he deserved it. Sometimes life outside was more humiliating than it had been inside.

'Don't say anything,' said Grant as he walked into Cameron's office. He'd decided to go in early and face the music rather than await the summons. 'I know how stupid I was, how unprofessional, et cetera, et cetera. You can save your breath.' He helped himself to a coffee from Cameron's machine.

'We're quoting on two other jobs from the same agency,' said Cameron. 'Did you know that? I reckon we're a sure thing with one and a bloody good chance with the other. How do you think we'd go if you'd planted one on that deadshit's face?'

Grant's shoulders slumped.

'I didn't know.'

'We need at least one of those jobs. The business needs at least one of those jobs. Have you any idea how hard I've had to work just to get our foot in the door?'

'Guess it's lucky you came in when you did.' Grant sat down heavily in the chair opposite Cameron.

'Luck had nothing to do with it. One of your drinking mates rang me.'

Grant thought back hard to the night before. He remembered looking over towards his table when the editor had called out to him and occasionally glancing in their direction. He didn't recall anyone getting up to use the phone. His blood turned cold.

'You've got someone watching me?'

'Let's just say it was one of my mates, not one of yours, who rang me.'

'Fuck you, Cameron!'

'We have a strike rate of one in four. That's all jobs, not just good jobs. We're taking pissant jobs just to pay the rent. Your strike rate is one in eight — no, make that one in nine.'

'What do you want me to do? Rack my cue? Go somewhere else?'

'No. What I want is for you to get rid of the chip on your shoulder and try to get used to the idea that the world doesn't owe you a living and the industry doesn't give a shit what you once were. Times have changed and you have to change with them or you won't make it. It won't be a question of me pissing you off, because the industry will do that for me. What have you got on?'

'A re-stripe. We're putting down a new voice-over.'

'Anything else?'

'I'm taking my reel in to FMH. They've asked me to go third quote on a job. They're pretty straight. If I do the right thing by them they'll give me a job down the track.'

'Good.' Cameron picked up a manila folder and tossed it to Grant. 'I want you to have a go at this.'

'What is it?'

'A series of three commercials for Garuda. Three sixties with thirty-second cut-downs. The thirties will get most of the air time so make sure you get a good handle on them. They'll be used in Australia and internationally.'

'You're giving them to me?'

'I recommended you to the agency. I sold them on your ability to handle big jobs and some of the guys have been around long enough to remember your old stuff. I told them I'd also put Marty on the job as second director.'

'I don't need a second director.'

'There are special effects and Marty's way ahead of you on what video can do. He came out of video clips, for Christ's sake, and where video's concerned he's the flavour of the month. I reckon it'll do him good to work with you, and you can learn a bit from him. You can choose your own producer so long as it isn't me. I haven't got the time to get on planes.'

'Planes?'

'You'll have to go up to Indonesia to shoot some sequences. You can travel, can't you?'

'I'll have to clear it with my parole officer but I'm sure it'll be okay.'

'Then it's settled.'

'Why are you doing this, Cameron? I fucked up last night. Fucked up big-time. This job's not going to give any change out of a million dollars.'

'More like a million and a half. Why? I'll tell you why. Because big, complex jobs are what you used to do, what you built your reputation on. They're your specialty and exactly the sort of contemporary big-budget spots you need on your reel. You're the best man for the job and the business desperately needs it. I need it and you need it. It's piss-or-get-off-the-potty time, Grant. I won't settle for another close second, understand? Understand what I'm saying?'

'Produce or piss off,' said Grant. 'I guess that's fair enough.' He looked down at the folder in his hands. 'Thanks for keeping the faith.'

He rose and strode to his office, dropped the folder on his desk and sat staring at it. Produce or piss off. Reclaim the high ground or tumble into the abyss. There were no more ropes to steady him if he stumbled or nets to catch him if he fell. His career hung in the balance, but Cameron had been dead right in saying this was exactly the kind of job he was good at. This was the kind of job he'd made his name on and built his business on. Built *his* business. He savoured the bitterness and anger long enough to harden his resolve. He picked up the folder and opened it.

'No worries,' he said to confirm his feelings. 'No whucking furries.'

He pressed the Play button on his tape deck. Louis Armstrong sang, 'What a Wonderful World'.

Chapter Seventeen

Billy's opal bought back almost half the number of sheep that they'd sold, even after his father had surprised the bank with a few placatory pounds and cleared their credit at the general store. The beasts they bought were in a sorry state and the price they paid for them reflected it. Their neighbours thought they were mad. Over the next few days the boys helped their father dole out the last of their feed while their sisters sulked and their mother fretted. More than any of them, she'd opposed the purchase of the sheep. As far as she was concerned, the opal had been a godsend, offering sustenance and hope, providing the means to ease their plight and carry them through till the rains came. It broke her heart to think that what might have been was wasting away and dying out in the paddocks. She blamed her husband for his weakness in taking advice from a twelve-year-old boy but mostly she blamed Neil for interfering. Such matters were not for children. What distressed her even more was her husband's gradual acceptance that listening to Neil had been a mistake. She sensed his shame.

Then, late one afternoon, she heard the black cockatoos and, biting her bottom lip unless she again dared to hope, watched them settle way out on the old ironbark. She noticed Braden had been drawn out of the work shed by their call and stood staring up at the sky. The clouds had been building all day, but they'd done that off and on for months, promising rain but failing to deliver. The sky looked the same as it had on so many previous occasions, grey and sullen, lacking the green tinge of an impending storm. But the cockies, which had been absent for so long, were insistent in their protestations that rain would come. The family went to bed that night cautiously optimistic but privately suspecting that the black cockatoos had got it wrong. At around three in the morning the pitter-patter on their iron roof announced that the cockies had delivered. The rains came in a perfect soaking drizzle that hung around for ten days, putting life back into the soil, vindicating the risk they'd taken and making a hero of Neil.

That was the funny thing. Billy had found the opal which had made their gamble possible, but it was Neil who bathed in glory. The family fortunes were on the rise again, just like the weeds breaking through the parched soil as the land awakened. The native grasses followed close behind, sprouting with vigour and volume, eager to compete. Showers followed the initial deluge at perfect intervals, as though God had decided graziers deserved a reward for their endurance. Braden claimed he could hear the wool growing on the sheeps' backs. Neil was given credit for all of it.

With Japan and Europe both greedy for wool, the promise of fat wool cheques and surplus cash was in the air. Banks offered to extend overdrafts and stores had no problem extending credit. Payday was coming at last and everyone manoeuvred for a share. Neil and his mother clashed again when he spoke out against extending their loan, arguing that they already owed the bank more than they could afford and that their existing debts were a millstone that prevented them ever getting ahead. He did the sums that proved his argument. His mother pointed to the girls' threadbare clothes, the sheets she could spit peas through and the bald patches on the towels but knew her pleas were wasted. Neil was the hero and had runs on the board. He could do no wrong.

Braden borrowed just enough money to pay the shearers, while the boys and their sisters skipped school to do the work they normally paid jackaroos to do. Their mother cooked the shearers' meals and reined in her impatience. The hard work, the making do and the deprivation had pushed her to the end of her tether. But all her trials were forgotten when the wool cheque arrived.

Braden took the family down to Dubbo and gave his wife and daughters freedom to shop. Thriftiness was ingrained in them so he hadn't the slightest concern that they'd waste money on trifles and luxuries. As far as the Dwyer womenfolk were concerned, necessities were luxuries. When the boys weren't watching movies, Braden knew he could find them in the main street with their noses pressed up against the shop windows taking their first look at television. Having a movie show in their lounge room was an almost unimaginable luxury, and they wondered if the day would ever come when they'd have a television set of their own.

When they got home, Braden sat down with Neil to draw up a budget. He'd convinced himself that Neil had a nose for the land and decided to start preparing him for the day when he'd take over the running of the spread. He paid off all the interest owed to the bank and a little of the principal, forgetting that this had been Neil's original suggestion. He settled his debts with suppliers and set aside a portion to replace and repair machinery, gates and fences. When they'd finished their sums there was hardly any money left, certainly not enough to make any noticeable change to the family's circumstances, but enough to see them through winter, when they could sell some lambs for meat, and for Braden to show a little magnanimity towards his two sons.

Neil and Billy never minded that their sisters did better than them when largesse was being dispensed. Girls needed make-up, nail polish, shampoos, smart shoes and fancy clothes, things that didn't interest them. If the boys were given the choice between a new pair of pants or a new football, they'd happily play in their underwear. They had no expectation of any reward for their help in mustering, shearing, drenching, plunge dipping, marking or repairing fences. Their help was just part and parcel of life on the land, which, if things went well, won them a trip down the highway to Dubbo. So when their father walked in with a rifle and a box of cartridges just as they'd sat down to dinner, they were stunned speechless.

'Here you go, boys,' Braden said. 'I think you've earned it.'

He laid the rifle on the sideboard and sat down at the table as though it was nothing out of the ordinary. The boys' eyes bulged out of their heads. It wasn't a birthday, Christmas or anything. They struggled to comprehend the magnitude and suddenness of the gift and wanted to rush over to check it out. But some things were sacred in the Dwyer household and mealtimes were among them. Protocol insisted they finish their dinner and ask permission before they left the table, a fact their father was well aware of and deliberately exploiting.

'It's a .22,' said Neil in awe, when he could finally speak.

'That's right,' said Braden.

The boys had been holding out for an air rifle for the past three years, hoping as every birthday dawned that the day would bring one. Never in their most febrile dreams had they dared hope for a .22.

'It's a Winchester!' said Billy.

'Right again,' said Braden.

'Where'd you get it?' asked Neil.

'I got it off the Crowleys. Their boy Sam's gone to join his brother down in Sydney. They don't have a use for it. They threw in the box of shells which I thought was good of them.'

'I can't believe it,' said Billy. 'I can't believe we've got a .22.'

'It's for both of you,' said Braden. 'But for safety's sake, I'm putting Neil in charge of it, okay?'

'You can put me in charge of it,' said Neil. 'But I think it should be Billy's. It's only right. He deserves it for finding the opal.'

Billy's jaw dropped and he held his head in his hands as he tried to come to terms with everything that was happening. He thought he'd died and gone to heaven just at the prospect of sharing the Winchester. Owning it and having the right to say 'my rifle' and to oil and clean it was almost too much to take in.

'Do you mean it?' he asked, dazed.

'Of course,' said Neil. 'You deserve it.'

'Yes!' Billy threw his arms in the air with sheer joy, his face radiant. He couldn't imagine any kid having a better father or brother.

'That's very generous of you, Neil,' said Millie, her pride evident, and it was also clear she was speaking for the entire family.

Neil's apparent thoughtfulness and kindness made them all feel good and, once again, he managed to appropriate the limelight even though it was his father who deserved it. What they all overlooked was that Neil's gesture in no way diminished his control over the rifle or his access to it. It simply didn't occur to anyone at the time and, even if it had, it would have seemed churlish and petty to remark upon it. It was only later, much later, that Billy realised how manipulative Neil was.

By then it was too late.

The following twelve months were as good as it ever got in the far northwest, helped by regular rain and buoyant wool prices. Graziers in the lush pastures further east tripped over each other in their scramble to buy new cars, tractors and equipment. Those out west picked up their discards for a song. It would have been easy for Braden to sit back and enjoy the good times. His ewes had reacted to the ready availability of quality feed with the best lambing season he'd ever known. The numbers of lambs were up and the losses were down. It never ceased to astonish him how bountiful his normally desperate land could be when the rains were reliable. The wool clip increased to the point where he could start making inroads into his overdraft and still have a bit left over.

The change in the weather pattern blinded them to other changes that were taking place. When Glory finished year eleven, she left both school and home to train as a nurse in Dubbo General Hospital. No one realised it at the time but she was the trailblazer, setting a precedent for the others to follow. Neil began to shoot up as though he, too, had been dependent on the rains. He seemed to get out of bed an inch taller than he'd got into it the night before. His voice alternated uncontrollably between soprano and baritone before settling on a pleasant tenor. His shoulders bulked up and his muscles acquired enviable definition. His size added authority to his ideas and his influence on Braden grew accordingly.

Neil's ideas didn't hail from sudden blinding flashes of inspiration or any intuitive understanding of the land. He'd grown up with radio but now he listened to it for news, weather and comment on regional matters instead of just to hear his favourite serials or the latest songs from Slim Dusty or Elvis Presley. Most days he managed to find or scrounge a copy of the local rag, *The Spectator*, or a day-old copy of the *Sydney Morning Herald* and read it on the school bus going home. Coincidentally his schoolwork, which had never been a priority, began to show marked improvement and more accurately reflect his intelligence.

He continued to cultivate friendships and contacts among elders in the Aboriginal community and showed respect for their knowledge when not too many in the white community were prepared to show them any respect at all. Alcoholism and violence were rife among the blacks, but not all blacks were alcoholic or violent. Neil chose his contacts carefully and listened and learned from them. He also listened on the occasions when his family visited others on nearby spreads and the men gathered around a few beers to discuss the business of wool-growing. In particular, Neil took keen note of their observations and speculations, learned whose opinions and comments were worth noting, tried to guess their intentions and weighed them against their natural conservatism. It intrigued him that they all promoted the advantages of being first to market, whether they were buying or selling stock or putting aside fodder, but for the most part were content to adopt a wait-and-see attitude. Neil saw opportunity in their hesitancy.

When New Zealand and Argentina stepped up their wool production, he used stories he'd clipped from the papers to persuade his father to diversify into cattle. With the wool cheque due any day, his timing was ideal. The two of them were sitting around the dinner table that had been cleared of dishes. His father was finishing a bottle of Dinner Ale and allowed him a glass. Neil could hear his mother in the kitchen, drying dishes, and knew she'd also be eavesdropping.

'All our neighbours are talking about doing it,' he argued. 'They can see the possibility of a wool glut, particularly as the use of synthetics increases. We should act while they wait to see what happens and buy some steers before they're in demand.'

'What do you propose?' asked Braden.

'Buy a mob of steers for fattening so we get some income in twelve months' time, and buy a decent bull and some heifers so we can start a breeding stock.'

'What are we going to use for money?'

'If it was up to me, I'd just pay the bank the interest that's due and put everything else into buying stock.'

'I dunno, Neil.'

'Come on, Dad. You know you're going to have to do it sooner or later. Why wait for the price of cattle to go up?'

'I don't know much about raising cattle.'

'According to Mr Crowley, they're hardier than sheep, can survive longer on scrub and are a lot less work. And look at these articles I've kept.' He pushed them in front of his father. 'The papers reckon beef prices are on the up.'

'You and your papers.'

Neil wasn't just selling his father on the idea of running cattle but on the prospect of breaking the cycle of debt, of getting ahead, of security and a level of comfort other Australians took for granted. Of course Braden listened to him. His own endeavours had barely succeeded in providing for the family in the most basic way, and his greatest achievement amounted to nothing more than not going completely broke and being forced to surrender the property to the bank. Neil's ideas raised the possibility of improvement in their circumstances and no one else had ever offered Braden that. Of course he listened. Even his mother, eavesdropping in the kitchen, began to listen and dared to dream. Neil was still only fourteen years old yet he came to embody their hopes and aspirations. Braden and Millie congratulated each other on having a son who was so bright. Neil also had other ideas, but he kept those to himself.

Other changes occurred over the following months and these were to affect Billy most. Despite their eighteen-month age difference, the brothers were inseparable, a mutually supportive partnership that seemed unshakeable and eternal. From the beginning, their relationship was integral to everything they did and, as they grew up, life for either without the other was unimaginable. Some things were just accepted. It was a given that Neil, with his advantage in age and size, would always be better than Billy at whatever they did. It was also accepted that Billy could rely on the unfailing support and encouragement of his older brother to help bridge the gap. When teams were being chosen, Neil always picked Billy ahead of older and bigger boys and Billy rewarded his brother's faith by giving his all. Neil always boasted that Billy fought a couple of divisions above his weight, and his delight when Billy pulled off a tackle against a boy twice his size or scored a try were the moments Billy lived for. He worshipped his older brother and revelled in his praise. But the eighteen-month gap in their ages when one was ten and the other twelve was easily measured in terms of ability. When Billy was twelve and Neil fourteen, however, the differences became more marked and complex. Neil moved into another age group with different priorities and desires. Billy became increasingly left behind. For a while, the .22 Winchester rifle obscured the differences as both boys enjoyed the novelty and explored the possibilities of their new acquisition. But there was another unexpected and profound change in their dynamics to take into account. Skill with the rifle was not dependent on age or size and it was immediately apparent that Billy was not only a better shot than Neil but a gifted marksman.

The boys graduated from shooting rabbits and hares to tracking and shooting feral pigs. More than anything Billy loved hunting pigs and loved it most when a boar turned on them and charged. He became hooked on the frantic rush of adrenaline, standing his ground while Rodney and Neil headed for the nearest tree, calmly releasing the safety and sighting along the barrel at the charging beast, making certain that his shot would strike between the beast's shoulders and rip through its heart. He stood his ground even as the beast's momentum carried it to within centimetres of his legs, the extent of its injury and the accuracy of his shot not apparent until its final collapse. Neil screamed abuse at him for the risks he took, but for Billy that only added to the magic. What if his shot had caught the boar's skull and deflected? What if he'd missed and only wounded it in the shoulder? Everyone knew the damage a boar could do to a man let alone a boy, but Billy only laughed at the danger. He saw the grudging respect in his brother's eyes and Rodney's open admiration. For the first time in his life, he was number one and that was the best feeling he'd ever known. Besides, he boasted, the closer the boar came the harder it was to miss.

But while the rifle was Billy's, Neil was still responsible for its use, and their father imposed rules which Neil was charged to uphold and which would result in the rifle's confiscation if flouted. The golden rule was that neither boy could take the rifle out on his own, whether to go hunting or just for target practice. It was a sensible rule, made for all the right reasons, but it was also unrealistic.

There wasn't a day when Billy didn't want to go hunting and, in the initial bloom of excitement and through the summer holidays, both Neil and Rodney were eager to accommodate him. If one couldn't make it, the other could and the golden rule was never an issue. But as time passed, things changed.

Rodney wasn't always available, and when his father thought he was onto a particularly promising dig, Rodney had to help sift through the opal dirt and wasn't available at all. That left Neil, and Billy found him increasingly unreliable and difficult to understand. In the mornings, on the bus to school, he'd make Neil promise to go hunting with him after school only to have him renege on the bus home. This infuriated Billy because the prospect of going hunting was the only thing that kept him going through the interminable, boring lessons. Even worse, Neil's reasons for not going shooting often beggared belief. How could anyone put homework ahead of shooting? And there were shameful times when Neil ignored the jeers and scorn of their mates and sat with the girls on the school bus. Billy had never felt more mortified in his life and it hurt him deeply that Neil seemed not to care. He got into fights defending his brother's reputation when other boys baited him by claiming Neil was a sissy or some girl's boyfriend. The only times Neil was like the brother he'd known all his life were when they were playing football or out hunting. Then he reverted to his committed, uncompromising self. That was the brother Billy liked and that only made him keener to go hunting together.

Things came to a head one afternoon when Neil reaffirmed his promise to go pig shooting while they waited for the bus to pick them up and take them home. Billy ignored the fact that Neil chose to share a seat with a girl called Pauline Pridle because he knew that his brother would be back to normal once they took the rifle out of the rack. He pretended not to notice when Neil held open a copy of the *Sydney Morning Herald* and Pauline leaned into him so she could read it with him. At least, that was what Billy thought they were doing, although he was darned if he knew how anybody could read fine newsprint at arm's length with the bus bouncing around. He failed utterly to appreciate that neither was the least bit interested in reading anything. Billy ignored the giggles and whispers of the other girls and the snide remarks of his mates in the back of the bus. Pauline had the best breasts of any girl in the class and they all reckoned Neil was onto a good thing. But Billy had no time for that sort of talk. Both of his sisters had grown breasts and they'd just been a matter of curiosity and no more. In fact he hadn't even been aware of that particular development until he'd bumbled into the bathroom and caught Glory half naked. Nudity had never been an issue and Billy hadn't realised that the time had passed when he and his sisters could share baths. He'd looked at his sister and her burgeoning breasts in absolute astonishment. 'Where did they come from?' he'd asked, and still smarted whenever anyone reminded him of his remark. But his naivety only served to underscore the fact that he wasn't the least bit interested in girls and, as far as he was concerned, Neil wasn't either.

When they got off the bus Neil surprised Billy and his sister by waving as it pulled away. Neil never waved goodbye. It just wasn't cool. His sister smiled knowingly and walked on ahead towards the house.

'What are you doing?' said Billy as they began to follow.

'Nothing,' said Neil, but he looked somehow guilty.

'You're an embarrassment.'

'Is that right?'

'Yeah.'

'Why?'

'You know. Why'd you sit with Pauline? The guys reckon you like her.'

'They would. Nah, she just wants me to help her with her maths. I said I'd ride over.'

'When? You can't today because you promised to come hunting.'

'Maybe we'll have to go hunting tomorrow.'

'We can't. Tomorrow's Saturday and we promised we'd help Dad paint the shed.'

'Sunday, then.'

'No! Today. You promised.'

'Yeah, well, I promised Pauline as well.'

'That's not fair! You promised me first.'

'I changed my mind.'

'You can't just change your mind. You promised. I've been looking forward to it all day.' Billy's face reddened and he clenched and unclenched his fists in anger and impotence.

'You'll just have to do something else. I promised Pauline.'

'You promised me! You promised me first!'

'Well, tough.'

The betrayal was too much for Billy. He punched Neil as hard as he could, aiming for his bicep where he knew his punch would hurt but do no lasting damage. Neil wasn't as considerate in his response. He retaliated with a solid blow to Billy's solar plexus, dropping his younger brother to the ground.

'You bastard ... you bastard ...' sobbed Billy as hot tears spilled from his eyes. 'You promised me ... you promised me!'

Neil ignored him and continued up the drive, rubbing his sore arm.

'It's true, isn't it? You just want to see her tits, that's all!' Billy let his tears run unchecked into the dry red dust where they disappeared in an instant. He couldn't believe his brother could break his promise for a girl. At least his sister was out of sight around the bend in the drive so she couldn't see him crying.

Billy waited until Neil had saddled up his stockhorse and ridden off before taking the .22 out of the gun rack and heading off to the stables himself. He saddled up his horse, Grasshopper, and waved to his mother as he passed the kitchen window, making sure he followed in Neil's tracks so she'd think they were going off somewhere together. His mother was as aware of the golden rule as he was. Once out of sight, he swung west towards the sand ridges. The funny thing was, he'd never really had any intention of trying to hunt down a pig. There was always a chance they'd come across one or two, the way they were breeding up in the good conditions, but Billy had something else on his mind. He'd seen some emus a few days earlier, when he'd ridden out to help his father tension wire in a fence he was repairing to stop his sheep wandering into the lignum swamp and becoming bogged. Billy was certain their tracks would lead him to eggs somewhere in the warrambool. The family enjoyed the occasional emu eggs and, if he ever wanted to get on the good side of his mum, all he had to do was bring a few home. They were about thirteen centimetres long, dark green in colour and had a strong, gamey flavour. Once accustomed to the taste, they became something of a treat, especially in a bacon and egg pie.

Billy had gone out looking for emu eggs on his own often enough and knew to keep a sharp lookout for the male birds, which had the job of incubating the eggs and could be fiercely protective. Whenever he found a male hanging around, he'd try to scare it off by throwing sticks and shouting. If that didn't work, he'd leave the eggs alone and try his luck the following day. Mostly he hunted eggs with either Neil or Rodney because that made things easier. If there was a bird around, one of them could distract it while the other swooped on the prize. But today he had the rifle instead of company. The .22 and the three bullets in his pocket gave him all the confidence he needed. One shot would scare off any bird and leave him a couple of bullets in case he got the chance to nail a pig. The idea of shooting a pig without dogs or anyone to help appealed to him. He'd really have something to brag about, so long as it never got back to his parents.

He checked the position of the sun above the horizon and calculated that he had about two hours of light left. Two hours wasn't much time to track down anything, but it was enough if you knew where to look and certainly long enough to gather up a few emu eggs. The big birds mostly laid around seven to ten eggs and Billy never took more than three from the same nest, partly out of consideration for the parents but mainly because three was all he ever needed. He consoled himself with the thought that emus couldn't count and, so long as there were still eggs in the nest to hatch, the birds were happy. The only time he really felt anything for emus was when he found them hanging from fences they'd tried to jump over. The birds died a horrible, slow death when they caught their toes in the top strand and hooked their heels on the second. The twist in the two wires trapped their legs so tightly there was little possibility of escape.

He startled a flock of galahs in the buffle grass, feeding on seed, and watched as they rose shrieking only to settle fifty metres away and continue feeding. Billy couldn't recall a time when there'd been so many birds. The scrub thickened around the edges of the warrambool but it was still easy going for the horse. Billy rode to the point where he'd observed the emus and dismounted, leaving Grasshopper in a bit of a clearing where it could graze if it wanted to or simply lie down. He thought briefly about tethering it but the stockhorses were well trained and knew to stay put. If it did decide to wander, he figured it wouldn't wander far and certainly not in the short time he expected to be away. He checked the sun. He still had about an hour and a quarter of light. Half an hour to find an egg and three-quarters of an hour to ride back home.

Billy put a bullet in the chamber, checked that the safety was on and began his search. Emus had left tracks everywhere so it wasn't so much a matter of following them as trying to work out where their nests were likely to be. Emus weren't especially particular about where they nested, but they did tend to favour small depressions and hollows and it was these that Billy looked for. The blacks always knew where to look and he fancied that his 'abo eyes' put him on a par with them.

Billy tensed when he spotted the pig tracks. He could tell they were recent because they overlaid the tracks of the emus. He slowed his walk and looked carefully around. There were plenty of scars where emus had gouged the ground looking for insects, but that wasn't what he was looking for. His eyes soon picked out the darker-coloured soil and the holes where a pig had been rooting under bushes. His excitement began to build. A pig and emu eggs all on his own and all in the one afternoon would be too much. It occurred to him that the pigs probably fancied a meal of emu eggs themselves, which meant the male birds would more than likely be on guard over their nests. Standing one-point-five metres tall, weighing up to fifty kilos and with big, powerful three-toed feet as weapons, the emus were intimidating opponents.

Billy spotted a male emu about forty metres away, in a slight depression just as he'd expected. Only its dark grey head was visible. The quick short movements of its head suggested that it had seen or heard something and was on the lookout. Billy was certain it was sitting on eggs and began to circle towards it using the thicker clumps of bush and thorns for cover. His plan was simple. He intended to get as close as possible before firing a bullet into a branch above the bird's head. Emus could run at fifty kilometres an hour and Billy figured the bird would get such a shock it would probably hit fifty before the report of his shot had died.

Because he was concentrating so hard on the emu he didn't pick up the snorts of the pig as soon as he should have, but he heard the lignum explode in front of him and knew before he even sighted the pig that he had only seconds to react. He brought the rifle up to his shoulder, flicked off the safety and aimed at the sound, tracking with it as the grey-black blur crashed into the clear. He stood his ground as he always did, making sure of his shot, making sure to aim between the bones of the shoulders, making sure his bullet penetrated the beast's heart. He fired, certain of his accuracy but not of the speed of his reactions. This pig didn't collapse at his feet. In fact, it barely slowed. It barrelled into his legs with the force of a runaway locomotive.

Billy was sent flying up and backwards into the base of a coolibah. The force of hitting the trunk punched the air out of his lungs and caused him to drop the rifle. He knew he was hurt but wasted no time thinking about it. Despite the pain in his legs and chest, he reached instinctively into his pocket for another bullet, snatched his rifle up off the ground and rammed the bullet into the chamber. Time was everything. Everything! Where was the pig? Where was the pig!

He found it three metres away to his side and slightly behind him, a big brute of a boar, still standing head down, scuffing the ground with a front hoof as it prepared for another charge. For a moment, astonishment vied with Billy's fear. A big boar! He hadn't been expecting such a major trophy. But why wasn't the beast dead? Why was it still standing? Billy was certain of his shot and the blood spilling down the boar's shoulders seemed to confirm his accuracy. But this pig was so much bigger than the others he'd shot and it suddenly occurred to him that maybe his .22 wasn't up to the job. Billy tried to roll over on his stomach so he could prop on his elbows and make sure of his second shot up through the beast's chest, but his legs didn't want to respond. The pig started towards him, wobbled, started again. Billy tried desperately to pivot around from the waist, tried to drag his legs into a position where he could bed the rifle into his right shoulder and aim. But his body rebelled and failed to respond. The boar charged. Billy screamed. His only chance was to shoot blind and hope his bullet struck something vital. Just as he began to squeeze the trigger the boar's front legs gave way. It pitched head first into the ground, collapsed and lay there mere centimetres from his face, kicking, frothing, squealing ... and dying.

Billy dragged himself up so he could lean against the trunk of the coolibah. Feeling was gradually coming back into his legs and with it came the worst pain he'd ever experienced. His jeans were dark with blood below the knees and he knew the pig had caught him good. Even as it had hit him he'd sensed that it had tossed its head to rip with its tusks. But how much damage had it done? He tried to stand, but abandoned the attempt immediately as a wave of pain engulfed him. He began to sob quietly, not just because of the pain and shock but because of the hopelessness of his situation. There was another golden rule he'd broken — *the* golden rule — one drummed into every outback kid from the time they could walk. *Always tell someone where you're going*.

Billy forced himself to stop sobbing and to take stock of his situation. How many times had Neil told him that the key to solving problems lay in understanding them? The trouble was, the more he understood the more frightened he became. He'd told nobody where he was going. He couldn't move and nobody even had a clue where to start looking for him. His shot had probably scared off all the other pigs in the vicinity, but he knew they'd be back. The locals hated pigs not just for the damage they did to the land, but because they didn't wait for fallen sheep or cattle to die before they started eating them. Billy was all too aware of where he stood on that score. He was bleeding, immobile and vulnerable.

What if the pigs came for him?

What if they tried to eat him alive?

Chapter Eighteen

Billy sat facing north on his veranda, his feet in their customary position up on the rail. His mug, drained of tea, sat alongside the apricot jam tin. A rollie burned slowly between his fingers. The late April sun burned off the light drizzle which had done little more than freshen up the pastures. Nevertheless, they had a good cover of grass and clover, which augured well for winter. Billy didn't have a lot on his plate. The sheep were freshly shorn and protected against flystrike and the steers were fattening nicely. The only thing concerning him was Linda.

For the past four months they'd been seeing as much of each other as circumstances permitted, but they hadn't permitted much. She'd gone away to Bali with her daughter for a month over the December-January holidays and had spent a week in Dubbo twice since then. When she was back home, often it was his work — first the mustering, then the mulesing, the paring away of the wrinkles and folds of skin around the lambs' hindquarters, and finally the shearing — that kept them apart. Billy was acutely aware that they'd see a lot more of each other if she moved in and was at a loss to understand why she hadn't. She'd admitted that she loved him and he'd admitted he loved her. That had surprised him because he couldn't remember ever telling anyone that he loved them before. He supposed he must have told his wife at some stage before she left him, but if he had he doubted that he'd really meant it. Not like he meant it with Linda. That was the thing. That was the crux. He'd meant it. She'd meant it. Yet she still resisted his invitation to move in. She was still his tenant, someone who paid him rent, and he was damned if he knew why.

He understood that she didn't want to involve him in her problems, but he was involved. How could he not be involved when he loved her? How could she possibly be safer on her own than under his protection? Off to the east, a flock of red-winged parrots settled into a stand of acacias. Their sharp, metallic contact calls were unmistakeable but for once Billy failed to notice them. He took a long drag on his rollie before butting it into his jam tin. Tea-break was over and he had work to do. Thinking about Linda was getting him nowhere.

Billy was a few days late going into Walgett for supplies, but that happened when there was shearing to be done. Nevertheless, he was out of beer and potatoes and that meant Rodney was as well. He mentally raised the trip into Walgett to the top of his list of things to do tomorrow. He wandered over to his shed where he kept his poisons. Today he had rabbits to kill and warrens to rip up, tomorrow he had Walgett and he'd kept the day after free to do all the odd jobs he'd been putting off. His life was returning to the kind of order and familiarity he was accustomed to, except for the emptiness inside him and inside his home that desperately needed filling. She rang him every night and he looked forward to her calls, but they added to rather than solved his problem. In fact, the memory of her amazing laugh followed him around like an echo. After years of nothing there was now something, a justification for persevering, but it remained tantalisingly beyond his grasp. The emptiness nagged at him incessantly. Unfortunately there were no treatments in his shed that could rid him of that.

Billy drove into Walgett without kicking up the customary comet tail. Enough moisture still held near the surface to lay the dust. He cashed Rodney's pension cheque first, bought his supplies at the supermarket and made sure Jimmy was out and Peter on duty before calling into the stock and station. Billy didn't need much and the main reason he dropped in was to find out who'd got the best of what little rain they'd had, how many centimetres and what was tipped to happen next. Peter claimed they could expect a few wet months, that the weather pattern was similar to the autumn of 1969. Billy could hardly argue. He'd spent the autumn of '69 in another country with more important things on his mind.

He wandered over to the RSL for a pie and a beer and a chat with anyone else who'd come into town. There was always someone and this day was no exception. He was enjoying a friendly conversation with some cockies who had properties near Collarenebri when Jimmy strolled into the bar. He spotted Billy almost immediately and ambled over with a smirk on his face.

'G'day, boys,' said Jimmy.

Billy responded and managed not to show his irritation.

'Seems I owe you an apology,' said Jimmy.

'Oh, yeah?' said Billy. 'What have you done?'

'Me? Nothing. I've done nothing. It's that city sheila I sent you.'

'City sheila?' said Billy. 'Oh, yeah. I guess you mean the one I've got set up in a love nest.'

'Yeah, sorry about that. Seems I got it wrong.'

'Only took you eight months to figure that out.'

'Anyhow, I saw her down in Dubbo a couple of weeks back. She was in the Country Club looking a million dollars, getting cosy with some city guy. He was pouring wine into her like he was on a promise.' He slapped Billy on the back. 'Bad luck, mate, but you can't say I didn't try my best for you.'

* * *

Just like Vietnam, thought Billy, you never hear the bullet coming that gets you. The kelpie sat alongside him on the passenger seat, ears flat, sensing his mood. It had taken all of Billy's self-control not to react when Jimmy had dropped his bombshell. He'd laughed. Ordered another round. Carried on like he'd carried on in Vietnam when all he wanted to do was scream and hide. He'd kept his emotions under tight control as he'd made his farewells, bought his slabs of beer and thrown them on the back of the ute. By the time he'd turned the ute around he no longer felt sickened to the point of despair and numbness had replaced shock. The hollowness inside him expanded into a void that knew no boundaries. He'd felt that way one other time, when he heard 'Motsa' had been killed in an ambush. Some of his mates claimed the sadness was always tinged with relief that someone else had copped it and not them. His emptiness then had been coupled with an overwhelming sense of disbelief, as though there'd been a mistake. Costa didn't take risks. He was a backup man. He never went up the pointy end. Costa had borrowed ten bucks off him that morning to settle a debt and reckoned he was going to pay him back that night. He thought he still had a future.

An acquaintance in a Toyota ute waved to Billy as he sped past towards Walgett. Billy's wave in response brought him back to the present. He dared to recall what Jimmy had said to him and felt a wave of the same disbelief wash through him. He couldn't reconcile the stock and station agent's words with what he knew about Linda, what she said to him when they lay together in bed, what she said to him over the phone every night they were apart, how she felt about him and how he felt about her. If he had to choose to believe one over the other, Jimmy wouldn't get a look-in. But why would Jimmy make up a story like that? What did he have to gain? Why would he bother when it could only put him in a situation of having to apologise? Nothing made sense. He consoled himself with the fact that Jimmy was a lowlife who liked dragging everybody down to his own level and whose observations were tainted and unreliable. So what if Linda had seen somebody down in Dubbo? There could be any number of explanations. Maybe she had other things to do there, things which required her to go for five days and which were none of his business. He was aware there were gaps in his knowledge of her, just as there were gaps in her knowledge of him. Billy did his best to be dismissive of Jimmy but his speculations led inexorably to the issue he found most difficult to deal with: why hadn't she agreed to move in with him?

Did it have anything to do with Dubbo?

The emptiness inside him seemed bottomless.

Chapter Nineteen

A change came over Grant Sinclair the moment he began work on the Garuda project. He was back on familiar ground, with the kind of budget that suited his expertise, and he revelled in it. Staff who'd wondered why Cameron put up with him suddenly saw Grant in a new light and even the young directors, the boy wonders, glimpsed the greatness that had once made him the hottest property in town. He pulled together an A-list crew which read like a directory of the best at their craft. He even managed to convince a lighting cameraman who'd gone to shoot features in Hollywood to come back as his director of photography. He tracked down fixers in Bali and Java who'd worked for other film crews and could act as local producers, smoothing the way with villagers and officials, negotiating payments for extras and for the use of locations and, importantly, arranging transport and local drivers. Grant rang people he hadn't spoken to for years, sold them on the project and won their support. He was flying and nobody, least of all the agency creatives, could remain unaffected by his enthusiasm.

Grant worked as hard on the agency people as he did on any other aspect of his quote. He kept them up to date with developments and won them over with the grandeur of his ideas, the visual touches and effects that made great images exceptional. Grant had anticipated difficulties with his second director, the video whiz, but the kid backed him to the hilt, finding cheaper and slicker ways to pull off the effects he proposed. For the first time since his release on parole, Grant was happy and it showed.

His daughter, Jasmine, couldn't believe the change that had come over him and their Sunday lunches became boisterous affairs. He let her bring girlfriends from school and sometimes he invited along the agency creatives. There was never a dull moment and never a second when Jasmine wasn't proud of her dad. She told her aunt all about it and about the commercials that were going to make Grant famous again. She was so full of it, Fran could not be other than convinced. She picked up the phone and rang Linda to tell her what was happening and heard the relief in her sister's voice. Grant was back, or at least on the verge, and everyone breathed easier.

While it wasn't normal to nominate a crew before being awarded the job, Grant used the big names he'd attracted to bolster his chances. He and Marty, the video whiz, spent some of Cameron's money to buy video time to develop and demonstrate the visual effects they proposed, and overlaid it on pirated footage of the ancient Buddhist temple of Borobodur in Central Java. The final result was spectacular. Grant made certain that he ticked every box, dotted every 'i' and crossed every 't'. The agency people were knocked out and made no secret of the fact that they wanted him to shoot their commercials, even to the extent of providing him with financial details of his competitors' quotes to make sure his came in on target.

On the day he had to formally present his quote and proposals to the full agency team, the creative director advised him that, as a courtesy, the new marketing director from Garuda's Australian operations had been invited to the meeting. Grant arrived at the agency with Cameron, Marty and his project producer, knowing that acceptance of their quote was a formality. The smiling faces greeting him as he led his team into the meeting room confirmed that his life was back on track and the glory days were about to roll once more. But then he saw another face, one that abruptly ceased smiling, and his soaring hopes plummeted to earth like a shot duck. His parole officer had warned him that such things happened and so had other inmates.

'You never stop serving your time,' they'd told him. 'You never stop serving your time.'

'What's the matter?' whispered Cameron urgently.

Grant only realised he'd stopped dead in his tracks when Cameron took his arm and guided him to his seat. He didn't even try to answer. What could he say? When Grant had last seen him, Garuda's new marketing director had been a mid-level executive with Continental Airlines who'd taken time off from his job to attend a trial.

The trial of the man accused of causing the death of his sister.

* * *

'Neatly done,' said Ramon appreciatively. 'You've contrived to bring us to the edge on three fronts.'

'Yes, well done,' said Milos. 'The wait while I told my story and while I was away has certainly done you no harm. Perhaps even sharpened your narrative, no?'

'There is no skill in simply relaying events as they unfolded,' said Neil. He pushed himself back in his chair and rubbed his eyes wearily. 'That is the point I keep trying to make you understand. Fiction is more difficult and we've done ourselves a gross disservice with our flirtation with true stories. Truth may not have the convenience of fiction, but neither does it have the burden of inventiveness, the difficulties of plotting and structure or the quest for credibility. The events I've described are not my doing. Ultimately they're my undoing. I think we'll all end up regretting the fact that I chose to walk in your shoes and tell this story. I know I do.'

'You may well be just relaying events as they happened,' said Lucio hurriedly before Neil had a chance to relapse into one of his moods, 'but I agree with Ramon and Milos. It takes skill to bring these events together and leave so many threads of the story dangling. I must admit I'm worried about young Billy.'

'I'm more worried about the older Billy,' said Ramon.

'As a man who has seen the inside of prisons, I have some sympathy for Grant,' said Milos. 'I don't think he deserves this latest setback. I want to know how it impacts on him and on Linda. This is the turning point of your story, no?'

'No comment,' said Neil.

'There's something else I want to know,' said Lucio.

'What's that?' said Neil guardedly. 'If you want to pursue more speculation about Linda, you can do so without me.'

'I'm not asking about Linda. No, I want to know if you had it off with the girl? You know, the girl on the school bus who had the great breasts?'

‘Pauline?’ Neil smiled as though at a fond memory. ‘Yeah, but not for some time. Not until we’d both turned sixteen.’

‘And along the way?’

‘Let’s just say I reached a few bases before I hit a home run.’

Ramon smiled along with the others but beneath the surface he’d begun to worry that it was Neil who’d missed the point. He, Milos and, to some extent, Lucio had all played with the truth, used it mercilessly but also skilfully to provide their stories with credibility, seamlessly mixing fact with fiction. All along he’d felt Neil was playing the same game, but what if his claim that he was simply describing events was true? What if he had misread the real nature of their game and mistaken their fictions for fact? What then of his frightening admission?

FOURTH THURSDAY

Chapter Twenty

'I have been thinking,' said Ramon. 'I have some concerns and I would like to voice them before Neil arrives.'

Milos and Lucio stopped discussing the problems of parking and turned to their friend. In Neil's absence they'd gone straight to their table, as had been their custom before Neil instituted the detour via the bar for a beer.

'It is not like Neil to be late but his lateness does provide us with an opportunity.' The blind man paused to give his audience time to clear their minds and think about what he had to say. 'I am concerned about Neil. I fear he has overreacted to our stories and the way we have used a core of truth as a basis for our fictions. At first I thought he was playing the same game, but now I am not so sure.'

'I think we all share your concerns, no?' Milos turned to Lucio and received confirmation.

'The question is, do we let him continue?' said Ramon. 'I am not sure that we are ready to deal with unalloyed truth, particularly when it has the potential to jeopardise our lunches. Neil seems intent upon revealing aspects of himself that we are better off not knowing. We have been careful over these past years to keep our true selves away from this table, to let nothing imperil our role as storytellers or interfere with the simple joy of telling and listening to stories. At times we may have deliberately given the appearance of breaching our conventions as a device to make our stories more involving and convincing, but that is all it has ever been: a device, nothing more. It is part of our skill that we appear to tell the truth, but that subtlety seems to have eluded Neil. Perhaps we have been too clever for our own good. I'm afraid his story has more than just an appearance of truth.'

'What do you suggest?' asked Lucio.

'We admit to our creative use of the truth and offer to release him from his obligations to complete this story. We then invite him to tell another. How do you feel about that?'

'You make too many assumptions,' said Milos. 'First, I am not prepared to concede that my last story, mine and Gabi's story, was anything other than the truth. What happened is what happened, exactly as I told it. Even if my story had been fiction with a core of truth I would not readily admit it. Such an admission would undermine my credibility as a storyteller. To me, the telling of stories and the manipulation of my audience is as important as the stories I tell. Neil believes my story was true and that is how it should be. I will not sanction anything that undermines my skills.'

'Regardless of the consequences?'

'It is a risk I am prepared to take. It is a risk we have all taken before, particularly with you, Ramon, with you and your story about Rosa and Eduardo. You'd have us believe that your story was a contrivance, but at the time we were all convinced it was true. Not only true, but that it was your confession masquerading as fiction. We gave you the benefit of the doubt and our lunches survived. I believe the risk adds a dimension to our storytelling and, while I fear Neil may again take us close to the brink, who's to say we're going to fall over? Eh?'

'Lucio, what do you think?'

'I hear what you're saying, Ramon. You may remember I tried to talk Neil out of telling the story right at the beginning. But I think I agree with Milos. On reflection it is good that we take risks. Even if we've misled Neil into taking a bigger risk than we ever intended, I still wouldn't change a thing. Besides, like Milos, I'm not prepared to concede my story was anything other than God's truth either. I also wish to protect my credibility.'

'So we let Neil continue, even though the outcome of his story may jeopardise our relationship with him and perhaps even jeopardise our lunches?'

'We survived your story, Ramon, and we will survive Neil's.'

'Milos?'

'I sympathise with your concerns, Ramon, but I think your solution is more a threat to our lunches than Neil's story.' Milos paused while he weighed up his next words. 'Your insistence on dismissing our stories as fabrications makes me wonder if you have a selfish motive. It occurs to me that you could be using this as an opportunity to further convince us that your last story was a fiction and so extinguish any lingering doubts we may have about you.'

'That is grossly unfair!'

'Is it? I admit to being selfish. I have a selfish motive for wanting Neil to continue. I am protecting my interests. I am also involved in his story. I want to know what happens.'

'Of course you do,' said Ramon. 'We all do. Once a story begins, I like to know how it ends. But we can't sit back and do nothing.'

'Perhaps we should repeat this conversation in front of Neil,' said Lucio. 'It would give him the opportunity to weigh up the risks and to alter his story if he feels it necessary. He is not so far into it that the ending is set in concrete. Once he realises how concerned we are, he can make adjustments. He is certainly clever enough.'

'It's a possibility,' said Ramon but he was less than enthusiastic. The debate had not followed the course he'd planned and Milos's accusation had stung. He was considering ways to proceed when he was distracted by the sound of someone approaching their table. He half turned, expecting Neil, and heard Gancio's voice instead.

'Excuse me, gentlemen. This young woman has a message from Neil.'

A message from Neil? Ramon's mind raced as he considered the implications. He heard chairs being pushed back and the haste with which they moved suggested that the young woman, whoever she was, was also attractive.

'I'm so sorry to interrupt and sorry for keeping you waiting. I couldn't find anywhere to park. Neil wanted me to telephone but I couldn't resist this chance to meet you all and express my thanks in person. I'm Barbara, Neil's PA. He'd kill me if he knew I was here.'

'Allow me to do the introductions,' said Milos. 'I am Milos, this is Lucio and Ramon.'

'I've heard so much about you,' said Barbara. She shook each man's hand.

'Please, sit down,' said Milos. He pulled back Neil's chair and held it for her.

'Thank you. I promise I won't stay more than a few minutes.' She let Gancio pour her a glass of wine.

'I take it Neil will not be joining us today?' Ramon made his enquiry politely but he'd listened to too many stories and played too many games to take the appearance of Neil's PA at face value.

'No. He apologises but it's hardly his fault. He's in hospital. He was nearly killed last night in a car accident.'

'My God!' said Lucio. 'Is he okay?'

'He escaped with a broken ankle and a few cuts and bruises but it could easily have been a lot worse.'

'What happened?' asked Milos.

'Someone smashed into the back of his car at traffic lights and pushed him into a van coming in the opposite direction. His BMW is a write-off.'

'And he escaped with just a broken ankle?' Ramon showed the right amount of concern.

'It's hard to believe when you look at his car. He was operated on this morning and I'm going straight from here to the hospital. He'll be in a cast for some months.'

'Please convey our sympathies and best wishes,' said Milos. 'If there is anything we can do for him, please let us know.'

'I'll pass on your regards but he has everything he needs. They'll probably release him tomorrow.'

'You mentioned thanks,' said Ramon. 'Why do you feel a need to thank us? What have we done for you?'

'What have you done? You must be aware of the effect you've had on Neil.'

'What effect?' said Ramon, clearly mystified.

Barbara stared at the blank faces of the three men. 'Oh, come on!' she said.

'We have no idea what you're talking about,' said Milos. 'As far as we're concerned Neil is Neil. He is the same now as he has always been. I can't say we haven't tried to change him, to smooth his rough edges and moderate his extremes, but we've met with little success. I made him the target of my last story but I don't know what good that did.'

'I can't believe you.' Barbara's voice bordered on amazement. 'If it wasn't for you, Neil and I wouldn't be getting married.'

Her news was greeted by stunned silence.

'You and Neil are getting married?' said Ramon cautiously.

'Yes.'

'But I thought ... didn't you just leave Neil for the ... how did Neil put it? The competition?'

Barbara put her head back and laughed.

'I had to do something or our relationship would have drifted on and off for another ten years. I don't know what Neil told you, but I never actually joined the opposition. I decided to take a week off between jobs and that was all it took for him to come to his senses. He called and asked me to come back. He said I had no choice, that I was his Gabriella.'

'Neil said that?' Lucio turned to Milos who was speechless in astonishment. 'He said you were his Gabriella?'

'Yes. Now do you see what I mean? Neil told me enough of your story for me to understand what Gabriella means to you, Milos. A few years ago Neil would never have said anything like that. He wouldn't have asked me to come back either.'

'I'm sorry if we appear dull-witted, but we don't see,' said Ramon, oblivious to the irony. 'You must help us out. Clearly there is a side to Neil which he has kept well hidden.'

'His recklessness, you must have been aware of his recklessness?'

'No.'

'Dear God! What do you men talk about when you meet?'

Her question hung over the table with no one anxious to respond. How could they admit to deliberately withholding information about themselves without discouraging Barbara from continuing? Ramon's reply, when it came, evaded the issue.

'I take it Neil's recklessness is connected with your need to thank us.'

'Oh, yes. I can't believe you weren't aware of it. His recklessness was legendary. He was reckless in business, in relationships and unbelievably so behind the wheel. You needed nerves of steel to be around him. He always put everything on the line. He took the most outrageous risks with the business. If anyone challenged his proposals, he confronted them head-on, no matter the cost or consequences. The in joke was that we had our own suite of rooms at the Land and Environment Court. Planning authorities lived in fear of him and our competitors are convinced he has balls the size of watermelons, pardon the expression. The truth was much simpler than that. The truth was, he just didn't care.'

'Didn't care?'

'That's right, Ramon. He didn't care if he lost everything. He didn't care what risks he took or how overextended we were at the bank. He took the business to the brink of collapse so many times it became the normal state of affairs. But his gambles paid off. We not only survived but flourished. Neil is the reason the business is so successful. He used to laugh at our concerns and, you know, if the whole thing had collapsed I don't think it would have worried him a bit. He didn't care, just didn't care.'

'You mentioned relationships.'

Barbara hesitated momentarily.

'Neil told me you're relentless. Like a dingo on a scent, he said. For me this is the painful bit. I think from the time we met Neil has always loved me. I know I've always loved him, but I wouldn't have hung around if I hadn't been certain of the depth of his feelings for me. He put me through the mill more times than I care to think about. It was as if he couldn't accept his feelings, as though he was in denial. I can't tell you how many women there've been. He'd live with this one for a while and then that one. Inevitably these relationships ended and usually ended badly. Believe it or not, I have a good deal of sympathy for these women. Neil often left them deeply hurt and emotionally scarred. But he didn't care. Didn't care about them and, seemingly, didn't care about me. He was like a stone skipping across water, leaving ripples everywhere he touched. Then your lunches started and he began to change. Oh, it was slow going at first, but the fact was, he was changing. It was as though you collectively provided him with a platform from which he could rebuild his life. You were an example to him. You came to this country with nothing and rebuilt your lives from scratch. You became his inspiration. You made him believe he could do the same.'

'And now you and Neil are getting married.'

'We'd talked about it off and on but it took Milos's story to bring him around. Even then he wouldn't commit to a date. That was why I walked out on him. I don't know what you said to him, Milos, on your return from Hungary but it affected him deeply. Your story got to him all over again.'

'I would never have suspected it,' said Milos. 'Never.'

'Unbelievably, he has even begun to talk about himself and some of the terrible things that happened to him. This is a major breakthrough. His brother and I have been trying to get him to open up ever since the lunches began and he gave up therapy.'

Lucio gasped out loud. Brother? Therapy?

'His brother?' said Ramon quickly. 'How many brothers does he have?'

'Just the one, and two sisters. Why?'

'And this brother is still alive?'

'Ramon! That's enough!' Milos glared at Ramon. The blind man may not have been able to see Milos's anger but the warning in his voice was clear enough.

Barbara looked from one man to the other, clearly puzzled. But her bewilderment was quickly displaced by a look of horror.

'Oh my God!' she said. 'I've blown it, haven't I? I've blown his story!'

'No,' said Milos quickly. 'In truth you have raised questions about one aspect of his story, that is all.'

'Oh God, Neil will kill me!'

'Don't blame yourself,' said Milos. 'We encouraged you to be indiscreet when we had every opportunity, even an obligation, to stop you. We have behaved abominably and you deserve our apology.'

'Neil told me to ring. He insisted I rang. He must've known what would happen. Now I've ruined everything.' She pushed her chair back and stood up, clearly upset.

'Please, your indiscretion is inconsequential,' said Ramon. 'Yes, we should have stopped you earlier, but your comments have merely confirmed what we suspected. Nothing of substance has changed, I assure you. Please don't be upset. There is no need. Neither is there a need to inform Neil of your visit here. He will certainly not learn of it from us.'

'Ramon is right,' said Lucio. He rose and took both of Barbara's hands in his. 'Nothing of substance has changed. Neil can continue his story none the wiser. Right, Milos?'

'Indeed.' He, too, rose from his chair. 'Neil is a very special friend to us and your revelations have only raised him in our esteem. I am both proud and astonished that we have had such a beneficial effect on him. Please convey our best wishes and tell him we look forward with great anticipation to the next instalment of his story.'

'Are you sure I didn't say too much?'

'Absolutely,' said Milos. 'I overreacted to Ramon's questions, that is all.' He glanced away towards the front of the restaurant. 'Once again I ask you to excuse our lack of courtesy. Gancio is coming to walk you to the door, but if you'd rather stay we would be honoured if you would have lunch with us.'

'Thank you, but I'd better go. Neil will be wondering where I am.' Barbara smiled but her smile was tenuous. She began biting her bottom lip the instant she turned towards the door.

The men sat in silence until she was safely out of earshot.

'So Neil's brother is still alive. Interesting.'

'You are incorrigible, Ramon,' said Milos angrily. 'You had no right to persist with your questioning.

Neil will be furious if he finds out and justifiably so. It is ludicrous to suggest nothing of substance has changed.'

'You accuse me of encouraging her but you did nothing to discourage her or restrain me. To use your own argument, Milos, you had every opportunity and — what was your word — obligation to stop Barbara talking. But you didn't, and neither did Lucio.'

'Let's calm down,' said Lucio. 'There is nothing to be gained by pointing fingers at each other. We are all equally to blame. We were all fascinated by what she said. None of us could have anticipated the mention of Neil's brother.'

'Or the comparison with Gabi,' said Milos quietly. 'Who could have anticipated that?'

'Or the comment about therapy,' said Ramon. 'Neil and therapy? These are two words I never expected to hear in the same sentence.'

'And what were the terrible things that happened to him?' said Milos. 'Dear God, he sat here just a few months ago listening to me talking about Gabi and her therapy and gave no indication that he'd had first-hand experience. I feel so foolish.'

'Perhaps we are all fools,' said Ramon thoughtfully. 'Perhaps Neil is a good deal cleverer than we think.'

'Explain yourself,' said Milos.

Ramon took a few moments to assemble his argument.

'First let me ask you, do you believe Barbara?'

'Yes,' said Milos without hesitation. 'Why, don't you?'

'We need to be sure. Doesn't it occur to you that Neil's accident is altogether too convenient? Here we are debating whether to call a halt to his story when he injects new information which turns our assumptions upside down. The timing is impeccable.'

'Surely you're not suggesting that he faked the accident?' said Lucio indignantly.

'We have no evidence that he is in hospital or that he has a broken ankle. We only have Barbara's word for that.'

'That's ridiculous,' said Lucio. 'We have an advantage over you and I apologise for bringing it up. We could look her in the eye. Believe me, Barbara was not acting.'

'So you are certain she is telling the truth?'

'Yes.'

'One more thing. Milos, you must be aware that Neil has borrowed elements from your story. The use of the third person when he refers to himself, the fact that he is telling the story of his brother, and now the involvement of his fiancée.'

'I think perhaps Neil may have unwittingly borrowed elements from my storytelling. It makes sense to use the third person. It is a convenience that lends detachment. We discussed this earlier. Also, my story was principally about Gabi and me. As for bringing his fiancée to the table, I cannot accept that this was part of his plan. I prefer to believe the evidence of my own eyes. I believe Barbara disobeyed instructions by coming to see us. I believe she is genuine in everything she said and I further believe her dismay was genuine when she thought she'd given Neil's story away. Her eyes did not lie. She panicked. Your concerns are justified, Ramon, but in the end I think they are groundless. I believe Neil had a car accident and that he will show up here next week with his leg in a cast.'

'So, we are to take Barbara's comments at face value,' said Ramon. He sat thoughtfully while Gancio served their entrée. 'If she is to be believed, then everything changes.'

'What do you mean?' asked Lucio.

Ramon surprised his friends with his sudden solemnity.

'We came here today fearing the effect Neil's story might have on our lunches. Specifically, we were concerned about our relationship with Neil once we learned how and why Neil took his brother's life. Now his fiancée tells us his brother is alive. So what really happened? Barbara tells us Neil has changed, from not caring about anything to caring enough to get married and rebuild his life. She tells us he has started talking about the terrible things that happened to him, things that required him to undergo counselling. Think about that in the context of his story. Think where it leads us. What made him not care in the first place? We must face the possibility that Neil is in fact playing our game and combining truth with fiction, but not the truth we were led to believe. Oh, no. He is engaging another truth and I suspect it is even more appalling. Let us hope Neil is playing games with us and we are victims of a stunt. Let us hope for his sake. Dear God! Poor Neil. If my suspicions are correct, this other truth does not bear thinking about.'

FIFTH THURSDAY

Chapter Twenty-one

Ramon, Milos and Lucio sat at their table as twelve-thirty came and went and the restaurant began filling with diners. They were fearing another postponement of their storytelling when Neil came swinging clumsily into the restaurant on crutches. The friends had been unsure what to expect. Milos had all but convinced them that Barbara would have confessed to ignoring Neil's instructions and relayed every word of their conversation to him. He was certain that Neil would arrive furious, if he bothered to come at all. But Neil was anything but furious. He had a broad grin on his face as he entered and now laughed as he shared a joke with Gancio. His use of the crutches was hardly expert but he managed to negotiate his way between the tables to his chair.

'Sorry I'm late. I got stuck trying to get out of the cab. I had to get some passers-by to give me hand. The only one who didn't think it was funny was the cabbie.'

'Neil, it's good to see you back and in such good spirits,' said Lucio.

'Good to see you too,' said Neil. He shook hands with his friends, rested his crutches against the table and slowly lowered himself onto his chair.

'I thought you would be more used to your crutches by now,' said Milos for Ramon's benefit. He wanted to make sure the blind man missed nothing. 'After all, it has been a week.'

'Bloody doctors,' said Neil affably. 'Wouldn't let me put any weight on my leg until yesterday. And would you look at this bloody cast. I break my ankle and they plaster my leg all the way up to my groin. I asked the doctor who did it if she'd whack some on my old fella while she was at it. Save a fortune on Viagra.'

'Your PA also said you suffered bruising and cuts. I was expecting to see your face swathed in bandages.'

'The windscreen shattered, of course, but fortunately stayed in one piece. I don't know whether it would have mattered much if it had fragmented because airbags popped out of everywhere. Those things actually work. God knows how many went off. The only problem is they don't make airbags for legs and they managed to slam into everything within reach. I got a few bruises across the shoulder and chest from the seatbelt as well, but it's nice to know they work.'

'It sounds like you were very lucky,' said Ramon.

'I think the fact that I drive the X5 off-road Beamer helped. I had weight and height on my side. Even so, if I'd been knocked into the path of a semi or a bus instead of a van, it might have been a different story. In fact, it might've been the end of the story. Think of the consequences of that. Young Billy would have been left facing the pigs, the older Billy would still be wondering whether Linda is on the level, and Grant would be left more bitter and twisted than ever. The good news is I would have been spared the necessity of baring my soul. I wish you guys had never started me off on this true story business. I'm not enjoying it. I was almost glad when the dickhead behind me forgot what his brakes were for.'

'What happened to him?' asked Lucio.

'He got the use of the first ambulance, which I thought was a bit unfair since he caused the accident. He's married with three young kids, a mortgage, a fractured skull, punctured lung, ruptured spleen and God knows what else. Last I heard he was still in intensive care. Apparently he was working two jobs to try to make ends meet and fell asleep at the wheel.'

'Poor bastard,' said Lucio.

'Poor bastard be buggered,' said Neil. 'He interrupted my story. I don't even let Ramon do that. Now, I know you guys are a bunch of pathetic winos but I would like a beer.'

Lucio caught the eye of a passing waiter and ordered a Peroni.

'What about the driver of the van?' asked Milos.

'She got the second ambulance. It was quite amazing really. I sat in my car with my ankle trapped, blood streaming down my legs and a young cop holding my hand while everyone else got proper attention. I heard she suffered head injuries, but she was blonde so I guess there was no change to the status quo. You know, the young cop even tried to get me to give him a statement while I was still trapped in the car? Dear God. You guys accuse me of insensitivity.'

'Seems you got off lightly,' said Ramon.

'The X5 is expensive but you get what you pay for. Ah, here's my beer. Cheers. I hope you didn't get up to any mischief in my absence last week.'

'Absolutely not,' said Ramon without hesitation. 'We had a quiet meal and went home early.'

He was pleased with the way the lunch had begun and he could tell the others were as well. Neil gave no indication that Barbara had admitted to her indiscretion, or that he was poised to reveal a dark secret about himself. In fact, the Neil that Barbara had revealed and the crass Neil joking about his accident could have been different people.

Both Milos and Lucio had pressed Ramon to elaborate on his dire warning of the week before but he'd resisted. In the days since, he'd replayed their conversation with Barbara endlessly in his mind and nothing had shaken his conviction that Neil was somehow using them as a means to confront his past — provided Barbara had been genuine. Everything depended on her credibility. Neil's explanation for his awkwardness with crutches was plausible, but his ineptness could also mean that he'd just that morning had the cast put on his leg. But if he was faking, would he have had a cast made all the way up his leg rather than just to the knee? The absence of any marks on his face was also suspicious despite Neil's ringing endorsement of airbags. Everything hinged on Barbara's credibility. Ramon felt for his wine glass and raised it to his lips. Whether Neil had planned it or not, interesting possibilities were opening up in his story.

'Which thread of your story do you intend to pick up first?' asked Lucio.

'Give me a break,' said Neil. 'Can't I enjoy my beer and your company first? And what about lunch? I can't tell you how much I'm looking forward to Gancio's cooking. My story has reached the stage where it takes on a life of its own and there's nothing

I can do about it. But I tell you what. When I was lying in hospital there were plenty of times that I thought about ditching it. I wish you bastards hadn't started me on it. But you did so I'm obliged to finish it. Ah, what the hell. You never know, it might even do me some good to finally get this load off my chest.'

Chapter Twenty-two

Billy tried to think like Neil and started arranging the things he had to do in a logical order. He discovered he could move his toes, even though the tensing of the muscles alongside his shins made him wince. He got the same reaction when he moved his ankles. Neil had always told him that if you could move your toes and ankles then your leg wasn't broken. The pain did seem to come from the flexing of a wound rather than the grating of broken bones, which was encouraging. Using his hands to draw his knees up, he untied his boots, removed them and peeled off his socks. His father had shown him how to tie a tourniquet in case of snakebite and claimed that socks did the job as well as anything. Billy figured the blood from the gashes on his legs was already beginning to clot and applied the tourniquets as a precaution so he wouldn't lose too much more blood once he tried to move.

He pulled his boots back on over his bare feet. Flies were already homing in on the dead pig and he wanted to get well away before other pigs sniffed it out. A dead comrade was a tasty meal as far as wild pigs were concerned and he wanted them filling up on the boar's flesh rather than his.

Billy had no choice but to try to move on. The coolibah he leaned against was a poor specimen and no good to him. While it was tall enough to get him out of reach of the pigs, if he did somehow manage to climb it there were no branches that he could sit on or straddle, at least none strong enough to support his weight. He straightened his legs and shuffled his bottom forward towards his heels, straightened his legs and shuffled forward again. He kept this up for around ten metres before the pain forced him to stop. He could feel blood trickling down his legs again and flies swarmed all over the dark patches on his jeans. Billy realised there was a limit to how far he could shuffle and looked around for another tree he could climb. But most of the trees were mallee-form and their thin spreadeagled trunks offered no hope of refuge. The rest were too thin and scrubby to support his weight. He had to keep going until he found a more substantial tree and groaned at the prospect. He looked for other options and realised immediately what he should've done earlier. He put two fingers in his mouth and whistled.

'Get over here, Grassie!' he yelled. 'Over here!'

He whistled again. He had no doubt that his horse, Grasshopper, would hear his whistle in the still air and maybe even his voice. But would the stupid animal act on it? He hoped it would have the wit or at least the curiosity to come and investigate. But that was the funny thing about horses. He hadn't bothered to tether his mount because, like all of their horses, it had been trained not to wander off. Now, in all likelihood, the training was working against him. He could picture Grasshopper raising its head dutifully at his whistle, then going back to its grazing. He whistled as loudly as he could and stared back towards the clearing, looking for any sign of movement.

'Get over here, Grassie! Over here!' He hoped the horse would hear the anger in his voice and that it would jolt some sense into it. His father always maintained Grasshopper was a couple of swallows short of a drink and had been undecided whether to keep it or put it down. Billy wished his father had put it down. It continued to ignore his whistle.

Billy shuffled forward another ten metres and rested. The sun had dropped well and truly below the tops of the trees and was within a few minutes of disappearing altogether. A sudden flurry overhead made him look up. The crows had found the pig he'd killed. Soon they'd start ripping into the carcass and, if other pigs couldn't already smell the blood, the sound of the crows squabbling would act like a homing beacon. Billy looked around anxiously. He wished he'd taken more notice of the trees on his way in but at the time trees had been irrelevant. They were just cover, a backdrop that defined the area he occupied. Yet he knew there was always one big tree in among the coolibahs and scrub, a good-sized gum or box. There was always something and he had to find it. Ignoring the pain in his legs he shuffled forward, aiming for a pauper belah tree about forty metres away. The forked trunk gave off low branches that he could use to haul himself to his feet so he could take a good look around. He whistled intermittently as he dragged himself along, hoping his stupid horse would finally take notice.

An explosion of screeches and beating wings told him what he didn't want to know. Pigs had found the carcass and chased off the crows. How long since he'd shot the boar, he wondered. Twenty, thirty minutes?

Pigs were normally more cautious and he was shocked that they'd returned so quickly. He doubled his efforts, despite the pain, and dragged himself forward as fast as he could go. Climbing the belah tree had never been his intention but he was coming to the conclusion that it might be his only option. At least it'd be better than being caught out in the open. How many pigs were there? How long before a pig that couldn't get at the carcass decided to come after him?

The pain in his legs almost caused Billy to pass out as he used the lower branches to pull himself to his feet. Once he'd steadied himself and sucked in a few deep breaths, he considered the problem of climbing the tree. Both forks of the trunk ran smooth and the lowest branch was a good metre off the ground and slanting sharply upwards. It was a typical pauper belah and hopeless for climbing. There was nothing he could stand on to support his weight as he hauled himself up. He groaned in despair. Everything was going wrong! Everything. But the commotion behind him left him little choice.

He jammed his rifle between the fork of two branches, took a firm grip on the thickest branch and heaved. It was like pulling himself up a thick rope without the help of his legs and his arm muscles trembled under the strain. He kicked his legs upwards, ignoring the pain as they collided with the trunk and the underside of other branches, desperate to hook them over something so he could take some of the weight off his arms. He managed to haul his right buttock up over a branch and rest it there while he gulped in air. When he was able, he worked his bottom more firmly onto the branch and tried again to lift his legs. It took all his strength and courage but he finally managed to hook his right leg up over a branch and then his left. He lay there sprawled across the lower branches with his bottom taking most of his weight. Despite his efforts, his backside was still barely a metre off the ground. Any reasonable-sized pig could rise up on its hind legs and have a chomp at him. Billy sized up the branches above him and realised there was little to be gained by trying to pull himself higher. Pauper belahs were often called scrub she-oaks for good reason. The trees were poor specimens, tapering quickly into a spindly network of branchlets. There was little to climb up on even if he had two good legs to help him.

Overhead the sky had faded to pale blue and was beginning to take on the translucency that precedes night. Billy unhooked his rifle and held it across his body. The sound of something moving through the scrub made him glance back the way he'd come. He was hoping to see Grasshopper but instead saw two pigs, snouts down, trotting towards him along the tracks he'd made in the soil. Their eagerness was sickening. Billy had never felt more frightened or vulnerable in his life.

'Piss off!' he screamed as loudly as he could.

The pigs propped and retreated a few metres. They lifted their snouts and sniffed the air, trying to gauge the extent of the danger. They hesitated, torn between their natural caution and the smell of blood with its promise of a feed.

'Piss off!' Billy screamed again.

The pigs retreated another ten metres before spinning around and holding their ground. Billy turned from them and whistled. Surely with it getting dark Grasshopper would take notice and come to him.

'Get over here!' he yelled. 'Get over here!'

The scrub cut his visibility to around one hundred metres but sometimes you could see movement further away. Billy strained his eyes but saw nothing. When he turned back to the pigs they'd come closer. And there were now four of them. Billy started sobbing. He couldn't help himself. The pigs took that as a sign to come closer.

Billy decided to lie still and let the pigs come to him. They were bolder now that there were four of them and they jostled for the lead. He slowly brought his rifle up to his shoulder and sighted along the barrel. He had only two bullets left, one in the chamber and the other in his pocket. One was for the pigs and he was too scared to even think about what he'd do with the other. But pig shooters all said the same thing. Always keep your last bullet in case something goes wrong.

Billy closed his mind to all thought and lined up the leading pig. Missing or wounding was not an option. He let it edge closer and closer until it closed to within five metres. He waited till the pig raised its snout, exposing the target area, and squeezed the trigger.

The sudden explosion sent birds screeching into the air. The three surviving pigs spun and bolted. The fourth dropped onto its side mortally wounded, its legs kicking uselessly in its death throes. Billy lowered his rifle. He had one bullet left. One bullet. He started to cry.

The crows came first to investigate the kill in the last of the light. That was how it worked. Birds came first then the pigs, and the pigs left nothing but a few bones and a memory of what had been there. Billy couldn't help wondering what would be left of him apart from his clothes and rifle. He could picture the search parties starting out at first light to scour the bush for him. But there was so much country to cover and he hadn't told anyone where he was going. Where would they begin to look? What chance did they have of finding his remains? He tried to drag himself up higher into the tree but the truth was he had nowhere to go. The tree simply wasn't big enough.

Billy wiped his sleeve across his eyes to dry his tears. He tried to think what Neil would do. One thing was for sure: Neil would never give up. Billy stuck his fingers in his mouth and whistled again for his horse. He stared hard in the direction of the clearing but nothing stirred.

'Grasshopper!' he yelled, in case his horse had responded but he hadn't been able to spot it in the gathering gloom. 'Get over here! Get over here, you stupid nag!'

Billy glanced up at the sky through the foliage. It was now dark enough for Venus to show and in ten minutes it would be so dark he wouldn't be able to see his hand in front of his face. A sob escaped from his throat. How would he deal with the pigs if he couldn't see them?

He reminded himself he was tough, and thought of all the times Neil had boasted about his courage when he'd made a tackle and especially the time when Blackie had nearly got him. Neil would expect him to put up a fight. Billy put his fingers in his mouth and sucked in his breath. This time Grasshopper had to hear him and come. It had to! He whistled louder and longer than he'd ever whistled before and strained his ears for a whinny or the soft sound of hooves on the heavy soil. For a moment there was nothing. Then he heard it.

A faint echo.

His whistle echoed?

Had he whistled so loud it had echoed? His whistle sometimes echoed up around Rodney's place, but it had never echoed before out on the plains. He filled his lungs and whistled again, held his breath in case he was imagining things. But back came the reply, faint and unmistakeable. Everyone had their own whistle and the whistle returning to him was no echo. No way! He knew exactly who'd made it: his dad. His dad was coming to get him! Billy stared in disbelief towards the clearing, hoping to catch sight of the light from his father's torch, but his eyes blurred hopelessly with tears. His father was coming to get him! He tried whistling again but a sob choked it off in his throat. What would Neil do? Neil wouldn't cry. His father whistled again, much clearer this time but still a long way off. Billy knew his dad would be waiting for him to respond. He wiped his nose on his sleeve, swallowed hard and whistled.

'Coo-eee!'

That was Neil.

'Over here!' shouted Billy. 'Over here!'

He started crying uncontrollably, out of relief and the certainty that the pigs wouldn't get him. His father called to him every thirty seconds and each time Billy had to swallow hard and take a deep breath before responding. Darkness had fallen like a blanket before he saw the first flicker of lights through the scrub. There were three of them, spaced about ten metres apart.

Billy knew they'd be walking their horses, making as little sound as possible so they could get an accurate fix on where he was. He wanted to rush over to meet them, crawl to them if necessary, but his legs had grown stiff and useless from being stuck in one position. It was all he could do to wipe his eyes so they wouldn't see that he'd been crying.

'Billy!' called his father.

'Over here!'

Torch beams flickered over the ground all around him before one finally pinned him.

'Got him!' he heard Neil say. 'He's in the belah. Can you see?'

Another beam came to rest on him.

'Got him,' said Braden.

'You okay, Billy?' It was his sister calling and he could hear the worry in her voice and sensed that she'd been crying. He'd thought his mother would've come after him but it didn't matter. Kath would do fine. He was dimly aware of more lights flickering through the scrub, approaching from the east.

'We got him, Doug,' called Braden.

Billy couldn't see past the glare from the torches but guessed his father was talking to Doug Pridle, Pauline's father. Billy hadn't a clue how they'd known where to start looking but it didn't matter. They'd found him. Somehow they'd found him and that was all that counted. For the first time since the pig had attacked he began to relax and was immediately overcome by the greatest weariness he'd ever known. It took all his strength to smile when he felt his father's strong hands reach beneath him and gently lift him out of the tree.

'You all right, son?'

'Looks like a pig got his legs,' said Pauline's father. 'Got him good.'

Billy was surprised at how distant the voices sounded.

'Yeah, I can see,' said Braden. He turned his torch

on the dead pig and the tracks Billy had left. 'Reckon if you track back you'll find the one that got him.'

'I'm sorry, Dad,' said Billy. He tried hard but failed to keep the choke out of his voice. 'I'm really sorry.'

'There's time for that later, Billy. The main thing is you're all right. Now, do you reckon you can ride home with me? Sit in front so I can hang onto you.'

He was dimly aware of Neil taking the rifle off him and Doug Pridle helping him up on his father's horse.

'Thanks, Doug,' said Braden. 'And thank your boys for me. I'll bring them over a dozen.'

'No worries, mate. Glad the kid's all right. I'll see you later.'

'How'd you find me, Dad?' Even through his tiredness Billy had to know. 'How'd you know where to look?'

'You can thank Neil for that.'

Thank Neil. Billy felt a surge of love for his brother. Neil never let him down, never! He settled back between his father's arms and closed his eyes. Now that he was saved, the pain in his legs didn't feel quite so bad any more. He was asleep before they'd hardly turned for home.

The doctor drove out from Walgett to spare Billy the pain of the trip in. One phone call to the Pridles and word about the missing boy had spread all over the shire and all the way into town. No one was really surprised by the doctor's gesture, although it was noted and appreciated. Under the circumstances, everyone automatically did what they could to help. He cleaned and stitched the gashes in Billy's legs and, to everyone's relief, found nothing to indicate that the bones were anything other than severely bruised. However, he qualified his diagnosis by recommending X-rays. Braden said he'd wait and see how Billy shaped up. The hospital over in Walgett had an X-ray machine but nobody went there unless they were pretty sure something was broken. It was a long way to go to prove bones were still in one piece.

With the help of local anaesthetics and two sleeping pills, Billy slept through to lunch the following day. He woke up sore and sorry. His mother made him finish a bowl of soup before giving him two aspirins. He slept through to dinner. Only then, with the family sitting and standing around his bed, did he tell them what happened.

'I reckon you've been punished enough,' said Braden when Billy had finished. 'I hope you realise now that rules are there for good reasons.'

'I'm sorry, Dad.'

'Yeah, well, you kept your head and did the right thing. You gave us a chance to find you, although God only knows what would've happened if Neil hadn't twigged to you.'

Billy turned to Neil.

'How did you know where I was?'

'It wasn't hard to figure out. I heard the first shot while I was at Pauline's. We were doing homework out on her front veranda. It was pretty faint but it made us both look up. The key thing is, we both looked in the same direction. I had a suspicion that it was you though I honestly didn't think you'd go hunting on your own. I lined up the sound of the shot with a veranda post and the edge of their cattle yards. I left about ten minutes later. I was more than halfway home when I heard the second shot. I still didn't think it was you because I didn't think you'd stay out so late. But just in case, I dismounted and scratched a big arrow in the ground pointing to where I thought the shot had come from. I stuck a stick through a couple of sheets of paper and wedged it into a bush in case I needed to find the arrow in the dark. Then I found Grasshopper trotting home on its own. That's when I realised you were in trouble. I galloped home and got Dad.'

Braden took over the story.

'Neil rang the Pridles and gave them the bearing he'd taken and we set off with your sister. Mum stayed here in case you made it home on your own. We found Neil's arrow and started looking, knowing Doug was working up from the east with a couple of his hands. I tell you what, though, we weren't very hopeful once it started getting dark. But Neil's directions were right on the ball. I reckon if we hadn't found you, Doug would've. The fact remains though, Billy, you'd still be out there if Neil hadn't been watching out for you and had the brains to take bearings. He's the one who saved your skin.'

Billy didn't even try to suppress the smile that enveloped his face. It felt so good to have such a wonderful brother and he couldn't think of anyone in the world he loved and admired more.

'I'll pay you back one day,' said Billy, and he meant it with all his heart. 'I'll pay you back, I swear I will.'

Nobody had the slightest inkling of the terrible price Billy would pay keeping his promise.

Chapter Twenty-three

Linda woke with the feeling that she'd turned a major corner in her life. The day before, she'd returned from a trip to Dubbo where Al had confirmed everything her sister had told her. Grant was a certainty to get the Garuda job and she knew there'd be no turning back for him. A few more jobs and he'd have the apartment, the car and the lifestyle, and too much to lose by trying to settle old scores. However, while she was delighted at the prospect of being able to return to Sydney, she had mixed feelings about leaving Jindalee Downs. She'd become extremely attached to her little house between the ridges and the lack of stress. And then, of course, there was Billy. She couldn't think about him without smiling, but their relationship did beg the question of what would happen if she returned to Sydney. Would he want to leave the farm for the city or would she divide her time between both places? Happily it was a question that didn't require an immediate answer.

She'd just sat down to begin working on another painting for which she'd done preliminary sketches when she heard Rodney's call. She didn't know whether to feel irritated by his arrival or pleased, because her garden was certainly in need of his attention. In the end she just shrugged. What did it matter whether she began her painting then or in half an hour? That was one of the attractions of living in the wilds. She rose and made her way towards the kitchen. At least Rodney was obeying her request to give her some warning when he was coming instead of just appearing at the back door.

He wasted no time coming down from the ridge and strode angrily towards her. He stopped and propped his shotgun in the crook of his arm. Linda had learned how to tell when something was up because Rodney's lower jaw hammered faster than normal and his eyes shone abnormally brightly. Something was definitely up.

'I god sum-thing for you.'

'Something for me?' Linda tried to sound pleasantly surprised as Rodney started fishing around in the pocket of his trousers. Rodney's trousers hadn't improved since the day they'd met and she couldn't imagine what his pockets might contain that she wouldn't normally run from. She was no wiser when he pulled out a grubby matchbox.

'Thid id for you.' He shoved his gift at her as though defying her to refuse it. His eyes blazed.

Linda had no choice but to take the matchbox from him. It felt so light that for a moment she thought it was empty.

'O-pen id.'

Linda slid the matchbox open and discovered a bed of cotton wool. She looked at Rodney questioningly, the obvious eluding her.

'Oh, give id to me!' Rodney snatched the matchbox from her hands and lifted the first layer of cotton wool. A black opal the size of a little fingernail stared up at Linda, glowing with blue and red and flashing green as it diffracted and refracted light.

'My God,' said Linda.

'I done id for you,' said Rodney defiantly. 'Go on. Take id.'

Linda took the matchbox from Rodney's hand and held it almost reverently.

'Black deam o-pal. Id dol-lid bud a bid brid-dle. No good for a ring bud id make a nide brooch.'

'It's beautiful,' said Linda. 'Did you find it?'

'Of course I found id! Down a-boud twelve me-tahs. I pol-lid id my-delf. I done id for you.'

'For me? Oh, Rodney, you're very sweet but I can't accept it. You've worked too hard for it. Why are you giving it to me?'

'Id a pred-dent.'

'Why? We've had Christmas.'

Her question appeared to have Rodney stumped for an answer. His jaw hammered furiously.

'Be-caud I like you!' he said, and began backing away as though his admission was something to be frightened of.

'I know you do and I like you too. But you don't have to give me a present to prove it.'

'Keep id. I made id for you. I'm going to do the gar-den now.' He strode angrily towards the garden shed. 'I need your pade and mad-dock.'

'I'll make tea in a while and we can talk about this,' said Linda.

She waited until Rodney's back was turned and slipped into the kitchen. Having recovered from the initial shock, she gently lifted the opal from the matchbox and examined it. Rodney had done a beautiful job of polishing and shaping it. It was clearly a labour of love and that had worried her momentarily. The opal was a statement, but not the one she'd at first feared. While it was a labour of love it was not a declaration of love. He knew that she and Billy were seeing each other and had even encouraged them. A smile spread across her face as she continued to stare at the opal and the way it flashed different colours at her depending on the angle she viewed it. She couldn't recall anyone thanking her for her friendship before, and if they had, they certainly hadn't done it so touchingly. A wave of affection for the little man swept over her.

She'd invited Billy to a romantic dinner of fresh prawns and ocean trout which she'd brought back from Dubbo and wondered how he'd react if she invited another guest. Rather than speculate, she rang his home and was lucky enough to catch him on his morning tea break. She told him about Rodney, the opal and her wish to reciprocate.

'I think that's a great idea,' said Billy without hesitation. 'Rodney doesn't get invited to dinner much.'

Linda smiled at the understatement.

'You don't mind?'

'Why would I mind?'

'See you about five,' said Linda. 'And don't work too hard and wear yourself out. I have a big night planned.'

As she hung up, she realised that her life in Jindalee Downs was too precious to ever give away entirely. She had family in Sydney and a company that employed twenty-two people full-time and countless others on a job-by-job basis, but no one made her feel more valued or appreciated than her two country neighbours. The phone rang and she thought immediately that it would be Billy ringing with some smart comment or to see if she wanted him to bring any extra vegetables from his garden.

'Yes, Billy Dwyer,' she said.

There was no response yet she could tell that somebody was there.

'Billy? Say something. Hello? Who is this? Who's there?'

The continued silence began to alarm her. But it wasn't quite silence. When she pressed her ear to the earpiece she could hear something, something familiar.

'Hello? Hello ...'

Whoever had called gently placed the phone back on its cradle but not before Linda recognised the music playing faintly in the background. Had she been meant to hear it or was it an oversight, or even a coincidence? Her blood turned to ice and she stopped breathing. It didn't matter that *Kind of Blue* was one of the greatest jazz records of all time or that millions of copies had been sold. There was only one person she knew who admired Miles Davis to the point of playing his music almost compulsively. And he was the last person Linda wanted to hear from.

In a panic she rang Al.

'Al, I think Grant just called me. What's happened?'

'I was about to ring you. I just heard.'

'Heard what, for Christ's sake?'

'About Grant's presentation to Garuda. You'll never guess who Garuda's new marketing director turned out to be.'

'Who?'

'Sharna's brother. Can you believe it?'

Sharna's brother. Linda mouthed the words but no sound passed her lips. She had a dim recollection of

Sharna's brother sitting grimly in court, never missing a session, the only member of the family to put in an appearance. She'd wondered at the time whether he was there out of a sense of duty, as the family representative — Sharna had hardly mentioned him — rather than because of brotherly love and the pain of loss. Maybe they'd been closer than she thought. She listened numbly as Al told her how the meeting had been aborted before it had even begun, with Sharna's brother threatening to fire the agency if they insisted on using Camera.

'I don't know what the situation is between Grant and Cameron but the word is, Cameron has had enough,' said Al. 'It's only gossip at this stage and, as you can imagine, the whole industry is buzzing with it. The only thing that's certain is that Grant will not be making the Garuda commercials.'

Linda gripped the phone so hard her knuckles turned white. The more Al said the more she was convinced that it was Grant who'd called her and the more certain she became of his motive. She started shaking uncontrollably. He had nothing to lose any more, nothing to lose by coming after her.

* * *

Linda's management training had taught her how to focus on a single issue at a time and not be distracted by other matters. Her training got her through dinner, although she was aware that Billy sensed something was amiss. Her job was made easier by Rodney's obvious excitement. He was like a child on an outing. He'd arrived wearing suit trousers that were ancient but spotless, and a white shirt several sizes too big. Only his boots, hat and shotgun were part of his regular garb and he left them at the door. His eyes sparkled and his ever-changing expressions did their best to settle into a smile. His joy was infectious and, despite everything, Linda couldn't help but get caught up in it.

Nobody ever ate a prawn with greater reverence or ocean trout with more wonder. The tastes fascinated Rodney and his determination to love everything on his plate even got him through the shock of the wasabi mayonnaise accompanying the fish. It wasn't just Rodney's delight in his discoveries that made her laugh but the tales he and Billy told about their years growing up together. However, it was the chocolate mud cake dessert Linda had bribed the Country Club chef to make that really stole the night and captured Rodney's heart. Prawns and fish were rare and exciting but chocolate was something he understood.

His excitement had him bobbing about and almost dancing when Linda wrapped up the remainder of the cake and gave it to him as he was leaving. Rodney paused on the veranda and forced himself to stand still. Goodbyes weren't part of his repertoire. He came and went, usually in a fury and always with purpose, real or imagined. But happiness had transcended his anger and he stalled in uncertainty. Without hesitating Linda leaned forward and kissed the little man lightly on his cheek. Rodney stood there stunned, immobile, so uncomprehending that even his hammering jaw for once stilled. Then, tentatively, he reached forward and kissed Linda's cheek. For a brief instant afterwards their eyes locked and it was Linda's turn to be taken aback. Whether Rodney's eyes just happened to catch the light at that very moment or somehow generated it internally, they blazed with the brilliance and colour of the opals he spent his life digging for. Without a word he spun around, grabbed his shotgun and took off into the night. Linda heard him chuckling all the way up to the top of the ridge.

When she went inside she found Billy had cleared the table and gone to sit outside on the front veranda. He'd poured himself a beer, her a wine, and sat with his feet up on the rail, smoking.

'That was a nice thing you did for Rodney,' he said.

Linda turned off the lights, came up behind him, kissed him on the neck and settled into the chair alongside him. A slight breeze, warm from the dry lands to the northwest, brushed over them. Gradually Linda made out the silhouettes of the ridges and the horizon across the treetops to the north. Overhead the Milky Way appeared as a low cloud almost within touching distance. Somewhere a small creature shrieked as it fell victim to an owl.

'You didn't drink much.'

'Couldn't,' said Billy. 'I couldn't drink more than Rodney and Rodney can't drink much. He watched me the whole night. Only drank when I drank. He and I both know what happens when he goes at it too hard.'

'Poor Billy. Do you ever stop looking after people?'

'Sometimes.'

'Was that story about the football and Blackie true?'

'Every word. Blackie got put down after he ripped into an Aboriginal kid. One of his mates threw his schoolbag over the fence and he went to get it back. You should've seen the mess Blackie made of him.

The doctor had to put fifty or sixty stitches into him. All I could think of was it could've been me.'

'You were lucky.'

'Funny thing is, we lived in fear of that dog but, Jeez, we missed him when he was gone.'

'It's often the way.'

Billy stubbed out his cigarette and dropped it into the jam tin.

'Linda?'

'Yes?'

'Are we going to talk about nothing all night or are you going to tell me what's up? Something happen down in Dubbo?'

'Dubbo? No, why would you think that?' She leaned back and gazed up at the stars, wondering what to say. 'Grant rang this morning.'

'Your ex-husband rang you?' Billy sat up. 'What did he say?'

'Nothing. That was the whole point. I guess he was just checking out the numbers from the phone account he took and I answered. He knows my number. He knows where I am.' She told him about the music in the background and about her phone call to Al.

'Hold on a minute,' said Billy. 'You have a film company? You're running it from here? I thought you were a schoolteacher.'

'It's a long story.'

'I think it's time you told it.' He turned and looked at her. 'Don't you?'

Linda took a long sip of her wine and stared out across the plains. She wondered whether the moon was still on the rise or had already been and gone. She remembered the lack of moonlight driving back from Dubbo the previous day and guessed the moon's appearance had been both early and brief.

'I don't have a clue where to begin.'

'Start when you were a schoolteacher.'

Linda took another long sip of her wine. Billy reached for the bottle and topped up her glass. It was a clear indication to her to take her time and leave nothing out.

'Billy, do you know what a westie is?'

'Someone from Sydney's western suburbs.'

'The term didn't exist when I took up teaching but the condition did. Being a woman and a westie meant having limited horizons and even more limited ambitions. My parents' only hope for me was that I'd do well enough at school to get a job somewhere nice, where I could meet nice people, marry someone nice, live in a nice house and produce nice children. I exceeded all their expectations when I did well at school and went on to university. They were ecstatic when I decided I wanted to become a teacher. Whoop-de-do. Kids nowadays complain about lack of opportunity but they should go back to the late sixties, early seventies. Girls didn't go into interesting occupations like marketing, finance or management. We were encouraged to become nurses or secretaries and only the very brightest and most determined hung on to become doctors, dentists, lawyers or accountants. The only other alternative was teaching.

'Initially I wanted to teach in primary school so I could teach a broad range of subjects. But I grew increasingly interested in art. Art opened my eyes to a world I never knew existed, a world of unlimited scope where any dream was possible. It was a world of unrestrained ambition and unbounded imagination where things didn't have to be nice, proper, orderly and respectful. Indeed, a lot of the work I loved was deliberately disturbing, disruptive and anything but nice. When the government bought Jackson Pollock's *Blue Poles* I could hardly wait to see it. I went up to Canberra and just stood in front of it, staring at it in absolute awe for hours on end, day after day. I couldn't believe that something so wonderful, so fresh and groundbreaking, actually existed. I went home and raved about it to parents who couldn't believe the government had wasted so much money on something so ridiculous. And do you know what? Almost everyone I spoke to outside of art school thought the same thing. For the first time in my life I began to suspect I didn't belong. But if I didn't belong there, where did I belong? I was a westie. What did I know about anywhere else?

'I discovered I had an aptitude for painting. My parents encouraged me and nearly fainted when they saw the drawings of nudes I did at life class. Nice girls didn't draw naked people. I think I was supposed to do watercolours of African violets. But I persevered despite their reservations and graduated with honours in art and distinctions in English and history. When I finished my training I thought, given my passes and the kind of person I was, I'd be sent to a nice genteel school somewhere, the kind of school my parents imagined, where the kids were well behaved and eager to learn. Instead they sent me to a school further west, where few of the kids were well behaved and even fewer could give a damn about learning anything.'

'Sort of thing the army does,' said Billy.

'I knew that in my little westie world I'd been sheltered from the sophistication and progressiveness of the eastern suburbs. Not even university cured me of that. I felt intimidated by students from the eastern suburbs. They all seemed so worldly and with it and knew so much more than I did. When I was posted to my first school I discovered how sheltered my life had really been. I knew nothing about life in the poorer suburbs. I went there bursting with optimism, remembering how I'd felt when I'd discovered the liberating effect of art. It was like a precious gift that I wanted to pass on and inspire others with. Dear God! You know, every lunchtime panel vans lined up along the streets outside the school and girls from years ten, eleven and twelve used to go and hop into them. They'd have sex with their deadbeat, unemployed boyfriends — kids who'd been students at the school only a year or two earlier — and then amble back to class where I was supposed to teach them. Can you imagine it? I was still a virgin. I was their teacher and still a virgin while they were having lunchtime sex with no more thought than I'd give to a peanut-butter sandwich.

'Some of the boys in the vans were also dealing drugs but I had no idea. I knew students at uni who smoked a bit of marijuana but these kids were popping pills and God only knows what else. I'd be talking about Renaissance painters and the revelation of perspective to a class in which half of my students were no longer capable of stringing two words together. So much for my gift! So much for opening their eyes! It didn't take me long to realise I didn't belong there either.

'Time passed and I didn't so much teach as cope. There were days when even coping was a triumph beyond all expectations. I turned to colleagues for sympathy and understanding. The sympathy and understanding turned into invitations to parties and to dates. I suddenly realised I was in the "meeting nice people" phase of the cycle and that the "marry someone nice" phase was next on the schedule. The fact was, my best prospect was to marry another teacher. That was what teachers did. We were so wrapped up in our little world that we didn't meet anyone else. I felt suffocated, and every day the walls closed in tighter around me.

'After three years I was transferred to a school closer to home, where the students were a whole lot better behaved and with whom I felt some affinity. I was back in my comfort zone and that made me vulnerable. I started going out with a maths teacher ten years my senior. He was a gentle giant with a big full beard and an easy-going, tolerant nature. He was like a big bear and this bear was looking for a mate with whom he could settle down for life. Of course my parents loved him, and for a while I thought I did too. He had a wider, more gregarious circle of friends, most of whom came from outside teaching. We went to dinner parties where people actually talked about politics, religion, money, the arts and even philosophy. It didn't dawn on me that it was this contact and conversation that I loved, not my big cuddly bear.

'Our interests embraced movies. We got involved in a film club that hired the local cinema one night a month to show classics like Kubrick's *Dr Strangelove*, Ingmar Bergman's *The Virgin Spring* and Milos Forman's *The Fireman's Ball*. Afterwards we'd debate the movies endlessly over pots of coffee and cheap wine. I loved it. It was like discussing art. One night one of our friends brought along a guest speaker who was a real live film director. Even though he only directed commercials, he'd actually been to the Cannes Film Festival and won awards in the advertising festival. He was utterly amazing. He stood up on the stage after the show and talked about the processes of making film, the people he'd met in Cannes and the magic of cinematography. He held us spellbound. I was over the moon when he agreed to come back to our friend's place for a drink. I'd never met anyone like him before. He was so cool, so with it, so handsome, so entertaining, so enthusiastic and so worldly. He lived on another planet, a world I craved. He must have sensed something because he asked for my phone number. I responded by asking for his. My friends looked on in astonishment. They couldn't believe this little westie could be so brazen. My big bear sat across from me with a sad half-smile on his face. He knew. He knew his future mama bear had slipped the shackles, kicked open the door of the cage and walked.'

'I take it Mr Wonderful was your husband-to-be?'

'Yes, it was Grant. I adored him. No, I worshipped him. I thought I'd died and gone to heaven when we started going out together. He took me into a world I knew existed but had never dared venture into. It was like I'd been reborn. His friends were all clever, witty, outrageous and utterly irreverent. They said things I didn't even dare think. He took me to restaurants where the meal cost more than I earned in an entire week as a schoolteacher. He took me to premieres of movies, to jazz concerts and art gallery openings. On a couple of occasions when I saw paintings I thought were outstanding he bought them for his apartment. Just like that. Money no object. Despite everything that's happened since, I have to say they were the most magical days of my life. I'd never been so happy. I felt that I'd finally found where I belonged. Oh, I didn't belong at first but I was like a giant sponge. I absorbed everything around me. I became one of them by osmosis. Everything about my new life was perfect, except for the fact that I was a modern-day Cinderella. At the end of play I still had to go home to my parents' house in westie-world and to my school to teach.

'Shortly after Grant split with the company he worked for and set up on his own, he asked me to move in with him. I didn't hesitate. My parents were appalled. For a while my teacher's salary helped keep us afloat but then things started to happen. He convinced me to give up teaching and go to work with him. He didn't have to ask twice. With my art background I began as a stylist-cum-wardrobe lady, running around and organising props and clothes for shoots. It was exciting, but exciting mainly because it was different. It didn't take me long to see what I really wanted to do. I wanted to become a producer and cost, organise and coordinate entire productions. I wanted to be the florist not just one of the flowers. Grant encouraged me. He took me under his wing and taught me the business. He claimed I was a natural and, I tell you what, I was a bloody natural. It had taken me a long time but I'd found my true vocation. I loved my job to the point where there weren't enough hours in the day or days in the week. Grant had to drag me out of my office, away from the set or out of a sound or videotape studio, to take me to dinner. I was the third of three producers but within six months I was winning more business than anyone else. Grant took on another couple of directors and the company grew.

'I thought I was a genius, but in truth Grant was the genius and his directors weren't far behind. It was their talent the agencies and advertisers wanted. I put the polish on the production and did the numbers that made things possible. I was only ever the facilitator. But in an industry where egos raged, when Grant called me a genius I was more than willing to believe him.'

'Can I get you some more wine?'

'God, where did it all go?'

Linda put her head back and tried to relax as Billy took the empty bottle to the kitchen. Once she'd started telling her story the floodgates had opened. Her torrent of words had surprised her and so had the intensity of her feelings. It was so unlike her to be so open, yet she had no regrets. She felt up and primed, as though she was pitching for a commercial. She heard a cork pop followed by Billy's footsteps and exhaled to release some of the tension that had built up inside her.

'It's a verdelho,' said Billy. 'Whatever that is.'

'So long as it's cold and wet.' She waited while Billy refilled their glasses and rolled a cigarette. The Milky Way looked closer than ever.

'When did things go pear-shaped?'

'They probably always were but I was too blind to see it. I was dazzled by my new life, Billy, and by my success. It's easy to look back now and be critical, but I wasn't stupid. I was just blindly in love: in love with Grant, my job and my new life. Despite the fact that Grant had walked into my little westie-world and literally charmed the pants off me, I guess I was naive enough to think I was the last girl he'd ever charm. It never occurred to me to question our relationship. We were Grant and Linda, Linda and Grant, a dynamic duo, entwined and inseparable. We lived together, worked together and went on wonderful overseas holidays together. I was blind to the fact that, between times, Grant went away on location with beautiful young actresses and models, gorgeous make-up ladies, wardrobe girls and stylists. Beautiful people were just a fact of our lives. We were surrounded by beautiful people. Heavens above, we were beautiful people ourselves. I was blind to the looks some of the girls in the office exchanged when we announced we were getting married. I was blind to the guarded nature of their congratulations. Grant was the sun around which I revolved and I was made blind by his brilliance.

'I had mixed feelings when I discovered I was pregnant. Having a baby meant change at a time when I didn't want anything to change. My life was perfect the way it was. On the other hand, Grant was ecstatic. When I voiced my concerns he dismissed them. This was the new age of women's liberation. He told me to keep working and doing what I loved until the baby was ready to drop. He talked about putting a crib in my office and how cool it would be to breastfeed the baby while I was pitching our quotes to agencies. He made it sound like another glamorous stage of our glamorous life.

'Six months later Grant took on a new producer and I was promoted-stroke-relegated to office manager. Producers need to be able to fly and I was becoming increasingly reluctant to because of the baby. The new producer was called Sharna and we clicked immediately. She had fire in her belly, bubbled with energy and confidence and could reduce the whole office to fits of laughter with her cheek. We loved her. Our clients loved her. She had big flashing eyes, jet-black hair and could not be intimidated. She was drop-dead gorgeous and, the funny thing is, I didn't expect my wonderful husband's producer to be anything but.

'Sharna became my best friend. She often shared meals with us and when the baby came along she often babysat for us. The two of us had girls' nights out together, shopped together and went to movies together. Some of the things we got up to were outrageous. She was my best friend. My mistake was thinking I was hers.' Linda paused as though reviewing a flood of memories, not all of them pleasant.

'So what happened?'

'What do you think happened? Jammy, my daughter Jasmine, grew too big and disruptive to take into the office and preschool would only take her two days a week. I tried leaving her at Mum's, but by the time I'd driven out west, had the cup of tea and the third degree, half of the day was gone. The changes I'd feared took place and my perfect life slipped away from me. I became housewife, mother and spectator to the life I craved.

'Things changed between Grant and me. Naturally I blamed myself. Grant wanted a lover who was also a beautiful, ebullient, effervescent companion and as wrapped up in his daily affairs as he was. I was wrapped up in nappies, NapiSan, reading stories, fund-raising, keeping house, shopping. The highlight of my day was seeing someone I knew at the supermarket. I used to breathe a sigh of relief when Grant brought Sharna home with him for dinner because it made things easier. I didn't have to deal with Grant on my own. I couldn't instantly get up to speed with his world and he wasn't interested in mine. Sometimes I'd chat away and think I was being bright and entertaining and then I'd catch a look on his face that told me he'd give his right arm to be anywhere else. I didn't blame him. I blamed myself.

I hated what I'd become. I was boring, a boring little westie housewife. The only good days were the one or two days a week I managed to spend in the office. I consoled myself that once Jammy started school, my life could get back to the way it was.

'I went back to work the week Jammy started school. I got myself an assistant and started producing, not for Grant but for the other in-house directors. Either my assistant or I picked up Jammy after school and brought her into the office. Strangely enough, it worked really well. My one or two days a week had kept me up to speed on costs and changes in production. I took my directors' reels around and started hustling for work. I surpassed everyone's expectations, even my own, with the number of bids I won. I felt my relationship with Grant was getting back on track now that we had work in common again. Grant seemed happy and, of course, my directors raved because they were paid on the basis of the jobs they did.

'One day one of them took me to lunch to say thanks. I chose the restaurant, one I hadn't been to for a while and which Grant used to take me to. It was midweek so I didn't bother making a reservation. The director dropped me off at the restaurant while he went to park his car. I opened the door and looked around to make sure there was a table free. I stopped dead in my tracks. Honestly, if my dear mother had been doing a strip on one of the tables I wouldn't have been more stunned. Somehow I managed to turn around and leave before anyone saw me. I intercepted the director and told him the restaurant was full. We went to some other place. The director kept asking me what was wrong. He said I looked like I'd seen a ghost. I may as well have seen a ghost. I'd just seen my husband at a table kissing Sharna. If that wasn't bad enough, they were supposed to be in Perth shooting a commercial and weren't due back for another two days.

'When we returned to the office I went through the call sheets and production schedules for the jobs where Grant and Sharna had gone away together on location. Surprise, surprise. According to the schedules, Grant invariably returned a day or two before he told me he was coming back. I had no doubt where he'd spent the time in between. I was amazed that he'd got away with it. The days following a shoot were always pretty intense with everyone wanting to see the rushes. It slowly dawned on me that everyone knew. They had to know for business to go on as usual. I don't know what was worse, the hurt of the betrayal or the shame and humiliation. My whole world, my wonderful world, had flipped upside down. There are no words to adequately describe how I felt. Hurt, betrayed, abandoned, humiliated, crushed, you name it. Lump them all together and you still don't even come close. Grant and Sharna were having an affair and, as far as I could tell, had been for a number of years. And everyone had known but me.

'I told my assistant I'd pick up Jammy and left the office. I had quotes to finish and people to call back but none of that mattered. I picked up Jammy and went straight home. If it had just been a fling I think I could've handled that. But it wasn't. Sharna was his mistress and had been for some time. She probably slept with him more than I did. I wanted to scream and poke her eyes out when I thought of her deceit, of all the times we'd gone out together and how she'd played along with the best-buddy act. Advertising and the film business are full of predatory girls who are prepared to sleep their way to the good life and cold-bloodedly target their bosses, but I never thought it would happen to us. I dismissed Sharna as one of them, a gold-digger, someone who wanted the high life without putting in the hard yards. I was Grant's wife and I decided to fight for what was mine.

'For two days I carried on like it was business as usual while underneath I seethed and plotted how I'd deal with Grant on his "official" return from Perth. I wanted Grant to open the bowling and ask me what was wrong. All I had to do was give him the silent aloof treatment and he'd give me the oportunity. The trouble was, things didn't quite go according to plan. He arrived home complaining of jet lag, gave me a perfunctory kiss and a hug and handed me his carryall full of dirty laundry. It was the laundry that did it. That seemed to define my place in the scheme of things. He'd spent the last three days screwing his mistress then brought his dirty laundry home to his wife.

'It's silly, isn't it? A bag of laundry. The devil is always in the detail. You know, people in the industry sprinkle obscenities around like confetti but it wasn't a habit I had acquired. But the gloves came off at that instant and I let Grant have it with everything I had. I don't think he'd ever heard me swear before. The words I used were chosen to hurt and had hardly been devalued by over-use. They didn't miss their target. For a moment Grant stood there absolutely stunned which encouraged me to really go for it. The next thing I knew I was sprawled on the floor. I didn't realise Grant had hit me until he lifted me up and slammed me against the wall.'

'He hit you?'

'And how. Two seconds I think was all it took for my emotions to go from righteous rage to abject terror. I felt so utterly helpless. He pinned me to the wall and said, "Don't you ever speak to me like that again." The sense of threat and violence was overwhelming. I'd never experienced anything like this in my life. Next thing I was apologising. *I* was apologising. I was begging him for forgiveness. Somehow his deceit, his infidelity and his violence were all my fault. He let go of me and I just crumpled to the floor. He stepped over me, walked to the fridge and got himself a beer and sat down to watch the seven o'clock news. Business as normal. The whole side of my face was throbbing where he'd hit me. I could barely comprehend what had happened. Suddenly the dam burst and the tears started. They flowed uncontrollably. I heard a noise and looked up. Jammy was sitting on the top stair, watching. She must have heard her father come home, run out of her bedroom and seen the whole thing. I'll never forget the look on her face.

'She crept fearfully down the stairs and came up and put her arms around my neck. "What did you do wrong, Mummy?" she said. She was only five years old and, in hindsight, she equated what had happened to me with the spankings I threatened her with when she misbehaved. But her question reinforced the fact that what had happened was somehow all my fault.'

'What did you do?'

'I should've grabbed Jammy and gone home to Mum's. But what would I have achieved? I would've been back where I started, suffocating in sympathy and I-told-you-sos. I would've lost everything. I was also certain Sharna would've walked in five minutes after I walked out and there was no way I was going to let that happen. I figured I'd let things cool down.

'I couldn't show my face in the office the next day because of the bruising. You know, it was only when I was trying to cover the bruising with foundation that I made the connection with the times Sharna had taken days or mornings off after she'd slipped in the bathroom or walked into a door. I suddenly realised the true reason for her bruising. A bag hadn't fallen out of the overhead locker and hit her on the face. A set hadn't collapsed on her and bruised her arms. The truth was appalling but all I could think was, the bitch deserved it.

'For days I did nothing but think about my situation. The solution seemed obvious to me. Grant and I had never been happier than when I'd acted as his producer. I decided Sharna had to go. I told Grant he had to get rid of her, that I'd be his producer and that everything would be rosy again between us. I told him I wasn't going back into the office until she'd packed up and gone. Grant had a different view on things. He'd listened to me, now I had to listen to him. He fired me and kept Sharna. She stayed on as his producer and I was banned from the office. He told me that I was ungrateful, that I was just a nothing schoolteacher he'd plucked out of suburbia, that I had money, a nice apartment to live in, a nice car and an easy life, and that millions of women would gladly trade places with me. He told me I should be happy with that. I wasn't happy but what choice did I have? I couldn't face going home. I couldn't admit, not even to myself, that I was a battered, bruised and emotionally abandoned wife.

'For three years we kept up an illusion of being a

happily married couple. We still had some good times, enough good times to put up with the nights he came home and mistook me for his punching bag. We went on holidays overseas together with Jammy. Sometimes I thought he still loved me, sometimes I thought I still loved him. One night we had an argument and, to be honest, I can't even remember what it was over. Probably a broken commitment. He may have failed to turn up to a dinner party we'd been invited to, or forgotten that I was waiting for him in a restaurant. It was the sort of thing we'd argued about before but this time it got a little out of hand. He hit me and for once I fought back. I wound up in hospital with a broken collarbone and a cut on the back of my head that needed stitching.'

'Nice guy, your ex.'

'I took some comfort, malicious comfort, from the fact that I wasn't the only one suffering. There were plenty of times Grant came home in a rage in the middle of the night after a row with Sharna. I knew she'd be taking time off the next day as a result. I still spoke to people in the office by phone from time to time when I needed to find Grant. Some of the staff were quite sympathetic towards me and I learned the cause of their rows. Sharna wasn't happy just being Grant's mistress and made no secret of her ambitions. She wanted her status upgraded and made official. She'd taken my job, now she wanted the rest of my life. She wanted to be Grant's wife and mother to his children.'

Linda looked down at her glass, surprised to find it empty once more. When Billy went to refill it she shook her head.

'I'm nearly finished. Then you can make me a nice cup of tea.'

'No worries.'

'I'll cut to the chase. Grant came home one night about ten o'clock. His face was flushed and he was clearly agitated. I knew something had happened but I didn't dare ask until he'd calmed down. He poured himself a scotch and slumped down in a chair, staring into space. When I took him a coffee, he grabbed hold of my hand and said, "If anyone asks, I was home all night, okay?" "Why?" I asked. He hit the roof. "Just do as you're bloody told!" he said. "For once in your life, just do as you're bloody told."

'I ran away into the kitchen. When you've been hit a few times you learn when not to hang around. But I was also worried for Grant. He looked scared and I'd never seen him look scared before. I couldn't imagine what had happened. When he left for work the next morning he was really subdued, kind of apprehensive. I took Jammy to school, did some shopping and came home. I was just thinking about making a sandwich when the phone rang. It was Grant's secretary. She'd rung to tell me that the police were interviewing Grant in his office. The police! Sometimes your mind makes connections without any conscious thought guiding it. "Where's Sharna?" I asked. I was told she hadn't come in and hadn't rung to say where she was. I'd just hung up, fearing the worst, when my doorbell rang. I opened the door and found two detectives there. They asked if they could come in. I was too stunned, too stricken, to argue.

'They introduced themselves and asked me what time Grant had come home the night before. I told them I wouldn't answer any questions until they told me what Grant was supposed to have done and why he was being interviewed. They asked if I knew

Sharna. Then they told me that she'd been found dead in her apartment, that it appeared she'd been assaulted and that the assault had resulted in her death. I might not have the words quite right but that's the gist of what they said. They didn't say killed and they didn't say murdered but they said enough. I went into shock. Sharna dead? The detectives helped me over to an armchair and sat me down. They brought me a glass of water and apologised for having to break the news and apologised for having to ask me questions. They told me witnesses had seen Grant enter Sharna's apartment early in the evening but so far no one had seen him leave. They again asked me what time he'd arrived home. What could I say? Grant had asked me to lie and say he'd been home all night, but how could he have been home all night if they had witnesses that saw him go into Sharna's apartment? The detectives must have guessed what was going through my mind. One of them asked if my husband drove a red Porsche. When I nodded he said, "We haven't found anyone who saw your husband leave Sharna's apartment, but, if it helps jog your memory, a red Porsche was seen driving away just before 10 pm. The driver seemed to be in a bit of a hurry."

'I don't like lying, Billy, and it's something I've never been good at. I told the police that he got home just after ten. It seemed ridiculous to say anything else. They thanked me for my cooperation. One of them used the phone in the kitchen and then they left. A little while later I got a phone call from a solicitor who said he was representing Grant. He asked if the police had been and what I'd told them. He told me Grant had been taken to Mosman police station for questioning.

'Grant came home by taxi around nine. He closed the door quietly and stood in the hall looking at me. "Grant, what have you done?" I said. He ignored me. He just glared at me. "You stupid bitch!" he said. "I told you what to say, but did you? You had to open your big mouth, didn't you, you stupid, stupid bitch!" He clenched his fists and started towards me, as if he was going to thrash the daylights out of me. "Go ahead!" I yelled. "Beat me as much as you like. But what are the police going to think when they come back tomorrow?" That stopped him. "What have you done?" I demanded. "Tell me!" He just shrugged. "Nothing, I've done nothing. It was an accident," he said. "We argued. I pushed her and she fell and hit her head on the edge of the table. It was an accident. The cops can think what they like but it was an accident." I asked him what the argument had been about. He did this sneering, incredulous sort of laugh. "The stupid bitch went and got pregnant on me. Can you believe it? Pregnant, for fuck's sake." He shook his head and laughed again, as though it was the most ridiculous thing he'd ever heard. "Why the fuck did she have to go and do that?"

'As soon as Grant left the next morning, I packed up Jammy and as many of our things as I could fit in the car and drove to my parents' place. I'd had enough. One of the detectives had given me his card so I rang and told him where I was. They came out to see me later that afternoon and asked if Grant had ever hit me. I told them he had and told them about the collarbone. They asked if I would stand up in court and testify that he'd hit me. I told them I would. It turned out that they'd found bruising on Sharna's body that was inconsistent with her fall. They'd also found old bruising. The office receptionist had told the police about the number of times Sharna had come to work covered in bruises and her suspicions as to the cause. They charged Grant that evening.

'The police argued that Sharna didn't fall but was knocked down by a punch. She hit her head first on the edge of the table and again when her head whiplashed against the floor. Grant got bail and used every trick in the book to delay his trial. I lost count of the times he rang threatening me with all hell if I didn't withdraw my testimony.' Linda sighed and drew her hand through her hair.

'Grant always maintained that Sharna's death was an accident and that he'd never hit her. He admitted arguing with her, admitted pushing her and admitted running away. He claimed he ran away because he was confused and upset and because he wanted to protect Jammy and me from scandal. But the police did their job well and built up a compelling argument of a violent man who one day went too far. Experts testified at his trial that much of Sharna's bruising was the result of blows and not caused by her impact with either the table or the floor. Neighbours told how they'd heard arguing that night and Sharna screaming. But for all the good work the police had done, they needed a clincher. The thing was, nobody had witnessed Grant hitting Sharna and, of course, she'd always denied that he had. She'd always had some excuse. The evidence against him on that score was purely circumstantial. But my testimony gave the evidence credibility, particularly in regard to my broken collarbone and the lacerations on the back of my head.

'To this day Grant believes the case turned on my testimony. Jammy had seen him hit me, of course, but

I wouldn't let her testify. His barrister grilled me for hours but I stuck to my story. They knew how important it was. Grant is convinced it was my testimony, and mine alone, that got him convicted and sent to gaol.

'There was this strange period between his conviction and sentencing. Even the police seemed relieved when Grant was found guilty. They thought the verdict could've gone either way. While nobody who knew Grant believed for a second that he intended to kill Sharna, I know he would've wanted to punish her. He didn't hold back when he hit and he seemed to enjoy the power it gave him. Grant undoubtedly caused her death, but I was prepared to concede that there'd been an element of misfortune. It was because of this ambivalence about his degree of guilt that half the people in the office expected him to get off with weekend detention or six months at worst. Yet the judge saw things in very black and white terms. I think he saw through Grant to the kind of man he really is.

'His summary was frighteningly blunt. According to him, Grant deliberately attacked Sharna because she told him she was pregnant. He hit her hard enough to cause her to fall and in the process suffer fatal injuries. He ran away and, in running away, showed callous disregard for the victim. At no stage had he shown remorse for what he'd done. He showed no sympathy towards relatives or friends of the victim. He showed no regret over the loss of what would have been his child. My testimony confirmed Grant as a bully with a history of violence towards women. I know from conversations I'd had with the detectives that the police were hoping Grant would get up to four years. The judge gave him eight.'

'Christ Almighty. Eight years?'

'Eight years with a non-parole period of six years. The court was stunned by the severity of the sentence. I felt like someone had punched me in the belly and knocked all the breath out of me. Then I looked at Grant. However badly I felt, the effect on him was infinitely worse. He staggered and I thought he was going to fall. He turned, as though looking for his barrister or anyone who could help him, when his eyes locked on mine. For a moment he seemed to forget all about his fear. I'll never forget the look on his face. It was pure hate, the kind of look that turns the blood in your veins to ice. Someone stood in front of me and broke the contact. I all but ran from the court.'

'Eight years.'

'He only served six.'

'That's more than enough. Do you want me to make you tea now?'

'I haven't finished. Maybe I'll have some more verdelho. Just half a glass.'

Billy tipped a little more wine into her glass. The breeze had finally died away completely and there wasn't even the rustle of leaves to disturb the silence of the night.

'The accountants rang the following day and asked me to come into the office. They'd held off calling me because of the uncertainty over Grant's sentence. They told me Film Gate, which was the name of the company, was heavily in debt and that they needed my signature to begin the process of selling it or winding it up. I was stunned. As far as I knew, the company had never been anything other than successful. I went in and discovered how Grant had bled Film Gate dry paying his legal expenses. Because of the trial and the demands on his time from lawyers, he'd been doing a lot fewer jobs. All up we were doing a third of the normal number of jobs and we owed money all over town. I discovered something else, though discovered isn't quite the right word.

'In the early days of Film Gate, Grant assigned forty per cent of the shares in the company to me to minimise his tax. It was a simple income-splitting exercise. He paid himself director's fees on every commercial he made, took bonuses out of profits and paid me an inflated salary. At some stage, he'd allowed our two tied directors to buy ten per cent each from his sixty per cent but still left me holding my original forty per cent. Maybe he didn't want to pay the stamp duty on transferring my shares back into his name or realised the day would come when I wouldn't draw any salary and wanted to keep splitting the dividends. My shares had never been an issue because I knew I was just holding them for Grant. Suddenly they assumed enormous importance.

'The accountants gave us three choices: sell, close the door or try to trade our way out. Nobody thought we could trade our way back into the black without Grant, our biggest star, but I thought otherwise. There was plenty of work on offer and I still had two sought-after directors and the nucleus of a good team. Besides, I was desperate. When we'd separated, Grant had paid me an allowance directly into my bank account and he also paid Jammy's school fees. But now there was no money left. I had no choice but to go back to work and earn some. I needed Film Gate to keep going. I convinced the others that we could trade on.

'Grant still had debts to settle with his lawyers and the leases on the apartment and his car. I put a deal to them that I would settle his debts in exchange for his forty per cent. Grant didn't want to pay his lawyers another cent but they in turn put a proposition to him that included appealing the sentence. Grant had little choice. He was desperate to appeal. Of course he agreed. I don't know how much effort his lawyers put into the appeal but it failed miserably. I borrowed money from my parents and my sister and gained control of the company, distressed as it was.

'I set about reassuring clients that we were back in business and reassuring crew that they would get paid if they worked for us. I'd built up a fair bit of goodwill and drew on every bit of it. It was a battle, a day-by-day struggle. Just when we looked like getting our heads above water, we had a job go bad on us that nearly put us under for good. The two directors stuck by me and took equity in place of salary. I paid them and myself just enough to live on and ploughed the rest of our fees back into the business. We survived and I ended up still in control of sixty-two per cent of the business.

'It took me eighteen months to pay back the bank, my parents and my sister. When one of the directors decided to try his luck in America, I offered his equity to the accountant of an advertising agency I'd had dealings with. He was clever, young and ambitious but, more than that, he was a man in the wrong job. He was crunching numbers for the agency's head office in Chicago. I thought he was born to run a business and I was desperate for someone to take over the finances and administration of Film Gate so I could dedicate myself to producing and building the business back up to a position of dominance. He agreed to join us and that was the turning point.'

'Smart move.'

'Thanks. I'm proud of what I accomplished. It was hard work and tough times but, I'll be honest with you, I loved every second of it, every success and every knock-back. I rebuilt the business out of nothing.'

'Like I say, well done.'

'Grant, of course, doesn't see things that way. I think he somehow imagines Film Gate could have run itself while he was in gaol and delivered him a steady stream of income. It didn't help that one of my young producers, a guy Grant had picked up off the street and given the same instruction he gave me all those years earlier, had stayed loyal to him, visited him in gaol and put money in his prison account. When I found out he was visiting Grant and doing things for him, I didn't fire him or tell him to stop. In truth, I was blown away by his loyalty. I commended him. It didn't occur to me that he was also feeding Grant's hatred with distorted tales of my success. The end result is, Grant is convinced that I took advantage of Sharna's death to make sure he got locked away so I could steal his business. He also believes I did a deal with his lawyers to make sure the appeal failed and he'd stay locked away. As ridiculous as it sounds, that is what he believes and that's what's been eating away at him for the past six years. I'm sure he blames me for his latest setback. I'm sure he blames me for everything that's gone wrong in his life. That's why I came out here to hide.'

'I'll make you a cup of tea.'

Linda shook her head.

'I don't know. It's so late. Why don't we just go to bed?'

'You're not ready for bed. You're wound up like a watch. I want you to stay there and listen for the night parrot.'

'Night parrot?'

'Yes, the night parrot. It's what you do out here when you can't sleep. You have to relax and listen real hard.'

'How will I know if it's a night parrot?'

'I dunno. Nobody's heard one for more than fifty years.'

Linda laughed and her tension began to seep away. She swung her feet up on the rail and gazed into the darkness. Listening for a bird that was probably extinct wasn't such a silly idea. Her whole body relaxed as she began to let go of the thoughts whirling around inside her head and embraced the vastness of the outback.

* * *

'So,' said Lucio, when he realised Neil was breaking for coffee, 'so now we know why Grant was sent to gaol. I think Linda has every right to live in fear of him.'

'There is no excuse for a man hitting a woman,' said Milos. 'None at all.'

'I don't think that is what Lucio meant,' said Ramon.

'No?'

'No, Milos. Despite Linda's protestations that the police did a good job, I think it is clear her evidence was pivotal. Without her evidence I doubt there would have been a conviction. Look at the facts. They argued, he pushed, she fell, he panicked. Sharna has been described as fiery and not easily intimidated. I imagine she also had a quick temper. Of course they argued and maybe sometimes the arguments got a little physical. It is quite possible that, on some occasions, the volatile Sharna even threw the first punches. What worries me is that there is no evidence that Sharna ever suffered anything more than bruises. I'm not condoning what Grant did, but if he is half as violent as he's been portrayed, I would have expected broken bones. They were together for what — five, six years? If he was going to hurt her, I mean break her arm or fracture her skull, don't you think he would have done so earlier? I think she was unlucky to hit her head, and he was unlucky that she hit her head. I accept that Grant was a bully, but couldn't he also be a victim of bad luck? Six years in gaol is a long time for bad luck.'

'You overlook the fact that he broke Linda's collarbone.'

'Ahhh, Milos, the break that broke the defence. Linda's testimony.'

'That's right. You can't ignore it.'

'Let's just say that the collarbone was a lucky break for Linda. A very lucky break. Grant went to gaol and she wound up with everything she wanted.'

'That is preposterous,' said Milos. 'You are adopting Lucio's argument. It wasn't so long ago that you took the opposing view and lectured us on the characteristics of domestic violence offenders, how they blamed everyone but themselves for their situation. Make up your mind, Ramon. You can't ride two horses at the same time, no? Everything Neil has said about Grant suggests he conforms to the stereotype you defined. He sees himself as the victim. He is angry and bitter because he feels betrayed. Sharna betrayed him first by getting pregnant and then by getting herself killed. Linda betrayed him by testifying. It's everyone's fault but his that he is in gaol. The cold hard facts are: a woman is dead because Grant assaulted her. That is why he went to gaol. And his going to gaol did not make Linda successful. Linda became successful because she was brave enough, strong enough and clever enough to take a debt-ridden company and turn it into something.'

'I'd like to hear Grant's side of the story.'

'You don't think Linda's telling the truth?'

'Is she? Or is he? Truth is the big issue in Neil's story, is it not?'

'So who do you think is telling the truth?' cut in Lucio.

'I am,' said Neil plaintively, but it was clear he was also mocking them. He shifted in his seat to try and ease his cast into a more comfortable position. 'How many times do I have to tell you?'

Chapter Twenty-four

For the second time, Grant's world came crashing down around him. His life and career were in tatters and once again it wasn't his fault! He'd done nothing wrong. In fact, he'd done everything right. His bitterness at this latest injustice plumbed new depths. He stared at the television, oblivious to the twittering fools on the morning show, while his anger slowly built.

Cameron hadn't sacked him as he'd threatened to do but had sacrificed him nonetheless. He'd fired him off the job and successfully re-pitched the quote with a new director. He kept Grant on in acknowledgement of the fact that it had been his ideas and the star-studded crew he'd assembled that had really won the job. It seemed a perfect solution all round. Cameron would get the payday his fledgling company desperately needed and the client and agency would get the spectacular commercials they'd been promised. Only Grant was left out in the cold. With nothing.

Nothing!

Prison had taught Grant how to hide his feelings no matter how depressed, frightened or angry he was. He put on a brave face for Jasmine and his parole officer and shrugged off the commiserations of everyone who'd worked with him on the submission. He allowed no glimpse of the bitterness beyond his façade. He hit his pillow anaesthetised by Johnnie Walker only to wake up in the morning dead in the soul with nothing to do and nothing to look forward to. Cameron told him to take a month off on full pay and to go and sit on a beach somewhere up in Queensland. Grant agreed. He couldn't even contemplate going into the office, where he knew everything would be buzzing with activity and everyone running around doing the final pre-production on his job. Someone had to pay for the injustices he'd suffered and he didn't have to look far to be reminded who that someone was. It was hard to watch television for more than thirty minutes without seeing at least one commercial her company — *his* company — had made. Cameron had told him to go take a holiday. Grant decided instead to take revenge.

He turned off the television just as the weather girl excitedly told him there were lots of sunny icons up and down the coast. He put on a Miles Davis tape, pulled the phone account he'd taken from Linda's sister out of his desk drawer and started ringing the numbers he'd marked. Miles Davis had just begun to play 'Freddie Freeloader', second track, side one, when Linda spoke to him. The sound of her voice was as immediately recognisable as it was unexpected. He'd already cross-referenced the numbers on the phone account with those he'd taken from Fran's teledex. He had that number under J Downs. Who the hell was J Downs? And, more to the point, who the hell was Billy Dwyer? He smiled grimly when the tone of her voice changed from affection to apprehension. She had every right to be apprehensive, every fucking right! He gently replaced the handset.

Grant rocked back on his chair, deep in thought. He had a place. The phone account listed the number under the Walgett exchange. And he had two names: J Downs, which he assumed was the name Linda was living under, and Billy Dwyer who, judging by Linda's voice, was at the very least a close friend. All he needed now was an address. He rang directory enquiries.

'Hi,' he said brightly. 'I'm after the number for a Miss or Mrs J Downs. I don't have an address but I know she lives somewhere in the Walgett area.'

'Hold the line, please.'

Grant was happy to hold.

'Are you there? I'm sorry, there doesn't appear to be anyone by the name of J Downs but there is a G Downs who runs a general store up on the Ridge.'

Grant frowned. He could imagine Linda doing many things but never running a general store way out in the bush.

'Do you have an L Sinclair?'

'There are four listings under Sinclair but no L Sinclairs.'

'Do you have a Billy Dwyer?' he asked. 'Same exchange.'

'I have a W Dwyer, Stony Creek Road. Is that who you're after?'

'I guess so, unless there are two W Dwyers.'

'There's only the one. I'll give you the number.'

Grant wrote it down and double-checked it, thanked the operator and hung up. Where the hell was Stony Creek Road and what was the relevance of J Downs? There'd been a time when he could locate pretty well any place in Australia. He'd had a policy at Film Gate that any map bought for any production had to go into the map library after the shoot to supplement the maps they kept for each state and major city. The number of maps rapidly grew and they became a handy tool for finding locations and out-of-the-way places. Cameron had set up the same system but hadn't yet done enough jobs to build a worthwhile collection.

Grant had trained enough producers to know how to think like one. He recalled shooting commercials at Collarenebri and Lightning Ridge and how every large property and patch of dirt that produced opals acquired a name that often never appeared on anything but local maps, and even disappeared off them when the mines petered out. Rather than drop down to the newsagents for a Gregory's map of New South Wales, he rang the Department of Mineral Resources and asked if they had maps of the opal fields around Walgett. Of course they did. Did they have any maps that included farms as well? They had maps with all the major properties marked. Grant hopped in his car and within half an hour had all the maps he needed for the whole Cumborah, Grawin, New Angledool, Walgett region.

It was only when he'd had time to look at the maps in detail that the inconsistencies appeared. Trails that appeared on one map were absent on others and none were named. The main roads, if the dirt tracks between the dots on the maps could be called main roads, seemed fairly consistent although the distances between the towns varied, sometimes by as much as twenty per cent. None of the maps showed Stony Creek Road yet he knew that was the road Billy Dwyer lived along. Obviously Stony Creek Road was represented by one of the thin black or dotted lines, but which one? As he ran his eye over the maps a name jumped out at him. Jindalee Downs. J Downs. It was just a dot in an open area with no marked road running anywhere near it. With growing excitement Grant realised the answer to his search lay in somehow putting Stony Creek Road and Jindalee Downs together. His brain clicked into high gear. His life had regained both point and purpose and revenge was a powerful motivator. Once he found Linda, all his problems would be solved and hers would begin. Finding her was inevitable, merely a matter of process. It was the sort of thing film people did all the time. All he had to do was think outside the square.

Jimmy tried doing the quick crossword but didn't have any heart for it. The gloom inside the stock and station gave an illusion of cool but that was all. The day had started out bad and only gotten worse, the last malicious gasp of an Indian summer. Even without the hot dry winds blowing in from the west the day would have been intolerable. There wasn't a cloud in the sky. Peter, his offsider, was filling in time by stocking shelves. Neither expected to do much business that day. Every beast on four legs would have holed up somewhere in the shade out of the wind and every two-legged creature with half a brain would've done likewise. Jimmy knew he could fire a shotgun down any street in Walgett and not run the slightest risk of hitting anyone. Nobody came to town on days like this.

'Why don't you take an early lunch,' said Jimmy.

Peter stopped stacking and checked his watch. It was only half-past eleven.

'Lunch won't be on yet.'

'The bar will be open. Have a cold one or three and I'll see you back here around one.'

'Fair enough,' said Peter.

Deciding who should go to lunch first was the biggest problem Jimmy had faced all morning. He didn't think there'd be anyone in the RSL yet, other than the usual deadbeats watching the horseracing, but the prospect of a cold beer was pretty enticing. What decided the issue was the fact that whoever went first had to come back so the other could go to lunch. Whoever went second didn't necessarily have to come back at all. Jimmy had no intention of coming back after lunch. There again, he thought, he might just close at lunchtime and put the sign on the door that said where they could be found, not that he expected anyone to come looking, not on such a brute of a day. He watched as Peter took his hat off the peg and stepped outside into a heat that sucked moisture out of your body, your eyes and your lungs. Jimmy reckoned Pete would have more than twenty flies going for his mouth before he stepped off the pavement.

He turned back to his crossword and tried to think what a seven-letter word for trench or bomb shelter could be. When the phone rang its sudden sound startled him. He frowned. It could only mean somebody wanted him to deliver something, somebody who didn't want to venture out in the heat himself. His voice was surly as he answered.

'Jimmy Tremaine.'

'Good morning, Mr Tremaine. I'm John Wilson, executive producer of Gunshot Productions. We're making a film on the way communications shape society and we need a little help.'

'You say you're making a film?'

'That's correct. For ABC TV.'

'And you need my help?'

'Yes.'

Jimmy was suddenly interested. He didn't know much about films, but the occasional film crews that had been through the region had splashed money around like confetti. The possibility someone might want to splash some his way had his full attention.

'What can I do for you?'

'We're trying to locate the owner of Sydney's largest commercial film company. We believe she's living out your way temporarily. We need to film an interview with her.'

'Don't know about any film people living out here.' Jimmy found it hard to hide his disappointment.

'Her name's Linda Sinclair, tall, light brown hair ...'

'Had a good-looking sort come through here about September last year looking for somewhere to rent. Real good-looking.'

'That will be her.'

'She's not here. Last I heard she was in Dubbo.'

'No, we know for a fact she's living somewhere around Jindalee Downs. Do you know a man called Billy Dwyer?'

'Yeah, of course. Jindalee Downs is his place.'

'Apparently she's staying somewhere near him.'

'You're kidding!'

'No.'

'Well, bugger me!'

'So you know where she is?'

'I sent her to see Billy. Jesus, he's a sly bastard. He denies ever laying eyes on her, but I reckon he's got her shacked up in his parents' old place.'

'Where would that be?'

'Now you're asking. I know it's on the western end of Billy's property, but I'm not real sure how to get there. It's somewhere off Stony Creek, but, mate, there are tracks heading off everywhere. There are rumours of opal up there. It'd take a bit of finding. I could give you Billy's number but I think you'd be wasting your time.'

'There's another problem there.'

'What sort of problem?'

'Apparently Linda Sinclair has taken a year off away from work and doesn't want to be disturbed. Our only chance of getting an interview is if we arrive unannounced. I can't ring Billy Dwyer without tipping her off. I want someone I can trust to be discreet to find her for us. We're prepared to pay.'

'How much?'

'You tell me.'

Jimmy thought for a while. He had a pretty good idea where the house was even though he'd never been there. Given half a day and a bit of luck he was pretty sure he could find it, particularly if there was a buck in it.

'I could do it but I reckon it'd take me a couple of days. Pretty wild country out there on the red ridges.'

'But you can do it?'

'Reckon. Thing is, we're pretty busy right now. I'd have to pay someone to cover for me.'

'What's the bottom line?'

'A hundred a day for each of us. That's four hundred dollars.'

'Be cheaper to get a helicopter.'

'You still gotta know where to look. Maybe I can do it in a day and a half. Three hundred.'

'When can you start?'

'Tomorrow. Bit too hot today and I've got things to arrange.'

'Okay. I want detailed maps and instructions. I'll send you one hundred dollars up front, one hundred dollars on receipt of your maps and instructions and another hundred on the day we do the interview. There's no point in you finding her if she's not there when we go to do the interview, understand? You can't say a word to her or anyone until after the interview, okay?'

'Sounds fair.'

'We might want to interview you too, explaining how we found her. People always like a bit of local colour. That'll be covered by a separate fee, normally four hundred dollars.'

'Four hundred dollars?' And he'd be on TV? Jimmy couldn't believe his luck.

'That's the going rate and not negotiable. Take it or leave it.'

'I'll take it. What address do I send the information to?'

'Do you have a fax machine?'

'No, but I can use the one in the council office.'

'I'll ring you in two days' time with a number. Send the material to me as soon as I give you the number because I'll probably be out on the road somewhere.'

'No worries.'

'I'll get the first one hundred dollars off to you this afternoon. I haven't got time to get a bank cheque. Will cash do?'

Grant allowed a grim smile of satisfaction as he hung up. The promise of cash and the possibility of appearing on TV was a combination that rarely failed to get him what he wanted. The only issue was what fax machine to use. He didn't want to give a number that could be traced back to him. There were public fax machines he could use at the post office and in the library which were suitably anonymous, but also fax machines in the restaurants he frequented. He'd lost count of the number of times he'd had material sent to him during the course of a long lunch. It was what people in his industry did.

Grant leaned back in his chair, satisfied that in two days' time he'd have a map showing him exactly where to find Linda and surprised that she ever imagined she could hide from him. She disappointed him. He thought he'd trained her better than that. He picked up the phone again and made an appointment with a law firm he'd singled out the previous day. They had a reputation for being smart and, importantly, he'd had no prior dealings with them. He needed them to do a company search on Film Gate and draft an agreement which would transfer all of Linda's holdings in the company to him. The agreement had to be watertight and incontestable. He wanted Linda to know exactly how it felt to have her company stolen and to be left with nothing.

Well, next to nothing.

His next task was to make sure that, when he finally caught up with her, he'd have her full and undivided attention. He dialled an acquaintance who'd begun a business supplying props to the film industry and subsequently built it up by supplying props of a different kind: marijuana, ecstasy and cocaine. He claimed he could provide anything at a price. He heard Grant out then told him his terms. The two-week hire of the rifle would cost five hundred dollars, with another five hundred dollars on top if the box of cartridges was opened. The fee would be deducted from the two thousand dollar deposit, which would be forfeited if the rifle was not returned. Grant accepted. That was something else Linda would have to pay for.

* * *

Jimmy closed the stock and station at midday when the temperature hit forty-two degrees. Keeping it open was a lost cause. Instead of going straight to the club, he went to the council offices and asked for the records to Billy's property. He had to smile. As he had expected, Billy had taken out a development application before beginning work on his parents' house. It showed the location of the house and a track leading up to it. But Jimmy knew better than to trust tracks indicated on maps. They tended to change every time there was a decent downpour or when trees fell over and blocked them. He looked at a larger map, which showed the boundaries of Billy's property and those of his neighbours, and used it to get a clearer idea of where the house might be. He worked out where it was in relation to Rodney's house and Stony Creek Road, which was one of the few named tracks on the map, and concluded that the house had to be up on one of two sand ridges. In country that sloped northwest at the rate of two centimetres every kilometre, the red ridges were hard to miss. The three hundred dollars was beginning to feel like easy money.

Jimmy went to the RSL, ordered a plate of crumbed cutlets and chips, bought a beer and started making plans. If he was going to go snooping around somebody's property it made sense to do it in fading light. He didn't want to blow his three hundred dollars by being spotted. Allowing an hour for the drive and another thirty minutes to get his bearings, he figured five o'clock would be a good time to set out. The temperature would have dropped to bearable levels and, if he discovered he'd jumped the gun, he could always drive into the bush and hole up for a while. He looked forward to a pleasant afternoon slowly sipping on a succession of beers, followed by a profitable evening.

The temperature hadn't fallen as much as he'd hoped when he set out in his four-wheel drive Toyota ute but it was headed the right way. He kept the windows closed and cranked the air-conditioning up as high as it would go. Even so, the heat kept him dipping into the esky on the passenger seat for a can of beer. Cumborah was like a ghost town from a western movie as he drove through it, with clumps of roly-poly blowing along the road like tumbleweed. He turned onto Stony Creek Road and drove straight towards the setting sun. There was no dust in the air, which was a sure sign nobody had come by in the previous hour. The chances of encountering another vehicle grew ever more remote.

Jimmy started paying attention once he passed the track leading up to Billy's place. He slowed to a stop as he crested the first of the big sand ridges. According to his calculations he was still a kilometre short of where he should start looking seriously. He engaged gear and motored along in second, searching for a promising track. The first track he took petered out into the bush. It didn't worry him. He hadn't expected to get lucky first time. He spotted fresh tyre tracks and followed them into the bush, but they terminated at a campsite where somebody had spent a night. Half a kilometre further on he came across a track that was obviously more used. He followed it full of expectation, only to discover that it looped back onto Stony Creek Road. He'd noticed trails radiating out from the loop and backtracked to investigate them. He chose the one with the freshest tyre tracks and drove slowly up it, heartened when the track began to climb and arc towards what looked like a knoll or rocky ridge. Natural caution and a desire to protect his three hundred dollars made him turn off the track and park out of sight among the cypress pines.

He'd barely covered a couple of hundred metres when the track forked. The right fork speared off into the bush but the left one, scoured by fresh tyre tracks, continued to climb. Jimmy kept to the bush so he didn't leave any telltale footprints on the track and followed the left-hand fork up the hill. When he spotted the Toyota parked in the car shelter he knew he'd struck gold. Even so, he had to be certain the four-wheel drive was Linda's, although he couldn't imagine who else it could belong to. He knew most of the cars in the area and the fact that he didn't recognise this one strengthened his conviction. He circled the carport, climbed up to where the rocks poked through the soil and sat down behind a boulder. The sun had dropped below the opposite ridge but it was still too light to go nosing around. He figured he had a twenty-minute wait and cursed the fact that he hadn't thought to bring a beer with him. His shirt was soaked with sweat and his throat was so dry it hurt to swallow. He thought of the three hundred dollars and the beers still in his esky. Happiness was just half an hour away.

The sandflies found him just as he recommenced his climb. He cursed. Forgetting to take a beer with him was an oversight. Forgetting to spray himself with repellent was sheer stupidity. They attacked his face, his legs and his hands. Cockatiels flitted among the mulga which had taken over from the pines. Jimmy looked up and realised immediately why the sandflies had begun to swarm. The wind had finally died down. He cursed again. Why couldn't it have kept up for another half an hour? He climbed higher, impatient now, and stopped abruptly when the dark solid shape of a house appeared in front of him. He crept further up the ridge until he was level with the windows, froze when a light turned on. Then he saw her come to the window. The sandflies feasted on his exposed skin but he didn't dare swat at them in case the movement caught her eye. She had a towel wrapped around her and was drying her hair with another. The light was behind her so he couldn't see her face clearly, but her build was right and he remembered her having long, slim legs. In truth, there was no one else she could be. He briefly thought about hanging around in case she dropped the towel covering her, but just as quickly dismissed the idea. His three hundred dollars were in the bag and the sandflies were giving him hell. He turned away but not without regrets. The woman was really something.

Once out of sight of the house, Jimmy wasted no time making his way back to his Toyota. Apart from keeping off the track, he threw caution to the wind. The money was as good as in the bank. All he had to do now was keep an eye on his odometer and record the distance back to the loop, the distance from there to Stony Creek Road and the number of kilometres back to the turn-off to Cumborah. He pulled the driver's door open.

'Tand dill, you thie-vin bar-tid!'

Jimmy nearly screamed with fright.

'I know whad you're af-der.'

Jimmy recognised the voice, exhaled with relief and hoped his galloping heart would slow before something broke.

'Jesus Christ, Rodney. What did you do that for? You scared the living shit outta me.' Jimmy raised his hands in the air and slowly turned around. Rodney lifted his head from the sights, lowered his shotgun slightly but kept it pointed at Jimmy.

'Whad you do-in creep-in round oud he-yah?'

Jimmy's mind raced. He was pretty sure Rodney wouldn't shoot him but his three hundred dollars were definitely under threat.

'It's a secret, Rodney. Can I trust you with a secret?'

'De-pend.'

'You know the woman who lives up there?'

'Lin-da?'

'Yeah, her.'

'Whad do you wand wid her?' Rodney raised his shotgun threateningly.

Jimmy had begun lowering his arms but raised them again immediately.

'Hey, it's okay. I'm not going to harm her. In fact, I'm doing her a favour.'

'A fay-va? Whad kind of fay-va?'

Jimmy saw immediately that Rodney had a soft spot for Linda and decided to exploit it.

'These people want to interview her for TV and asked me to help them find her. Apparently she's quite famous.' Years of snooping and playing with suspicions and innuendo had taught him the merits of sticking relatively close to the truth. 'They're making a film about all the good things she's done but it has to be a surprise. They want to film her in her little hideaway here.'

'Why?'

'Put the shotgun down and I'll tell you. I've got some beer in the esky. Do you want a beer?'

Rodney lowered his shotgun and clicked the safety on. He still stared at Jimmy with the utmost suspicion.

'Here,' said Jimmy. He opened a beer and passed it to Rodney. 'Mate, if you tell anyone you'll ruin the whole thing.'

'Whad a-boud Bil-ly?'

'Definitely not Billy. He'd tell her and that would be the end of it. Look, the film guy said it's going to be a tribute to Linda. You know what a tribute is?'

'I'm nod tu-pid.' Rodney's eyes blazed with fury.

'Sorry, mate! Sorry! It's just that if anyone deserves a tribute, she does. That's what they reckon. You don't want to spoil that, do you?'

'I don wand fil-lum pee-pul craw-lin all oh-ver the place.'

'They won't, Rodney. God's truth. They told me they'll be in and out in a morning. They've got helicopters.'

Rodney looked unconvinced.

'Do it for Linda. Mate, when it's all done, she'll thank you.'

'They bed-da nod hang a-round if they know whad good for them.'

'They won't, mate. Now promise you won't tell anyone.'

'Prom-id.'

'Good on yer. Finish your beer and have another?'

'No. You bed-da go now be-fore I change my mind.'

* * *

Grant made the call to Jimmy from Riccardo's restaurant in Paddington. His timing was perfect as he was forced to wait in line behind a real estate agent while the fax machine printed out a sale contract. The restaurant was full of business men and women, all demanding service at the same time. Grant had to press up against the wall in the narrow corridor to let the waiters pass by with their plates. The real estate agent gathered up his contract and raced back to the table before his buyer cooled off. The fax rang almost immediately. Grant picked up the pages addressed to John Wilson, Gunshot Productions. The map and instructions were perfectly clear. It was also perfectly clear to him that, if anyone ever asked, nobody would have a clue who'd used the fax that day.

Chapter Twenty-five

Billy hated homework but he came to hate Neil's homework even more. Whenever something needed doing Neil always had homework, which meant Billy was always the one who had to help his father with the hundreds of jobs that kept cropping up. He couldn't understand why Neil hadn't left school after completing his school certificate like his sisters had done. The younger of them, Kathleen, had just gone to join Glory in Dubbo and scored a job as a secretary. They seemed to be having the time of their lives, which made Neil's decision even harder to comprehend. Neil had stayed on to complete his Higher School Certificate and, worse, was actually taking his studying seriously. Billy suffered all the extra work because he saw a benefit at the end of it all. He assumed he'd leave school when Neil did at the end of the year and they'd go down to Sydney together to look for work. Though neither of them had ever been to Sydney, they'd heard all about it from other kids. They had Test matches down in Sydney and live bands in pubs. Billy didn't share his plans with anyone because he didn't want to be lectured on the importance of finishing schooling and gaining qualifications. Besides, he didn't think for a second Neil would go without him. What he didn't know was that his parents had already made plans for him and they ran at odds to his own.

The future had never been an issue with Billy. It was just something that was going to happen and would be good when it did. He rarely looked further ahead than the next football match, pig shoot or party. When anyone asked what he intended doing with his life, he just shrugged. If pressed, he'd admit that he'd like to do an apprenticeship and become a builder or a mechanic. Everyone knew he was good with his hands and both occupations seemed logical choices. Not once did he say he wanted to take over the farm.

Things began to unravel one Saturday morning after the wool cheque arrived, when his father tossed Billy the keys to his old Holden and asked him to drive him into town. Billy was a bit annoyed because Neil was just sitting around and he'd intended to talk him into tracking down a couple of pigs. He noticed his father had put on a clean shirt and moleskins and even let his mother trim his hair. Something was up.

'Where are we going?'

'You'll find out when we get there.'

Billy sighed and nursed the car down their rutted track onto the road. He let the speed slowly build up to seventy k's and sit there. Any faster and the old Holden bottomed out in the dips and jarred rust free every time a wheel hit a pothole.

'We're going to have to do something about these shock absorbers,' said Billy, after a hammering over a strip of corrugations.

'One day,' said Braden.

'Should do the suspension while we're at it.'

'Probably not worth it.'

'What do you mean? It's still a good car. There's nothing wrong with the motor. Or the gearbox.'

'What about the rust?'

'I can fix that,' said Billy.

'Then fix the suspension at the same time.'

Billy turned towards his father and was surprised to see a wry grin on his face. They didn't talk much the rest of the way into Walgett.

'Where to?' said Billy as they motored slowly down the main street. The town was always pretty busy on a Saturday morning. 'Stock and station?'

'Just keep going.'

'How far?'

'Start slowing down after the intersection.'

Billy was mystified.

'Stop here.'

Billy pulled over outside the Holden dealership.

'What are we doing here?'

Braden climbed out of the car.

'Come with me and you'll find out.'

Billy followed his father into the car yard. It felt odd just walking in there. The owner, 'Smiling Bob' Smart, greeted his father like a best mate. Billy had lost count of the number of times Smiling Bob had chased Neil and him out of the yard for leaving fingermarks on the duco and windows of new models. New-model cars were one of the most exciting things that happened and all they'd wanted to do was gawk at them and try to imagine what it would be like to ride in one.

'Bob, you know my son, Billy?'

'Of course. How're you going, Billy?'

'Good, thank you, Mr Smart.'

Smiling Bob greeted him like a long-lost buddy too, which was really odd given their previous encounters.

'Well, what do you think of it?' Smiling Bob opened the door of a brand-new Holden utility. The white paint dazzled in the morning light and the new tyres, free of dust, glowed with a blackness they'd never achieve again in their life. The red vinyl upholstery hadn't a mark on it.

'It's great,' said Billy cautiously. He'd never thought the day would come when Smiling Bob would actually invite him to look over his cars.

'Why don't you give it the once-over while your dad and I finish the paperwork?'

Paperwork? Billy turned from Smiling Bob to his dad. The sly grin was back on his father's face. Billy looked at him incredulously. His father just nodded but the nod said it all. He turned back to the ute. His father had bought it? A brand-new ute? Billy couldn't recall his father ever buying anything brand-new. But, as unbelievable as it seemed, there were his father and Smiling Bob walking away to the office. His father was laughing. Billy turned his full attention to the ute, his eyes devouring every detail. It was the six, not the V8, but the six was plenty good enough. He took in the column change, the radio in the dash and the heater. Billy had never even ridden in a car that had a heater. The bench seat had an armrest that folded out. Billy struggled to take it all in.

'What are you doing with the old rust bucket?'

Billy spun around. He'd been so absorbed in the new ute he hadn't heard Smiling Bob and his father return.

'I'm giving it to Billy.'

Billy's jaw dropped. Was there no end to the surprises? The old car was his?

'God love him, what's he done wrong to deserve that?' said Smiling Bob. He started laughing. 'Billy,

I'd think twice before saying thank you, if I were you.'

A phone rang in the office. 'Excuse me a sec.' Smiling Bob ducked back inside to grab the phone. When the wool cheques were in, every call was a potential customer.

'What do you think?' said Braden.

'About the ute?'

'About taking over the old car.'

'What do you think? I'm blown away. But what about Neil?'

'He won't need it at university.'

'University?' Billy reeled. Things were happening far too quickly.

'Well, he might need it at university but he won't be able to afford it. Amounts to the same thing.'

'Neil's going to university?'

'Of course. You knew that, didn't you?'

Billy hadn't known. Nobody had said a thing to him about university. University was somewhere other kids went. Not Neil. Not him.

He followed his father home so he wouldn't cover the new Holden with his dust, and tried to make sense of the morning. He'd been blown away to discover his father had bought a brand-new ute. That was enough to blow anyone away. Then he'd been blown away to discover the old car was now his. He'd made no secret of his desire to have his own car but had thought he was years away from acquiring one. The old car even felt better to drive now that it was his, now that he nursed it along with the respect that comes with ownership. Billy should have been elated but instead felt strangely deflated. It should've been one of the best days of his life, yet all he felt was confused and somehow betrayed. Why hadn't Neil told him he was going to university? And what about their plans to go to Sydney? He kept his thoughts to himself while his father showed off his new acquisition and took them all for a ride in it. But as soon as they sat down to lunch he asked the question uppermost on his mind.

'If Neil goes to university,' he said, 'what am I going to do?'

'Stay here,' said his father, as though the answer was obvious. 'Someone's got to stay and help me run the place. Can't manage it on my own.'

Billy had the oddest feeling that somehow the whole world had moved on while he wasn't looking and he'd been left behind. He was assailed by so many thoughts and emotions they roadblocked in his brain. But one thought emerged with blinding clarity. He'd just been shown his future and it looked like a lonely version of his past.

'I'll give you a hand with the rust,' said Neil.

* * *

'Why didn't you tell me you were going to university?' said Billy.

He'd taken Neil out for a test run in the old Holden, ostensibly to work out what repairs needed doing most, but really just to get away so they could have a talk. He'd driven out towards the Grawin and stopped where floodwaters at some time had carved out a broad warrambool. The depression gave way at the southern end to a lignum swamp. The change in vegetation was so abrupt it was as though someone had drawn a line in the ground as a boundary. The road, which was raised above the level of the floodplain, provided an uninspiring view which reflected Billy's state of mind. It had dawned on him that the car was his consolation prize. Up ahead, lousy jacks were picking over the carcass of a galah that had been hit by a car.

'I wasn't sure I was going myself. I wasn't sure Dad could afford it. Even with government assistance, Dad will still have to help me out until I get a decent part-time job.'

'How can he help you out? He's just bought a bloody new ute.'

'It's leased. I helped him arrange the lease.'

'You knew he was buying it? And you didn't tell me?' They weren't questions so much as accusations.

Neil shrugged. 'You know how Dad likes his little surprises.'

Billy got out of the car, picked up a stone and hurled it as far as he could into the warrambool. A cluster of small parrots scattered as it burst through the trees.

'Why do you want to go to university anyway?'

Neil joined Billy, propped against the Holden's mudguard.

'To get away from this. I'm sick of being poor, Billy. I reckon we've all been poor long enough.'

'What do you mean?'

'For Christ's sake, I want to make something of myself. Make some money. Real money.'

'How?'

'I don't know yet, Billy. I don't know. But I'll find a way. All I know is there's a big world out there and opportunities I can't even begin to imagine.'

'What about me? I don't want to stay here. Don't you think I want to make something of myself too? Don't you think I want to be rich? Stuff it, why should I be the only one left here?' Billy angrily hurled another rock into the bush.

'Which of us do you reckon has the best chance of making it?' said Neil quietly. 'You or me?'

'You,' said Billy reluctantly.

'That's right. I have. I've thought it through and I've got a plan. Once I finish uni and start making some real money I'm going to send for you, okay? Whatever I'm doing, I'll make you part of it, if that's what you want.'

'When will that be?'

'I don't know. But it'll be as soon as possible.'

'Fair dinkum?'

'Of course.'

'Promise?'

'Cross my heart.'

'What about Mum and Dad?'

'They're part of the deal. If things go well, I've promised to pay them back by setting them up in a little house somewhere where they can retire.'

'So I'm not stuck here for ever?'

'No way.'

'Well, you better make a shit load of money real fast, that's all I can say.'

'Trust me,' said Neil. 'I promise I'll get you away from here.'

Chapter Twenty-six

'This place needs screens right around the veranda,' said Billy irritably. 'Don't know why I didn't do it when I built it.' He was fidgety. Being indoors for any length of time always made him fidgety and the fact that Linda had set the table inside didn't help. He belonged outside, with his feet up on the rail, but that wasn't an option. The hot spell had continued into May and the sandflies and flies were ferocious. They clung to the outside of the window screens in their thousands. 'I feel like a bloody prisoner in here.'

'Thanks,' said Linda. She joined him from the kitchen with a beer in each hand. 'For goodness' sake, stop prowling around and sit down.'

Billy took the beer from her, pulled his chair out from the dining table and sat facing the window. He didn't feel quite so hemmed in so long as he could look outside. She sat down opposite him. She'd aimed a fan at the table but all it did was shift the warm air from one place to another.

'I think it would be a good idea if I brought you a shotgun.'

'A shotgun? I don't know anything about guns.'

'I could teach you all you need to know in five minutes.'

'Why? So I can shoot my ex-husband if he happens to find me?'

'There's nothing wrong in defending yourself.'

'You've convinced me it won't come to that.'

'It doesn't hurt to be prepared. It would be different if you came down and stayed at my place.'

'I really don't want to drag you into my problems.'

'I'm dragged, Linda, I'm here. What's the difference? Me coming to your place or you coming to mine? Come and live with me. If I'm off somewhere on the spread, at least you'll have the dogs to protect you.'

'Maybe.'

'Maybe what? One, you'd be safer and, two, we wouldn't have to sweat it out in here. We could sit outside on my veranda. Catch a breeze.' Billy got up and walked over to the window. His eyes narrowed. 'Uh-oh, you've got company.'

'What!'

'Come here and I'll show you.'

'It's not him, is it?' Linda rose from her chair and ran over to the window. Billy was pointing towards the track up the western ridge that Rodney used when he came to do her gardening.

'Just to the right of the trail,' said Billy. 'In front of that scrubby gidgee.'

'What? Oh, my God!'

'Want to rethink the shotgun?'

'Is it poisonous?'

'Yeah, it's poisonous all right.'

'What is it?'

'Red-belly black. It'll make you mighty sick but probably won't kill you.'

'It's coming towards us.'

'It most likely lives under the house. Probably been

living there for years. That's not necessarily a bad thing though.'

'What do you mean?'

'They're territorial. They keep the brown snakes away and they're the real nasty buggers. Get bitten by a brown, all you can do is hope that your will's in order. Most people out here don't mind having a black around for that reason.'

'Ugh,' said Linda. 'I hate snakes, I hate them all.'

'So come and live at my place.'

'Have you got a snake?'

'Yeah. The dog lives under the front veranda and the snake lives under the back. We've learned to get along with each other. Funny thing is, the dog chases all the other snakes away except that one.'

Linda watched the black snake slither out of sight under the lip of the veranda, headed beneath the house.

'Your place is looking better all the time.'

'Then come home with me.'

Linda smiled and shrugged with resignation.

'If the only alternative is sitting here like Ma Baker with a shotgun on my lap and being nagged to death I really don't have a lot of choice.'

'Good,' said Billy. 'Come home with me tonight.'

'Whoa, boy. I need time to wash and pack things. I'll have to clean out the fridge and freezer. It'll take me all day tomorrow.'

'I'll give you a hand.'

'Did you talk to your friend in town?'

'Peter? Yeah. He hasn't heard of anyone snooping around but he'll keep his eye out. By the way, where's the kelpie?'

'Bella's in the kitchen, keeping an eye on our dinner. I think I'll go give her a hand.'

'Dogs belong outside.'

'My place, my call,' said Linda.

Billy watched her go then sat down at the table, relieved that she'd finally come to her senses. He hadn't told her about the tyre tracks he'd found down below the house because he hadn't wanted to frighten her. They'd prompted him to ring Peter at the stock and station and ask him to be his eyes and ears. All the signs suggested someone had been snooping. If it had been an opal miner who'd taken the wrong turn, he would've just done a one-eighty and driven back the way he'd come. Why detour off into the bush out of sight? And whose were the footprints? There appeared to be two sets. He'd tried to follow their tracks but his abo eyes weren't much use once they got in among the rocks and he'd lost them. But he'd seen enough to know that they'd headed uphill. But how far up? And why? He'd stayed over with Linda that night and the following night, just in case. He figured there was most likely an innocent explanation. Maybe some campers wanted to climb high enough to photograph the view. God knows, the relentless northwesters had made it too hot to climb all the way to the top. While that seemed the most reasonable explanation, it sat uneasily with him. Why now? He couldn't recall anyone doing it before, though he appreciated he was hardly in a position to know. Nevertheless, it smacked of coincidence and Billy distrusted coincidences. He finished his beer and walked into the kitchen to get another.

Grant turned off Stony Creek Road onto the loop and reset the odometer of his rented Nissan Patrol. So far his instructions had been pinpoint accurate, clearly the work of a man anxious to protect his third instalment of one hundred dollars. Though his lights were on low beam, Grant was acutely aware of how obvious they were in the vast blackness around him and to anyone on the lookout. Occasionally pairs of rubies stared back at him in the spill of the beams but he didn't give a thought to which animals they might belong. He only had eyes for the road and his odometer. Dealing in tenths of kilometres was bad enough given the normal variation between odometers, but tenths of tenths was inviting trouble. What were his chances of finding the right track at 'a whisker under point-six-five kilometres' when every gap in the scrub looked like it could be the start of a trail? Grant slowed down to fifteen k's. Even with the airconditioner running at full bore he was sweating. As the odometer tripped over point six his headlights picked up wheel ruts arcing to the right thirty metres ahead of him. Grant grunted with satisfaction. It had to be the right track. His instructions told him to proceed for another one-point-one kilometres and to park alongside the car shelter, but they allowed for a different kind of surprise to the one he had planned. Instead, he angled off into the bush after covering just two hundred metres, stopped behind a thicket of pines and turned off his lights.

Before leaving the Nissan, Grant covered his face, arms and hands with Rid insect repellent. He slipped the Rid, his torch, the contract, a bottle of water and the opened box of cartridges into his backpack, picked up his rifle and followed his tyre marks back to the track to make sure his Nissan was well enough hidden. Satisfied, he set off on foot up the sand ridge towards Linda's. He'd dressed completely in black and even considered blackening his face, but it had been apparent from early on in the evening that the precaution would be unnecessary. Although the first crescent of the new moon lay on its back low above the western horizon and the sky was filled with stars, it took all of Grant's concentration just to see the track in front of him.

It was so dark he would've missed the fork if he hadn't been looking for it. He continued uphill, more cautious now, but was soon forced to stop. Unbelievably, where he stood was even darker than it had been down where he'd left his car. He had no choice but to use his torch. He'd focused the lens on his Magnalite so that it gave a narrow beam with very little spill but he still didn't trust it not to reveal his presence. He cupped his hand over the lens before turning the torch on and allowed only a sliver of light through his fingers. He realised he was in a gully surrounded by trees, the canopies of which had joined to completely block out the stars. He dared to raise the filtered beam of his torch so that it shone uphill. The moment he caught the dull reflection of something metal way up ahead of him he switched the torch off. It had to be Linda's car or the car shelter. He slowly and deliberately made his way forward, arms out in front of him in case there were tree trunks or other obstacles in his way. It reminded him of the nights he'd woken up in strange hotel rooms, with no idea where the bathroom was or where the light switch was, and found his way entirely by touch. But that was before, when he'd had the world at his feet and travelled so often he sometimes couldn't even remember which country he was in. The memory caused bitterness to rise like acid in his throat. He carried on up the hill until he was no longer certain he was headed the right way.

He risked another quick flash of light through his fingers and almost gasped out loud. It wasn't just the closeness of the Toyota that stunned him, even though it was less than two metres in front of him and he'd had no idea it was there, but the fact that there were two cars. Two cars! At no stage had Grant considered that Linda would have company and he'd made no provision in his plans. Yet he should have considered the possibility. He had little doubt that the Toyota in the car shelter was Linda's or that the ute alongside belonged to the person called Billy Dwyer. Natural caution told him to turn around and try again another night, when Linda was alone, but he couldn't face the delay. What if someone found his car tracks? What if Linda decided to up anchor and take off? Grant shook his head. He couldn't risk it. His grip tightened on his rifle. The presence of Billy Dwyer changed nothing. The only difference was that Billy might have to learn that friendship with Linda always came at a price.

'I'm really going to miss this place,' said Linda. She picked up her coffee, leaned back in her chair and took a sip. 'The funny thing is, it's the opposite of everything I thought I wanted.'

'What did you want?'

'What everyone wants. Big beautiful house, fabulous water views and stylish furniture. But this place has really got to me.'

'You've done a good job on it.'

'Thanks, but it's more than that. Everything here is basic but the truth is, it's enough. The cooker's a dinosaur but it works fine. Same with the washing machine. I haven't missed not having a dishwasher. In fact, I've enjoyed doing the dishes, especially with you drying.'

'You can do the dishes down at my place.'

'You're too kind. What worries me is that once I leave here I won't come back. These canvases will remain unfinished and so will the garden. The house will go back to the way it was when you first showed it to me, and that would be a real shame.'

'I don't see why you can't come back.'

'My life's in the city, Billy. Like the house, sooner or later I'm going to have to go back to the way I was too. One way or another the issue with Grant will have to be resolved. The last few days have made that blindingly clear. Maybe I'll have to take the initiative, although God only knows how. Damn it! If only he'd got those Garuda commercials.'

'Do I have to go back to the way I was or is there a place for me in your plans?'

Linda rocked forward and put her coffee down. She reached across the table and took Billy's hands in hers.

'Billy Dwyer, how could you possibly —'

The kelpie's sudden explosive bark cut her short. Billy leaped to his feet. Linda spun around screaming as the kelpie raced past her towards the veranda and threw itself snarling at the screen door. The figure standing there was little more than a dark shape but his rifle was hard to miss. It was pointed at the kelpie.

'Bella! Heel!'

The kelpie turned around obediently and crept back to Billy, tail between its legs. It lay down at Billy's feet, growling softly, eyes fixed on the intruder as he pushed open the screen door and stepped inside.

'Good move, cowboy, you just saved your puppy dog's life,' said Grant. 'And maybe even the bitch's.'

He swung his rifle around so that it pointed directly at Linda. 'Hello, Linda. What's the matter? Aren't you pleased to see me?'

Grant closed the screen door behind him and moved carefully into the room until he was level with her. All the while in gaol whenever he'd imagined this moment it had always begun with a punch that had been six long years gathering force and momentum. He knew exactly how it would happen. He'd watched it replayed endlessly in slow motion and super slow motion, seen his fist smash into her jaw from every angle as though it was TV coverage of the knockout punch in a title fight. He'd seen her face split open, the explosion of blood, spittle and splintered teeth. He'd seen it, felt it and rejoiced in it. But in his imaginings she'd always been alone, his hands had been free and not gripped around a rifle, and common sense had never been a factor. It took a supreme effort to restrain his fists, to rein in his fury and put the lid on his bitterness. There was plenty of time for revenge, he told himself, and plenty of ways of taking it. He found he was breathing hard and gulping air, not so much from the effort of sneaking up the hill but from the tension, and took a couple of deep breaths to calm down. He looked into Linda's eyes and felt a surge of satisfaction when he saw the sheer terror there. It was as though she'd been reading his mind, reading his intentions, watching the replays. All the blood had drained from her face and stripped the colour from her lips. Her whole body shook with fear. He'd seen her scared before, but never so scared and never without so much reason. Christ Almighty, he wanted to slap her, his whole being cried out with the need, but he knew if he started in on her he wouldn't be able to stop and that could ruin everything. He forced his gaze away and onto Billy. It was time to check out the boyfriend.

Grant smiled. He couldn't help himself. If he'd had to cast an archetypal, strong, steadfast, honest-as-the-day-is-long country boy for a film, Billy would have been a shoo-in for the part. He was a living cliché, right down to the moleskins and RM Williams boots. Grant couldn't help wondering what Linda was doing with a bloke like him. He wouldn't have picked Billy as her type at all. But clearly Linda saw enough to like to take him into her bed, which made Billy a problem and one he had to deal with. He swung his rifle off Linda and onto Billy and went immediately on his guard when there was no reaction. Grant had expected to see something, at least a flicker of nervousness or apprehension. But the eyes that met his didn't waver. Grant kept staring at Billy, trying to figure him out as he addressed his ex-wife.

'Where are your manners, Linda? You know I like a beer when I come in.'

Linda immediately backed away towards the kitchen, as though scared of what he'd do if she took her eyes off him.

'Make it two,' said Grant. 'Save yourself a second trip. And don't even think of doing anything silly or I'll give lover boy here a second navel.'

He scanned the room while he waited for Linda to return. He had to get Billy — in fact, both of them — into a position where they were no threat. When he noticed the deep sofa he smiled. Linda had bought a similar sofa for their apartment. It looked great and there was no doubting its comfort, but people sank so deeply into it they almost needed a crane to get back to their feet. He couldn't remember the number of times he'd complained about it. It suddenly occurred to him that maybe the sofa was the same one from their apartment. It looked pretty much how he remembered it. Maybe it was something she'd kept when they'd separated. Whatever, new or old, it would serve his purpose.

'Okay, just put the beers down on the table. Now I want the two of you to go and sit on the sofa. And take the dog with you.'

Grant opened one of the cans and knocked back half of the contents in a couple of gulps. He smiled again with grim satisfaction when he saw Billy's dismay as he realised the helplessness of the position the sofa had put him in. Grant perched on the edge of the table, laid his rifle down alongside him and slipped off his backpack.

'You must be Billy Dwyer.'

'That's right. Mind if I smoke?'

'What?' Billy's simple request caught Grant off guard. 'No, go ahead.' Grant watched carefully as Billy pulled the pack of tobacco from his shirt pocket and began to make a rollie. As a director, he couldn't help but be fascinated by the contrast between the two. Billy could've been watching grass grow while Linda looked like she was about to piss herself. It was hard to believe they were playing the same scene. 'I suppose Linda got you up here for protection.'

'It was my choice.'

'Ah, Billy, why do we all make the same mistake? Thing is, super bitch here doesn't need your protection, or mine, or anyone else's for that matter. It's us who need protecting from her.'

'That's not the way I heard it.' Billy rolled his cigarette and licked the edge of the paper. He tamped both ends twice before sticking it between his lips and lighting it.

'Well, it wouldn't be, would it? You're being played for a fool, Billy. But don't worry, you're not the first and Linda's fooled better men than you. She's good, Billy, really good. You managed to fool the judge and the jury, didn't you, Linda, and, as far as I can tell, the entire police force as well? That's right, isn't it? See? She's not denying anything. Doesn't that tell you something? Believe me, Billy, as long as you live, which may not be all that much longer come to think of it, you will never meet a more cold-hearted, calculating, ruthlessly ambitious bitch than this little schoolteacher here. She's the Queen of Bitches. Right, Linda?'

When Linda didn't respond he screamed at her: 'Right, Linda!'

'Yes!' It was more of a sob than a word.

'What are you?'

'Queen of Bitches.' Linda was shaking so badly she was barely coherent.

'Sorry? What did you say?'

'She said, Queen of Bitches.' Billy drew deeply on his cigarette and looked for somewhere to butt it. 'When you finish with that can I'd like to use it as an ashtray.'

Grant took a last pull from the can and tossed it to Billy. The beer had hardly put a dent in his thirst. He took another deep breath to let his anger subside. But, Christ, there was so much anger it was hard to keep it bottled up.

'Well, Billy, you heard it from her own mouth. She is the Queen of Bitches, self-confessed. The question is, are you convinced? Do you believe her?'

'No.'

'That's a shame. You disappoint me, Billy. Here I am, trying to help you understand what we're dealing with, but you won't listen. I can see that I'm just going to have to tell you my side of the story. You don't mind if I tell lover boy what really happened, do you, Linda? Tell him how you put your sweet little hand on the Bible and swore to tell the truth but told a whole lot of porkies instead? Why are you staring at the floor? Is it really so hard for you to look me in the eye and face the truth? Christ, you're pathetic! You should've seen her in court, Billy. My God, what a performance! She wasn't pathetic then. I had no idea she was such a good actor. You know, I almost stood to applaud. I've directed a lot of very fine actors, Billy, the best in the country, but I've never got a performance like that out of any of them. Never! Doesn't it make you wonder, Billy, if she's been putting on a little act for you?'

'No. She seems pretty genuine to me.'

'You sure?'

'Yeah, I'm sure.' Billy began rolling another cigarette.

'I hear she's been running her business — sorry, my business — from here. Did she tell you that?'

'Yeah, she did.'

'I also hear that she has regular meetings with her accountant in a motel somewhere.'

'Actually it's a Country Club,' said Billy evenly. He felt Linda tense alongside him. She hadn't mentioned the Country Club to him and he hadn't mentioned his conversation with Jimmy.

'A Country Club? Of course. Nothing but the best for my little schoolteacher. I'm pleased for your sake that Linda has been so forthcoming. Did she tell you her accountant was also her lover?' Grant caught the quick intake of breath, not just from Linda but also from Billy. Yes! He was starting to really enjoy himself. 'Oops! Am I right in thinking she didn't tell you he was her lover? Why would that be? Never mind, Billy, I only just found out myself. Apparently shares in my company weren't the only inducement she offered around. Right, Linda? Right, Linda!'

'Right.'

'Right. Good, we've got that cleared up. I should tell you, Billy, just so you know who you can trust around here, that the accountant is now married with a kid. Happily married, apparently. You can make up your own mind whether anything's still going on between them. But don't you think she should've told you? Been entirely forthcoming?' Grant ripped the tab off his second beer.

'You know, I should have realised what a calculating bitch she is right from the start. I'd hardly met her when she drops her almost-fiancé and all but giftwraps her pussy and presents it to me on a plate. Right in front of everyone, including the poor pathetic bastard she'd just abandoned. I was young and full of myself, and naive enough to think it was all down to my good looks and charm, but Linda ... well, she had a much clearer grasp of the situation. My charm and good looks didn't enter into it, did they, Linda? It wasn't who I was that mattered but what I was. And what was I? I was her ticket to freedom, Billy, her ticket out of triple-fronted brick veneer land, meat and two veg suburbia, her ticket to the bright lights and the high life. I was the pathway to her ambitions. Well, hardly a pathway, more a doormat really.

'Again, I should've guessed what she was all about when we started going out. She was just a westie schoolteacher. She knew nothing. Nothing! The first time I took her to a restaurant she didn't recognise a single dish on the menu. Had no idea what a risotto was or a salsa. No idea at all. But a month later, guess what? She's an expert. You name the restaurant, she could name the chef and his signature dish. She was an art teacher and knew all about art history but hadn't a clue which contemporary artists were hot and which weren't. A month later she's throwing their names around like confetti and even getting me to invest in them. I could hardly keep up.' Grant took another swallow of beer. 'Christ, beer gets warm quickly out here.

'In the interests of fairness, Billy, I have to tell you Linda was not ungrateful. She could not find enough ways to thank me. And she was great company. She was excited by everything we did and her excitement was infectious. She made me want to take her to different places, show her new things, have new experiences. She made me appreciate what a fabulous lifestyle I had. When she asked if she could move in with me, well, it kind of seemed a natural progression. Big mistake. Give the bitch an inch, Billy, and she takes a mile.

'Next thing I knew she wanted to give up teaching and become a film producer. She'd already moved into my apartment, now she wanted to move into my office. Why not, I thought. One of the prerequisites for working in film is boundless energy and she had energy to burn. She took to the business like a duck to water, Billy, and I was proud of her. I taught her everything I knew. I even made her my producer. How about that? But you've got to stop and think here, Billy. I mean, what more could a little westie schoolteacher want? She had a good job, made good money and lived a life only a few privileged people like me could afford. What more could she want?

It turned out she wanted a lot more, Billy, a whole lot more. The bitch wanted everything I had.

'You know what a spreadsheet is, Billy? It's the sheet girls like Linda spread 'em on. That's how they get to the top in the film business. They marry the boss. She proposed, I accepted and we got married. Do you know why I married her? I'll tell you. Yes, she was gorgeous. Still is, don't you think? She said she loved me and I had no reason to doubt her. She was fun to be with. She was good to work with and we had lots to talk about. There was never a dull moment. But you know something? I didn't marry her for any of those reasons. They're reasons to live with someone, not necessarily marry them. No, I married Linda, Billy, because I was very aware of where she'd come from and who she really was. I thought I was marrying a schoolteacher, a good old-fashioned girl with good old-fashioned values, someone from the heartland of Australia. I wanted a wife who would be a good, diligent, loving mother to my kids, someone who'd keep the house neat and tidy and my clothes clean and pressed. In short, Billy, I wanted a good old-fashioned wife. Tell me, was that such a bad thing to want?'

'I imagine there are a lot of men who think that way.'

'You are so right, Billy. There are lots of good-looking women around who give you a great time in bed but they're not necessarily the ones you want for your wife. I thought I'd made the right choice with Linda.

'I thought she'd give up work and become a housewife once she got pregnant, but no. She kept on as my producer until her belly grew so big she could no longer travel. What did she do then? Go home and make sure she was eating the right food and doing the right exercises so we'd have a bonny bouncing baby? No way. She made herself office manager. I was a bit busy, Billy, otherwise I would've put a stop to it right there. Linda didn't need to work. We didn't need money. But what does she do? She has the baby and next thing I know she's bringing her into the office, breastfeeding her while she's working and changing her nappies during meetings with clients. Does that sound right to you, Billy? Does that sound like the actions of a caring mother? As soon as the kid was old enough she was shunted off to kindy. Then to school. The poor kid's feet didn't touch the ground. I have to tell you, Billy, this wasn't exactly what I had in mind for the mother of my children.

'We started arguing about it. I thought Linda should quit work, have another child and become a fulltime mother, but she wouldn't have a bar of it. She was violently opposed to the idea and I mean violently. She went off like a cheap alarm clock every time I mentioned it. It took me a while to realise that she hadn't even wanted the first child. Why? Because it interfered with her ambition, Billy. It interfered with her precious plans. You know, a lot of commercials Linda worked on won awards, but I tell you there's one award she'd never win in a million years. She'd never win Mother of the Year. Believe me, Billy, I don't think she'd win a single vote.

'I don't know what your plans are, but I hope you weren't thinking of marrying her. Bad move. It's a funny thing but, for some reason, women change when you marry them. It doesn't matter how much fun they are to start with, they soon get tiresome. No matter how much fun they were in bed, sex becomes an imposition. And you know what the worst thing is, they start telling you how to live your life. That's what happened to me. She never let up and the problem was, there was no escaping her. I had to put up with her at home and in the office. So I fired her, Billy. Got her out of the office. I mean, what's a man supposed to do? It was not what she wanted, God knows, but it was the only way I could keep my sanity.'

'That so?'

'You doubting me, Billy?'

'My understanding is that there was another woman involved.'

'Billy, please, there's always another woman involved. Man is not monogamous, especially when what he's getting at home is monotonous. The wise man gets his life in order, Billy, makes sure each thing is in its place. Don't think I'm not loyal, because I am. Linda was becoming a total pain in the arse but all I did was fire her. I didn't divorce her or abandon her. She was my wife, for heaven's sake, the mother of my child. I had responsibilities. I made sure she had a nice home, a nice car and plenty of money to indulge herself. We went out together, took holidays together and had good times together. I even threw my leg over as duty required. Yes, there was another woman, Billy, but I felt I was entitled to that. She was a tiger between the sheets, a real tiger. I worked hard and deserved a little R & R.'

'Maybe you should've divorced Linda and married her.'

'Men like me don't marry girls like her, Billy. Sharna — her name was Sharna, in case you didn't know — well, she had that wrong-side-of-the-tracks quality about her. Know what I mean? Great head, great body but lacking a bit in the breeding department. Voice a little too harsh, manners a little too coarse, a tad loud, that sort of thing. I really looked after Linda, Billy, I really did. Everything could've been so fine. I'd finally got her to understand her place in my life and I thought Sharna understood hers. But would you believe it, Sharna had ambitions too. It doesn't matter what you do, Billy, how reasonable you try to be, women always want more. They always want what they can't have.'

'You got Sharna pregnant.'

'Correction, Billy. Sharna got Sharna pregnant. She thought if she got pregnant I'd piss off Linda and marry her. I'm loyal, Billy, I told you that. Marrying Sharna was never an option.'

'So you lost your temper and killed her.'

'Ah, now we're getting to the crunch. You see, Billy, this is the bit where everybody gets it wrong. I have to admit I wasn't overjoyed to learn she was pregnant, but that sort of thing happens and it wasn't something I couldn't deal with. I mean, I had three choices, right? I could divorce Linda and marry Sharna, which was never going to happen. Take care of Sharna and the kid financially, which I was prepared to do. Or pay for an abortion, which, to be perfectly frank, was the option I favoured. I said as much but that wasn't what Sharna wanted to hear. I told you Sharna was a tiger in bed — well, sometimes she was a tiger out of it as well. As soon as I mentioned abortion she went off her brain. When I tell you she flew at me, believe me, that's what she did. Un-fucking-real. She'd had a few goes at me before, to be honest, and I can't tell you how many times she'd sunk her knee into my nuts. But this time, Christ Almighty, she lost it completely. She would've scratched my eyes out if I hadn't pushed her away.

I didn't even push her particularly hard. We had scatter rugs on a polished floor, Billy. Scatter rugs. She slipped as much as anything. Anyway, she fell and the edge of the table pretty much did the rest. I didn't kill her, Billy. I didn't even harm her. What happened to her was an accident and an accident of her own making. She chose to get pregnant. She chose to attack me. If you knew Sharna you'd have no trouble understanding that.'

'I understand she had a few other bruises as well. I suppose she made a habit of slipping.'

'Here we go again. I wonder who told you that? I admit there were times when Sharna lost her temper and things got a little out of hand. But I never hurt her intentionally.'

'No, you just hurt her accidentally. Regularly, but accidentally.'

'Sarcasm, Billy? It doesn't do you justice, though I must confess justice has become a devalued concept. Tell me, Billy, did Linda ever tell you about the time Sharna and I were shooting a Colgate commercial? We'd spent a day building a set for a bathroom. We'd even had tilers laying tiles and plumbers rigging up taps that worked. Sharna came charging out of the make-up room, still talking to the talent and not looking where she was going. She hit the set so hard she demolished it. She knocked the whole damn thing down. Walls, sinks, tiles, taps. We had to pull her out of the wreckage and take her to Emergency to get patched up. She cost me a whole day's shoot, but that was Sharna. Then there was the time she bought a stone Buddha in Thailand that had been pilfered from Angkor Wat. She didn't want to risk checking it in with her baggage so she stuffed it in her flight bag and stowed it in the overhead locker.

I mean, write your own ending here. Sharna was a disaster area, an accident waiting to happen. And sure enough it did. The plane hit an air pocket, the locker flew open, Buddha popped out and head-butted Sharna. Buddha won on a TKO. Billy, there are a hundred Sharna stories.

'One time we went to a wedding. Sharna decided to take a photo of the bride and groom cutting the wedding cake. She rushed to get a close-up, tripped over the cable to the lights the official photographer was using and crashed into the table. The table collapsed at one end and the cake went down like the *Titanic*. It was amazing to see and fortunately somebody captured it on home video. The cake slid down the length of the table as gracefully as you like and the camera tracked with it. That was the bit I liked. The guy with the camera could've saved the cake but instead he filmed it. You have to admire his professionalism. But once again we had to dig Sharna out of the debris, this time with a split lip and a sprained wrist. Unfortunately, the cameraman missed that.

'Do you understand what I'm saying here, Billy? Sharna was accident-prone. She was a standing joke, a disaster area. There was never a time when she wasn't carrying bruises from one misadventure or another.'

'I take it Linda was also accident-prone?'

'Now I'm glad you brought that up, Billy. Obviously Linda's told you how I used to beat her up, use her as my punching bag, and doubtless you believed her. Why not? Everyone else did. And do you know what, Billy? It's true, I did hit her. Twice, actually. The first time was when she found out that I was screwing Sharna. She was hysterical, Billy.

I slapped her to calm her down. Let me see, we'd been married five years by then. Now, don't you think if I'd been a wife-beater, Linda would have found out a long time earlier? The second time was when she demanded the right to continue working. She got hysterical then too.'

'Was that when you broke her collarbone?'

'Ah, the collarbone. God, that played well in court. You know, despite the misguided testimony of my receptionist, I think the men and women of the jury accepted my evidence about Sharna's propensity for self-injury. In fact, I'm sure they did. I think they also accepted the truth about how Sharna had slipped and hit her head. At least, they were prepared to give me the benefit of the doubt. But then super bitch takes the stand and tells them I'm a habitual wife-beater. She tells them how she lived in mortal fear of what I'd do to her. Two slaps and she's in mortal fear, for fuck's sake! And then she claims I beat her up so badly I split her head open and broke her collarbone. She produces the medical records. It is so obvious to me that she is lying that I assumed everyone else could see that she was lying too. The judge, the jury, everyone.

'But I underestimated her again, Billy. I underestimated her acting ability. But most of all, Billy, I underestimated how ruthless she could be in pursuing her ambition. She was brilliant. By the end of the day she had the judge and jury eating out of her hand. Why just marry the boss when you can be the boss? You see, Billy, super bitch here saw the opportunity to get her ambitions back on track. Once she got me locked away she could take over. Take over my company and take over my life. Get everything she'd ever wanted from the day she met me. All she had to do was tell a few little porky pies. So she lied, Billy. My little schoolteacher put her hand on the Bible and lied her fucking tits off! I didn't break her collarbone, Billy. I didn't split her head open. I didn't, did I, Linda? Did I, Linda!'

* * *

'Neil, you bastard, you can't end the day here!' Lucio turned indignantly to the others for support.

'I meant to stop half an hour ago. My bloody leg's killing me.'

'Come on! You're just using your leg as an excuse. What's another fifteen minutes?'

'Agony, Lucio,' said Neil. 'No, that's probably too strong. Acute discomfort. And the discomfort has become so acute I'm not putting up with it for another minute, let alone another fifteen. You can't complain.'

'I think you've done well to last as long as you have,' said Milos. 'Coffee?'

'I don't think I've got the time. I've arranged for my PA to pick me up at five which is in exactly ...' Neil checked his watch '... two minutes.'

'Come now, Neil. I'm sure Barbara wouldn't mind waiting a few minutes.'

'Barbara, Milos?' Neil's eyes narrowed. 'I had no idea you were on such familiar terms with my PA.'

'I'm not,' said Milos quickly. 'You know she rang after your accident. People give their name when they call, no?'

'She rang you, did she, Milos? I was under the impression she rang Gancio.'

'When Gancio passed on the message he also passed on her name,' said Ramon wearily. 'The real issue is whether or not you have time for coffee. It would be a courtesy to Gancio to let him know how many to make.'

'I'll skip coffee,' said Neil. 'Maybe one of you would like to demonstrate some of your wonderful European courtesy and help me out of my chair. Ahh ... thank you, Lucio. Frankly I'm surprised I had to ask.' He gathered up his crutches and put them under his arms. 'Always a pleasure to see you, gentlemen. Till next week. Please feel free to talk about me when I'm gone.'

'Till next week,' the men responded and watched Neil make his way ineptly to the door, which Gancio held open for him.

'Till next week indeed,' said Ramon softly. 'Milos, what on earth possessed you?'

'I'm sorry, Ramon. My apologies to both of you. A slip of the tongue. What can I say?'

'No damage was done,' said Lucio. 'I think Ramon covered up your mistake.'

'Let's hope so,' said Milos.

'Hope,' said Ramon caustically. 'Hope is what a drowning man clings to before he goes under. You made a catastrophic blunder, Milos, and you hope no damage was done. How long have we known Neil? He is like a dog with a bone. He gnaws away at things until there is nothing but fresh air left to gnaw on. Do you honestly imagine for a second that he'll just ignore your "slip of the tongue"?'

Milos bowed his head in acknowledgement of his blunder.

'For God's sake! If Barbara hasn't already told Neil about coming to see us, she will within the next ten minutes. Neil will be giving her the third degree and, when he finds out, he will be furious. At her and at us. And I don't think we'll be Barbara's favourite people either.'

'I'm sorry, Ramon.'

'Save your apologies for Barbara. I'm sure she'll be relieved to know you're sorry. I think Neil has been way ahead of us all along. I think he is attempting something quite remarkable and would have pulled it off but for Barbara's intervention.'

'What are you talking about?' said Lucio. 'What is he attempting?'

'Use your brain for once. For God's sake, do I have to hold your hands and guide you as if you were little children? Haven't you been listening?'

Both Lucio and Milos shifted uncomfortably in their chairs.

'I think Neil's original intention was to cure us of the truth by shocking us, which is why he made the remark about taking his brother's life. But in developing his story he became more ambitious. I strongly suspect there is another story within the story he is telling but he has disguised it brilliantly. His intention is to lay all the facts out in front of us and yet not have us realise the real story he is telling. But for his accident, I don't doubt he would have got away with it.'

'Away with what?'

'You work it out, Lucio. Neil's story is all about belief and who to believe. I'm convinced he timed his exit perfectly, with us engrossed in wondering who is telling the truth — Grant or Linda. Whether deliberately or otherwise, he is deflecting us from debating the real issue, which is what transpired between himself and his brother. Soon he will tell us what he did to Billy and ask us to believe what he did is true. He said he took his brother's life but, thanks to Barbara, we know he didn't. But something equally unforgivable happened. What worries me is that your slip of the tongue might jeopardise the story Neil is really trying to tell.'

'Which is?'

'Oh, use your brain, Milos! You're as bad as Lucio.'

'Calm down, Ramon,' said Lucio. 'Despite your claim that Neil is a terrier — and I concede that he can be — I am not convinced that he didn't accept your explanation. Why wouldn't Gancio pass on Barbara's name?'

'For God's sake, Lucio. That is not the issue. The issue is why Milos used her name in such a confident and casual way. It assumed familiarity.'

'Ramon is right,' said Milos reluctantly. 'The question is, how do we respond next week?'

'That's entirely up to Neil,' said Ramon. 'He holds all the cards. He may choose to confront us, but then again he may not. He will do whatever he thinks is best to salvage his story and, whatever his decision, we owe it to him to go along with it. I don't think Neil has any choice but to complete his story exactly as he planned it. It appals me that neither of you can see what he's trying to do.'

SIXTH THURSDAY

Chapter Twenty-seven

'Today my story concludes,' said Neil. 'Today I rattle the skeleton in my closet. I hope you all feel proud of yourselves when I reveal the extent of my shame. Once Ramon decided to involve his murky past in his story, this outcome was inevitable. I suspect we've all done things we are not proud of. God only knows what Ramon got up to in Argentina but it's significant that he's never gone back there. The generals are long gone but wild horses couldn't drag him back, not even for a visit. And what about you, Milos? You told us about how you were on the run in Hungary with your brother and your desperate struggle to survive. It's clear to us that your brother would do whatever was necessary to ensure your survival. Whatever was necessary. Think about that. I'm sure a lot of it would not make for mealtime conversation. Milos, you couldn't have avoided being party to things your brother did, things that would shame you now, things you don't want to talk about and left out of your story. I have no doubt that you told us a sanitised version. As for Lucio, anyone who has been in as many bedrooms as he has should be careful throwing stones. You guys rewrite history to protect yourselves and the opinion others have of you, but I'm not going to play your game. I'm going to be very Australian and upfront about what I did wrong and let you judge me on the basis of it. But while you judge me, just remember who you really are.'

Neil finished his coffee. He'd let it get cold. He placed the cup back on the table alongside his empty wine glass. No one seemed eager to interrupt or comment.

'I don't know if any of you have ever gone into the chat rooms on the internet. I have. It's a wonderful Walter Mitty world where you can be anyone you want to be. You can be old or young, male or female, rich or poor. Ramon could get his eyesight back, Lucio his virginity and Milos could have virtual affairs to make up for the ones he's never had in real life. Chat rooms are a world of invention and fantasy. They're time out and an escape. That was what we had here before Ramon made his convoluted, thinly disguised confession. We had a world of invention and fantasy: each of us came here and could pretend to be anyone we wanted to be because we were both friends and strangers. We had the right here to be someone other than the person we were to the rest of the world. We had the right to sustain invention and, if we chose, to become characters who were no more real than those who inhabited our fictions. I want you to think about this when I conclude my story, my true story, and ask yourselves whether we weren't better off.'

'You overestimate the level of our frankness,' said Ramon cautiously. 'As I've told you before, my story was not my confession, thinly disguised or otherwise. However, I was happy to let you think that it was. It was a risk I was prepared to take to add tension to the telling. In this company, one has to be very careful of the risks one takes. Do you want to think about that?'

Chapter Twenty-eight

Billy reached into his top pocket for his tobacco and began to roll another cigarette. The calmness with which his fingers went about the task eased some of the tension inside him. He hoped it had a similarly calming effect on Linda who was still rigid with fear.

He'd discovered the sedating effect of rolling cigarettes in Vietnam. The infantry section he'd been attached to had been sent out on a five-day patrol and he'd taken his turn standing guard at night. He'd set mines around their perimeter that he could detonate electronically in the event that the Vietcong launched an attack, but they did little to comfort him. There were so many stories of how the Vietcong secretly watched the crescent-shaped claymores being laid and then crept in under cover of darkness to redirect them inwards. There were also stories of Vietcong silently infiltrating the perimeter and slitting sentries' throats. Billy had heard all the stories but thought he was up to the task. After all, he went down tunnels and there weren't many men who were prepared to do that. But the tunnels were silent and the jungles at night anything but. His ears, which had been attuned to picking up the slightest sound below ground, missed nothing above it. He lost count of the number of times he was convinced the enemy were creeping up on his position. He'd held fire, not wanting to risk shooting at shadows or straying animals and giving away their position, and held off detonating his mines in case they had been turned and he blew half of his section to bits. When his shakes got too bad he put his SLR down and rolled a cigarette to calm himself. He knew he couldn't smoke while he was on guard duty but there was comfort just in rolling them as though he was going to light up. He stuffed the rollies back in the plastic tobacco pouch. When he was relieved one and a half hours later he was stunned to discover he'd rolled over thirty.

'Well, Linda, are you going to tell lover boy what really happened?'

Billy ran his tongue along the edge of the paper, tamped the ends and reached for his matches. The match striking sounded abnormally loud. He felt Linda jump.

'Look, Billy, it seems super bitch has lost her tongue. Amazing, isn't it? Couldn't shut her up in court, can't get a word out of her now. Why do you think that is?'

'You tell me.'

'Oh, I will, Billy. You see, my little schoolteacher actress here told the jury I was a really nasty man who got a kick out of beating women. She told them she had cuts and broken bones to prove it. Billy, she had the jury sitting on the edge of their seats. They recoiled when she told them how I'd hit her so hard I'd split her head open from top to bottom. They wanted to gather her up in their collective arms and give her a hug. When she told them how I'd knocked her down so violently that I broke her collarbone, one of the male jurors turned to look at me and, I swear, if he'd had a length of rope on him, he would've lynched me right there.

'I watched my barrister get up, Billy, and I thought, here we go, he'll get the truth out of her. I mean, I was paying him three thousand dollars a day. He was a gun silk, Billy, the sort of interrogator the Gestapo would've treasured as a shining example of their craft. He told the jury what really happened, how we were getting ready to go out to dinner. Linda was rubbing one of her fancy oils into her skin when I got out of the shower. We were clowning about, Billy. I said something to her that was a bit naughty and when I turned around to get my towel she flicked me with hers. She can make towels snap, Billy, like cracking a whip, and she got me a beauty right on my arse. I spun around to grab her towel off her. Understand this, we were playing. It was a game. It was something we'd done a hundred times before. Linda was laughing. I was laughing. We were a happily married couple having our own naked tug of war in the privacy of our bathroom when she slipped and let go. Do you hear me, Billy? She slipped and let go of the towel. Slipped and let go. That's all. Bathrooms are unforgiving places, Billy, and nice, expensive Italian marble is especially unyielding. My little Academy Award-winner split her head open and broke her collarbone.

'I dressed her, Billy. I carried her out to the car and drove her to hospital. I stayed with her until she'd been stitched, sedated and X-rayed, then went home to take care of our daughter. The babysitter was just a kid herself, studying for the HSC, and had to get home. My daughter knew Linda had slipped and fallen, so did the babysitter and the doctors and nurses who looked after Linda in the hospital. But do you know something, Billy? Nothing my three-thousand-dollar-a-day barrister did could make Linda admit that she was lying, make her change her story, get her to retract a word. I was home free until she told her lies. I would've got off, Billy, I would've got off. But the judge and the jury believed the bitch. They believed her. And they thought it was too much of a coincidence that both Linda and Sharna fell and hurt themselves. The two events were years apart, Billy. Where is the fucking coincidence in that?

'She lied, Billy. Your little girlfriend put her hand on the Bible and swore to tell the truth and then lied through her teeth. In hindsight, you've got to take your hat off to her. She got everything she wanted and I got six fucking years in gaol. Six fucking years! Have you any fucking idea what gaol is like, Billy, have you any fucking idea at all?'

'Yeah, I do as a matter of fact.' Billy calmly butted his rollie in the beer can. He looked up at Grant. White flecks of spittle had gathered at the corners of Grant's mouth, a vein in his temple was throbbing and his eyes were bulging. Billy had the feeling Linda's eyes had widened a bit as well.

'You've done time?' Moments earlier Grant had looked like he was about to explode but the shock of Billy's admission somehow defused him.

'I got twelve months, served nine.'

'What for?'

'Assault. I was living in Sydney and trying to get my life back together. I was having a quiet beer in a pub when these student types, all long hair, sideburns and Uncle Ho T-shirts, came in. To cut a long story short, they got stuck into me for going to Vietnam.

Called me a killer. Accused me of murdering innocent women and children. There were seven or eight of them, some of them girls. One of the girls actually spat at me. I had three of the dickheads on the deck and out for the count before the barman and a couple of other blokes pulled me away. The barman stood up for me in court and said I'd been provoked. The judge said that I was a menace to society, all the more dangerous for being a trained soldier. In the end he gave me the benefit of the doubt. Gave me six months' suspended sentence and a caution that if I reoffended I'd go straight to gaol.'

'What happened?'

'I reoffended.'

'You're kidding.'

'No. A few days later. Same scenario. Vietnam vets weren't exactly the flavour of the month. None of us wanted to go to Vietnam but, when we got back, those of us who got back discovered we were saddled with the guilt of the nation and loathed for it. I decided I wasn't going to wear it.'

'But you knew you'd go to gaol.'

'I didn't care.'

'Christ. Where'd they send you?'

'Long Bay.'

'Twelve Wing?'

'For a while. Until I got reclassified from C1 to C3 and transferred to the training centre. Have to thank my parole officer for that. I didn't give a shit where I went or what I did.'

'There's the difference between you and me, Billy — I do give a shit. They tried to send me to Vietnam too. When I got the papers, Christ, did I curse the day I was born. May the fucking eleventh. Don't you think it's ironic that the day you're born should determine whether or not they're going to try to get you killed? I assume you got balloted in.'

'Yeah.'

'What was your birthday?'

'May eight.'

'There you go. The difference is, you went, Billy, like a lamb to the slaughter and I didn't. The rugby club doctor gave me a medical certificate saying my back was buggered and went on for eight pages about the treatment I was supposedly getting. Thing is, we were running second in the comp and they didn't want to go into the finals without their star breakaway. Nobody went to Vietnam who didn't want to go, Billy. You either had to be terminally stupid or you wanted to go.'

'I had no choice.'

'You had choice, just as you had choice over whether or not you went to gaol. That's the real difference between us, Billy. I'm the one who had no choice. No fucking choice at all. Super bitch here saw to that.' Grant picked up his rifle and pointed it towards Linda. 'Know what I want now, Billy? I want revenge. I want to get my own back, make Linda pay for her lies and what she did to me. It's time she paid for the two thousand, one hundred and ninety-three days I spent in gaol. It's time she paid for destroying the fabulous life that I had and the brilliant career. It's time she paid for stealing my company. I want to kill her, Billy, and that means I'll also have to kill you. Sorry about that, but when you hang around super bitch you have to expect to get hurt. I'll have to shoot you first, Billy, because just shooting Linda would be too kind, too quick. I really think she deserves to be roughed up a bit first. Roughed up until the bitch is begging me to shoot her, pleading with me. I'm told,

Billy — and you can probably correct me here if I'm wrong — that a bullet in the belly is the most agonising way to die. I do like the sound of that. The most agonising way to die. That's what she deserves, Billy. What do you reckon?'

'I saw worse in Vietnam.'

'What do you think, Linda? What's the matter? Cat got your tongue again? You know, Billy, when I left home a couple of days ago there was no doubt at all in my mind what I wanted. Above all, I wanted to get even in the way I've just described. But that's not all, Billy. I want more. I want my company back and my old life back as well. I want things back to the way they were before super bitch ruined everything. You know, it took me a whole day's driving and thinking to realise that I couldn't kill her and get my company back. Can you imagine what a bitter pill that is to swallow? I have to choose, decide what I want most. On the one hand I want to kill her, but that could complicate things when it comes to regaining control over my company. I mean, if she signed the company over to me and then disappeared, how would that look? I have the problem of making sure there's no suggestion of coercion or duress. Follow me, Billy? How unfair is that? How unjust? If I want my company back, the bitch has to go unpunished. Un-fucking-punished. What would you do, Billy?'

The tension began to seep from Billy's body as he realised Grant had already made his decision. He hoped Linda had realised it too, even though she gave no indication.

'If I were you, I'd show Linda where to sign.'

'Is that right?'

'It's hardly a tough decision, is it? If you shoot Linda, you'll be the first person the police will suspect. Even if you don't go back to gaol, you'll have no company, no career and nothing to live for. That doesn't make much sense to me.'

'You know, Billy, on balance I think you're right, although the decision is a lot harder to make than you think.' Grant reached into his backpack and pulled out the documents his lawyers had drawn up. 'You'll find I've been more than generous, Linda, far more generous than you deserve, but we want everything to pass the sniff test. Basically, you're selling your interest in Film Gate to me for half a million dollars. Ahh, you look surprised. I must admit, half a million is a very generous offer, but then again you have given me very generous terms. Very generous terms. You've agreed to let me make the payments over twenty years. I give you twenty-five thousand dollars every year for twenty years. I know I spend more than that each year on entertainment, Linda, but you know, I think you could live quite well out here on twenty-five thousand a year.' He looked around at the blank canvases on the walls. 'You'll be able to finish your paintings and maybe even sell a few. God forbid, Linda, but you might even end up thanking me.

'Now, I'm going to pass the papers to you, Linda, and you're going to initial every page and sign and date them where they're marked with a cross. When you've finished, lover boy here can witness your signature. I think that's a nice touch, don't you, having Billy act as witness?'

'Go to hell.'

Billy spun around. Linda was still shaking but her jaw was set and her eyes blazed defiance. 'I'm not signing.'

Billy turned back to look at Grant, alarmed. The

colour had gone from Grant's face and his lips, which had played with a sneering half smile as he'd taunted them, had retreated to two thin lines. At first there was disbelief in his eyes but it quickly turned to hate.

'Well, I guess you've just made my decision for me. You see, I was being absolutely honest when I said I didn't much care which way the decision went. I'm really going to enjoy breaking you, Linda, breaking you bit by bit. How many days would you like to spend dying? I mean, I'm not going to rush this. It might be the last real pleasure I get out of life. Billy's probably right in that I will be the main suspect when you disappear and there's no way I'll let them put me back in gaol. You're going to pay, Linda, you are going to pay in spades, not just for what you've done to me but for whatever happens next. You're going to suffer like you made me suffer. First, you're going to watch me shoot Billy. I'm sorry, Billy, that it's come to this but super bitch has left me no choice. But now do you understand what we're dealing with here? Now do you understand what a hard, ruthless bitch she really is? She'd rather watch me shoot you than sign away her company. She values her company and her ambitions more than your life. How do you feel about that, Billy? How do you feel about the bitch now?'

Grant raised the rifle and lined Billy up in the sights.

'Linda, for Christ's sake! Tell him you'll sign!' Billy turned to look at her but she wouldn't meet his eyes and kept her mouth resolutely shut. 'Tell him!'

'Yes, tell me, Linda.'

'Linda!' Billy was stunned. 'For Christ's sake, Linda, if he kills me he'll kill you! What good will that do? Tell him you'll sign!'

'Last chance, Linda. Three ... two ... one ... sorry, Billy.'

Billy knew he didn't have a chance but decided to at least die trying. He jerked forward, transferring his weight over his knees, and pushed down with his thighs and calves. At the same time he pushed down with his hands, felt the delay as the energy was partially absorbed by the padding in the sofa. He'd never pushed harder in his life or with more determination but he knew he was too slow gathering momentum and braced himself for the bullet. He was dimly aware of Bella reacting, her growl and the scrabbling of her claws as she struggled for traction. He saw Grant's finger tighten on the trigger, saw his life face extinction, and turned away before the explosion. Instinctively he covered up to protect himself and recoiled backwards. The closeness of the shot almost deafened him. His ears rang yet he could hear Linda screaming alongside him. Screaming and screaming. In blind panic he tried to work out where he'd been hit and why he couldn't feel the pain and why his brain was still thinking. You're not supposed to hear the shot that gets you. Everyone knew that! You never hear the shot that gets you, but he'd heard it, his ears still rang with it. Then he remembered there'd been another sound, something he'd heard and ignored and now understood. He dared to look down, leaning forward to see clearly. Her head had come to rest on his foot. Her lifeless tongue hung over the arch. Blood seeped onto the rug. Tears he'd never expected to flow again welled up in his eyes, tears of anger, sorrow, relief, disgust. Linda sobbed hysterically but words of comfort were the last thing on his mind.

'Well, soldier, what do you think? Pretty good shot? I haven't had a lot to do with guns but I've got a good eye. Flows on from my training as a cameraman. Do you think I got through to Linda, Billy, or was it just a waste of a dog?'

'You didn't have to shoot it.'

'I did, Billy. I had to shoot someone or something. It came down to you or the dog. I hope you agree that I made the right choice. Now it's just between you and the bitch. No more chances. No more choices. God, I'd like another beer. Billy, you look like you could use one too. The thing is, I don't think we can trust super bitch to go get them for us. I think once she got to the kitchen she'd do a runner. She'd sacrifice you, Billy. I mean, if she can do it once, she can do it twice, right?'

'I'll sign.'

'What?'

'I'll sign.'

Billy slowly turned to look at Linda. Her voice was barely audible, flat, lifeless, defeated. The defiance was long gone from her eyes. Tears filled them now.

'Louder, Linda, I can't hear you.'

'I said I'll sign.'

'Hear that, Billy? She's changed her mind. Changed it, just like that. If she'd exercised her woman's prerogative a moment ago your little doggy would still be alive. Thing is, Billy, do you think her new spirit of cooperation means we can trust her to get us a couple of beers? Can we trust you, Linda? Can we?'

'Yes.'

'Amazing, isn't it, Billy. Shoot a dog and the bitch comes to heel. Why didn't I think of it before? I'll tell you what you'll do, Linda. You'll get up slowly and stay in my line of sight. Stay in the doorway where I can see you. Reach around the fridge door for the beers. Understand?'

'Yes.' Linda stood shakily, and turned towards Billy at the sight of Bella's body. 'I'm so sorry, Billy. I never thought he'd shoot. I forgot about Bella. I'm so sorry.'

Billy nodded acknowledgement.

'She's sorry, Billy. Touching, isn't it?' Grant stood so Linda could pass in front of him but well beyond reach. 'Bitch was quite happy for me to shoot you but she's upset because I shot the dog. Well, at least you know where you stand. Now move it, Linda. Keep your arse in sight at all times. I want a target I can't miss.' Grant kept his rifle up and pointed at Linda as she made her way to the fridge and opened it, but his eyes flicked back and forth between her and Billy. He smiled as Linda straightened and made her way back with a can of VB in each hand. 'Put one down on the table, Linda, and open the other before you give it to lover boy. That's it. Okay now, Billy, I don't want you abusing my generosity and doing something silly like throwing your can at me, so would you put your right hand behind your head and keep it there. Okay, Linda, give him his beer and sit down.' He resumed his perch on the table and opened his can. 'Cheers, Billy.'

'Cheers.'

'Now, Linda, I believe you're going to sign some papers.'

'You'll have to wait until my hands stop shaking otherwise people will know I signed under duress. You could take the dog out onto the veranda or something. It's not helping me, having her lie there.'

'That's a good idea, Linda. Why don't you pick her up and put her outside?'

'Me?'

'You're the one who wants her moved. Billy and I are having a beer. Besides, I think it'll do you good to discover what a dead body feels like.'

Linda got up off the sofa and bent to pick Bella up. Tears spilled from her eyes. She struggled to get her arms beneath so that the body was evenly supported and staggered to the veranda door.

'I can't open it.'

'Use your feet.'

Linda kicked the screen door across and gently laid Bella down on the veranda. She ignored the insects that threatened to engulf her, rose to her feet and stood head bowed over the body. It slowly dawned on Billy what she was up to and the gamble she was taking.

'Shut the screen and sit down,' ordered Grant. 'It's time to get the business over and done with so we can all relax and have a good time.'

'My hands are still shaking. Look.'

'For Christ's sake, Billy, give her a sip of your beer. I'm starting to lose patience.' He picked up the envelope with the documents inside and threw it at Linda. He also threw her a pen. 'Practise your signature on the envelope and then get to it. Stop fucking me around.'

Linda opened the envelope and started reading.

'What the hell are you doing now?'

'I'm reading the documents. I want to see what I'm signing.'

'For fuck's sake, I've told you what you're signing! Get on with it!'

'What's the big hurry, Grant? Reading this is just the distraction I need to calm me down and steady my hands.'

'Okay, okay. Take your time. We've got all the time in the world, haven't we, Billy? How's the beer going? Good?'

'Can't complain.'

'You know, Billy, another time and another place I think I could get to quite like you. I must admit I'm not much of a VB man myself. I prefer the European beers — Lowenbrau, Becks, Peroni. And I always think beer tastes better out of bottles than cans.'

Billy pretended interest but his ears strained for the sound of a stealthy movement of someone slipping through the undergrowth, searching, creeping nearer and nearer. Alongside him, Linda read through the documents as though weighing every word. He no longer knew what to make of her.

'Tell me, Billy, did you kill anyone over in Vietnam?'

'What's it to you?'

'I want to know what I missed.'

'Believe me, that's the last thing you want to know.'

'Why? Don't you think I could handle it?'

Billy glanced towards the veranda windows. He sensed Linda silently urging him to keep talking.

'It doesn't matter whether you could handle it or not. That wasn't a choice they gave you.'

'Spare me the dramatics, Billy, just answer the question. Did you kill anyone?'

'Yes.'

'How many?'

'Hard to say.'

'That many? Soldiers or civilians?'

'Sometimes it was hard to tell which was which.'

'So you might have killed civilians. Any women and children, Billy? I got six years just for being in the same room as a woman who killed herself. How many women did you kill?'

Billy thought back to the bombed village in the rain and the villagers running screaming towards him. He remembered the woman who'd filled his sights and her crying children, saw her fall over and get back up again, and how he'd thought it was odd that there could be so much fire in the midst of so much rain. He remembered the noise of the rain and the bombs and the woman falling again, soundless amid all the sound. Saw her get up and reach for her children. Then someone lost his nerve and started shooting and others joined in before the officers restored control. He'd fired just one round, one single round, a nervous reaction to someone else's nervous reaction. Three people fell and didn't get up again. One was the woman he'd targeted. Her kids pulled her arm, trying to lift her back to her feet. Trying to bring her back to life.

'Hello, Billy? Hello? Anyone there?'

'Like I said before, you don't want to know. Want to know something else? I don't want to know either.'

'Whoa! Down, boy! Getting a bit touchy there. You know, some people looking in on us right now might think I was the killer. But my conscience is clear. I have no trouble sleeping at night. What about you, Billy boy? Having any bad dreams? Night sweats? Conscience troubling you?'

'No, not that I'm aware of.'

'Not that you're aware of? What kind of an answer is that?' Grant drained the dregs of his beer can and turned to Linda.

'Time's up. Stop reading. Start signing. And don't piss me about.'

'I've nearly finished.'

'No, Linda. You're not listening.' Grant picked up his rifle again to make his point. 'You've finished reading. Simple Simon semi-automatic says pick up the pen, do a couple of signatures on the envelope and start signing. I've had all the beers I want and all of your company I can stand.'

Linda picked up the pen and signed her name twice on the envelope. Her hand was still a little unsteady but it didn't show in her signature.

'Satisfied?'

'Get on with it.'

Linda worked through the document, initialling each page and signing and dating both copies of the agreement. She passed the documents over to Billy to witness, showing him exactly where to sign. Billy put his beer down and took the pen in his right hand. It was hard to concentrate on the papers in front of him when his ears were screaming at him to look elsewhere. The bottom step of the veranda had a sound all of its own, a short, barely discernible sound of wood rubbing on wood whenever weight was placed on it. He glanced up at Grant to make sure he held all of his attention.

'Do I witness both copies?'

'Don't you start pissing me about too, Billy. Just sign the bloody things.' He watched carefully as Billy added his signature to the second document. 'Good.'

Billy held his breath. For once he wanted Rodney to shoot first and ask questions after.

'Hand up, you bar-tid, hoo-wah, bitch!'

Billy's eyes shot to the screen door. He could see Rodney standing there, shotgun cradled into his shoulder. He turned to Grant, expecting him to freeze, but he was already pivoting. Grant fired and fired again, not with calm deliberation but from sheer fright, firing blindly, not aiming but pointing.

'Shoot, Rodney!' Billy didn't know whether he said it or just thought it, but he was too slow anyway.

Rodney's cry of pain cut through him like a knife to the heart. He lunged up out of the sofa but was too late. Rodney had disappeared from the screen door and Grant was crouched over, pointing the rifle at him.

'Sit down! Sit down, Billy!'

Billy sat back down. Grant was wild-eyed with fear and clearly panicking, swinging his rifle recklessly, finger tight over the trigger. Outside Rodney was howling like a wounded dog, his cries growing more desperate and anguished by the second. And also fainter.

'Oh God, Grant, what have you done?'

Linda had risen to her feet; Billy had no idea when. Her eyes were flared and staring, her hands covered her mouth.

'He had a gun! For Christ's sake! Oh, holy shit! He had a gun!' Grant was still in a crouch, uncertain whether to point his rifle at Billy, Linda or the punctured screen door. 'Who or what the fuck was that? Tell me!'

'He's my neighbour! You shot him!'

Grant was shouting and Linda was shouting back at him. Billy heard the sound of stones falling and someone sliding and whimpering. Rodney was trying to crawl back to his home.

'It was self-defence, you saw that.'

'Shut up, both of you,' said Billy forcefully. He got to his feet. 'I don't give a damn which of you ends up with the bloody company and I don't give a damn who did what to who. You hear me? Rodney's out there and needs our help and I'm going to help him.'

'You're not going anywhere!'

'Try and stop me.'

'Sit down!'

Billy realised Grant was panicked enough to squeeze the trigger either intentionally or unintentionally. He hesitated, torn between self-preservation and the need to help Rodney. Finally he sat back down, but only on the edge of the sofa.

'Grant, we have to do something.' Linda was pleading. 'He could be badly hurt. I've signed your document. What more do you want?'

'Shut up! Sit down! I need time to think. Shit!'

'We haven't got any time!'

'Shut the fuck up!'

Linda sat down but, like Billy, barely on the edge of the seat.

'Now everyone and his fucking dog will know you signed the documents under duress!' said Grant. 'Don't you see? You want proof of duress? How about a fuckwitted neighbour with a bullet hole in him?'

'I promise I won't contest it.'

'Jesus! How stupid do you think I am? Like I'd take your word.'

'You can take mine.'

'What's that, Billy boy?'

'I'll back you up. I'll swear in court that Linda signed of her own free will. I'll confirm that you shot Rodney in self-defence.'

'Why should I trust you?' Grant glared at Billy, all his composure and arrogance gone. 'I suppose you also have a simple explanation for why I just happened to be sitting here with a loaded rifle?'

'I'll square things away with Rodney. He'll do whatever I tell him. Provided he's still alive. Provided we get to him before he dies.'

'Listen to him, Grant. Rodney does whatever Billy tells him.'

'You don't have any choice.' Billy stood up again. 'You can either trust me or shoot me, because I'm going out after Rodney.'

'Okay, okay! We'll all go. You'd better not be lying to me, Billy. You know I've got a low tolerance for liars. Linda! Pass me the agreement.'

Linda handed the documents to Grant. He was too jittery to give the pages anything more than a cursory check. With shaking hands he stuffed them back into their envelope and put the envelope in his backpack. He took out his torch.

'Any more torches? We need more torches.'

'I've got two,' said Linda. 'One's in the kitchen, the other's in my bedroom.'

'Get them. And grab your first-aid kit. She's got one, hasn't she, Billy?'

'She's got one.'

'Good. I'm trusting you to keep your word, Billy. But take one step out of line and I'll fucking shoot you.'

Billy nodded. The only thing that mattered was helping Rodney.

'Right. You go first. Linda, give him a torch and follow him. I'll follow you. Just don't try anything, okay?'

Billy paused as he stepped over the body of Bella. There was a splash of blood beside it, too fresh to have seeped from the dog's body. There was another drip on the top step. He felt a rage surge inside him that he'd rarely felt since he'd been sent home from Sydney. First things first, he thought. Help Rodney, if Rodney could still be helped. Everything else could wait. He strode quickly to the trail up over the ridge, hoping he wouldn't find Rodney lying dead beside it.

And shit scared of what he'd do if he did.

Chapter Twenty-nine

Billy stopped when he reached the crest of the outcrop where the ground was stony and barren but for a scattering of gidgee trees. Below him both Grant and Linda were yelling at him to slow down but that wasn't why he stopped. The fact that Rodney had made it to the top heartened him and gave him hope that he hadn't been hit anywhere vital, although there was still the possibility that he could bleed to death if they didn't get to him. He blamed himself for letting Linda use Rodney, although he'd no idea that Grant would panic and react so blindly and desperately. They had no right to put Rodney in that situation. It wasn't his argument. But what could he have done? Nothing could have prevented Rodney from coming running once he heard the gunshot that killed Bella. The sound of boots skidding on stones signalled that Linda and Grant had finally made it to the top. Grant was furious.

'Clear off like that again and I'll shoot Linda. Understand me?' Grant was puffing hard from the effort of climbing the ridge. Linda wasn't much better off.

Billy ignored them.

'Rodney could've gone anywhere from here and cut through the scrub any number of ways. We've got to hope that he's taken the most direct route and that he's still dripping blood. Once we get down on the sand, Linda, you come on my left, Grant, you come on my right. Look for blood spots, okay?'

They found Rodney's footprints once they reached the sandy soil and, though it was impossible to tell which were the most recent, they all seemed to channel towards the same gap in the scrub. Billy spotted blood, not on the soil but on the leaf of a bush Rodney had brushed against. It was the confirmation he was looking for.

'He went this way. Stay behind me.'

Billy realised he was the only one capable of following a trail. Neither Linda nor Grant could've spotted the blood on the bush. They didn't even know to look for it there; in fact, hadn't a clue what to look for. He found another blood spot and another and the semblance of a track. The further he went the more Billy appreciated what a creature of habit Rodney was. The pines and coolibahs in the saddle between the two sand ridges were well spaced yet Rodney had followed the same path as faithfully as a feral pig. It had only fanned out into a delta towards the outcrop above Linda's. Billy pressed on, flicking his torch from left to right, checking both sides of the track to make sure Rodney hadn't collapsed or stopped to rest. He thought it unlikely but he wanted to be sure. There were regular indentations and drag marks alongside the track, probably made by the butt of the shotgun. He guessed Rodney was using it as a crutch or for support.

He found another blood spot and another and more at regular intervals. There was never much, just enough to let him know he was still on the right track. His concern for Rodney made him slow to realise just how regularly spaced the drops were and how well placed. It was as though Rodney had deliberately dripped them there so they couldn't be missed. It slowly dawned on Billy that Rodney might be up to something. But then he'd heard his cry of pain when he'd been hit and his awful howling when he'd run away. He knew his friend was a tough little rooster but there was also his whimpering when he'd climbed back up the ridge. That hadn't been faked. Rodney was hurt badly, but how badly? And were the blood spots just natural seepage? He thought he was reading too much into the spots until he found another exactly where he expected it to be. His suspicions grew, though he felt it was still too soon to draw a firm conclusion. Rodney had probably rested somewhere on top of the ridge and he almost certainly would have stayed long enough to see the light from their torches and know he was being followed. It suddenly occurred to him that maybe Rodney had counted on it, realised he needed help and had also worked out the only way he could be sure of getting it. Billy groaned under his breath.

'Jesus Christ! How much further are you taking us, Billy?' Grant was puffing hard. 'We've come a long way, especially for a man with a bullet in him. You sure he made it this far?'

'There's a trail of blood. Come up here and I'll show you.' Billy hoped that Grant would come close enough so he could grab his rifle. He had to do something.

'Just point it out with your torch and back away. Right away. Linda, you stay where you are.' Grant stepped cautiously around her and up to the patch of soil lit by Billy's torch. The drop of blood was small, less than the size of a five-cent piece, but the colour was unmistakeable. 'Okay. But how much further?'

'His cabin's on top of the ridge and in a bit.'

Grant stepped back so Linda could pass in front of him and followed her on up the slope.

Billy slowed as they climbed higher. The soil became more gravelly and Rodney's tracks became harder to find. He was considering doubling back to look in another direction when the beam of his torch picked up a telltale splash of red. Billy wondered how anyone could miss it. It was sitting on top of a grey-white, football-sized piece of shin-cracker, as clear as any signpost. Billy bit his bottom lip. That was no accident. The odds of the drop of blood falling on the one spot where it could not be missed were astronomical. He was almost certain he knew what Rodney was up to. It was exactly what he'd do in the same situation, but that didn't make it right.

'Rodney!' he called out. 'It's me. It's okay.' Billy had to do something and calling out seemed his only option. But would it make any difference? 'Call to him, Linda. Tell him it's all right.'

'Rodney! Where are you? Tell me so I can help you.'

They stood still for a few seconds waiting for a response. When there was none they continued up the hill.

'Rodney!' Billy called again. 'It's okay. Don't be frightened. Linda's got the first-aid kit. Where are you?'

Rodney didn't reply but Billy was sure he was watching them or waiting for them to come into view. He wanted to tell Rodney to put down his shotgun but couldn't without alerting Grant and making him even more agitated. God only knew what Grant would do if he thought there was a chance Rodney would shoot at him. Of course there was always the possibility that Rodney had collapsed from loss of blood, but Billy doubted it. The signposts were too obvious. Rodney was still thinking clearly. He headed towards the cabin but suddenly a small cluster of spots showed that the little man had turned away towards his diggings. Billy's heart sank.

'Rodney! Don't be scared. We're only going to help you. Understand? We're only going to help you. Tell him, Linda.'

'It's okay, Rodney, don't be frightened.' Linda staggered and caught herself when she tripped on a piece of rock.

Billy led them on into the diggings, taking care to avoid the mineshafts and heaps of mullock.

'Bloody hell, Billy, where are you taking us? I don't like this.' Grant stopped and shone his torch around him, stunned by the incomprehensible landscape. 'What the fuck is this?'

'We're on Rodney's diggings. He's probably holed up down one of the shafts. Stay close.'

'Why?' demanded Grant.

'So you don't fall down any of the mineshafts.' That was just one of Billy's worries. With no moon and only torches lighting their way, the shadows were as black as the entrances to the shafts. But what he was really worried about was giving Rodney a clear shot at Grant.

'Rodney, where are you?' called Linda.

Billy's dismay grew when he realised Rodney was leading him towards the triple where, years earlier, he'd found the opal. Of course Rodney would lead him there and he knew exactly what he'd find when he got there. Blood spots on the rungs of the ladder. An invitation to descend, leaving Grant on top alone and a sitting duck. Billy had had enough. His dog was dead, Rodney was wounded and he didn't need any more drama. He had to gamble on Grant holding his nerve, or at least what was left of it.

'No, Rodney,' he called. 'It's okay. Don't do anything!'

'What do you mean, "don't do anything"?' demanded Grant immediately. His voice rose an octave. 'What the fuck's going on?'

Billy ignored him.

'Where are you, Rodney? It's okay. Trust me, don't do anything!'

'What are you doing?' screamed Grant. 'Tell me! What's going on?'

Billy could hear the panic in Grant's voice and it filled him with dread. The panic was just going to hasten what was probably inevitable anyway.

'Turn off your torch!' he ordered. He flicked his off. Linda followed suit.

'No way!' said Grant. 'I know what you're trying to do!' He raised his rifle, left hand holding his torch hard along the stock so he could see his target.

The sudden explosion from the shotgun made Billy jump even though he'd been expecting it. It came from nearby but not quite as near as he'd feared. Billy lunged towards Grant but collided with Linda. She fell to the ground, screaming. Billy staggered. He could see Grant's torch lying on the ground but he couldn't see Grant.

'Grant! Are you okay?'

'He shot me.'

There was more disbelief in Grant's voice than pain, which made Billy think the pellets had spread too wide to have done serious damage. He didn't know if Grant was still standing or not. He flicked his torch on and caught Grant in the beam. He was still standing, still clutching his rifle.

'Turn it off!' Grant's eyes were wide with fear and shock.

'Just drop your rifle and put your hands up. I've got to keep the torch on so Rodney can see you've surrendered.'

'Turn it off!' He raised his rifle and pointed it at Billy. 'Turn it off!'

Billy flicked the torch off and dropped to the ground. Then he heard the sound he least wanted to hear, the sound of Grant doing the most stupid thing he could possibly do.

'Stop!' he yelled. 'Don't run! Stand still!' Billy flicked his torch back on and searched for Grant. Just as he caught him in his beam, Grant disappeared. The scream that followed confirmed the worst.

'Oh, Jesus! He's fallen down a shaft! Linda, you go and attend to Rodney. And take the bloody shotgun off him. Rodney! Linda's coming to help you. Tell her where you are.' Billy used his torch to point where he thought the shot had come from. 'Head that way and watch where you put your feet.'

Billy turned and began to circle around to where he'd last seen Grant. He held his torch out to his side in case Grant had faked the fall to regain control. He doubted Grant was capable of thinking clearly enough but had to be sure. He crept up to the shaft from the opposite side, crouched down and turned off his torch.

'Grant, can you hear me?'

He heard a faint groan in reply and it definitely came from the shaft. He edged slowly towards the lip.

'Grant?'

A scrabbling came from deep down, a sharp intake of breath and something that sounded like a sob. Billy peered over the lip and turned on his torch.

Grant yelped in fright and tried to pull himself away into the cover of a tunnel that Rodney, or more likely his dad, had dug along a horizontal fault. The mine was old and decaying. Part of one side of the vertical shaft had collapsed, leaving a sloping ledge which had probably helped break Grant's fall. Still, he'd tumbled at least five metres and landed on rubble. Blood streamed from a gash in his head and there were red buttons of blood where shotgun pellets had struck.

'Mate, it's okay, it's okay. I'm not going to hurt you. Stay where you are and I'll go find a ladder.' Billy looked for a sign of acknowledgement but Grant ignored him. Instead, his hands groped around in the rubble as though searching for something and Billy realised what. The rifle had fallen in with him. 'For Christ's sake, no one's going to hurt you!'

'Where'd the bar-tid hoo-wah? Where id he? I'll ged him!'

Billy whirled around. A panicked cry of 'no' came from beneath him and he pushed himself backwards as Grant fired up the shaft.

'Where the bar-tid? Where id he!'

'No, Rodney!' yelled Billy. He could hear Grant desperately trying to find cover from Rodney's shotgun. Billy winced as Linda's torch finally located then held on him, blinding him.

'Get the bloody torch off me!' Billy shone his own torch towards Linda, centring the beam low around knee height. Rodney had his left arm over Linda's shoulder and his right used the shotgun to share his weight. Even in the spill of the torchlight he looked terrible. There was a dark wet stain on the left side of his shirt. 'Linda, for Christ's sake, what are you doing? Get him away from here! Take him to his cabin.'

Billy didn't dare stick his head over the edge of the shaft but called anyway, 'Grant? You hear me? They've gone, they've gone. I'm going to get a ladder and get you out. Okay? Just put your rifle down.'

There was no reply.

Billy rocked back on his heels, suddenly aware of what he'd promised and his lack of alternative. The consequences hit him like a brick. The beam of his torch flickered wildly as his hands started shaking.

'Jesus Christ!' he said softly to no one, not even himself. He forced himself to his feet and shone his torch about to get his bearings. He'd thought it was all over, finished, done with, consigned to his past. He forced himself to concentrate, to acknowledge the difference in circumstances. But were they so different? He doubled back to where he'd stood when Rodney had fired. He marked his start point and, with his boot, carved an arrow in the soil pointing towards the shaft Grant was hiding in. That done, he followed the blood spots to the triple, certain that was where Rodney had set up his ambush. If they'd got that far, there was no way Rodney would've missed. Sure enough, there was a ladder in the shaft and, as he'd predicted, blood spots on it. He put his torch on the ground and began hauling the ladder up. At any other time, Billy might have savoured fond memories, but a smile had never been further from his lips.

His brief look down the shaft showed him that Rodney, or his dad before he'd died, had been busy. The triple now had five separate digs radiating out from the main shaft at different levels. Obviously when other diggings had yielded nothing, they'd come back to it in the hope that it would again produce. Hope, a shovel and a bucket: the opal miner's holy trinity. Billy didn't bother checking the ladder. Rodney wouldn't have led him there if there were problems with it. He put his left arm between the middle rungs and hoisted it up onto his shoulder and backtracked. His heart rate increased and his breath came in short gasps when he realised there was no escaping the next step. Fate had turned the clock back and there was absolutely nothing he could do about it. When he reached the arrow he'd carved in the ground it felt like it also pierced his heart.

'Grant?' he called. His voice sounded scared, like someone else's. There was no answer. He put the ladder down and edged up to the lip of the shaft. 'Grant. It's me, Billy. I'm unarmed. Linda's taken Rodney to his cabin. She's also taken the shotgun. You hear me, Grant?'

Billy waited for a reply but there was none. He lined up his torch so that it shone down the shaft and put his finger over the flash button. One quick flash and he'd know if there was a rifle pointed up at him. One quick flash. He hit the button and instantly released it.

Nothing.

He hit the button again and kept it on, watching for movement.

Nothing. Just blood drying on the rubble. Somehow Grant had managed to crawl away into the tunnel. Billy pulled back from the lip, feeling as though someone had wrapped metal bands around his chest and tightened them a notch.

'You there, Grant? Can you hear me? I'm coming down. Put your rifle away. It's just me, and I'm the only hope you've got. Okay?'

Silence.

'Grant, for Christ's sake!'

More silence. The bands around his chest tightened another notch. He picked up the ladder and tentatively lowered it down the shaft.

'Here I come, Grant, here I come.'

Billy's palms were wet with sweat, his heart jack-hammered inside his chest and he struggled to draw breath. As soon as his head dipped below the surface he felt the whole weight of the world close in on him. Every fibre of his body screamed at him to climb back out.

'Here I come, Grant.' He said this as much for himself as for Grant. He braced himself and turned off his torch. 'Oh, Christ!' Darkness came crashing in on him. He closed his eyes as tightly as he could. He tried pretending he was up on the ridge in an attempt to slow his breathing and stop the pounding in his ears. He had to listen. Listen. Listen. Listen! But the walls were pressing in on him, closing over the entrance, entombing him. The metal bands tightened, squeezing the air from his lungs.

He forced himself to defy every instinct and step down another rung, eyes shut, trying to hear over the pounding, fighting back his terror. If he could only calm down. If he could only hear. If he could only stop the pounding inside his head. If he could only get the hell out of there. He stepped down another rung.

'Here I come, Grant, here I come. Take it easy, okay?' His voice sounded so distant and alien. Billy guessed his feet were now level with the opening of the tunnel and that he was entering the area of greatest vulnerability. He braced himself for the gunshot. This was the moment when the Vietcong cut intruders in half with a burst from their Russian-made rifles. He stepped down another rung, and another, his scrotum contracting, his knees trembling. Sweet Jesus! After all this time he was back in another tunnel. Another tunnel. Another live one.

His foot touched rubble. Billy had ceased breathing. He was no longer capable of calling out to Grant or to anyone. His concentration was hopelessly fragmented and he struggled to think through his next step — something which, years earlier, would have been automatic and calculated. His hand located the entrance to the tunnel. It was narrower than the width of the shaft but not by much. Nevertheless, he pressed himself hard against the shaft wall to protect as much of his body as he could. With his arm extended as far away from his body as it could go, he pressed the button on his torch. Just a quick flash, a quick look-see.

Nothing happened.

His torch failed!

Billy spun around to grab the ladder and climb out when he realised there was no problem with the torch. The problem was with him. He still had his eyes shut. He froze, opened his eyes, but was still as blind as he'd been with them closed. The darkness was absolute. As quietly as he could he pressed his body back up against the wall, even though he knew his precautions were futile. He'd given away his position. There was no doubt at all in his mind where Grant had his rifle pointed. The only question was, would he use it?

Billy sucked in air but had trouble forcing it down into his lungs. The bands around his chest made the effort painful. In an act as courageous as any he'd ever undertaken, he extended his arm again and depressed the button on his torch.

His nightmare exploded into life.

Billy opened his eyes expecting to see his veranda posts and hear the kelpie snoring under the steps. He couldn't understand why the darkness was so absolute. It had happened before on nights when there'd been a heavy overcast and it had taken time for his eyes to adjust, but sooner or later the veranda posts always materialised, sometimes barely discernible but always there. Something else was wrong and it took him a moment to realise what it was. The silence. The absolute silence. That was wrong, very wrong. There was always some sound: wind, creaking boards, something contracting or expanding, something moving — a mouse or a rat. There was always something. Why couldn't he see? Why couldn't he hear? Where was he? Why couldn't he remember going to bed? To Billy's horror, memories slowly resurfaced and he fought the urge to throw up.

Terror washed over him as remembered where he was, why he was there and what he had to do. He realised that he must have passed out, but for how long? Where was his torch? He felt about wildly with his hands, brushed something smooth and metal and grabbed it. He pointed it upwards. He needed to know the way out was still open, needed to know he hadn't been buried. His finger pressed the button and relief flooded through his body. But there was another demon still to face because he had to be sure. He slowly turned the torch so that it pointed back along the tunnel.

The rifle was in the same position, out of reach, and the hands were palm down. Only the face was different. But everything else was the same.

Chapter Thirty

'My God, Billy, are you all right?'

The concern in Linda's voice made him wonder whether something had happened to him and he hadn't realised it.

'You look like you've seen a ghost.'

That was exactly what he had seen. A ghost he thought he'd buried long ago. He'd climbed out of the shaft and collapsed onto a heap of mullock alongside it, staring wide-eyed at the sky until both his heartbeat and breathing had slowed to something approaching normal. Lying there exhausted had reminded him of the times when he, Neil and Rodney had rested from their underground explorations on probably the same mullock heap, staring up at a blue sky without a single worry in the world. It had taken a couple of rollies to regather his wits.

'How's Rodney?'

'Not good.'

Rodney lay on his back on his bed, one side of the sheet stained with blood and Betadine antiseptic. Billy couldn't tell if he was asleep, unconscious or had his eyes closed in pain. Linda had done her best and stuffed gauze into the wound in his side in an attempt to stem the blood loss and bound the dressing tightly with a crepe bandage. Even so, her efforts seemed hopelessly inadequate. Rodney's breathing was worryingly shallow. His face was grey.

'We've got to get him to hospital.' Linda sat by his bed, holding his hand helplessly. 'I don't know what else to do.'

'I'll go ring the doctor.'

'Where's Grant?'

Billy hesitated. So much depended on how she responded.

'Grant is dead.'

Her eyes widened in shock and she dropped Rodney's hand back on the bed. She seemed lost for words. As though aware of Billy's gaze she turned away from him, covered her face and started sobbing.

'The roof of the shaft collapsed and fell on him. Maybe he accidentally kicked over one of the supports.'

Or maybe — more likely — he triggered one of Rodney's dad's booby-traps but Billy didn't want to think about that. All his focus was on Linda. He couldn't tell whether she was crying from shock, a sense of loss or with relief. He waited for her to say something, anything, knowing that whatever she said could determine whether there was still hope for them.

'It's all my fault,' she said eventually. Her voice was soft and full of remorse, or was it shame? Billy had to strain to hear her and couldn't tell. She kept her face buried in her hands and wouldn't look at him. 'I should've signed straightaway.'

Billy turned and walked out into the night. Yes, she should've signed straightaway. Grant would still be alive and so would Bella and Rodney wouldn't be knocking on death's door. The fresh air was a balm and the vastness of the sky a comfort. He flicked his torch on and headed for the trail that led back to Linda's, already missing the company of his dog, missing the touch of the wet nose on his hand letting him know he wasn't alone. It occurred to him that the trail hadn't existed before Linda moved in and wondered how many times Rodney had walked over it. How many times had he worked on the garden? Was that often enough to make a trail? He thought of the way the trail fanned out in a delta where it reached the stony ridge above Linda's and guessed that in daylight he'd find cigarette butts and marks where Rodney had sat or lain down to watch her go about her business. If he could possibly have managed a smile he would've. Rodney wasn't a sneak or a Peeping Tom, but Billy suspected he was totally infatuated and had been for some time. How many women like Linda had ever given Rodney the time of day? How many had taken the time to talk to him, understand him and care about him? No wonder he'd rushed over so quickly after hearing the shot. But did Rodney know Linda any better than he did? Did either of them know Linda at all?

Billy hung up Linda's phone and walked wearily to the fridge. All the beer was gone. He made himself a mug of tea instead and slumped down at the table where only a few hours earlier he'd been in love and Linda had agreed to move in with him. It seemed a lifetime ago. He thought of the police sergeant down in Walgett, who'd listened incredulously to his story and was now waking up the doctor and the ambulance crew. How would the sergeant go at explaining what had happened? Even to him it all seemed unreal, improbable, more like the plot of a movie except that in movies everything ended happily and the good guy got off with the girl. He thought about walking back to Rodney's to see if there was anything he could do for his little mate, but realised he'd be more help waiting down at Stony Creek Road to guide the police and ambulance. Christ Almighty, he wished that he was back on his own veranda with his feet up on the rail. There was so much to think about — and so much he didn't dare think about. If he'd ever needed a white-out, he needed one now.

He tried to gather his thoughts and project forward rather than backwards but too much had happened to let go easily. His mind pinballed from thought to thought. Rodney lay badly wounded. Bella lay dead right outside the screen door. And Grant lay dead and all but buried in the mine. Billy grimaced as his mind flooded with nightmarish memories and fears but also with questions that begged answers. Old mines were hellishly dangerous but why had the roof collapsed right then? Was it just bad ground or something else? Had Rodney or his dad removed the supports to use elsewhere? Did Grant knock over a support in his panic or did he fall victim to one of Rodney's dad's infamous booby-traps? In the end it didn't matter. Grant was dead. And as far as he was concerned it didn't matter what Grant had done or intended doing. Nobody deserved to be buried alive in that suffocating darkness. Just the thought made Billy's hands shake and sweat bead on his forehead. He forced himself to his feet. He needed to go outside, to see the expanse of the sky again and feel the vastness of the outback. Besides, there were things that had to be done.

Realising that the police would probably want to see Bella's corpse to substantiate that part of his story, he could do no more than make preparations for her burial. He covered her with a hessian bag, took a mattock from the shed and chipped a deep enough hole in the flinty soil to accommodate her body and allow a reasonable cover. He collected stones to place over her grave, not so much as a memorial but to prevent Rodney digging there. But then it occurred to him that Rodney might have no reason ever to dig there again or tend the garden. The house didn't need a gardener if Linda didn't need the house. And she didn't. Not any more. She didn't need the house and he had no idea whether she needed him, or ever had. Was the Linda who'd pledged her love and shared her bed already gone from him, and had she ever really existed? All he knew for sure was that her going would leave a far bigger hole in his life than the one she'd filled.

He checked his watch. It was almost 1 am and time for him to drive down to Stony Creek Road to meet the police and the ambulance. He missed his dog.

* * *

The ambulance left with Rodney on board just on 2 am, with the intention of taking him directly to the hospital in Walgett. The police left shortly after, having decided that not much could be accomplished until daylight. The sergeant knew Billy well enough to know that he wasn't given to lying and had no trouble with his story, particularly after Linda's corroboration. But he was more accustomed to dealing with violent assaults, drunkenness and petty theft. Knowing that a more senior and experienced team would probably fly in from Sydney or drive up from Dubbo to investigate, he wanted his report to be both thorough and accurate so it would bring him credit not criticism and maybe even a transfer back east. He arranged to come back at nine when Billy could walk him through the chain of events from the time Grant first appeared at the flyscreen door.

Billy drove Linda home in his ute but was unsure how to proceed once he'd got there. So much had occurred he wondered if they'd both benefit from a little breathing space. In the end Linda denied him choice.

'Stay with me, Billy. Please.' She put her hand on his arm as though to prevent him leaving. 'Please,' she repeated.

'Are you sure?'

'Aren't you?'

Billy didn't know how to answer.

'Stop it! Don't do this to me, Billy.' Linda's voice was weak from weariness but there was no doubting her desperation. 'Don't you think Grant's hurt me enough? Don't let him take you away from me as well.'

Billy got out of the ute and walked around to her side. When he opened her door she fell into his arms.

'Hold me. Please, Billy.'

Billy held her but without conviction. Linda began crying softly.

'Let's go,' said Billy. 'We can talk better up at the house.'

Halfway up the drive Linda gave in to her weariness and despair. Billy handed her his torch and carried her the rest of the way. She buried her face into his shoulder and kept it there as he climbed onto the veranda and stepped over Bella. He put her down gently beside the table. For some reason he wanted her sitting in the same chair, with everything the same as it was before Grant had appeared. 'I'll make you a cuppa.'

'Thanks.' Linda slumped in the chair, put her elbows on the table and buried her head in her hands.

Billy put water in the kettle and switched it on. Doing something stopped him from thinking. He put two heaped teaspoons of tea into the pot and took two mugs out of the cupboard. He looked under the sink and found an empty apricot jam tin that Linda had kept for him to use as an ashtray. Despite everything he felt a pang of regret. The washed and scrubbed tin was an act of affection from the Linda he used to know and hoped still existed. There was some cause for hope. She hadn't mentioned the contracts or made any comments about recovering and destroying them. Then again, what would be the point? Under the circumstances, no court in the land would uphold them. He took the milk out of the fridge for his tea and cut a slice of lemon for hers. There were questions that needed answering and he wanted the truth. One lie, one evasion, and not even prison walls could keep him there. He poured the tea and took both mugs out to the table. Linda looked up as he placed her mug in front of her.

'Shoot,' she said lifelessly. 'Ask me anything you want, anything at all. I'll tell you anything you want to know.'

'I don't know where to begin.'

'Begin anywhere you like.'

Billy reached into his shirt pocket for his tobacco and began to roll a cigarette. The familiar action gave him time to assemble his thoughts into some kind of order. The jam tin down by his feet was a reminder of what was at stake.

'Tell me about your accountant.'

'Al? I hope one day you'll meet him, Billy. You'd like him. He's been a tower of strength for me and, to be honest, I couldn't have got by without him. Al's one of my best friends, Billy, but he's not my lover. Not now, and not for a long time. We did have an affair that lasted about three weeks when he first joined the company. He helped me so much I think I took him to bed out of gratitude, but that was no basis for a relationship. We were both relieved to get back to just being friends.'

'And Dubbo?'

'Purely business. Nothing personal, Billy, but I kept our meetings there a secret from everyone. I made no exceptions. It's the only way to keep secrets. By the way, how did you know where I stayed?'

'Jimmy told me. He saw you there, in the dining room.'

'And you didn't bother to tell me?'

Billy shrugged.

'Why, Billy?'

'Maybe I was frightened of what you'd say.'

Linda shook her head sadly at his lack of trust.

'You had nothing to be frightened of.'

'I'm sorry. What about the other things Grant said?'

'You're going to have to be more specific.'

'Your ruthlessness and ambition.'

Linda realised her tea was getting cold and took a couple of sips.

'I've already told you about my ambitions, Billy, and my determination. They have limits, despite what Grant said. I'm not ruthless or heartless.'

'That's not the impression I got when Grant had his rifle pointed at me.'

'I'm really sorry for that, Billy. I never thought for a moment that he'd shoot. He's a bully but he's not a killer. You've got to understand the effect his sudden appearance had on me. Just seeing him brought the whole nightmare back. He could have come through the screen door holding flowers instead of the rifle and I still would have been quaking in my boots. He's beaten me up, Billy, bashed me for no good reason other than that he was on a power trip and it made him feel good. He wanted an obedient, subservient, frightened little wife to wait on him and that's what he turned me into. For years I had no idea what to expect when he walked in the front door. I never knew whether I'd get a kiss or a thump in the ear. Do you know what it's like to live like that, Billy? Have you any idea what it's like to live in fear?'

'Yes,' said Billy softly.

'He's a coward, Billy ... was a coward. He'd taken everything from me — my self-respect, self-confidence, my notion of who and what I was — and he'd taken away all hope that things would ever change, ever be better. Just sitting there on the sofa, listening to him goading and taunting me, brought it all back. When he wanted me to sign so he could take my company away as well, something inside me just snapped. I decided it was time to make a stand. I've never been able to defy him, Billy, never stood up to him before, and you have no idea how much courage it took. When he pointed his rifle at you and threatened to shoot you, I nearly died.'

'*You* nearly died?'

'I'm sorry, Billy. Perhaps I wasn't thinking very rationally; in fact, I almost certainly wasn't. All I knew was that I was never going to give in to him again and I was certain, absolutely certain, that he didn't have the guts to shoot you. At that point I didn't care if he turned the rifle on me. But I didn't even expect that. I thought he'd just hit me again, like he always did. I never thought, never imagined for an instant, that he'd pull the trigger and shoot poor Bella. Oh, Billy, if I'd thought that would happen I'd have signed. I'd have signed anything. I'm so sorry.'

'Is there any truth in anything Grant said?'

Linda bowed her head.

'Yes.'

'What?'

'I lied, Billy. I did lie in court, just like he said. I broke my collarbone and cut my head exactly the way he described.'

'You lied in court? Christ Almighty! No wonder you came up here to hide.'

'Hear me out, Billy. I lied to get even with him. I lied to get even with him for bashing me, for humiliating me with his affair with Sharna and for causing her death. I lied first to the police and then the lie took on a life of its own. I thought maybe I'd retract in court, once it was clear that Grant would pay for what he'd done, but then his barrister twisted the truth and blamed all of Sharna's bruises on her clumsiness. Yes, she was accident-prone. She was headstrong and impetuous. She never walked where she could rush, but it was ludicrous to suggest she caused herself all those injuries. He bashed her, Billy, just like he bashed me. He bashed her and caused her to hit her head. He caused her death. All along the prosecutor maintained my evidence was crucial to gain a conviction. How could I change it? If I retracted my statement Grant would walk, and he deserved to be punished. I'm not proud of what I did, Billy. And I never thought for a second that Grant would get six years.'

'He claimed you lied so you could take over his company.'

'There was nothing left to take over! The company owed money everywhere. For heaven's sake, Billy, you heard him. How long do you think he could afford to pay his barrister three thousand dollars a day? That was on top of what his solicitors were charging and they were milking him with both hands. Grant put every last cent into defending himself, his own money and the company's. If I hadn't grabbed the reins, the company would've gone into liquidation. There would've been nothing for him to come out to either way.'

'Your retraction could've helped his appeal.'

'My retraction would've exonerated him and landed me in court charged with perjury. I would've been the victim once again. Do you think that would've been justice?'

Billy stared into the bottom of his mug. He couldn't remember finishing his tea or even drinking it. He felt absolutely exhausted.

'One last question. How did you feel when I told you Grant was dead?'

'How did I feel? Jesus, Billy. What do you think? I felt devastated. That wasn't how I expected things to end. That wasn't how I wanted them to end. I'm stuck now with telling my daughter that her father is dead and trying to figure out how I can stop her from blaming me. She knows I lied in court, Billy, and why. I've never hidden anything from her. Up until now she's accepted my reasons, maybe because with her father in gaol I was all she had. She never stopped loving him. She accepted that he'd done wrong but she still loved him. Why wouldn't she? He never gave her any reason not to. He never lifted a finger against her or even scolded her. He was never anything but kind and loving to her and I think she always suspected it was somehow partly my fault that Grant hit me. I'm frightened, Billy, frightened that my lie will come home to haunt me. If I hadn't lied, Grant wouldn't have gone to gaol, wouldn't have come out here looking for me, and I wouldn't have to tell my daughter that he's dead. What am I going to do if she blames me, Billy? You tell me.' Linda began weeping silently.

'I'm sorry, Linda.'

'No. Don't be.' She lifted her head defiantly. Tears streaked her face. 'I said you could ask me anything you wanted.'

'I had to know. I had to be sure. It's been a very confusing night.'

'And are you satisfied?'

'Yes.'

'Then hug me, Billy Dwyer. Hug me now! Hug me till your arms ache.'

* * *

Neil looked at his companions, inviting comment.

'What is this?' asked Milos. 'A coffee break or the end?'

'What do you want? A movie ending? Isn't that what you criticised me for wanting? Life's not like a movie, is it, Ramon? How many times have you told me that? Life is full of loose ends and unresolved issues. Right, Ramon?'

'But you can't just end there,' said Lucio.

'Why not?'

Lucio glanced at Milos and Ramon. It was obvious that Neil was provoking them and he wasn't sure how to respond. He decided to stall.

'There are things we're entitled to know, Neil.'

'Such as?'

'What happened to Rodney?'

'Broken ribs and a punctured lung. Like I said in my story, he's a tough little rooster. He was sore for a while but he went back to his diggings. By the way, I never mentioned that he was a hoarder. He might have sold a few opals from time to time but never any of his good ones. He said he didn't want anyone to know that Jindalee Downs could produce quality opals and give them a reason to rob him. But the truth was, the opals were so hard won, neither he nor his father could bear to part with them.

'When Billy visited him in hospital, Rodney asked him to take his opals into safekeeping. He told him where to find them, which room they were in and which floorboards to lift up. All the opals were in a shoebox. When Billy opened it, he found the same Smith Kendon sweets tin Rodney's father had shown him the day he got hit in the face by the black harlequin. It still had the same opals in it. He discovered the black harlequin in a tin all of its own, and there was nothing else that even remotely compared with it. All up, he found over sixty opals, all different sizes and colours and all immaculately polished. It sounds like a lot until you remember that Rodney's dad spent over thirty years digging and Rodney more than twenty after him. An opal a year isn't much. Billy reckons the opals were their entertainment. He reckons Rodney and his dad were like Scrooge McDuck and his money. The patterns on the tins were almost worn away by all the handling.'

Neil leaned back so Gancio could serve his coffee. 'Gancio, old mate,' he said. 'When you're done with the coffee we might have another bottle of that pinot grigio. And make sure it's really cold.'

'I don't tell you how to tell stories,' said Gancio sternly. 'Don't you tell me how to serve pinot grigio.'

Ramon waited until Gancio had finished serving coffee before asking the question they all wanted answered.

'Tell us what happened to Billy,' said Ramon. 'Isn't that what your story is about?'

'What do you want to know? Do you want the full movie ending or just the highlights?'

'It's your story, you tell it.'

'He sold the farm, except for the few acres our parents' house sat on, and moved to Sydney with Linda. They lived happily ever after.'

'Neil, stop treating us as though we're children,' said Ramon. 'It does you no credit. You told your story well and we appreciate it. But you haven't finished. You know it and we know it. You keep ducking the issue and I can only assume you need time to organise your strategy. Perhaps I can help. You said at the start of the story that you took your brother's life. You have continually maintained that the story will reflect badly on you and you've asked us not to judge you too harshly. What is there to judge, Neil? What did you do to Billy? Can I help you further? Early on in your story Linda invited Billy around for dinner. It turned out to be Billy's birthday. I can't recall the exact chronology but it would have been some time in October or early November. Right?'

Neil nodded.

'So tell us, Neil, when Grant was taunting Billy about Vietnam, why did Billy tell Grant his birthday was in May?'

'Ah, Ramon,' said Neil, 'you never let me down. Your eyes may be buggered but there's nothing wrong with your ears. What the hell? At least let me finish my coffee.'

Chapter Thirty-one

The year Neil went to university down in Sydney, the fates conspired to enhance the myth of his infallibility. First, the autumn rains stayed away and winter settled into one of the coldest in living memory. The bitter winds hardly let up and at night the chill factor regularly took temperatures down below minus two. Outback sheep are hardy beasts but the autumn shearing left them cruelly exposed. The pigs, wedge-tailed eagles, ravens and crows were the beneficiaries as they fed on a steady supply of animals that failed to survive. For the Dwyer family, with their newly leased ute and equipment, the stock losses were sufficient to put pressure on their budget.

The cattle fared better, with minimal stock losses, and there was enough feed around for them to maintain good condition. Then the cold dry winter turned into a hot dry spring when the rains failed to appear. Even more worrying were the mobs of kangaroos moving in from further west and the sunsets tinged amber from dust storms and the smoke of distant scrub fires. The number of kangaroos on the property quadrupled, all of them competing with livestock for the available feed. They surrounded the watering troughs and invaded the paddocks Braden had set aside for fattening the yearling steers. For a while the dogs and Billy's deadly shot managed to keep them at bay. But they continued to flood in from the desperate country further west until their population grew beyond control. With them came flocks of starving emus, many of which were too weak to clear the fences in their way and died hung up in the wires. Only the carrion feeders flourished. One day Billy saw three camels in the distance and couldn't even begin to imagine how bad things were further west to have driven them so far east. Over in Walgett the Kamilaroi elders pointed to rarely seen dry-country birds and the dearth of blossoms and seeds on trees. They knew and so did the graziers, growers and townsfolk. Everyone braced themselves for the worst.

Braden didn't panic. With the wool clip and the sale of the steers he figured they'd earn enough to meet their obligations so they could buy in some feed and still have enough to scratch along. But the collapse in wool prices that Neil had foreseen finally occurred and the value of the clip plummeted almost overnight by thirty per cent. Some traders blamed the Japanese, claiming they'd ganged together and were conspiring to force prices down. Others blamed a worldwide glut and the increased use of synthetics. It didn't matter much to Braden what had caused the fall. He was more concerned with what he'd use to buy stock feed once he'd met his commitments. When the bottom dropped out of beef prices he knew trouble was just around the corner.

What irked Billy was his father's conviction that if Neil had still been around things would've been different. Winter would've been warmer, spring cooler, the rains would've come and wool and beef prices would've held up. When Billy challenged his father and pointed out that even if Neil had stayed on the farm they'd still be faced with the same problems, his father countered by claiming Neil would've managed things better so they'd be squared away financially. Billy worked hard around the property after school and at weekends and resented the implication that somehow he wasn't doing enough or had failed to measure up.

When he suggested they sell as many beasts as they could and use the income to buy feed to support the rest, his father ignored him. When Braden rang Neil in Sydney and got the same advice, he hailed Neil as a genius. His father's blind faith in Neil bewildered and irritated Billy. His resentment grew.

He'd stayed on the extra year at school to complete his HSC but many of his friends hadn't. They'd left school and home for jobs wherever they could get them. Some went up to Brisbane, some to Sydney, and others made it all the way down to Melbourne. Kids who couldn't saw a straight line to save themselves got apprenticeships as carpenters and builders. Others, who knew next to nothing about cars, got jobs selling them or as mechanics. Billy couldn't escape the talk about what his old schoolmates were doing and what a great time they were having. Worse still, most of the good-looking girls he fancied had followed his sisters' example and flown the coop. It seemed everyone was off doing something, making something of themselves and having a ball doing it. Everyone except him. Billy's one hope was that Neil would come home for Christmas, but his brother had taken a summer job with a building development company to earn money so he could continue his studies.

Things went from bad to worse. There was never any question of him following Neil to university, of going anywhere for that matter. The farm desperately needed him. His father had often claimed hardship was an opportunist just waiting to strike. The drought opened the door and, before they knew it, their property was under siege. He and Braden spent long hours hand-feeding and attacking the roly-poly, boxthorn and Hudson pear. The plants threatened to take over pastures grazed bare by stock and invading kangaroos. Blowflies, which were always a problem in summer, swept in early from the west in plague proportions. Hardy ewes succumbed to flystrike despite having been crotched and lambs fared even worse, even though they'd been mulesed and sprayed in January. They worked long hard days, up before the sun and in bed not long after it set. Billy's life became as monotonous as the incessant droning of blowflies. He came in each evening to a home devoid of siblings and a social life that barely existed.

Life throughout the northwest became a desperate struggle as the rains stubbornly stayed away. Barber's pole larvae died on the barren soils; the pigweed, cat heads, wild tomatoes and other noxious weeds withered, but so did the last of the grasses. Roly-poly died and broke away, tumbling across the landscape and adding to the sense of desolation. With limited funds to buy cattle nuts or bales of feed, Billy and his father had nothing to look forward to except months of scrub-cutting and more hardship to keep their stock alive.

For Billy, the only saving grace was the old Holden. It was his link to a life that sometimes seemed impossibly remote. His parents understood when he climbed into the old car and, without a word, took off to a football game and the booze-up that invariably followed, or drove all day to a woolshed party or a bachelor and spinster ball. These were times when he just had to get out, to escape, to mingle with people his own age and remember that he was still young, still a teenager. But these contacts also served to remind him that there was another world out there that was passing him by. There was always someone else who'd made the break, or someone who'd come home for a visit full of stories about big-city life, pay packets he could hardly comprehend, movies, beaches and girls who apparently knew no shame.

In his despair, driving home to more isolation and thankless hard labour, he clung to Neil's promise to send for him once he got on his feet. But deliverance bore no deadline and Billy could see little difference between waiting for Neil and waiting for rain. There was little hope of either in his foreseeable future. He realised that he had to take his destiny into his own hands, but loyalty, obligations and his promise to his brother held him back. In desperation he took his troubles over to Rodney but Rodney couldn't help. His dad had him working fulltime digging for opals and Rodney had no problem with that. He'd always known he'd spend his life following in the steps of his father and, as far as he was concerned, that was what sons did. He couldn't understand what Billy was so upset about.

Winter brought relief from the heat but the winds settled into a pattern that everyone knew would not bring rain. Braden and Billy alternated between hand-feeding and cutting the guts out of scrub for livestock that grew thinner and weaker by the day. Braden extended his loan at the bank with no clear idea where the money was going to come from to support it. The shortage of cash got Billy thinking and brought a ray of hope. He got it into his head that everyone would be better off if he left the property, got a job down in Sydney and sent money home to help out. He refined his argument on the long days out cutting scrub, believing the family's best interests lay in selling off as much livestock as they could and putting the proceeds into feed for the rest. The logic seemed irrefutable. With their stock halved, there'd be less scrub to cut and less feed to buy. Any shortfall in earnings would be partly offset by the money he sent home. The light at the end of the tunnel blossomed, along with his hopes, until it dazzled him. Billy became convinced by his argument and equally convinced that he'd spend Christmas in Sydney with Neil. It was all he thought about during the day, all he thought about when his head hit the pillow at night and all that got him up out of bed in the morning. Christmas with Neil became an objective, a destination and an ambition.

When spring came around once more in a blaze of clear blue skies with little prospect of relief, Billy decided the time had come to raise the issue with his father. He thought his father would jump at it. He'd based his calculations on the wages he'd heard his old schoolmates were getting and figured that, if he stayed with Neil and counted his pennies, he'd be able to send back at least half of his take-home pay. Billy thought of the fuel and feed that could buy and saw himself as both selfless and the saviour of the property. It occurred to him that it was exactly the sort of proposition Neil would come up with and, in the full blush of youthful confidence, presented his case one night over dinner. His father slammed his fists on the table, cursed his lack of gratitude and told him to stop dreaming. Braden told him he was staying put and to get used to the idea.

A rift developed between Billy and his father that night which neither made any attempt to heal. It was as though each had found a focus in the other for their anger and bitterness at the hand fate had dealt them. They hardly exchanged a word and then only if it was necessary in the course of their work. Billy's despair and isolation grew. He came to hate the property, to see it as a gaol and the livestock as his gaolers. He wondered what he'd done wrong to deserve a lifetime condemned to hard labour. All his hopes lay in Neil's promise to rescue him. Then one night Neil rang to say he'd quit university.

Billy had just turned eighteen and was beyond tears but the news devastated him. When it was his turn to speak to Neil he discovered his brother strangely upbeat about it. The property company were keen for him to join them. Said he had a talent for the business. Claimed a degree wouldn't help him in his job. Maintained that leaving university meant he'd start earning good money sooner. His arguments sounded reasonable but they failed to conceal the truth. The reality was that without help from the family, Neil could no longer afford to study. Billy had a million things to say to him but they all amounted to a plea for help. In the end he said nothing. It was all too much for him. He couldn't see how Neil could possibly earn enough to rescue him if he didn't complete his degree. Without a degree, Billy was convinced Neil would wind up a builder, carpenter, mechanic, plumber or labourer, no better than the rest of their mates. If Neil couldn't rescue him, what hope was left?

Billy ran from the house and took off down the road in the old Holden without any destination in mind. Sometimes just the act of driving helped dissipate his anger and sense of helplessness. For a brief moment he considered driving until he ran out of petrol and then hitching the rest of the way to Sydney, but the tank barely had enough gas to get him to Walgett and he had no cash in his pockets to buy more. Without really thinking about it, he turned onto a neighbour's property where a girl he knew from school lived. He'd dropped in on her on other occasions, more out of lack of alternative than any other reason. He didn't particularly like her and she certainly wasn't pretty or even bright. Her only attractions were her proximity and the similarity of her plight.

Cheryl-Lynne was the only girl and eldest child in a family that included four younger brothers. Her mother had contracted an incurable degenerative disease that affected the nervous system and was confined to bed, unable to look after herself let alone anyone else in the family. At the age of sixteen Cheryl-Lynne had been forced to give up school and become nurse, housekeeper, cook and stand-in mother for her brothers. She was bound to her property by chains even thicker than Billy's. It was to her that Billy turned in his distress. He picked her up and took her for a drive, so she could have a break, however fleeting, from her family and her chores. They didn't have to drive far to find a spot where they could sit and talk before the inevitable climb into the rear seat for sex. Sometimes their coupling made them feel less lonely. They held each other tight and lied about the depth of their feelings for each other. But other times it merely highlighted the depth of their desperation. Cheryl-Lynne made him promise that if he ever got away he'd take her with him. She always made sure Billy wore a condom. At the age of nineteen, she'd done all the mothering she ever wanted to do. That was fine with Billy.

Rain came in the first week in November, when it was least expected. High temperatures in October had caused deep cracks to open up in the parched land. Just when everyone was bracing for another scorching summer, two weather systems collided over the Southern Ocean, sending cold, moisture-laden clouds streaming north across a broad front right up into Queensland. The rain pelted down for four days, causing the Macquarie Marshes and Narran Lake to flood. On the fifth day, the rains stopped as abruptly as they'd begun. Graziers and growers throughout the far west stepped down from their verandas to kick the toe of a boot into the soil and speculate on whether there'd been enough of a wet to bring on the native grasses.

Neil rang two days later with startling news. His company had promoted him into the marketing department and were sending him back to university part-time to complete a marketing degree at their expense. Billy was over the moon. He had no idea what marketing was or what a marketing degree entailed, but it was obvious that, whatever it was, Neil was good at it. He had to be or his company wouldn't be wasting their money on him. Billy was disappointed that once again Neil wouldn't be coming home for Christmas, but ultimately it didn't matter. The only thing that did matter was that his dreams and hopes had been brought back from the dead. For the first time in a very long time Billy felt like smiling.

The November rains were both a blessing and a curse. The first plants to recover were the noxious weeds and Braden and Billy had their work cut out trying to prevent their starving livestock from feeding on them. But then rain came again in January, a drizzling, soaking rain that hung around for two weeks. Braden claimed he could see the grass growing and reckoned the clovers weren't far behind it. But the clovers brought their own set of problems. The cattle ate so much clover it fermented and formed a foam over the top of their ruminant stomachs which prevented them from belching to relieve the build-up of gas. With no paraffin oil to break up the foam and no cash to buy any, Billy and his father resorted to dosing the cattle with diesel oil and stitching a cannula through the side and into the belly of the worst affected. Once the bloat was under control, Billy grabbed the opportunity to go into town and blow off a bit of steam. He took Cheryl-Lynne with him whenever she could get away from her endless chores, because he recognised that she needed a break as much as he did. He took her because he thought it was the decent thing to do. She saw it more as the beginning of a commitment.

Billy still came home from his trips into town or to woolshed parties deeply depressed. Kids who'd been three years behind him at school had left and found jobs in the city. But what hurt him more was the number heading off to universities. The one or two of his day had become a dozen or more and Billy couldn't help feeling he'd been cheated again.

When Neil rang in early April to say he'd borrowed a company car and was coming home for the weekend, Billy saw it as a progress report on his salvation. The visit gave him his first opportunity to sit down with his brother and discuss exactly what marketing was all about and when the big money would start to flow. He began to count the days until Neil came home and then the hours. He went out on the trail bike and scouted around until he'd found a place where he was certain they'd find pigs. He wanted to make sure his brother had the best possible time and enjoyed himself so much he'd be drawn back for more. Billy had a smile on his face all day Friday, knowing his brother had been given the day off and was already on the road. The last time he could remember feeling that way was when they'd been kids and either he or Neil had had a birthday.

Neil arrived home just after 11 pm, stepping out of what appeared to be an almost brand-new Ford Falcon, dressed to the nines. He'd let his hair grow long at the back and sides, wore a white shirt with the top button undone and a loosened tie. His charcoal grey trousers were clearly the bottom half of a suit and his moccasin shoes had tiny gold buckles. Neil caught Billy's look of astonishment and laughed.

'I had a quick meeting in Newcastle on the way up,' he said. 'If you want to be the part, you have to dress the part.'

They sat around the dining table, slowly sipping on cans of beer until two in the morning while Neil entertained them with his stories. He described a world which neither Billy nor his parents could really comprehend, but that didn't stop them swelling with pride at his accomplishments.

'When I took on the job with the developers I really landed with my bum in butter,' he said. 'They spend millions buying blocks of land with seemingly no more thought than we'd give to buying twenty or thirty steers. It was only after I'd been there a few weeks that I learned what factors influence their decisions. They got me in originally to help their accounts department crunch numbers, but I got so interested in what they were doing that within three weeks the boss had me helping to prepare proposals to put to councils. I loved it and I guess he loved my enthusiasm.'

'Well done,' said Braden.

'Do you know the really amazing thing?'

'No,' said Billy. Everything he'd heard so far sounded pretty amazing.

'My boss is only thirty. He left school when he was sixteen and he's already a multi-millionaire.'

Billy's jaw dropped.

'A multi-millionaire and he's only thirty? And he left school at sixteen?'

'That's right.'

'Then why does he want you to go back to university?'

'He reckons times have changed. Got tougher. He says marketing is the way things are heading and he wants me to learn all there is to know.'

'I don't understand how you can have a job and also go to university,' said Braden.

'I do eighteen hours a week at university and I make up the time after hours at work. Then I go home and, instead of getting into bed, I do my assignments. I do sixteen-hour days, Dad. It makes running this place seem like a holiday.'

Neil talked until they were all too filled up with news to hear more. Billy kept glancing at his parents' faces and wondered if the same look of astonishment and pride was reflected on his own.

Billy rose early the following morning and waited impatiently while Neil slept in.

'Let him have his rest,' said Braden. 'God knows he's earned it.'

Billy fidgeted and kept looking up at the sky. The sun blazed down with late summer intensity, pushing the mercury steadily higher. The sheep stopped feeding and lay down in the shade of any tree that threw a decent shadow. By ten, every living creature had gone to ground. It was after eleven before Billy and Neil headed off towards the western end of the property and the sand ridges where Billy had located the pigs. Even with the windows wound right down they sweltered.

'How badly do you want to shoot a pig?' asked Neil.

'How badly do you?' said Billy.

'I can take it or leave it in this heat.'

'Be lucky to get a shot at one anyway,' said Billy. 'They'll all be holed up somewhere in the lignum. I was only going for your benefit. What do you want to do?'

'Drive around till we find somewhere cool and drink the beer,' said Neil. 'Any shade up on the flat rock?'

'One way to find out,' said Billy. He turned the wheel and cut through the scrub to the top of the sand ridge where the mulga was thick and shady. Billy reversed under the trees so they had a view out over the plains. Nothing appeared to have changed since their childhood. Billy lifted the lid of the esky on the back seat and took out a couple of cans.

'Remember your promise?' said Billy.

'Of course,' said Neil. He punctured his can, put his head back and let the cold liquid pour down his throat.

'Are you still good for it?'

'Good as gold,' said Neil. He gazed out over the lifeless landscape. 'I'm going to get you out of here,

Billy, though it might take a few years yet. I'm going to be a millionaire.'

'Bullshit!'

'No, I'm serious. Look at me. If you know what you're doing in the property business you can make an absolute fortune. I've seen the projections, Billy. In fact, I even worked on some of them. Things are going good now but they'll really start to take off in five or six years' time, and from there there'll be no looking back. I'm going to make both of us rich. You're going to have so much money you won't know what to do with it.'

'Get off!'

'No, fair dinkum.'

'You're kidding?' Billy took a good look at Neil and he was as serious as he'd ever seen him. 'You're not kidding, are you?'

'No, Billy, I'm not. I know what I have to do and I know how to do it. When I've got a bit of a track record I'm going to start my own company. Don't tell anyone. There'll be room in it for you too.'

'What about Mum and Dad?'

'I'll put them into one of my developments, on a beach somewhere. I'll make sure they won't have to lift a finger ever again.'

'You reckon you're going to do all this?'

'Yeah. For sure.'

Billy looked hard at his brother, searching for any suggestion that he was having his leg pulled, and finding none. He leaned back into his seat and tried to comprehend what life would be like in the city with more money than he knew what to do with. His brother made it sound almost like a done deed.

'What's the timetable?' said Billy.

'All going well? Between eight and ten years. Ten years max.'

'Eight years?'

'Yeah, all things going well. But there is a bit of a problem.'

'What?'

'A glitch. Something that might throw a bloody big spanner in the works.'

'What, for Christ's sake?'

Neil turned to look at Billy as though weighing him up.

'What, Neil? What are you talking about?'

'I've got a problem, little brother, but it'll keep till dinner. Mum and Dad'll probably want to hear about it too.' Neil reached behind and grabbed another couple of beers. He passed one to Billy. 'Here. Don't say I never give you anything.'

Neil spent the afternoon with his father, helping him work out his finances. Meanwhile Billy stripped down and cleaned out the Holden's carburettor and fretted. He believed every word his brother had said about becoming a millionaire and tried to imagine what the problem could be. He'd pressed his brother for an explanation all the way back from the sand ridge but Neil had just smiled grimly and ignored him. By the time he'd cleaned up for dinner, Billy was convinced that whatever the problem was, his brother could figure a way around it.

When he sat down at the table he found his mother and father in unusually good spirits. Braden had butchered a lamb for the occasion and his mother had roasted a leg slowly until the meat just fell off the bone.

'Did Neil tell you how we're all going to become millionaires?' asked Braden.

'I didn't say you'd become millionaires,' said Neil. 'I said you'd just live like them.'

'That'll do,' said Braden gleefully. 'I can just see us sitting on a beach somewhere with nothing to do but eat, drink and grow old gracefully.'

'Neil said he's going to teach me the business and give me a job,' said Billy.

'Told me that too,' said Braden.

Billy and Braden made jokes about chauffeurs and cleaning ladies and trading cars in every time they needed to be filled up with petrol. Billy was so excited he failed to notice that Neil wasn't contributing to the merriment.

'So when is all this supposed to happen, Neil?' Millie had got up to clear the table and looked expectantly at her son.

Neil looked away momentarily, as though embarrassed.

'Sit down, Mum.'

If Neil had fired a shotgun he could not have grabbed everyone's attention more effectively. Smiles froze on faces and became looks of concern.

'I haven't lied to you,' said Neil. 'Believe me, everything I've said can come true and sooner than you think. I could promise you right now that you could be living in your own home by the beach in eight to ten years but for the fact that something's come up.'

'What?' said Braden.

Billy held his breath. A change had come over Neil and it scared him. Neil pulled an envelope out of his shirt pocket and placed it on the table.

'I've been called up.'

'What?' said Braden.

'My birthday came up in the ballot, Dad. They want to conscript me into the army.'

'What?' said Braden, but everyone knew he'd heard perfectly. His face had turned ashen. Billy stopped breathing.

'It's for two years. Even if I'm lucky enough not to get sent to Vietnam, it's still two bloody years. It doesn't matter whether I go now or after I've finished university. It's still potentially the end of my career.'

'Your company will take you back, won't they?' said Braden.

'Sure,' said Neil bitterly. 'But they're not going to sit around and wait for me. They'll get someone else in, give my opportunity to someone else.'

'What about our home by the sea?' said Braden, aghast. 'What about us all living like millionaires?'

'What can I do?' Neil shrugged.

'No!' said Braden. He leaped to his feet, shouting, 'No! I'm not going to stand by and see this family's future ruined. We're going to have to do something.'

'Like what?' said Neil. 'Send Billy in my place?'

* * *

Neil sat back. An appalled silence settled over the table. He lifted his cast with both hands and shifted his leg into a more comfortable position. Neither Milos nor Lucio would meet his eyes.

'I could see it coming,' said Milos eventually. 'But I didn't think you'd actually go through with it. I hardly know what to say. How could you do such a contemptible thing?'

'I told you at the start that I took my brother's life, though the reality is I robbed him of the chance of ever having one.'

'What was Billy's reaction?'

'What do you think? He didn't want to go but we didn't give him much choice. Everyone turned on him, not just me. My father bluntly reminded him of the promise he'd made after we'd rescued him from the pigs. He made it pretty bloody clear Billy owed me.'

'Dear God!'

'I'm not proud of what I did. But was it any worse than what you did on the run with your brother? Are you going to look me in the eye and tell me you never stole food from others who were starving? Wasn't that also contemptible? You can say what you like, Milos, but there's no difference between us.'

'No difference? You disgust me! I would have given my life to save my brother's. He would have given his life to save mine. You used your brother to save yourself. Used him shamelessly. That is the difference, the difference between us! What you did was despicable. I could never have done that. Never!'

'I kept hoping Billy would volunteer to go in your place,' said Lucio. 'If he'd volunteered, then what you did might possibly have been forgivable. Maybe not forgivable, but at least understandable. You deliberately contrived the whole thing by building up everyone's hopes. You made their future contingent on your own. That was nothing short of blackmail. Why you would want to admit this to us is beyond me. Do you feel better for it? Eh?'

'Never filled any of your little darlings' heads with promises you had no intention of keeping, Lucio? Just so you could throw your leg over?'

'That's different!'

'Of course it is,' said Neil. 'I kept my promises, you didn't.'

'You disgust me.'

'Do I? Look at the larger picture here, Lucio. You too, Milos. Don't you think my parents deserved a better life after all they'd been through? Don't you think they deserved to end their days peacefully and comfortably? Yes, I contrived things so that Billy went to Vietnam instead of me, but I kept my promises. I delivered! If I'd gone to Vietnam we'd all have ended our days on the property. None of us would've escaped.'

'And you think that justifies sacrificing Billy, no?'

'Oh, you can be wise now, Milos, but back then nobody had any idea of how hard Vietnam would be or the long-term effects it would have on the soldiers who went there. I had no idea it would affect Billy as much as it did. I just figured he'd come home and work for me. I always kept a job open for him.'

'You're too generous,' said Milos sarcastically.

'Have you any idea of the expectations the family placed on me? I was the only hope of a better life for my parents and for Billy. Have you any idea of the pressures that put on me to succeed? Jesus Christ! When property crashed in the early seventies it took all my savings and all my plans with it. I was devastated and I couldn't tell anyone. I couldn't tell my parents that their dream had just died. I couldn't tell Billy he went to Vietnam for nothing. I had to start all over again. I had to borrow money so my parents could build their little home on the ridge. I think the day they moved in was the saddest day of their lives. Moving in meant no more house by the beach, no more easy retirement, no more living like millionaires. It broke my heart as well as theirs but it seemed the only option. I'd done my best, but my best just hadn't been good enough. I realised then that I had to do even better.

'I'd grown up with droughts and living on the brink so I knew it was possible to recover. I put my head down and worked day and night to make their dream happen. It took quite a few years but I finally bought them an apartment up on the Gold Coast. I bought it before I bought a place of my own. Do you think Billy could've done that for them?'

'You were just working off your guilt.'

'I admit there was an element of that. I took care of Billy too. I felt responsible for everything that had happened to him. I can't tell you how many times I had to bail him out financially but I never got a word of thanks. Every time there was a drought he turned to Bank Neil. When he needed new equipment, more livestock or a new ute, it was always Bank Neil that got it for him. The thing is, if Billy had come back from Vietnam with his head still in good shape, everything would've worked out.'

'Of course, he could always have come back dead,' said Ramon quietly.

Neil spun around.

'That was the risk I took.'

'No, Neil, that was the risk Billy took.'

'Just be careful what you say, Ramon. We all know there are more skeletons to rattle in your closet than there are in mine.'

'So you keep saying. The point is, Neil, it really doesn't matter how many homes by the beach you bought your parents or how many times you helped Billy out with your money. What you did was unforgivable. Unforgivable, Neil, no matter how you attempt to justify it. Could you forgive anyone who did that to you? Could you?'

Neil's eyes narrowed and he studied Ramon intently.

'When were you going to tell me, Ramon?' he said quietly. 'When were any of you going to tell me?'

Milos and Lucio realised what Neil was alluding to and stared shamefaced down at the table. Only Ramon kept his head up.

'Before you say anything else, Neil, first let me congratulate you on your skill. If Barbara had not come to see us, I would never have guessed. None of us would have. You once accused me of dressing my confession up as fiction, an allegation I deny, but you have gone a step further and executed your story brilliantly.'

'I appreciate your compliments, Ramon, but let's face it, they are rather hollow. You had no right to interrogate Barbara the way you did. You talk about honour and respect and flaunt your European manners but the bottom line is, you can't be trusted. None of you can.'

'What's going on?' asked Milos.

'One moment, Milos. Yes, Neil, it is true that I probably asked Barbara one question too many. But you can understand how she caught us by surprise. You can understand how bewildered we were by the contrast between her descriptions of the gentle, sensitive person she claims you really are and the abrasive "chat-room" persona you adopt for us. What were we supposed to do? Just sit there with our mouths open? I had no intention of undermining your story. When she volunteered the facts that Billy was still alive and that you'd been in therapy, Milos quickly interceded to stop me asking any further questions. The truth is, Neil, she'd already told us too much before I asked any questions. Our only deception was not to tell you. It is not a decision we took lightly and we took it in what we thought were your best interests. We didn't want to spoil the telling of your story. And the truth is, we didn't. These two still haven't guessed, though I think they are now beginning to suspect what really happened.'

'What happened?' said Milos.

'Will you tell them, Neil, or will I?'

'Why don't you, Ramon? How could I possibly deny you when you're so obviously full of your own genius?'

'Four things gave you away, Neil. First, Barbara's description of you. Second, the fact that you were in therapy. Third, the fact that Billy was still alive. And fourth, the fact that you didn't care. You claimed Billy didn't care when he came back from Vietnam and got involved in fights. He didn't care that he got sent to gaol. You described Billy's mind-set exactly the way Barbara described yours when she told us of the massive risks you took building the business. She actually used the same words. She said you didn't care, just didn't care. She also gave us the impression that Billy is in fact your older brother. Is that correct?'

'Spot on.'

'So you engaged in role reversal to tell the story of how it was actually you — not Billy — who went to Vietnam, how you were manipulated to go in your brother's place. Why, Neil? Just to get it off your chest?'

'I don't know.' Neil exhaled wearily. He was aware of Milos and Lucio staring at him open-mouthed as they came to terms with this latest twist. 'I had this vague idea that it might be cathartic, provided I could do it in such a way that you guys would be none the wiser.'

'And was it?'

'Too soon to tell, Ramon. It doesn't really matter. I guess the main reason I told this story was because I thought I could get away with it. And, at the same time, present a compelling case for reverting to the telling of fictions at our lunches.'

'I suspect your real reason for telling the story was to gauge whether the resentment you still harbour towards your brother is justified, if what he did to you could ever be forgiven.'

'I like to think I forgave him a long time ago, but you're right — forgiveness is sometimes hard to maintain when I have to deal with the nightmares. Thank God, they're increasingly infrequent. At the end of the day, I have to concede that everything did work out for the best. The fact is, we did burden my brother with all our hopes and aspirations. And I did owe him for rescuing me from the pigs. I made a promise to him that some day I'd pay him back. I paid him back by going to Vietnam in his place.'

'My God,' said Lucio. 'Five minutes ago I thought you were the biggest arsehole that ever walked the earth. Now I have the pleasure of liking you all over again.'

'It is a pleasure the three of us share,' said Milos. 'Congratulations on a story brilliantly told.'

'What about Grant and Linda? How much of that story was true?' asked Lucio.

'As much as you want,' cut in Ramon. He was puffed up and clearly revelling in the fact that he'd guessed Neil's intentions. 'Neil did what we pride ourselves on doing. He used truth as a basis to contrive a fiction. Grant and Linda's story was simply the vehicle he used to tell his real story. Am I right?'

'No comment. It is the listener's prerogative to believe or not believe. Now, gentlemen, I'm going to leave you in peace so you can discuss my brilliance at length.' Neil pushed himself to his feet and took hold of his crutches.

'What? Won't you at least stay and have a celebratory drink?' asked Ramon. 'You've certainly earned it.'

'No, not this time,' said Neil. He took a couple of awkward steps towards the door before turning and smiling. 'My story's finished. I've achieved everything I set out to do. Now I'm going to go and take this bloody cast off.'

'What?' Ramon started as though shot.

'Yes, the cast has served its purpose. Really, Ramon, how could you ever believe anyone who described me as gentle and sensitive? Dear-oh-dearie me.'

It took Milos and Lucio a moment to appreciate the magnitude of Neil's deception. They looked at each other, then at the hapless Ramon, and burst out laughing.

'Think about it, Ramon. Think of all the clues I gave you.' Neil's demeanour had changed, his weariness gone. He hobbled back to the table and sat down, clearly enjoying himself. 'You of all people appreciate the structure of stories and the devices we use. Didn't you get suspicious when I employed the same devices Milos used in his story? No disrespect, Ramon, but Blind Freddie could see I was up to something.'

'We did discuss it,' Milos conceded.

'But not with me,' said Neil. 'That was your mistake. I kept waiting for you to challenge me and could hardly believe my luck when you didn't. That was all the encouragement I needed. Milos told the story of his brother. So did I. He referred to himself in the third person. So did I. He brought in Gabi to reinforce his story. I brought in Barbara. In Milos's story his brother took his identity. I took Billy's. Come on! Surely that must have set the alarm bells ringing. But you ignored them. Not just Ramon, but all of you. And shall I tell you why?'

'Go on,' said Lucio. Like Milos, he was beginning to share some of Ramon's discomfit.

'Because, for all your intellectual pretences, you're no better than a bunch of women gossiping over the back fence. You couldn't help yourselves. You saw the chance to peep behind my "chat room persona" to who I really am and you couldn't resist. Instead of concentrating on the story, you jumped at what appeared to be an opportunity to find out what makes me tick, what my strengths are and, more particularly, what my weaknesses are. You protested that the baring of my soul risked jeopardising our lunches, but you made no real attempt to stop me. The opportunity to paw through my dirty laundry was just too good. You should all be ashamed of yourselves. You claim to take pride in our anonymity and the fact that we choose to reveal little about our real selves but your actions convey the opposite. But for your sordid, morbid curiosity I'd never have got away with my deception. Your pettiness made it all possible. In the end, you learned nothing about me, nothing at all. You don't know me any better now than you did at the start of my story. But I learned something about you. Protest as much as you like, but I don't think there's a principle you're not prepared to sacrifice.'

'You don't think you're being a bit harsh?'

'You tell me, Ramon. Were you deceived by my story or not?'

'Fair point. But it may be that our only fault was that we dared to hope.'

'Hope?'

'Yes, Neil, hope that somewhere beneath your abrasive, often obnoxious exterior there lie some saving graces.'

'No way,' said Neil grinning. 'What you see is what you get.'

He started laughing and, one by one, the others joined him.

Acknowledgments

For most fiction writers, credibility is the key to good storytelling. It certainly is for me. I read a lot of books and spend hours in libraries researching the places, times and events about which I'm writing so that I can work from a solid base of knowledge. However, credibility often lies in the detail and books don't always provide it. There is nothing to compare with conversations with people who live in the places about which I'm writing and who experienced similar events or were witness to them. In the course of writing this book a lot of people gave up their time to speak to me and share their knowledge. I'd like to take this opportunity to thank them for their contribution.

I am particularly grateful to Peter Stonestreet, noxious weed inspector for Castlereagh-Macquarie County Council. Peter was kind enough to take me with him on his rounds through Walgett, Lightning Ridge, Cumborah, the Grawin and Glengarry, and showed me how to spray the prickly pear and other noxious weeds we found by the side of the road. Through Peter I met John and Jackie Brenerger of Eumenbah station and Fred Coliwell of New

Prospect who gave me the benefit of their knowledge gathered over years on the land.

I was doubly fortunate in that Peter's wife, Claire Scanlan, is the District Veterinarian for the Coonamble Rural Lands and Protection Board and was able to fill me in on all the terrible things that can happen to livestock out in the northwest.

Yet, for all the help that I was given, I don't doubt that there are a few things I didn't get quite right. However in talking to graziers — and I spoke to quite a few — it became apparent that every grazier has his own way of doing things and there is no set time for lambing, shearing or mulesing, to use a few obvious examples, and no universally agreed 'right' way of doing anything.

It's also particularly pleasing when friends and former colleagues step up to the plate to help. I'm especially grateful to:

Chris Baker, Probation and Parole Officer from the Long Bay Parole Unit, for his advice and insights;

My agent, Margaret Connolly, for her unflagging support;

My editor, Nicola O'Shea;

And the team at HarperCollins who worked hard and conscientiously to ensure that this book presents as well as it does.

Lunch with the Generals

DEREK HANSEN

Ramon, self-styled master storyteller, has steered his listeners down a sinister path littered with love and betrayal, secret police and death squads. But as the Argentinian's tale nears its startling conclusion, his audience is struck with horror at the possibility that Ramon's clever invention is nothing more than the cunningly disguised chronicle of his own shadowy past.

Is Ramon a gifted artist of the imagination or the perpetrator of a terrible act of revenge that defies all forgiveness?

'Hansen is a great novelist. Only the bravest and most confident writer could grant his characters such intelligence and insight and still remain in command.' *West Australian*

'blazes life and death and love from every page' *The Courier Mail*

ISBN 0 7322 7542 3

Lunch with Mussolini

DEREK HANSEN

Spring 1945: The quiet of a northern Italian village is shattered by an explosion of gunfire as eight innocent women are gunned down. But why have they been executed now, with the war almost over and the Germans standing to gain nothing from further reprisals?

Fifty years later, the daughter of one of the victims finds the German officer who ordered the executions living under an assumed name, and sets out to avenge her mother's death.

'It is no coincidence that two great novels linked with the Second World War have come out of Australia . . . Keneally's *Schindler's Ark* and now Derek Hansen's *Lunch with Mussolini.*' *Glasgow Herald*

'Derek Hansen take a bow. You have written one of the most entertaining, gripping and powerful novels of the year.' *Sunday Telegraph*

ISBN 0 7322 7543 1

Lunch with the Stationmaster

DEREK HANSEN

The eagerly awaited third novel in Derek Hansen's bestselling 'Lunch' series.

Lunch with the Stationmaster takes us back to Gancio's restaurant. It is a Thursday and, as usual, Ramon, Lucio, Milos and Neil have gathered for their weekly lunch appointment. It is Neil's turn to take the floor—except that Milos steps in and demands to tell his story. He has no choice in the matter, he says: 'This story has already been too long awaiting the telling. It must be told now. Time is running out. It is not just an obligation but a repayment of a debt.' With those words he hooks the three other men—and Derek Hansen hooks his readers.

We are taken back to Hungary in the 1940s, a time when Jews are persecuted and rumours of the terrifying death camps are circulating. This is a novel with huge range, set within a real historical landscape populated by figures like Adolf Eichmann and the Russian and Hungarian secret police. It is also a love story set during a time of turmoil and separation, a story which begins in Hungary and seeks its conclusion in Australia.

ISBN 0 7322 7508 3